# Everything in the Garden

A.K.Biggins

This is a work of fiction. Names, characters, businesses, places, events, locales and incidents are either the products of the author's imagination or used in a fictitious manner. Any resemblance to actual persons, living or dead, or actual events is purely coincidental.

Copyright © 2025 A.K.Biggins
All rights reserved.

Cover design view42photography.com

ISBN:

ISBN-13:978-0-9955905-7-1

For my wonderful family, amazing friends and to everyone who picked up this book; thank you for giving my words a chance.

Everything in the Garden

## A Confession

I think the first thing I want say is, I have never considered myself to be a serial killer and, after some research, I clearly see I don't fully fit the profile. For a start, I am female, which is pretty rare and my murderous spree was actually quite restrained. There were times when I wanted to murder quite a few more but managed, with enormous self-control, to curtail these desires. Also, my murders are spread over years rather than months.

The actual definition of a serial killer is: *'A person who murders three or more people in a period of over a month, with a 'cooling down' time between murders.'* As I did kill three or more people (murder is such an emotive word) and given that definition, I technically am one but please understand it's not that I killed for any sort of pleasure or gratification, these acts were committed purely out of necessity.

I am a woman of a certain age and a product of my generation. I was born in the late 1950's in a small village in Yorkshire. I have a nice home now, not in Yorkshire. I have lived in exile on the South Coast for more than thirty five years with a wonderful and loving husband, two grown up children and grandchildren too. On the surface, I am quite an ordinary, clothes from Marks and Spencer's type of woman, who just happens to have kept a part of her life and a few small acts of justifiable wickedness hidden. Until now.

Now, I believe my chickens are coming home to roost and so before I am judged for what I have done, I'd really like the chance to explain myself. Perhaps I should say here that I am on a fair bit of medication – it's supposed to keep me calm. It tends to fill my head with cotton wool but it does also soften the self-loathing and regret. I'm telling you this so hopefully you'll understand when I get muddled or go wandering off, as I am prone to do. So where to start, well, at the beginning of course but it's a long story so I'd better get on with it.

Everything in the Garden

## One

When she was sixteen, Barbara Cooper, my mother, 'got into trouble'. The source of this trouble was never named but Barbara was mercilessly shamed. Her discovered pregnancy in early 1957 was an absolute scandal in the small village where she lived. Although her parents, Jack and Mary, didn't disown her, they struggled to allow her to forget the disgrace she had brought to the family and the Cooper name. I, Rosemary Ann Cooper, am that disgrace.

Don't get me wrong, I am pretty sure my grandparents loved me and once the initial shock of my existence subsided, they treated me with love and kindness. The rest of the village though, were not quite as accepting.

Mum and I lived with Jack and Mary in their modest pre-war semi-detached house in Crigglestone, a village on the outskirts of Wakefield, where we all rubbed along reasonably well. I loved 'helping' Grandad in his garden where he taught me the names of his plants and how careful I had to be around them. My favourite job though was sowing seeds, ready for the next year.

Nana was a baking fiend, making cakes, pies and buns most days and I was her keen and willing helper but only after scrubbing my hands clean from the garden and she always let me lick the bowl and wooden spoon.

Mum struggled with the isolation her predicament caused. The village never allowing the scandal of her teenage pregnancy to be forgotten, her not revealing the identity of my father probably went some way towards keeping tongues wagging and her friends, concerned for their own reputations, quickly faded from view. However, everything changed after I'd turned five in the autumn of 1962.

Once I started school, Mum got a job in the village shop working for Mr and Mrs Parkes. It was there that she first drew the attention of Billy Flynn, a local man who didn't seem to mind the stigma of her unmarried mother status. Not only that, he was also happy to take on her illegitimate daughter. Billy was 31 years old, ten years older than Mum, and lived with his widowed mother on High Street.

His Dad had been killed in the 1941 Crigglestone colliery disaster, along with 20 other men. This was before the pits were nationalised so there was no compensation or pension payments for Mrs Flynn and her then eleven year-old Billy. Luckily, they lived in a small cottage which had been in the Flynn family for two generations so they had no rent to find but with no wage coming in it was hard on his mother, known and referred to by everyone as The Widow, and her boy.

Leaving school at fourteen, Billy went to work at Crigglestone West railway station. His mother made him promise he would not ever go down the pit. However, there were few other opportunities for a young lad, especially one who had shown little interest in school or learning, so he was lucky to gain this employment. Although he had dreams of being a train driver, he never made it further than conductor; his attitude and quick temper were doubtless barriers to promotion. There were two sides to Billy.

To my grandparents, he was charm itself and Mum revelled in his attention and flattery. He literally swept her off her feet with plans for us to be a little 'respectable' family. After a very short engagement, Billy and Barbara were married in April 1963 in a quiet little service at St James's church in Chaplethorpe. There were only ten people at the ceremony, including me, and the sun shone. Afterwards, we all went back to my grandparents' house for sausage rolls and egg and cress sandwiches and it was then I heard Nana say to Billy,

"I want you to promise me you'll look after our Rosie; love her like she were your own."

"Oh aye, course I will, Mary, she's like a little version of your Barbara and I'm gonna look after both of 'em." He took a swig from the bottle of beer he had just opened, gave her a nod and went back to the sitting room but the look on Nana's face told me she wasn't convinced.

There's only one surviving photograph of their wedding, the rest were destroyed in an anger-fuelled bonfire some years later, but I did manage to keep one, my favourite. I had secreted it away the day the film came back from the chemist. It shows my mother in a lovely white (much to The Widow's disgust!) satin, full length dress made with great care and relief by her mother Mary. On her head is a small white pillbox hat with a shoulder length veil attached. Her long dark hair is swept back in a French pleat and she is holding a large trailing spray of flowers. Even though the picture is black and white, I could always see the colours as my happy memory converted the sepia image into brilliant technicolour in my mind's eye. The deep red roses in Mum's bouquet and on Billy's lapel, Nana Mary's smart, light blue two piece, which she also made along with my pale pink satin dress with a deeper pink, wide ribbon waistband. The Widow, of course, wore black as per her general mood and never smiled once. Grandad Jack, the father of the bride, is beaming into the camera along with everyone else. Mum had laughed when she saw the pictures with him on.

"God love him, he's so happy that he finally got me married off!"

The reason I stole that picture was because of Mum's smile, she looked so beautiful, thinking she was about to start a much happier life.

Although there was never any official adoption, after the wedding I was told my name was now Rosie Flynn so that I had the same surname as my Mum. However, I was never asked or instructed to call Billy anything other than Billy. But he did tell me I should call The Widow 'Granny' which I did only when absolutely necessary.

Mum told me so many times in the weeks leading up to the wedding that marrying Billy was going to make everything alright and I believed her. So I took this picture as a memory marker of the day our perfect life began. Little did I know that it was one of the very few happy days of my new life as Rosie Flynn.

It was clear from the first meeting that The Widow Flynn didn't think much of Mum or me. Her boy had worked hard to keep the wolves from her door and provide for the two of them, now suddenly there were two more mouths to feed; she had always had a bad chest, along with lots of other non-specific ailments, so working wasn't for her. Her approval of the match was given reluctantly and only on account of what else came in the package along with the bride and her daughter.

This was something I only discovered years later. Grandad had indeed been happy to see his daughter married, happy and grateful. So grateful he had given Billy £500, a massive chunk of his savings, to help them get a bit of a start to their life together.

On the eve of their first wedding anniversary, Mum was dashed off to Manygates Maternity Hospital and, although she was three weeks early, she gave birth to a healthy baby boy, my brother David. Although she was never going to be accepted by The Widow, for a little while after this, she was granted a little more tolerance.

"A real grandchild!" she declared at the news, with a pointed glance my way, before sending me to Parkes's shop to buy a bottle of sherry to celebrate. Billy stopped me just before I left the house and told me to get some sweets, holding out a threepenny bit. Cautiously, I reached out to take it while keeping my eyes on his face. He let the coin go and ruffled my hair and I felt the hairs on the back of my neck prickle as I muttered my thanks and fled from the cottage.

On his arrival, this scrawny little bundle was instantly the apple of his father's eye. The Widow was initially full of praise for her beautiful grandson but that didn't last long. He soon became something else for her to complain about, criticising Mum for not looking after him properly. His birth had been long and difficult and Mum had only had one night in hospital before she brought him home. Unlike when I was born, there was no one to help. The Widow was cold and unwelcoming when Nana and Grandad came round to see her and their new grandchild and Mum tried to put a brave face on, telling them she was fine and very happy. But she was not fine and I saw her distress increase daily.

She really struggled with him for a while, claiming she felt clumsy, and couldn't get him to settle. She lost a lot of weight quickly and was forever saying she needed to go and have a lay down. To begin with, The Widow allowed this, as long as the baby was asleep or I was there to tend to him but she soon reverted back to her resentful self. She sniped and belittled Mum every chance she got, telling her to pull herself together and stop being lazy. Mum was still doing all the cooking and cleaning, The Widow's chest wouldn't allow for *her* to do anything and the baby was getting more crotchety, crying day and night.

One morning, when Davy, as he was now referred to, was about seven weeks old, there was a terrible row. We had all had a particularly bad night, Mum had not been able to feed and settle him and he'd been crying inconsolably for hours. At 7am, we were all downstairs and emotions were running high. I was washing my face in the back kitchen and Mum was walking around, juggling her screaming baby, while Billy sat at the table eating his bacon and eggs. I only caught half of what was said and didn't understand a half of that but I knew it was bad. I stayed by the old stone sink, out of the way, knowing Billy would be off to work soon, afraid to walk into his line of sight, knowing how much my presence annoyed him when he was in this mood. Billy was shouting about how the bloody hell was he supposed to work a full shift after being up all night. Mum started to respond but The Widow shouted over her, fanning the flames, saying Mum was useless, calling her common and stupid. Davy's crying seemed to get louder and I didn't catch what was said but Billy was speaking in his low furious voice. The Widow continued her shrieking at Mum and I heard her sob as she tried to speak but Billy's sudden bellow made me shrink back even further into the shadows.

"Jesus Christ! Will the pair of you just shut up and let a man have some peace." There was a thump and crash of breaking crockery followed by more shouting and swearing. I wiped my sudden tears on the back of my hand and edged towards the back door. I was out and running down to Nana and Grandad's house in seconds.

"Mum's not well and Billy and The Widow are being horrible to her," I blurted out as my startled Nana opened the door to my frantic banging. Putting on her coat, she walked back with me. I told her I'd sneaked out without anybody noticing so she told me to sneak back in again while she went to the front door.

Luckily, I hadn't been missed and managed to edge my way back into the kitchen. The Widow was still shouting at Mum, saying that she wasn't even capable of being a proper wife let alone a good mother. She stopped mid-sentence at the loud knocking at the door. I took my chance then to creep into the room and realised Billy had gone to work. The old woman actually got off her backside and went to the front door. Davy was in his pram, still clearly unhappy but more grizzling than crying. Mum was on her hands and knees by the table sweeping up the debris from Billy's breakfast along with the broken crockery. She looked up as I came towards her and it broke my seven year-old heart seeing how unhappy she was.

My memory of that incident gets hazy there, I was probably sent off to school. I've no recollection of what happened next, only what I later learned. Nana took her daughter and grandson back to her house for the rest of the day so she could rest. The following day she went with her to the doctor who told Mum she was run down and had a touch of nerves; very common after having a baby. This was making her milk thin so Davy wasn't getting enough from her feeding him. This would be easily cured by topping up with formula milk in between feeds and her getting a bit more rest. He also prescribed iron tablets which she got from the chemist and agreed with Nana's suggestion of a bottle of Guinness from the off-licence before bedtime.

I have heard that Guinness is an acquired taste and Mum very soon acquired a taste for it along with the odd nip of the clear liquid she referred to as Mum's medicine. The tablets and her bottle of mother's help seemed to do the trick and soon she started to pick up. Davy began to fill out and sleep better and the bubbling resentment between her and The Widow went back to a low simmer.

As Mum's postnatal depression was patched over with Guinness and gin, her worries and concerns about her son receded but my fears and anxiety grew. It wasn't that I felt Billy and his mother ganged up on Mum and me, although The Widow did try really hard to create this alliance, it was more that Billy seemed irritated by all the women in the house. He never did anything to stop his mother belittling and upsetting his wife or say anything to calm the situation down and started spending more evenings at the working men's club. There were no other major incidents but the atmosphere in the tiny five-roomed cottage remained tense and I found myself torn between trying to stay out of Billy and The Widow's way while keeping an eye on Mum.

My brother was a beautiful baby and grew into a very lovable child and, despite our seven year age difference, we were close. I was always happy to mind him and took pride in pushing his pram on the occasions I was allowed.

The Widow's favourite saying was that children should be seen and not heard and although she mainly meant me, I helped him learn the self-preservation skills I had mastered growing up in that turbulent and volatile environment. I wasn't just good at keeping quiet, I could probably have run a masterclass on how to practically make myself invisible, so for a while we managed, without too much physical harm, to rub along.

In August of 1965, things started to change. The announcement of the closure of Crigglestone West railway station, scheduled for the following month, was met with horror by all the inhabitants of 42 High Street. Billy was incensed at the news. Life was so bloody unfair. He had worked hard for an absolute pittance for all these years and now what? Now they were chucking him on the scrap heap like he was nothing and don't get him started on that tosser Beeching, the jumped-up posh bastard who was destroying not just the railways but the heart and soul of the country.

These were the times when my skills in concealment and silence were most required and I noticed that even The Widow cowered a little as her son shouted and barged about the small living space. I did my best to keep Davy out of the way, taking him to the park or just for a walk up and down the street, which usually ended up with a trip to Nana and Grandad's where I helped in the garden. But neither of us could fully escape Billy's anger for long; the hand marks on Davy's arms and legs were never as red, or lasted as long, as the ones he left on me.

During those days and for the weeks that followed, I prayed every night to a God, at that time I must have believed in, to make everything alright.

He took his time in answering my prayers, another three and half years to be exact, but on the last day of the summer holidays in 1968, when I was just about to start big school, I thought things might actually be about to get better.

## Two

Billy and Barbara Flynn were appointed as steward and stewardess of Crigglestone Working Men's Club. Whether this was an act of God or just, finally, a bit of good luck, it was a very welcome turn of events for almost all of us. The job came with accommodation and we got a three bedroomed flat above the club so for Mum, Davy and me it had an extra advantage. Billy was at pains to tell everyone he spoke to that he was still going to be supporting his mother financially but she wasn't moving with us.

It was entirely his decision but one that we were over the moon with. Despite The Widow's protestations, pleas and tears, Billy made it clear she was staying in her own home, which was, after all, only a five minute walk away.

It was big news in the village as everyone knew, or thought they knew, that Billy was devoted to his mother and yet he was abandoning her and they all knew who was behind it, that bloody Barbara Cooper. The hussy, with her sordid past, had put him up to it. I heard words along these lines in the post office and the grocers and even one of my school friends told me this was what everybody thought. I am fairly certain The Widow herself was the source of much of this gossip but the 'good' people of the village were happy to believe that the fallen woman was to blame for Billy's dereliction of family duty. No one considered for a second that Billy was equally relieved to be finally out of his mother's cramped and dingy little house and away from her sharp, spiteful tongue.

We moved into the club at the end of October when I was eleven and

Davy was four and life without The Widow was a massive improvement. My brother and I still spent time at Nana and Grandad's house, giving Mum and Billy some 'relaxation time' after working hard behind the bar. This relaxation time mainly consisted of sleeping off the afterhours drinking, which happened most weekends.

Billy slotted easily into the club steward role, making it his own and becoming a firm favourite with the regulars. He enjoyed his new position, being in charge, and worked hard in the cellar to keep the pipes clean and the beer good. He also soon learnt the art of creative stock control which enabled him to make a bit of extra profit for himself and felt no need for all four of the existing bar staff, confident that two would be adequate for busy times and only one for afternoons. Mum worked behind the bar in the evenings while I looked after Davy and helped with the housework. Another one of Billy's money saving schemes had been to sack the two cleaners.

"No use paying them for a simple job you an' your Mam can do."

Some mornings, before going to school, I helped Mum clean up the previous night's debris if it had been really bad, cleaning ash trays and wiping over the tables. For this task I was rewarded with half a crown a week from Billy. If he was around as I finished, he would often point out bits I'd missed, his complaints about my work generally dependant on how hungover he was. But we slotted into an easy routine and he seemed to be much less angry with everyone and everything, especially me, so I let my guard down a little as we moved towards the festive season.

The week before Christmas, Billy got cross when I made my reluctance to take Davy round to see The Widow a bit too clear. The old woman's hatred of me had reached a new high since we'd moved out. She blamed me, even more than Mum, for us leaving her behind, a grudge created by Billy. He told her it was because I needed a bedroom of my own that there was no room for her. So my visits to see if I she needed me to do anything for her were always a trial.

It was the day after I'd broken up from school and I wanted to go to the park to meet my friend Julie. I said I'd take Davy with me but Billy said no. He said I had to go to The Widow's and give her a bit of company. His eyes flashed with the temper I hadn't seen for a while but feeling the unfairness, knowing full well that she didn't want company from me, I ignored the warning. I was on the verge of raising further objections when I caught sight of Mum's face. She was standing a bit behind him, eyes wide in horror at my refusal and shaking her head. There was no mistaking the pleading look she was sending me. I knew my stepfather had been about to lash out and slap me and was ready for it, feeling a hint of sudden bravado, but the look on Mum's face stopped me in my tracks. I bit down on my disappointment and gave in.

"Alright, I'll take Davy round to see The W…Grandma. I can go to the park another day." I would have got a slap anyway for calling her The Widow, even if everybody else did. Billy managed to recover his affable face again but kept his eyes narrowed at me as he took in my face, searching for defiance or mockery. I tried to return his insincere smile but something in the way his mouth turned up made me drop my gaze and I turned round to get Davy into his coat.

When The Widow died six weeks later, at the age of 66, local gossip was that she died of neglect and a broken heart, especially as the death certificate assigned heart failure as the cause. I heard Billy say to Mum that maybe the weak chest she had forever complained about wasn't quite so exaggerated after all. However, they were all wrong.

I killed her and even now, after all these years, I am not sorry.

I could claim it had been an accident, or something I did on the spur of the moment in a fit of anger, but it was neither of these. I hated that woman so much for the things she said and did to purposely hurt Mum and me and I decided the week after we'd moved out of the cottage that she needed to die. It was simple logic, she didn't want to live on her own and we didn't want to live with her. I couldn't risk Billy giving in to the pressure from her and all the local gossip. I needed her to be gone and so I planned how I would make this happen.

It was Wednesday, the first week of February. I had just got home from school, having collected Davy from Nana's on the way. As we walked into the small kitchen, Billy was waiting, sitting at the table smoking. He looked up from the Daily Express and told me Granny was feeling poorly. I looked over at Mum who had her normal, *'please don't upset him'* expression. My stepfather told me I needed to go over and make her tea and stop with her for an hour or so for a bit of company.

This had begun to be a regular occurrence, once or twice a week she would guilt Billy into sending me round. She was always so poorly, she could barely move, but always fit enough to go to the bingo. Mum was busy with the club, housework, laundry and Billy's demands and so the job was mine.

This actually suited The Widow very well as she could release more of her malicious jibes and general nastiness at me. Her goal was to make me cry; she'd mastered the technique over the years, occasionally needing to give me a sharp slap or whack with her walking stick as I'd become immune to her verbal abuse. Since moving out and moving up to secondary school, I'd developed a much harder exterior and realised that if I just smiled at her and did not respond, this would actually rile her more.

Davy came with me that day and as soon as we walked in she began saying what a grand lad he was, asking him about school before giving him a threepenny bit and telling him to help himself to a biscuit out of the tin. Scowling at me, she told me to go and put the kettle on and make her some tea.

"There's a bowl of pea an' ham soup in the pantry you can warm up for me and butter me some bread," she called from her reclined position in her overstuffed armchair, "an' hurry up you lazy little sod" as I walked towards the back kitchen.

"Okay, Granny," I called back in my sweetest voice as I took the bowl of thick dark green soup from the window sill of the tiny pantry with a smile. "Perfect," I muttered to myself as I poured it in to a pan. Stepping out of sight towards the three-ringed gas cooker, I reached in my pocket for the folded piece of paper containing dried and crushed foxglove leaves and, once I'd lit the ring, I stirred them in.

As I brought the tray in five minutes later, Davy was keen to leave. He was desperate to go up to Parkes's shop to buy sweets with his threepence. I said he should wait with me and help clear up once Granny had finished.

"No need for him to sit around if he wants to get off," she said immediately, as I knew she would, "You go an' get your spice love," she beamed at him, "Rosie can clear up." Looking at me with a spiteful smile and narrowed eyes she added, "You can sweep up an' all and dust the ornaments while you're here."

"Go straight home when you've got your sweets, and mind the road," I told him.

Back in the dark, crowded little room, I watched as she ate greedily, dunking the thickly buttered bread and taking big mouthfuls, saving a piece to wipe round the bowl when she'd finished. I busied myself with the small brass knick-knacks she kept on her fireplace, watching her out of the corner of my eye.

"Ere!" she called, holding out the empty bowl and spoon to me, "An' where's me cup of tea?"

"Sorry Granny," I said dashing across to take it, "I'll get it now."

"Get me a biscuit an' all and don't you be helpin' yourself to one, I know how many's left, you thieving little shit."

I waited out of sight by the cooker and counted slowly as I lit the ring underneath the kettle. I'd only got to thirty when I heard her making a funny noise.

"What's wrong Granny?" I asked in mock concern, going back to stand in front of her, "Are you alright?" Her eyes were rolling in her head and both her hands were at her throat as she continued to make a gasping attempt at a cough, her face very red. I crouched down slightly to the side of her, not sure if she was going to be sick, and gave her my biggest smile. "Oh dear, Granny, are you choking on your nasty words? Has all your badness finally filled you up? You look like you're going to explode." I tilted my head as she tried to move her hands towards me and say something. My smile got bigger as I saw panic and confusion on her face, her lips turning blue, and I felt satisfied that she was dying.

"Good riddance you mean old bag," I said softly as she gave one last strangled croak before losing consciousness. I got up and went back to the washing up, paying close attention to the bowl, spoon and pan.

When I got home at half past five, I told Billy she was fine. I'd made her tea and done some dusting and tidying and left her watching telly. I'd added that she still said she wasn't right but she looked okay to me and she'd eaten three slices of bread and butter with her soup as well as two chocolate biscuits. Billy chuckled saying,

"There's nowt wrong with her that tomorrow night's bingo won't cure, she'll probably outlive me the wicked old crow," and with a slight shake of his head he finished his mug of tea and got ready to open up the club.

The next morning, he was just getting up as I was about to leave for school. Mum was at the cooker, the bacon already sizzling, and I smiled widely at him as I went to get my coat. I asked Mum if she wanted me to collect Davy from Nana's again and she said that would be a great help. I nodded and set off for the twenty minute walk to Kettlethorpe Secondary, hardly able to contain my smile, knowing how much better things were going to be and reminding myself to practise my shocked and then sad face for when I got home.

So there it is, my first murder at just 11 years old. Well, something had to be done, didn't it?

## Three

There was quite a buzz around the village for the next couple of weeks. The death of Agnes Joan Flynn was not so much mourned as exploited in the continued campaign against my mother. The quickly arranged and basic funeral raised even more eyebrows and insinuations about The Widow's 'untimely' death. Luckily this gossip and rumour made its way to the ears of Doctor Bendelow, who had signed the death certificate, and he immediately put a stop to any suggestion that the death had been anything other than heart failure brought on by bad diet and inactivity. I always liked Dr Bendelow.

Still, people like to gossip and they had more fuel for their fire when, after the funeral, all that was on offer was tea and shop bought cakes and the following day, Billy put her cottage up for sale.

Billy had seen an opportunity and was in need of a quick sale. He wanted the money to add to his already substantial nest egg which would enable him to fulfil his new ambition; becoming the licensee and owner of The Old Swan public house.

To the village, again this was *'that bloody Barbara Cooper'* making him leave his poor widowed mum to die alone just so she could have a pub. I think Mum was hoping that having the pub, a place they owned with no boss or committee to answer to, would be yet another new start for us. I was hoping that it might make Billy a little less angry. And it did, for a little while.

Almost a year to the day after we'd moved into Crigglestone WMC, we moved out. It turned out it was a of jumping before he was pushed as

Billy had not actually been popular with some of the committee members and his creative accounting had not been as clever as he thought.

Our first Christmas in The Swan was almost wonderful. Not having the sour faced Widow scowling and criticising was, of course, great but it was as if Billy had undergone some sort of personality transplant and seemed to be going out of his way to be nice to all of us. He still drank a lot, as did Mum, but Davy and I were left to our own devices with the generously extravagant presents they'd bought us.

Davy and I tipped out our gifts from big black bin liners while Mum drank her Andrews Liver Salts and chain-smoked in front of us, Billy's snores faintly resounding from the open door of their bedroom. I thought that sending The Widow off to her maker was the best thing I'd done so far in my life; of course, it didn't last.

After the excesses of Christmas where the pub was full most evenings and dinner times, January saw the takings down and Billy's good humour in decline. He was constantly yelling at all of us over the slightest things and Mum retreated back into her sadness cloak, popping out only to serve in the bar where she served herself along with the customers. One early evening, I was surprised to hear Billy laughing as I washed glasses in the corner of the bar. He'd been in a particularly foul mood all day and my right cheek was still smarting from a slap he'd given me for some made up reason. Mum was pushing her glass under the optic, helping herself to a double gin, as Billy began to chuckle, telling a customer that she was drinking away the profits. He always had the knack of slipping seamlessly from a rage-filled bully into jovial mine host but, on this occasion, I remember shivers down my spine as I saw something very scary in his nasty smile.

Davy started school that January and it was a particularly cold start to the year. The one gas fire in the living room of the rooms above The Swan did little to warm the flat and we weren't allowed to have it on very much when Billy wasn't there. Davy was always complaining of being cold and he was permanently hungry and Mum said more than once that he must have a tape worm as he ate so much but stayed so scrawny. The answer to both these problems for me was to take my brother to see Nana and Grandad on the walk home from school every day. There was always a coal fire burning in their living room and the kitchen was warm from Nana's baking and we were given hot meals followed by a slice of the cake of the day.

If Mum or Billy noticed we were late home, they never mentioned it. In fact, most times Mum would be having a lie down in the bedroom *'sleeping off her dinner'* as Billy would say with a nasty laugh, chain-smoking in front of the telly.

Then came the February half term.

No school meant were trapped. The weather turned colder and roads and pavements were icy and, for the first couple of days, Billy's temper echoed around the walls of the flat. Thankfully, Tuesday night saw a slight thaw and Nana turned up at not long after nine the following morning while Mum and Billy were still in bed. She announced to the bleary-eyed pair that she was taking Davy and me into Wakefield to buy us new coats and then enlisting our help in Grandad's garden as he wasn't feeling too good. I thanked a God I was starting to not believe in.

We caught the bus from half way down Durker Lane, shivering as we ate the butterfly buns Nana had brought for us, guessing correctly that we hadn't had any breakfast. We went to C&A first where she bought us both new warm coats which we kept on, putting our worn thin anoraks in a carrier bag. She also bought Davy a jumper and me a cardigan before we went to the underwear section. She bought us both vests, even though I really wanted a bra, before marching us quickly over to the market. She bought us warm sausage rolls from one of the stalls which we ate while following her around as she filled up her shopping bag with her weekly essentials.

We had corned beef hash when we got back, Nana's speciality, with mashed potatoes and swede. The four of us sat round the table, Grandad making us laugh as he tried to sing along to songs on the radio he clearly had no idea of the words to, Nana smiling at him telling him not to be so soft. This is such a strong memory with me that I swear I can smell the food as music floats around my head. Little did any of us know that this day would be one of the last times the four of us were this happy.

Events overcame us four weeks later in the early hours of a cool and dark morning. Someone banging at the front and then back door of the pub broke into my sleep and, as I came round, I heard shouting and Billy opening his bedroom window. It was two of Nana and Grandad's neighbours and at twenty past four on the morning of Saturday 21st March they had come to tell Mum that Grandad had died and Nana needed her.

In the days following, Mum tried to comfort her mother and cope with her own grief without disappearing completely into a bottle of gin. Billy, on the other hand, seemed to rise to the occasion, behaving like the dutiful son-in law, providing support and comfort to his wife and her mother but with sudden lapses into his own particular humour,

'Jack Cooper, known to his friends as Tommy is gone,' just like that!'" was the joke that he never ceased to find funny, even at the funeral.

After the service at the crematorium, everyone was invited to The Swan where sandwiches and sausage rolls were on offer along with other delicacies and a free drink – just the one mind – to raise a glass to a wonderful bloke. Billy was of course delighted that most people stayed well after Nana had left. I'd spent the night with her after Grandad died, which Mum and Billy had been happy about but the next day when I'd asked to stay another night I, saw a flash of anger cross my stepfather's face but much to my surprise it vanished and he agreed. As long as Davy stayed there too, we could both stop with her till after the funeral but no more.

It had been so nice, despite the circumstances, staying with Nana in her warm and comfortable house, I tried to spin it out a little longer. While the pub was still full of mourners, now paying customers, Nana said she was tired and wanted to go home and I volunteered to go with her and take Davy and stay one more night. Everyone within earshot began nodding at this and I knew Billy couldn't refuse. However, his cold smile left me under no illusions that I would be punished later, but it was worth it.

In public, Billy's consideration and offers of help continued in the weeks after the funeral and only stopped when Nana told him, in no uncertain terms, that she was in no need of any help with the management of her money. She also had no intention of selling her three bedroomed house and moving somewhere smaller. I was listening in from behind the sitting room door when I heard her angrily retort, *"You'll just have to wait till I'm dead to get your hands on Barbara's inheritance."*

I've often wondered how I survived those years living with Billy. The improvement in our lives following the demise of The Wicked Widow was short lived and, after Grandad died, I had to worry about Nana as well as Mum and Davy so things were pretty bleak at times.

Sometimes at night, as I lay in the stripy nylon sheets, I wondered if Grandad had died because of me. If I was being punished for seeing off The Widow; God moves in mysterious ways and all that. But I generally talked myself round, her presence had cast an evil shadow of hate but of course it was her son who continued to supply the misery.

So perhaps you might be thinking that my second murder was Billy, the bastard, but I'm afraid you're well off the mark; I didn't plan to kill Billy. Don't get me wrong, I wanted to, hundreds of times, I mean every time I saw the wonderful foxgloves still growing in Grandad's garden, my mouth would turn up in the corners and I would visualise the look on his face as the digitalis made his heart explode. But the truth is, I wasn't just scared of him, I was terrified.

I'd instinctively ducked and dived my way through my childhood, managing to mostly avoid his temper and spite. The slaps, mainly on the back of my legs, were sometimes a daily inevitability but I took my mother's lead in trying to keep as low a profile as possible and accepting that he was never to be argued with. As I got older, I began to realise that, in fact, my stepfather was in better control of his temper than his shouting and lashing out led us to believe. Mostly, his flying off the handle was part of his control strategy.

One of my buried memories still forces its way into my consciousness from time to time. It was a January evening a week before I turned fourteen and I was getting ready to go to a friend's birthday party. Nana had agreed to babysit Davy who was then seven and Mum had gone to collect her while my brother was watching TV in the sitting room. I thought Billy was downstairs in the bar, stocking up ready for opening time so I almost screamed in surprise as he walked into my bedroom. I was spraying my neck with the orangey smelling perfume Nana had bought me for Christmas. I saw him take in my appearance, looking me up and down with a worryingly strange grin, before telling me I looked like a tart and demanding to know where I'd got the money to buy all that muck I'd plastered on my face. Forgetting myself, I started to answer, telling him it was a bit of eye shadow and I'd bought it with Christmas money. I realised my mistake instantly, seeing the look on his face. I had risen to his deliberate provoking. He stepped forward, his teeth clenched, his eyes gleaming as he prodded me hard in the chest with each word.

"Just – who – the - bloody – hell - do - you – think - you - are - talking - to?"

Each prod pushed me backwards until I hit the wall. He smiled and told me I was lucky he was such a tolerant man, his face so close I could smell his whiskey soured breath. Frozen in dread, my heart beating in my ears, his eyes locked on mine and I felt his hand brush my bare leg at the bottom of my skirt as he licked his lips.

"Rosie!" Davy's voice as he walked towards the bedroom, made him drop his hand and step back. That was when I knew I had to get away.

# Four

The next day while Billy was outside with the draymen unloading the weekly beer delivery and Davy was in his bedroom, I attempted to tell Mum about what had happened. But it was difficult to get the right words, she got annoyed and told me to stop trying to wind him up. She even said I should be grateful for all he'd done for me, that he'd made us a proper family and provided me with a good home. I felt my anger rise and before I could think about what I was saying I blurted out,

"Don't you mean he provides you with gin, keeping you topped up?" In an instant, my error was apparent as I felt the force of Mum's right hand across my face. She yelled at me to go to my bedroom and I obliged instantly.

I began spending as much time as I could out of the house, deciding not to say anything to anyone. I just needed to stay on my toes at home and make sure I wasn't on my own with Billy. Mum never mentioned it again and I've often wondered if she knew what I'd tried to tell her or if, by that time, she was too far gone.

The only person I actually confided in was Julie, the friend whose birthday party I had gone to that night. I'd met her on the first day of school back when I was five but we'd only really started being friends when we'd started at secondary school.

After we moved into The Swan, I'd been allowed, very occasionally, to have her round after school for a while and on even rarer occasions, I was allowed to go to her house. Julie lived near the school so I could only go to her house if Nana would collect Davy from the infants.

We did sometimes hang around together at weekends. When I told her about Billy touching my leg and being all weird, she said he was creepy which was why she'd not wanted to come round the last couple of times I'd asked her. She suggested that I should go and live with Nana and I explained he would never allow that. It was my job to look after Davy and keep the flat clean and anyway, I'd be worried about Mum.

On the first anniversary of Grandad's death, the week before Easter, I was in the kitchen with Davy eating toast and dripping when Billy walked in, wearing only his pyjama bottoms. He had an odd expression on his face and ruffled his son's hair as he passed behind him. If he noticed Davy flinch, he made no acknowledgement. I was immediately on high alert. It was only just gone 8am and Billy never surfaced before ten on a Saturday morning.

"Your Mam's not right well this morning," he said, with his back to us as he filled the kettle, "she had a bit of an accident last night, walked into the door, silly old cow." He finished with a chuckle that made my blood run cold.

"Can I go an' see her?" Davy asked.

"Not just yet, I'm taking her a cup o' tea and letting her have a bit of a lay in. You two make yourselves scarce and leave her in peace," he said, finally turning to look at us.

"I was going to take Davy round to Nana's for a bit, is that alright?" I asked in my meek, compliant voice. He thought for a moment and, afraid he was going to say no, I added, "It's the anniversary of Grandad dying so it might cheer her up."

"Oh aye, well, yeah, I suppose you'd better get round there, I don't want her coming here upsetting your Mam, yeah go on get your sens off now."

He nodded as he spoke with a furrowed brow, there was clearly something not right but I knew better than to question it. Davy still had a slice of toast on his plate and I could see he was about to argue so I stood up and said, "Come on Davy, you can eat that on the way." I shepherded him into the hall and into his coat, grabbing my own, without a backward glance.

Nana was sad of course but the smell of baking that hit us as we walked in told us she had decided not to sit around and mope. The cake cooling on the table, along with the one still in the oven, told us that she had started early.

Her mood was pragmatic and almost buoyant and so I decided not to tell her about Mum. Billy had made it clear he didn't want her turning up and I knew if I told her what he'd said, or even that he was taking Mum tea in bed, she would smell a rat and be straight there. We had a pleasant morning; Davy made some biscuits and I helped make the butter cream for the second cake and to ice a tray of buns. We had beans on toast for our dinner and then ate large slices of cake. Nana put the second cake, along with the buns and all the biscuits, in her big tin for us to take home.

She was going to see one of her friends in the afternoon and so we all left the house at the same time. We had just got to her garden gate, about to go our separate ways, when she told us to tell Mum that it would be nice to see her the next day if she wasn't too busy.

"She's poorly and Billy…," Davy started to say but I cut him off, giving him a shove at the same time.

"She had a bit too much to drink last night that's all. I'll tell her," I said with what I hoped was a *'you know what she's like shrug and shake of the head'*.

"Yes well, your mother drinks far too much every night from what I've heard," she responded primly with a nod of her head, "Anyway, you two get off home."

"Why didn't you tell her that Mum's had an accident?" my brother wanted to know as we set off down the hill.

"I just don't want her worrying," I lied.

Mum was up when we got back but she wasn't behind the bar. She was in the sitting room watching telly from the sofa. I went to the kitchen to put the tin on the table as Davy charged in, telling her loudly about the baking and things we'd brought home but he stopped mid sentence and cried out. I moved quickly to see him almost in tears standing in front of her and turning to look at her I could barely believe my eyes. Her face was so swollen on the left side that her eye was closed. The swelling was a dark purple and the side of her mouth was split.

"Oh no what's happened?" I cried out.

"It's alright love," she began softly, "I'd had a bit too much to drink and walked into the storeroom door, silly bloody fool that I am."

"Does it hurt?" Davy was close to tears.

"Only a bit," she said and smiled which made her wince in pain. Swinging her legs off the sofa and stood up, "Come on, let's go and see what you've made."

She didn't work that evening and instead watched TV with us. It was the only time in my life that the three of us did that and it was wonderful. Billy arranged for one of the women who'd been asking for a bar job to come and cover for Mum. This was quite a feat as he hated having to pay bar staff and did it only when he was sure it would be a busy night.

"I'm not payin' her much as she's not worked behind a bar before, so it's like a trial," I heard him say as he polished his shoes.

As he was about to go downstairs to open up, he told me to go down to the bar with him as he wanted to give me something. I was instantly full of panic and followed him down warily. A few moments later, I had to pinch myself to be sure I wasn't dreaming. As we walked into the stockroom, he pulled out three bags of crisps and put them on a tray with two bottles of fizzy orange pop with straws. He measured a triple shot of gin in another glass and topped it off with a splash of orange cordial before handing me the tray and telling me look after Mum. Then he turned and went over to unlock the big double doors.

Mum didn't want her crisps; she said it was painful eating so Davy had them with two slices of thickly buttered bread in a sandwich. I put her drink on the coffee table in front of her and she didn't touch it for ages but I did see her keep glancing at it. She'd taken a bag of frozen peas out of the freezer and kept pressing them to her face to help the swelling go down and the drink stayed untouched for almost an hour. Morecambe and Wise was on and it was lovely to see and hear her laugh. Davy was curled up beside her and as she leaned forward to pick up her glass, I saw her expression change. She took three quick sips before leaning forward again as if to put the glass back but changed her mind, leaning back, the drink firmly in her hand. Ten minutes later she told me to go downstairs and get her another drink, claiming it was helping with the pain.

At 9pm, she took Davy to bed and I heard her tell him it was too late for a story, her voice a little slurred. She'd taken her empty glass with her and as I listened, oblivious to whatever was on TV, I heard her in the kitchen opening bottles and refilling her glass. She did that twice more before I helped her to bed around half past ten when I went to bed myself.

It took me ages to get to sleep that night. I lay under my covers staring at the ceiling and thinking about why we lived like this and why Mum had to drink so much? Of course, I knew the answer; it was Billy, the emotional hand grenade, that we all had to tread so carefully around.

He got worse when he'd left the railway but things got better when we moved to the club and lost The Widow. Getting the job at the club gave him a new found power and freedom. Living on licensed premises, he could have a pint anytime he wanted. This was the real reason he left his mother in her cottage. The widow was famously disapproving of any more than the occasional glass of sherry, constantly criticising Mum for her nip of gin in the evenings. I remember many a time, while we were still in cramped little cottage, the old witch having a go at her, saying she was a slovenly tart and drinking away her son's money, but I cannot remember a single time seeing Mum drunk then. Billy was five pints loud and belligerent most Friday and Saturday nights but I couldn't recall

Mum being even tipsy in those days. When we moved to the club there were lock-ins, when from my bedroom in the upstairs flat, I heard the drunken booming chatter of Billy and his cronies and Mum's voice, slurring sometimes, and once or twice she was a little unsteady on her feet and yet, and yet... When was it then that she became known for liking a drink? 'Of course', I thought, 'No one could live with Billy without some sort of coping mechanism' but when had her drinking become so bad she had started walking into doors?

I'm pretty sure you're ahead of me on what was going on but please remember I was fourteen and had a very closeted life and I know I had murdered my step-grandmother but I knew very little about grown up relationships. I had only two examples really, Nana and Grandad's non tactile, happy closeness and Mum and Billy's, which was 'complex'. He bullied Mum, like he bullied me and Davy, well me mostly but I actually thought he loved Mum and Davy; I was never in doubt that he did not love me. And he was always quick to lash out at my brother and me with a sharp slap to the back of the legs, which had progressed to a slap across the face for me as I'd got older, but I had never seen him raise a hand to Mum and never imagined he would. Perhaps I shared Mum's need for denial as I reasoned that the wide, solid, wooden storeroom door must have been the cause of the injury and Mum really did need to cut down on her drinking.

The next day, her face was still bad, well I actually thought it was worse, more bruising had come out but perhaps her eye wasn't quite so swollen. It seems the peas had not been wasted in vain. However, Billy insisted she had to work in the bar, she would just have to try and cover it up with makeup.

"I can't manage Sunday dinner on me own Barb an' I'm not paying that bloody Denise to work again. She were bloody useless."

I thought about pointing out that maybe if he'd asked one of the other people he knew, who actually had experience of working behind a bar, instead of the tarty Denise who always had her goods on display, it might have been better, but obviously I didn't. There wasn't a great deal Mum could do about her face, slapping an extra layer of Max Factor on, in my opinion, made it look worse and I could clearly see she was in pain as she tried to rub it over the swollen skin. I said I'd help and sat Davy in the storeroom with a colouring book and some crayons. As soon as she got downstairs, Mum pushed a glass under the optic and used a double gin to help her swallow two paracetamol before fixing a smile to her face as the front door opened and a couple of the regulars came in.

I busied myself collecting and washing glasses for the first hour, losing count of the amount of times Mum had to explain her injuries, but I did notice the reactions to her explanation. Just after 1pm, I dashed upstairs to check on the Sunday roast, sort out the vegetables and mix up the Yorkshire pudding batter. I had registered that Billy had been a little quieter than normal when they had first opened up but for the last hour he seemed more like himself, perhaps thinking people were accepting the story of how Mum got her injuries. To be honest, I think *she* believed it by then.

We sat down to eat our Sunday dinner at exactly 2.40pm and as Mum struggled to chew, she looked pale and drained, even through her double coat of foundation. As soon as he'd finished, which was always before anyone else, Billy put his knife and fork together and stood up. He gave a loud burp and nod of satisfaction before announcing he was off for an hour on the bed, telling me I could clear up and let Mum have a lay down with him. Mum gave a little cough before announcing she was going to see her mother. Billy's face contorted and I closed my eyes wishing him to disappear but Mum continued,

"It'll be all round the village now about my accident, if I don't go and see her and tell her meself what happened, she'll be thinking the worse." There was silence as we waited to see if he would buy it, finally he nodded his head slowly.

"Aye, mebe your right, you should go an' see her and tell her." His nodding became a little vigorous before raising his index finger and pointing at her, "and tell her I weren't even in the room when it happened an' you were pissed up." He almost spat the last four words before turning round and walking out of the room but shouting over his shoulder, "an' don't you be there all bloody afternoon, I want you back here to iron my shirt for tonight."

Hearing the bedroom door close, I sprang to my feet and took my plate over to the bin, scraping away my mostly untouched meal. My brother put his knife and fork down in the 6.30 position and looked at me hopefully; smiling, I took his plate away as well.

It didn't take long for the three of us to clear up and twenty minutes later we were walking down towards Nana's house, where we found her watching The Golden Shot. Davy ran straight over to her and she gave him a quick cuddle before moving to stand up. That was the point she saw Mum's face.

Apart from the odd quick glance, I noticed Mum could not look directly at her as she told the tale of her drunken clumsiness. I tried not to make a sound when she added at the end that she was definitely cutting down now and had not had so much as a sniff of gin since it happened. At this point, Davy shushed us, sitting cross legged on the floor barely a yard from the screen. "Bernie, the Bolt!" he exclaimed at the same time as Bob Monkhouse, completely oblivious to our conversation.

Nana took a sharp sniff of a breath, turned up the volume on the TV and told me to sit down before turning to Mum and, in a clipped voice, said,

"Come in the kitchen and help me make some tea." It was not a request and as soon as they got in kitchen, she pushed the door closed. I stood up and went as close as I could to listen.

"So has he hit you before or is this the first time?"

"Billy didn't do this, he'd never hit me," Mum's voice was wobbly, "I told you I'd had one too many and I walked into the storeroom door, it were half open an' I tripped a bit and hit me face smack on the edge."

"You must think I'm simple," Nana sounded really angry, "If your Dad were alive he'd be round there right now blacking both his eyes, Good God, Barbara, I've never thought much of him but hitting a woman, that's low even for him."

"Mum! Please will you stop, this isn't helping, it's not going to happen again," Mum was crying, "he didn't mean it and he's sorry, I'd drunk too much and I started it, please just let it go."

They came out together with cups on saucers and Nana said there was some pop and cake on the kitchen table for us and we weren't to make any crumbs.

We stayed only another ten minutes or so before Mum said we needed to get back. Nana suggested that Davy and I stayed a bit longer but Mum said Billy wanted us all to have a bit of tea together before they opened up. Nana shook her head and said nothing but her face showed her disbelief-tinged anger. Billy, of course, could not care less about us having a bit of tea together and didn't actually come out of the bedroom until gone half past six, leaving him only just enough time to get washed and changed and down to open up for seven. The reason Mum wasn't letting us stay was she didn't want Nana asking me questions about how things were. How she thought that would continue I've no idea but then my mother never really thought very far ahead.

Looking back now, I suspect that was the first time Billy had raised his hand to her and possibly he had done it while he was under the influence himself, but it had clearly been more than one punch. However, seeing the effects of his actions once he'd sobered up seemed to have shocked and frightened him and perhaps, for a while, he did feel genuine remorse but it didn't last too long, I guess he just couldn't help himself.

## Five

My stepfather's attempts at behaving like a normal human being were still in effect three weeks later when he gave me and Davy £2 each to spend at the Heath Common Easter Fair on Good Friday. I was delighted when Mum, who had first glanced at Billy before answering, had agreed to me going on the proviso that I took my brother. Julie's Mum and Dad were taking us and would leave us there while they went to Pinderfields Hospital to visit her granny. We were getting two and a half hours of freedom to enjoy the rides, eat toffee apples and try and win a goldfish. I would have Davy in tow but I knew he wouldn't be much trouble, he was so excited about going and I warned him he had to be on his best behaviour. Julie didn't mind him coming, she was just happy that I was allowed to go.

We had been twice before, both times with Nana and Grandad. My brother had been too small to remember the first time but the second time he'd loved it; the merry-go-rounds, candy floss and riding on the dodgems with Grandad. I had similar memories but also of seeing small groups of happy unsupervised teenagers. Julie was also keen to sample this little bit of freedom. She was an only child and her parents tended to be on the over-protective side.

We often talked at length during playtimes and dinner breaks at school about what it would be like to have parents that allowed us to stay out later and hang around with other kids of our age. Julie got Jackie magazine delivered to her house every Thursday and would bring it to school on Friday and we would read it together. She kept all her copies in her bedroom and on the rare occasions I'd been allowed to go to hers, I'd poured over the pages of back copies, reading articles about how to get clear skin and to make yourself more attractive to boys. We chatted about boys more and more as our teenage hormones swamped our minds and started to change our bodies and imagined what it would be like to fall in love and get whisked away from our boring, in her case and terrible in mine, lives.

Then, of course, there were our pop idles. Julie had posters, not all just from magazines either, pinned up on her bedroom wall and we fantasised about meeting our favourites and them falling in love with us.

Mum had always had a record player when we lived with Nana and Grandad but it had not been a requirement when we moved into the cottage. There would not have been room and even if there had been, The Widow would never have let her play her records. But when we moved into the club, Grandad gave it to me, along with her small collection of LP's. They were mostly the Beatles and Elvis but with one Frankie Valli and the Four Seasons that was my particular favourite. I spent hours listening to them in my room and learnt most of the songs by heart. Sometimes, when Mum was sorting the washing or cleaning, she'd ask me to put on her favourite Beatles album, Rubber Soul, and she would sing along to that as she busied herself tidying. Julie had her own much newer record player in her room and her collection was mainly her own although she too inherited some Beatles LP'S.

Mum reminded me for about the tenth time that I had to keep an eye on my brother at all times and told Davy that he had to listen to me and not go running off. Julie's Mum told us both that we were not to talk to strangers and we were to stay together at all times. She gave her daughter £3 and told her not to spend it on lots of sweet stuff that would make her sick. Her Dad told us they would be back to pick us up at half past five and we should be exactly in that same spot or else we would never be trusted to do this again.

We climbed out of the car mumbling 'yes' and 'of course' and walked quickly across the damp grass towards the sound of the bass heavy music, bright coloured lights and all the fun of the fair.

We were giddy with excitement as we stood just inside the periphery, the gorgeous sweet smells and joyful activity all around us, pulling us this way and that. Davy shrieked with pleasure pointing at the candy floss stand but I said we should all go on a ride first and Julie grabbed my arm, yelling, "The Big Wheel, come on, the Big Wheel!"

We squeezed into a swinging seat of the Ferris wheel, Davy between us, and the lad who pulled down the barrier to fasten us in gave Julie a wink before turning away and *'Ticket to Ride'* boomed from the massive speaker. As the wheel filled up and we were lifted high above the ground, my euphoria soared and Julie and I sang along. I felt Davy tense and squeeze my hand as we reached the top of the arc so I squeezed back and told him it was all fine and *'look we can probably see The Swan if we look hard enough, wow Davy, we're like birds in the sky,'* my voice full of the wonder I truly felt and he began to relax and look around as the wheel lowered us for another assent. As we swooped past the control box, the lad that had fastened us in grinned at us and winked again.

"Do you think he's a proper Gypsy?" Julie asked.

"Yeah," I said, "I think you have to be to work on the rides."

"How old do you think he is?"

"I dunno," I shook my head, "twenty or something?"

"Yeah, that's what I thought," she said and turned to look to the side as we reached the top again. We went round twice more before it was time for us to get off. It was a different lad who unfastened us and as we exited the ride, I saw the other one chatting with two older girls in very short skirts and white knee-high, wet-look boots. The girls were laughing at something he was telling them and he was standing really close to the one who had the very low top on. I glanced at Julie who was also watching them. After a second or two, she led the way right past them. No one even registered us as we moved over to the dodgems.

Our money ran out just before five. We had spent £2 each on the rides and Julie used her additional pound to get Davy candy floss and us two a toffee apple. She had just enough left then for either the coconut shy or the win-a-goldfish and asked Davy which he'd prefer. His eyes were big with gratitude and he chanted '*Goldfish, goldfish!*' as he jumped up and down. My lovely friend paid for the three balls and we all had one attempt to get one in the display of small fish bowls to win. I won't bother building up the tension, we all missed and I could see my brother was disappointed so I reminded him what a great day we'd had and the stoic little chap managed a smile as we walked towards the road to wait for our lift home.

Davy was buzzing all the way back, telling Julie's parents how brilliant it had been. He said being on the Big Wheel was like being at the top of the world and he could see all the way to Australia from the top. They laughed and her Mum encouraged him to tell her more about the fair. As it was almost six when we they dropped us off, Billy and Mum were both in the kitchen. Mum was putting away the ironing board and four of Billy's crisp white shirts hung from the door frame on hangers while my stepfather sat smoking at the table with a mug of tea and looking at the Barnsley Chronicle.

Davy was still in hyper mode, talking quickly and loudly about how he'd had the best time and he'd been flying like a bird and he'd nearly won a goldfish and he was really good on the dodgems and....

"Alright!" Billy cut him off, "We get the picture, now calm down will ya. It's been nice and peaceful while you were out," nodding his head towards Mum and giving her a narrow-eyed smile, "an't it love?"

Mum responded with a mouth only smile and a nod before unhooking the shirts and taking them into the bedroom.

"Is it alright to make me an' Davy some beans on toast?" I asked.

"I can do you some chips and egg to go with it if you want love," she replied coming back in to the room, "That's what we've had so the chip pan's still hot."

The next morning, even though I knew I was probably pushing my luck, I asked if I could go down to Julie's house as her Mum and Dad had said I could. This wasn't actually true but I was sure they wouldn't mind. Much to my surprise and without checking with Billy, Mum said yes, I could go, but I had to be back for my dinner at half past twelve to mind Davy for the afternoon. I ran back to my room, picked up my cardigan and shoulder bag and was out of the door within a minute.

The weather was drizzly so I was quite damp when I got there. Julie's Mum let me in with a smile and told me to go up to Julie's bedroom, after taking off my shoes. We had a lovely couple of hours, lying on her bed, flicking through her comics and magazines and talking about what a great time we'd had at the fair. Three times Julie mentioned the good looking lad on the Big Wheel and after about half an hour she brought out a copy of Just 17 magazine where she found a picture of a girl wearing the wet-look boots we had see the older girls at the fair wearing.

"I'm getting some of these," she said, pursing her lips and nodding her head, "and I'm getting some hot pants."

"Really, will your Mam let you?"

"Well I've told her I need new clothes, ones that don't make me look like a kid and she's agreed to let me pick some stuff myself. We're off into Wakefield next Saturday."

I nodded, impressed, and thought about asking Mum or Nana about me getting some teenage clothes but sighed, knowing full well what the answer would be. Mum would just say no, I was too young and Nana, well she would get really cross. The week before, Mum had sent me up to Parkes shop, flustered about forgetting to get bread and brown sauce. I'd been in my room experimenting with my recently purchased eye shadow and mascara and I had rolled my skirt up at the waistband and was looking at myself appreciatively in the wardrobe mirror when she'd called me from the kitchen. There was a pound note on the table and she was standing over the cooker with her back to me.

"Make sure you go straight there and back," she said, not turning around, "and be quick." I picked up the money and set off. Nana was coming out of the shop as I reached the door. She took one look at me, her face went white and she grabbed my arm and pulled me to the side, away from the door. I was about to protest that I had to hurry up as Mum was making Billy's dinner but she didn't give me a chance.

"You go home and wash that muck off your face now, young lady." She was proper angry and went on to ask how old I thought I was and didn't I know I was asking for trouble parading around like that. I did eventually manage to get my words out and tell of my urgent errand so she finally allowed me entry to the shop but not before I had unrolled my skirt back to it's just above the knee length.

Of course, I knew the origins of this outburst; my mother and her teenage pregnancy. I suppose now would be a good time to address this and why I have not mentioned my biological father before now. You would think that the way Billy treated me and how much I hated him, I would have been curious to know who my real Dad was, that perhaps I would have dreamt about him coming round and punching Billy's lights out and taking me away to live with him where I would be treated like a princess. But no, I never thought or wished for any of that. When I was younger, all I knew was I did not have a Dad and that was wrong but I didn't understand why and I knew not to ask. After moving in with The Widow, there were several cruel taunts and nasty remarks she made about Mum being 'soiled goods', 'a fallen woman' and 'a dirty little liar' being the least nasty of them. I did ask Mum once why she said these things and what she meant. She just smiled sadly and said that she was an old woman and in a lot of pain so she lashed out at everybody and I was not to take any notice.

I tried not to mind and to think of her as an old woman in a lot of pain but all I could see was an evil old witch who hated me and Mum. To give him some credit, and believe me this is hard, Billy did occasionally tell her to shut up or give it a rest, which she did grudgingly. It was around this time I first heard the word 'bastard', surprisingly not from The Widow but from one of her neighbours, while I was in the shop looking at the penny sweets. I forget this nasty old woman's name but she bustled her way in and walking straight to the counter and handing over her list, began speaking,

"I've had a terrible night's sleep, me an' Arthur was kept awake all night with the noise from next door. I don't know what Joan was thinking, letting that Barbara Cooper and her little bastard move in with her, and why their Billy wanted to take 'em on God only knows." She did have the good grace to blush as Mrs Parkes shushed her and pointed at me before giving her shoulders a quick shake of indignation, implying that she only said what everybody else in the village thought and then asked if there was any news about the new Empire Stores factory opening, as her son in law was hoping for a job there.

I had to wait three days before I got the chance to ask Mum what a bastard was and if I was one. We were on our way to school, one of the few times we were on our own and Mum wasn't fetching and carrying for The Widow or her son. She stopped walking and asked where I had heard the word and I told her. She sighed before shaking her head and setting of in a brisk walk, pulling me along.

"It's a horrible word and you're not to say it again. It's what mean and nasty folk say," she said, crisply. Stepping quickly to keep up, I left a small pause before asking,

"But what does it mean and why did she call me it?"

"It means somebody who doesn't have a Dad," she said carefully, "and as you have one now you certainly are not one."

"But..."

"No, I don't want to hear any more of that from you. Never use that word again, ever, and forget what that mean old bag said."

She never heard me use that word again, but I heard it more than a few times. Children can be cruel as they try to work out their place in the hierarchy of the school pecking order. This can be compounded when they are brought up by ignorant, belligerent and small-minded parents, in my experience, and this was definitely the case at Mackie Hill Junior and Infants schools. But what I'm letting you know here is that, although I never spoke about the origins of my birth with my mother again, I was party to the rumours and gossip that surrounded it. However, it was almost a decade later that I finally discovered who my biological father was, but that's for later.

Nana's reaction to my makeup reminded me of the things I'd heard as I progressed through the school system. Barbara Cooper had been a right little madam, spoilt by her parents and allowed too much freedom. She wore makeup and tight tops and stayed out till all hours of the night. That was how she'd got herself into trouble and then she'd refused to tell anybody who the father was, mainly because there were so many to choose from. Practically all of these biographies of my mother were totally untrue by the way.

Anyway, I am deviating from what happened, so back to Easter Saturday 1971. Julie let me take two old copies of Jackie magazine home with me. I put them under my cardigan against my developing chest to keep them dry from the still drizzly weather. Mum smiled briefly and nodded as I walked into the kitchen and told me to go and get my brother from the bar and tell Billy she'd be down in half an hour.

I spent the afternoon looking through the magazines, lost in a world of possibilities I knew were beyond my reach as my brother played with his Lego in the sitting room. I was engrossed in a story about a shy girl who worked in a typing pool and met a gorgeous boy with shoulder length, curly hair at the bus stop, when I heard the downstairs door being locked and Billy and Mum coming back up. Glancing at the mantelpiece clock, I was amazed to see it was 3pm and quickly put the magazines under the sofa seat cushion and sat on the floor next to Davy. He grinned at me and pushed a pile of bricks towards me so I could help him build his fort. Billy came into the room, ruffled his son's hair and flopped straight across the sofa, taking up all three seats.

"Put the telly on Rosie," he instructed me, "stick it on number three, I want to watch World of Sport for the half time scores." Billy wasn't interested in football, only the games that ended in a draw. He had, apparently, filled in the football pools coupon every week since he was sixteen, always sure that one day he'd win big and buy himself a big house and a flashy car. Looking back now, I would like to go back in time and tell him not to be such a greedy pig. He had already hit the jackpot when he had got Mum to marry him.

## Six

Julie got her white, wet-look, knee-high boots and a pair of hot pants. Not the ones she had wanted, which were actually just very short shorts but ones like short dungarees, purple with a white wave pattern and I thought they were fabulous. The low cut top she had wanted, not that she had anything to show off in it, was point blank refused and she settled for a short-sleeved, skinny, ribbed orange round-neck one; the whole outfit was amazing. She let me try it on and looking at myself in the mirror, I thought I looked like someone else, someone better, and I knew I needed to get new clothes, whether Mum and Nana agreed or not.

It was another three weeks before I managed to move further with this reinvention of myself. Since decimalisation at the start of the year, I'd been getting fifty pence a week from Billy for my weekend cleaning of the pub. My stepfather was such a dinosaur, he was struggling with the new money and Mum wasn't a lot better. I could see how stressed they got over the changes and so made myself useful with the knowledge I'd acquired from school. As I was tactful in my help, Billy almost forgot I was the subject of his displeasure for a lot of the time and I had a reasonable few months, although I stayed on my guard - I wasn't about to make that mistake again and Billy was never going to change his spots.

I had nearly two pounds left over from my Christmas money and as I'd been mostly saving my cleaning money for months, I had twelve pounds and sixty pence in my very well hidden savings and decided the time had come to spend it. When I first started to collect this little stash of money, I thought of it as my 'running away money' even though I knew I would never have the courage to go nor would I abandon Davy, but I still thought of it as my escape fund.

Saturday 22nd May. While everyone else was still sleeping, I took the keys for the pub from the kitchen, from behind the bread bin where Billy always left them. This had been agreed the night before. If I went down and got all the cleaning done in the lounge and tap room, doing it all by myself so Mum could have a lay in, then I was allowed to go to Julie's on my own and could even have my dinner there, as long as I was back by the time The Swan closed for the afternoon.

Being invited to have my dinner with Julie's parents was just one of the many embellishments of the story I'd told Mum, although I'm pretty sure I would have been welcome to have my dinner with them, had Julie and I actually been there. I met her at the bus stop down by the school, having made sure that Nana wasn't planning a trip to Wakefield that day. We got off the at the bus station and went straight to C&A. Julie suggested we go and see what they had in Clockhouse before going to Dolcis to get my boots.

The great thing about the big department store was I got to try on things to see how they looked on me, which was really good fun. I tried on three mini dresses, two pairs of hot pants and a very short skirt along with various tops. Julie was still finding things for me to try on when a shop assistant came into the changing rooms and told us it was not a dressing up play area but a serious shop and if we were not buying anything we had to leave. As I had not found anything that made me feel the way Julies clothes had, we left and went to the market.

At quarter past one, as we made our way back to the bus station, I had three carrier bags. I'd bought a small check mini skirt in brown, beige and cream, a cream and yellow round neck short sleeved top and an orange and yellow mini dress. I didn't have enough money for the boots from Dolcies but found a pair of brown ones in the market. Julie lent me two pounds to complete all my purchases and bought us both a sausage roll to eat while we waited for our bus home. Billy had not paid me for that weekend yet so I promised my friend I would start to pay her back the following week. She said she was just glad to see me happy but did wonder what my tyrannical stepfather would say when he saw my new attire. I said I was more worried about Nana than him and asked if I could leave my clothes at her house for a bit and just take the boots home.

As soon as I walked in, I could tell something was wrong, Davy was sitting on his bedroom floor in the middle of scattered Lego, his back to the door and his head hunched; I could see his little shoulders shaking. I quickly tossed my carrier bag into my room and went to him. The rest of the flat was silent, like that calm before the oncoming storm, and I was praying that it wasn't anything to do with me. I was back well before my curfew time and had done all my jobs before going so it could only be that someone had seen me getting on the bus. The sitting room door was open but it was empty and silent. "Hey, what's up Davy?" I asked, sitting next to him.

"I've been bad," he managed to say between sobs. He had his knees bent and his arms wrapped around them, "I have to stay here till Mam comes back and if I move an inch I'd gonna get another crack." I looked him over quickly and could just about make out the red hand mark his leg.

"Was that Mam?" I asked.

"No," he said shaking his head, "it was Dad, he wanted Mam to go down and help him but I said I didn't want to be up here on my own."

"Is that why you were bad?"

"No, I was bad cos I tried to hit Dad when he hit Mam. Mam said I were naughty an' all." He let out another long sob and the all the joy I had been feeling that day disappeared in a flash.

I knew there was nothing I could do but try and keep things calm and not antagonise Billy any more. I was no match for him and running off to tell Nana would do more harm. Apart from the fact that she had become a lot more frail since Grandad died, bringing her in on the trouble would only make Billy worse and Mum would side with him. God knows why but I knew she would.

When I'd left my clothes at Julie's house, her Mum had given us both a Jacobs's Fruit Club biscuit. I had been delighted and even more so when she had given me a second one for my brother. I started to eat mine as soon as I'd got through their gate and as I got to the top of the hill, I thought about eating the other one. Now I was glad I hadn't as I passed it to him and told him to stay there while I went down to see if they were still mad. His smile at the chocolate bar started to crumble as I stood up but I promised him I'd be really quick.

Mum was serving one of the regulars in the taproom bar as I came through the stock room, stopping in the doorway. She glanced over at me and I was relieved to see she her face was unmarked. Not a punch this time then.

"You're back," she said over her shoulder with half a smile before turning back to her customer, "Twelve pence love." As she rang up the money in the till, she pushed a half pint glass of bitter lemon under the gin optic. I closed my eyes briefly before taking a deep breath in and, in the cheeriest of voices, asked if she wanted me to take Davy to the park for a bit. She took a big gulp of her drink, her eyes rolling up in her head in clearly defined relief before she said, "Aye take him to the park for an hour and you can call in an' see your Nana if you want, she'll give you both your tea. It'll give me an' Billy a chance to get an hour's peace after we close up."

I didn't stay to hear anymore, I was aware that Billy, who was in the lounge bar serving a couple I didn't recognise, had started to walk back towards Mum.

Davy was delighted to be leaving the flat and we both quickly distanced ourselves from the pub. He still had chocolate round his mouth so I spit on my hankie and wiped it off.

"That were the best chocolate biscuit I've ever had," he grinned at me.

"Julie's Mam has got a big tin full of them, and there's orange and mint flavoured ones as well."

"Wow, can I have one of them next time and can we ask Mam to buy some." His eyes were like saucers. I agreed that we would.

"Can we just go to Nana's?" he asked, walking really close to me.

"Yeah, if you want, she dunt know we're coming though so she won't have jelly in the fridge."

"She will have cake though," he laughed, "she's alus got cake."

When we got back, around five thirty, Mum was coming out of the bathroom, a towel on her head and another round her body, the bruises to her arms shockingly clear. I averted my gaze and ushered Davy into the sitting room where Billy was standing in front of the fire combing his Brillcreamed quiff in front of the big mirror.

"Ay up, how was your old Nana, what's she sent for us?" he nodded at the big hexagonal Quality Street tin I had in my hands. He was clearly in an excellent mood so I decided to take a chance. I showed him my new boots, telling him that Julie's Mum had bought them for her from her catalogue but Julie didn't like them so she was going to send them back. I put them on and walked up and down in the sitting room, my brown crimplene trousers rolled up to show them off.

"I love them, so I've said I'll buy them off her. What do you think?"

"Oh aye, they're alright." He lifted his head slightly, giving me the briefest glance. His mouth was full of half a rock cake and, not waiting to finish chewing, he asked "How much are they?"

"Four pounds, but I can pay it off twenty five pence a week," I said as Mum came in to the room, an instant frown on her face.

"What can you pay off?"

As I repeated the story, her frown deepened and, shaking her head, she told me she didn't like me getting things on tick, it was a slippery slope. I opened my mouth to argue but Billy got in first, still spitting crumbs as he spoke.

"Your Mam's right Rosie you don't wanna to get caught up in this buying on the never-never." He paused to cram the rest of the cake in his mouth and wipe his nose with the back of his hand before saying, "I'll buy 'em for you." Standing up and taking his wallet out of his back pocket, he peeled off four pound notes.

"Here ya go, pay it off, like your Mam says an' don't be getting in debt."

"Thanks Billy," I beamed at him, "I'll take it down tomorrow after I've finished the cleaning, I'll take Davy with me. Julie's Mam really likes him." I glanced over at my brother who looked thrilled at the prospect of a trip to a house that had a big tin of chocolate biscuits.

That night I put the two pounds to repay Julie in my small purse and the two pounds profit in my running away jar before hiding it back under the loose floorboard under the bedside rug, smiling at my ingenuity.

## Seven

Towards the end of the following month, Julie and I were trying to work out how we could go to the Whitsun Fair at Thorne's Park on our own. We could get the bus there and back which wasn't a problem but her Mum had said that now her granny was out of hospital, they would take us and enjoy the fair with us. Julie, apparently, had immediately snapped at them that she was not a kid and didn't need them to go with us. For her back-chatting she had received a smack, *'hardly felt it, they hate having to hit me'* and was told she wasn't allowed to go at all. I was crestfallen at this news but she said not to worry, she would guilt them into letting us go; I just had to try and get Mum to let me go without my brother.

I asked Nana if she would look after Davy so I could go with my friends. I told her that there were four of us going and none of the other three had to take their little brothers. She sighed and pointed out that Davy would be really disappointed not to go, he'd had such a good time before. She went a bit quiet before asking which day my friends were going. The fair was on Saturday, Sunday and Monday and Julie said her Dad was taking her and her Mum to York on Sunday to see her aunty and they would be staying overnight so it had to be Saturday for us to go. She said we would need to get there as soon as it opened and stay as late as possible to have a good look round. I knew she meant looking for the good looking lad off the Big Wheel but nodded my agreement.

After what seemed like ages, she agreed to look after Davy at her house on Saturday, provided I was home by a reasonable time and behaved myself. Then she said that it was only fair for her to take me and

Davy to the fair on Monday so nobody, including her, missed out. '*What a result*', I thought.

I picked my moment to tell Mum about this plan. It was about half past ten in the morning, she was frying some mince and onions and I was peeling carrots. It was the Saturday before and she'd been telling me she wasn't feeling very well ever since she'd got up. It was quite hot in the kitchen, even though the window was open but Mum kept her heavy woollen cardigan on and seemed to be shivering. As I started to ask her, she suddenly shook her head jerkily and dropped the spatula, turned the gas off and said she needed to get something for her headache. I started cutting up the carrots and putting them in another pan and waited for her to come back. She was gone about five minutes and when she returned she seemed a little less shaky. She relit the gas and continued with her cooking and I went back to asking her if my two trips to the fair were alright with her. She seemed distracted, pushing round the meat, but after a couple of seconds she reached across me for an oxo cube and said in a gin-scented breath, "Yeah, that's alright as long as you take him to your Nana's afore you go."

That night, again I pondered Mum's behaviour and Billy's treatment of her. I was sure that my stepfather would make a teetotaller turn to drink if they had to live and work with him twenty-four seven, so Mum had no chance. It seemed that Billy encouraged her to drink but I didn't understand why.

I'm certain the main reason Billy married Mum was how it made him look. Billy Flynn, the good man, prepared to take her and her bastard on, giving them a home. Of course, what Billy and everyone else seemed to have forgotten was that he wasn't actually that popular and no other lass or woman would have touched him with a barge pole. But why was he encouraging her to drink so much and why hadn't he noticed how ill she was looking lately.

Julie's parents did relent and so on Saturday 29th May, shortly before midday, we got on the bus in our new trendy clothes, a light dab of blue eye shadow and a sweep of mascara, for our second visit to experience all the fun of the fair. The layout was fairly similar to how it had been at Heath Common and the rides looked the same and Julie, who had raced from the bus, slowed down when we reached the candy floss stall.

We didn't see him as we approached the ride. There was another lad leaning on the railings talking to an older one inside the operating booth but there were no customers yet. In fact, there weren't many fairgoers at all and not all the rides were open. Julie linked arms with me and pulled me slightly away and deeper into the enclosure. Somebody whistled at us as we passed one of the rides but I suddenly felt self conscious so I dare not look round. Julie's face lit up with a massive grin but she didn't look round either.

"What shall we go on first?" she asked excitedly. We were standing between the Waltzers and the Speedway.

"I don't mind," I shrugged, mirroring her smile, "which one do you want?"

"Let's go and stand up there and watch the Speedway go round for a bit." We walked carefully up the wooden steps, me suddenly wishing I'd gone for the hot pants and not the short skirt as I was certain people behind could see my knickers as I climbed. Once we got onto the platform, we chose our little spot, opposite the booth in the middle of the ride and leaned on the rails trying desperately to look more grown up than we felt. Watching the wooden shapes spinning round and the handful of riders whizzing past was making me feel a bit light-headed.

"Come on," Julie tapped my arm, starting to walk towards the steps, "let's go on the Waltzers." This ride was just coming to a stop as we climbed up to the platform. A man with long dark curly hair in a ponytail and a gold earning, about Billy's age, was helping a couple get out of one of the curved seats. Seeing us, he stepped to the side and held out an arm as he said,

"Well, well, well, what have we got here? Look at you two beauties, you must be models. Come on then, climb in here for the thrill of your life." We both giggled and Julie pulled me back towards the rail saying,

"Yeah, maybe in a bit, not sure if we're ready for all that spinning yet."

We turned away and looked across the fairground to see what else there was. I could see a few people getting into cars over at the dodgems and suggested we go there next before going back to the Big Wheel; it was starting to fill up and get busier.

We paced ourselves a lot better than we had the previous time, I'd only brought two pound fifty of my own money plus another pound that Nana had given me and although Julie had said she did not mind paying for me to go on some rides, I didn't want to take advantage of her. I was also quite hungry as I had not had time to have any breakfast, not that there'd been enough milk for both Davy and me to have our cornflakes, so I really wanted a hot dog. It was just after eating this delicacy, along with a ridiculous amount of tomato sauce, that we went back to the Big Wheel.

"Oh my god!" Julie squealed, "He's here!" I was still wiping my mouth on the back of my hand when she grabbed my arm. I looked across at the same good looking lad we had seen seven weeks before. He was standing in front of the booth talking to the man inside as the wheel turned. Julie took in a deep breath and dropped my arm before strolling towards the ride. There were a few people already there and as we got closer, I saw two girls who went to our school. They were in the year above us and looked us up and down and whispered something to each other before smiling and turning away to look over at the good looking lad.

"Let's have another walk round," I said and she nodded. "I really want to go on the Waltzers, let's see if that creepy man has gone."

When we got to the ride, the creepy man had moved into the middle and was operating the ride. There were two lads walking round between the whirling c-shaped carriages. One of them looked very much like the lad from the Big Wheel so we made a beeline for the carriage nearest him. Julie squealed with delight as he brought the safety bar forward, touching her leg 'accidently' before moving back to give us an initial spin. The creepy guy had a microphone and kept shouting, 'wave your hands in the air' and 'scream if you want to go faster.'

Julie screamed and screamed even though I kept hitting her arm and telling her to stop. I did not scream, I did not like it at all, in fact I hated it. I could feel the as yet undigested hot dog threatening to make a comeback appearance.

"Let's go on again," Julie yelled as the ride stopped and I leaned forward waiting to be released.

"No!" I said sharply, "I need to get off before I'm sick." The good looking lad was there helping us out. I staggered on wobbly legs onto the wooden decking and straight down the steps. I put my hand on the side of the wooden structure to steady myself, head bowed, as I took in deep breaths. Julie was at the side of me a few seconds later, laughing.

"Oh my God Rosie, that was great," she said and then, only just noticing my distress, "Sorry, you didn't like it, you're not going to be sick are you?"

I started to feel better after about ten minutes of sitting on the steps while my friend kept giving the Waltzers lad the eye. Unfortunately for her though, his attention was elsewhere with a couple of older girls.

"Shall we go back to the Big Wheel?" I asked.

This time we were first at the gate and as the ride came to a stop, the first object of Julie's desire gave her the widest of grins.

"Hello gorgeous," he said as he helped her in to the swinging chair. I climbed in after her with no help and smiled at how happy she looked. As the ride filled up, she kept leaning forward and backwards trying to see him and making the seat rock.

"Steady," I said, "I've only just stopped feeling sick."

'In my Rainbow Valley' by the Love Affair was playing as the wheel filled up and at the line where someone says '*Meet me where the rainbow ends*' I felt a little shudder of something down my spine and suddenly felt anxious but had no idea why. I was about to say something to Julie when the song stopped and Gary Puckett and The Union Gap began singing 'Young Girl' and the feeling was gone. We looked at each other with excited pleasure and started singing along, carried away with the music, as the wheel sped up for five full rotations. Afterwards, Julie insisted the very good looking lad had put that record on just because of her. Not quite the fantasist that she was, I thought they probably had a stackable record player like Mum's and the records were just put on six at a time so it was actually just coincidence, but I didn't say anything.

Even though we hung around the gate to the Big Wheel, the boy of Julie's dreams did not come over and talk to us and so we had one more walk around the stalls and rides before going to get the bus back home. I went to Julie's again to change back into my brown trousers and checked cheesecloth shirt but I did take my new clothes home in a carrier bag. Julie's Mum gave me two Club biscuits again, both orange ones this time, and I set off to Nana's house to collect my brother.

# Eight

Nana had saved sandwiches and a big slice of cake for me, which I devoured in about five minutes, I was so hungry. Davy wanted to know if I'd tried to win him a goldfish and I said no but I would definitely try really hard when we went on Monday. I saw Nana giving me a funny look and hoped that when I'd washed my face at Julie's house, I'd got all the eye makeup off but she didn't say anything. She told me to tell Billy she hadn't done much baking that week so had nothing to send up but she might do some before Monday.

"And it's about time I got some of me tins back," she said as we walked to the door and as she opened it, added, "We'll be getting the half past one bus on Monday so I'll make you both some dinner if you get yourselves here by twelve." I agreed with a smile; things were looking good.

I had experienced some independence and freedom and things seemed to be on a much calmer and slightly brighter footing at home but I knew better than to push my luck with Billy. He would be disappointed I hadn't brought any cakes from Nana so I gave him the two Club biscuits from Julie's Mum. I told him they were for me and Davy but as we'd had the last bit of Nana's cake, I thought he should have them. He looked at me with narrowed eyes as he reached to take them from my proffered hand and I had to use every ounce of strength I possessed not to let him see the shudder of fear as he licked his lips.

"Well aren't you the good little girl these days," his tone confirming I was on shaky ground.

"Where's Mum?" I asked turning away from his intense stare.

"She's having a lay down, sleeping off her lunch," he said with a shake of the head, "If she's not up an' making her sen presentable in half an hour, wake her up and tell her to get a move on." He ripped open both chocolate biscuits and ate them both in four bites before washing them down with the last of his mug of tea.

"Right, that's me off to get ready to open up." And thankfully, he left the room. Davy had said nothing since we'd got in but had sat on the floor to one side of me, staring at the telly. As soon as the bathroom door shut, almost as if she'd been waiting for him to leave, Mum came out of their bedroom.

Julie had sulked a little bit when I told her I was going back to the fair on Monday and then tried to cajole her parents into only going to York for the day but they weren't having any of that. She was livid with them for their selfish arrangements which used up all her red energy and so she stopped being quite so sulky with me and just said to find out when the next fair was.

The fair on Monday was a different experience and actually a nice one. As soon as we walked into the fairground, I saw the two girls from our school. They were leaning on the railings of the Ferris wheel and the very good looking lad was leaning on the other side and laughing with them. They didn't notice me this time, with my Nana and my little brother.

Davy was really excited and bounced up and down at the side of me as we walked round. Nana stood on the edge of the ride smoking a cigarette while we went on the dodgems. I let my brother steer and of course there was no dodging done, he just kept trying to plough into the other cars. He went on a couple of rides on his own with Nana and me waving as he rotated to the tinny music and then all three of us went on the carousel horses. Nana was really laughing, saying she hadn't been on a ride at the fair for more years than she'd like to remember, it had really taken her back. Then she looked a bit sad so I suggested we have a go at winning a goldfish. Davy's intensified jumping up and down as he held her hand pulled her out of her sorrow and she nodded with a smile.

She paid for three ping-pong balls so we all had a go and we all missed. I thought Davy was about to cry when the woman on the stall came over and said to Nana, 'If you have another go, I'll give you six balls so you can have two throws each." Nana looked at her grandson and sighed before getting out her purse and after five balls, we were still without a win, just Davy last to go. As soon as he'd thrown it, the woman walked in front of the bowls and I saw her drop a ball in a bowl on the second row as my brothers ball fell between two others.

"We have a winner!" she declared, pointing at the bowl. Nana gave her a nod and a smile and I thought Davy would explode. Nana had to get her purse out once more to buy some fish food but assured the lady she had a bowl at home so did not need to buy another.

"I won, I won, I won!" His face was an absolute picture as he was handed a goldfish in a plastic bag. Worried about the fish not liking to be spun around, he was content to just wonder round for another ten minutes or so. He allowed me to hold his new pet while he ate candy floss but after that we got the bus home, during which he took his responsibilities very seriously; sitting up straight on the seat and holding the bag carefully, watching the tiny orange scrap swim anxiously to and fro.

As soon as we got to her house, Nana helped him transfer the fish into its new round home and explained how much food to give him. Davy was certain it was a boy and had decided to call him Troy, after Troy Tempest in Stingray. We had ham and tomato sauce sandwiches and jelly and custard and watched a bit of telly before it was time to go home.

Nana was allowed to carry the bowl as she accompanied us back to the pub. I was given the tin of butterfly buns to carry and Davy held the container of fish flakes. I was pretty sure she had timed it so that Billy would be in the bar when we got there so she didn't have to talk to him.

Mum was putting her makeup on when we got in. I thought she

looked really tired and clearly Nana did too. Once the goldfish bowl had been placed carefully on the sideboard and admired by all of us, Mum and Nana went into the kitchen and Nana pushed the sitting room door closed. I could hear them talking in low voices. Try as I might, I couldn't catch anything of their conversation but Mum was quiet after Nana had gone home, in fact the only thing she said to me was that I needed to mind Davy every day for the rest of the week until we went back to school, adding that she'd give me an extra pound at the weekend if I kept him out from under her feet.

Things muddled along pretty well for a while and as the weather got warmer and we got closer to the summer holidays, I actually began to think that everything was okay. Boy was I wrong.

It was a Tuesday or Wednesday, not sure which, but I'd just got in from school. I wasn't collecting Davy any more. Mum or Nana collected him between them which meant I was allowed to go to Julie's house, only for an hour and I had to be home by five and only a couple of times a week. This day had been one of these times. We'd been sitting in her garden playhouse, which was actually amazing and full of lovely things including a lovely sheepskin rug and lots or cushions. She had a wooden box in the corner full of Sindy dolls and outfits for them. It had become a habit to play with the dolls although we'd pretend we were doing it ironically as we dressed and redressed them. I can't recall how many dolls she had, I do remember she only had two Paul dolls but we both mainly played with our favourite. Julie's was the Sindy with the long amber coloured hair, exactly the same shade as hers, and she called her Juliette. Mine was the one with dark shoulder-length hair that flicked up a bit and looked like Mrs Peel from The Avengers, my absolute favourite TV program, and so I called her Emma. We had been so engrossed in our chatting about how we were going get a flat together and have wardrobes full of clothes and have fabulous jobs and good looking boyfriends, I had lost track of the time. It was only when Julie's Mum came to tell her that her tea was ready that I realised it was already quarter past five.

Running all the way home, I had a massive stitch in my side as I ran down the side of the pub. I noticed the lights were on and caught a glimpse of Billy behind the bar which gave me a slither of relief. Coming to a stop at the back door, I took a deep breath before opening the door and walking quickly upstairs, bracing myself.

Mum was sitting at the kitchen table smoking, her face red and blotchy and a picture of misery. Nana was washing up. I started to say I was sorry for being late but Mum shook her head and told me to go and play with Davy in the sitting room. No one offered me any tea and I decided not to ask for any. I didn't hear Nana leave but just after seven, Mum put her head round the door and told me to sort Davy out and get him to bed, she was needed in the bar. I did as I was told and, after reading him a story from one of the three children's fairy story books we possessed, I went to the kitchen and made myself some toast before going to bed myself.

Two days later, Nana took Mum to the doctor's and as a result of this visit, she really cut down on her drinking. At first, I put this down to the fact that the doctor must have given her some new pills.

Julie told me that an uncle of hers had been told by his doctor that he had to stop drinking but he couldn't so the doctor had given him some medicine or something that made him feel sick just at the smell of beer and it had worked. I hoped it was going to work for Mum.

The last two weeks of the school term, things seemed okay and Billy was in a permanently good mood. He had started a darts team and takings were up and they had a new reliable bar maid, Shirley Blenkinsopp, who *'wore the right sort of tops to keep the punters happy'*.

Mum was quiet and spent a lot of time having a lie down but I was confident that this was not because of gin and believed the headaches she professed to have were the cause. Of course, that was rubbish as I discovered on the morning of Saturday 17th July, the day before my 14th birthday. My brother and I were in the kitchen eating cornflakes when Billy's voice boomed out,

"How the bloody hell has that happened? You stupid cow!" His rage building as he added, "You've done this on purpose just to spoil stuff, you, you..." the sound of a slap ended this sentence followed by, "I should have listened to me Mam, she said you'd ruin my life, well I'm not havin' it, you hear me?" Another slap and Davy got off his chair and came over to stand at the side of me. I took his hand and led him out of the kitchen and knocked on their bedroom door.

"Mum, Davy's not feeling well," I said quickly. There was silence for a few seconds then Billy said in a slightly less angry voice,

"Take him in the kitchen and give him some water, your Mam'll be there in a minute." We didn't move, just stood very still listening. "Get some bloody clothes on and go and see to my lad but don't think I've finished with you."

We went back to the kitchen and waited. Mum appeared a few moments later looking dreadful.

"Shall I go and get Nana?" I asked as she walked gingerly across to the sink to fill the kettle. She shook her head but kept her back to us. Davy went over and hugged her hip. She winced slightly before turning to crouch and give him a hug.

"The two of you get dressed and then go down to your Nana's, she knows you're coming. I'll come and get you after dinnertime closing."

"What about the cleaning?" I asked.

"Don't worry about that, I'll sort it today." She waved her hands in a 'go away now' gesture. I wanted to say that I wanted to do it, I wanted the money for doing it, but the look on her face stopped me so I nodded.

As we walked down the road, I replayed in my head what we'd overheard and as a small glimmer of realisation began to unfurl, I had an idea what the cause of Billy's latest fury was and Nana confirmed it.

Mum was pregnant, she had suspected it for a while, and had it confirmed at by the doctor two weeks before, but only told Billy that morning. She cried at the doctor's, telling him she could not possibly have another child. The doctor told her she should have thought about that before she'd made one and anyway, she'd left it much too late, she was at least four months gone.

"Goodness knows how she'll cope," Nana said, shaking her head, "She's not much of a coper your mother, well I'm sure I don't have to tell you that!"

Unable to solicit medical intervention, she tried to do something herself. A very hot bath and half a bottle of gin had scalded her skin and made her very unwell but the baby remained. Needless to say, my birthday was a bit of a non event. Nana gave me a card with three pound notes in which I quickly added to my running away fund and also a long, skinny ribbed cardigan that was really trendy.

"Thanks Nana," I squealed, "I love it."

She'd also bought a card for Davy to give me and made me a cake. Mum gave me a card in the morning with a five pound note in and said that was to make up for missing the cleaning money the day before. She needed me to help her with it then though as she'd not slept well. Billy wished me happy birthday when he came down to the bar and gave me a pound note once I'd finished in the tap room but he clearly wasn't happy.

The next few days were terrible. Billy snapping at everybody, especially Mum and surprisingly, she snapped back a few times. I tried hard to steer clear of these arguments that always ended in Billy shouting and Mum screaming before the inevitable slap. I started to think Mum was actually provoking him, testing his limits of control, the way she started to square up to him, the new life growing inside her making her bolder. During these shouting matches they seemed to try and outdo each other with reasons why they didn't want the baby. Billy's were financial; the inconvenience of Mum not working and the cost of everything they'd need. Mum screaming at him that she couldn't go through it again and how hard it was already, cooking, cleaning, fetching and carrying. She had apparently told the doctor all of this but he was deaf to her plight. Even though they agreed this was an unwanted pregnancy, they continued to argue about it like it would make some difference. At one point when Mum must have given him the date the baby was due; around the second week in December, I heard him yelling "not only had she ruined his life, she'd ruined his Christmas an' all".

As school had broken up for the summer, not that the weather had realised it was summer, I tried to get Davy out of the house as early as possible and stay out as long as possible but I didn't want to spend any of my saved money. Neither Mum nor Billy were forthcoming in giving us any more than the odd two pence for sweets for Davy. Billy said I had money of my own, he meant the fifty pence a week I got for cleaning and I could hardly tell him that this was my running away money. With the way things were, that was well back on the cards and might be happening sooner rather than later. But my little brother was the problem.

Davy shrank further into himself and spent most of the time, when we were home, in his room with his Lego and his cars. I sat with him sometimes trying to get him to laugh or even speak but he looked permanently miserable. I knew I couldn't ever leave him and so I had to think of another way to save us both.

The last week of the school holidays, it rained almost every day and on the Tuesday, after we had spent the morning at Julie's house where even the Club biscuits hardly raised a smile, we called in at Nana's hoping for some dinner. She quickly made us egg and chips and as we ate began putting stuff in her big black shopping bag. As soon as we'd finished, she hurried us out saying she would walk back home with us as she needed speak to Mum.

Again, mother and daughter were shut up in the kitchen and talking in low voices. Davy and I were told not to disturb them as they needed to sort something out. After almost an hour, Nana came and told us Mum was laying down for a bit and she would stay and keep us company but first she was popping downstairs to have a word with Billy. This was all very strange behaviour and as soon as she went through the door, I shot into the kitchen to look for clues as to what was going on.

In the sink there was a mug and a small, empty glass bottle. On the draining board was a bottle of orange juice Nana got from her milkman but half of it had gone. I picked up the bottle from the sink, the label was old and faded so I couldn't read what it was and the bottle was greasy. I put it back where it had been. Nana's shopping bag was on the floor by the table and I was about to look inside it when I heard the downstairs door open and realised she was on her way back up. I moved quickly back to Davy's bedroom and flung myself on his bed. My brother didn't look up; his head bowed as he ran his favourite car up and down the same piece of rug.

"What's going on Nana?" I asked when she came to stand in the doorway.

"Your Mam's not well, it's the baby," she said matter-of-factly, "Anyway, I've brought some scones with me and I've fetched jam as well as I know Billy eats all yours." She looked at her grandson, waiting for a reaction and when there was none she said, "Davy, did you hear me?" He raised his head, nodding at her before dropping it and refocusing on his car.

"Right, well I'll just go and clear up the kitchen, you two stay here a bit," she said, wiping her hands down her sides and looking distracted. We ate the scones with thick layers of strawberry jam and she poured out the remainder of the orange juice into three glasses as she sat at the table with us.

An hour later, Mum started to make a noise. It sounded a little bit like a cow mooing; it was so deep and guttural. Nana got her purse out and told me to take Davy to the shop and get some sweets and gave me two ten pence pieces. As we got to the door, she added that we had to stay out for at least an hour. I didn't bother trying to argue that it was actually throwing it down and just grabbed our coats and led the way out.

I let Davy choose five pence worth of sweets, deciding we might need the rest on other days. I didn't have any. He took his time in choosing and I encouraged him to think long and hard about what he wanted until Mrs Parkes' patience ran out and she said to either choose something or go home as she'd better things to do than stand here waiting for him to make his mind up. The rain had eased off slightly but we were getting soaked so we went across the road to the bus stop and got a bit of shelter there for a while before walking up and down the street. I had no idea if we had been out an hour or not but when the rain started again, I took us both home.

Nana was waiting for us in the kitchen. Her shopping bag was at the side of her along with another bag. She put her mug down, stood up and told us we were both going to sleep at her house. She had got all our stuff and we were going straight away. Davy looked at me, his eyes like saucers. I nodded at him and he reached for my hand and we followed her out without another word or a backward glance.

# Nine

After a lovely fish and chip supper, Davy and I had a bath, me going first for a quick wash and leaving Davy in his own little world, playing with three rubber ducks that had once belonged to me, until his skin wrinkled and the water got cold. Nana made us hot chocolate and left us watching telly while she popped back to The Swan to see how Mum was, saying she'd not be long; she was gone three hours.

At half past ten and after my brother had fallen asleep on the sofa, I carried him up to the freshly made up spare bed and waited anxiously, sitting on the bottom step of the stairs, staring at the front door. As soon as it opened, I asked if everything was alright but her expression told me it absolutely was not even though she said yes and told me to get myself off to bed.

The next morning as she made us boiled eggs and soldiers for breakfast, she told us that Mum was in hospital and she would probably be there for a couple of days but we weren't to worry.

"Can we stop here while she comes home?" my brother asked.

"Well, probably," she replied vaguely, as if this had not been considered by anyone, then after a pause, "Yes, I think that'll be best." Davy's face lit up in a smile I hadn't seen for weeks.

I immediately surmised that whatever it was that Nana had brought round for Mum was something to make the pregnancy go away but Nana didn't mention the baby so I wasn't sure it had worked. Then I suddenly remembered,

"What about the cleaning? It's Saturday and I need to go and do the cleaning, especially if Mum's not there. Billy won't do it."

"No, I don't suppose he will," she said wistfully, "Finish your breakfast and we'll all go up there. We need to get you both some more clothes anyway and me an' Davy will give you a hand to tidy up."

I wanted to ask about the baby but was too scared of how I would react to the answer, whatever it was, so decided to wait to be told.

Walking up to the pub without a word, we almost had to run to keep up with Nana's wide and determined strides. We arrived shortly before nine and the building was quiet and firmly locked. Nana had to bang on the back door for about five minutes before we saw Billy move the bedroom curtain. He came down to open the door in a string vest and some baggy and not too clean y-fronts. Nana tutted and pushed her way past him, we followed sheepishly and he turned to follow us, slamming the door.

"What's 'appened then?" he asked once we were all in the kitchen. He pulled out a chair and placed himself heavily on it. Not waiting for a response, he nodded his head towards me, "Get me a cup a tea an' some toast an' drippin', Rosie."

"I'll do that," Nana said, "while you go and get washed and dressed. Rosie you go and get some clothes for you and Davy, you better get your school stuff an' all."

"Ay up, what's goin on?" Billy's eyes narrowed as he put both hands on the table and gave Nana one of his warning looks.

"They're stopping with me while Barbara's in hospital," she replied, in a tone that said he did not frighten *her*, "They're back to school on Monday and I can't see her being home before then."

"Just how bloody long is she gonna be laid up?" he said angrily, "I need her here." He stood up. "You need to tell them doctors she needs to be home," he said, waving his finger. I scuttled out to my room and Davy followed close on my heels.

I started pulling out socks and underwear from my drawers and putting them on the bed and then reached up for the small suitcase on the top of my wardrobe while Davy sat on the edge of my bed watching. We could hear the discussion continuing in the kitchen, Billy's voice getting angry but Nana's remaining calm but firm. After a few minutes, my stepfather stomped into the bathroom.

"Has Dad hurt Mum again?" Davy asked in a quiet voice.

"No," I started to say but then realised I didn't actually know. "I don't think so; I think she has had to go into hospital because of the baby."

"I don't want her to have a new baby," he said piteously.

"I don't think anybody does," I took a deep breath, "Anyway, shall we take the Lego and your cars to Nana's as well."

As the three of us walked back down the hill an hour and a half later, I asked how long Mum would be in hospital. Nana replied she had no idea but was going to see her that afternoon and she needed to take her some 'bits' so she was going almost straight away. She was back at just gone five and looked exhausted.

"Right, well your Mum's lost the baby, which is probably for the best but she's still going to be sad so you are not to mention it again."

It's funny really how much of our lives we were told not to talk about or mention, well not funny, bloody tragic really.

Mum stayed in hospital for two weeks, which I remember thinking was a bit extreme but when she did come home, her arm in plaster and her face and legs thin and colourful, I realised my assumption had been far from correct. In fact, Mum had lost the baby because she had fallen downstairs. She also had a dislocated shoulder and a broken arm.

We stayed with Nana the whole time. I still went up to do the cleaning but didn't go up to the flat. I'd been surprised Billy had not wanted me to clean up there as well but he muttered something about 'him managing' so I gratefully left it at that. It was a glorious fortnight but in the last few days there was a horrible foreboding of what would happen when Mum came home and we had to go back.

When we walked into the flat, I could tell something was different. For a start, it was remarkably tidy and Mum was sitting on the sofa with her feet up on the pouf and a mug of tea in front of her. Billy, who had opened the door to us, asked Nana if she wanted a cuppa but she declined, following him into the kitchen.

"The flat's looking tidy," she commented loudly; she'd brought rubber gloves and Vim with her expecting the place to be a pig sty.

"Aye, it is. I got Shirley Blenkinsopp to come round and do a bit for me so it'd be right for Barbara coming home," he said in an artificially bright voice.

"Oh aye, she's been doing a bit for you in the bar an' all I've heard," Nana said under her breath as she turned to check out the rest of the flat. Billy said nothing but I'm sure he heard.

I went to take our bags of clothes to the bedrooms but dropped them in the hall as I took in what I saw through the open doors.

"Oh aye, we've had a bit of a swap round," Billy said with something that strangely sounded like nervousness in his voice, "I bought these bunk beds from a mate so you an' Davy can share a room." My belongings were piled up in the corner of my brother's room on top of a small chest of drawers. I looked over at Mum for an explanation.

"It's just for a bit love," she said, not making eye contact, "while I'm better, it'll be more comfortable for me to have a bed to meself."

Davy, oblivious to my shock, was over the moon about the new sleeping arrangements, asking me if he could have the top bunk. I looked over at Nana and saw that she was in agreement that Mum should have my room so I forced a smile and said, "Yes, course you can."

Mum never moved back into the marital bed and I suspect she was more than happy with that. She started to make a slow recovery but still used gin to wash down her painkillers and antidepressants.

I almost didn't go to the fair at the end of September at Agbrigg. Mum was still looking broken but she smiled a bit more often. I mentioned it on the Thursday when I'd got home from school but only as a statement.

"There's a new girl in our class who's moved from Ossett. Her an' Julie are going to the fair on Saturday."

The new girl was called Karen and she had two older sisters and didn't seem to be in the least bit bothered about getting into trouble at school and Julie thought she was great. In the two weeks I'd stayed with Nana, I only saw my friend at school as afterwards she hung out with the new girl who lived in the same street. As their friendship grew, I became the third wheel; they didn't exclude me but I was very much an afterthought.

It was Karen who told me of their plans to go to the fair, having heard plenty about the good looking lad on the Big Wheel and she was confidant she could help Julie to 'get off' with him.

"Do you want to go with them?" Mum asked, not taking her eyes from the TV, although I was pretty sure she wasn't watching Deputy Dawg.

"Yeah," I said tentatively, wondering if I'd timed it right with her medication, "it'd be nice to go."

"Well you should go then," she said, giving me a half smile but then with a big sigh added, "I'll manage."

"I could take Davy with me," I said sadly.

"That would be better for me," she said reaching out for her mug of tea, "or you could ask your Nana if she'd mind him," adding vaguely.

Nana said she would have him but only if I was back before six as she didn't want to have to walk us home in the dark. I agreed although I knew Julie and Karen's plan was to stay until as late as possible.

On the bus I took the seat behind my two friends, sitting forward trying to be involved in their chatter. It was a grey and overcast day and the field was wet and muddy. Julie wore her white boots and Karen had a similar pair and they'd both opted for hot pants. I wore my mini dress, the cardigan Nana had bought me and my brown boots. As the three of us walked towards the funfair, the sound of the music made us quicken our step and we practically ran towards the red and yellow fencing around the Ferris wheel.

We climbed, with the help of the good looking lad, into a carriage and as he fastened us in with the safety bar, he winked. After our five turns, he helped us all out, Karen being the last, keeping hold of her hand for a bit longer than necessary. She gave him her widest smile as she tottered towards the exit, saying we should go back on straight away. Julie wasn't quite so smiley.

"Let's go on the Speedway and the Waltzers'," I said, stepping away from them, "we can go back on here later." I saw the look Karen gave me but she shrugged and said alright, pointedly linking arms with Julie as they walked at the side of me.

I loved the Speedway, although Karen kept calling it the *'cocks an' hens'*. I was sitting on a motorbike on the inside of the ride, Julie in the middle and Karen on the end. The lad who took our money, not very good looking but still nice, came back to stand in front of Julie as the ride set off and pretended to sing along with Peter Sarstedt, miming the words to *'Where do you go to my lovely.'* As the ride came to a stop, he stepped forward and, leaning towards her, said, "You're lovely you are, hope you're staying on for another ride." She blushed so much her face was almost scarlet. I walked over to lean against the fence but my friends stayed where they were, fumbling in their pockets for the fare.

As their second ride came to an end, the lad went over to Julie and whispered something in her ear that made her squeal before getting off, nodding enthusiastically and walking, a little unsteadily, towards me.

"He says he fancies me and wants me to come back at nine o'clock when they've finished."

"Will you?" I asked incredulously.

"Maybe," she laughed, "if I don't get a better offer. Deciding not to say this lad looked about twenty and he probably wasn't looking to be her boyfriend, I said instead, "Come on, let's go on the Waltzers." As I was walking away, I saw Julie pull Karen back and whisper something that made her look at me briefly before shrugging.

After the Waltzers they bought some brandy snaps before going over to the dodgems. I guessed what was coming and waited for them both to get into a car before getting in one on my own. Maybe I was a little bit paranoid but Karen, who was steering, did seem to enjoy ramming in to me for most of the ride. As soon as the cars stopped, I climbed out, ignoring their calls that they were having another go. As I stepped away from the ride, I was wondering if I should just go home when I tripped slightly and someone caught my arm.

"You alright love? You look like you've lost a pound an' found a penny," he said with a laugh, not letting go of my arm.

"Oh," I said, startled, "Yeah, well I'm not havin' a great time." I tried a small smile and he pulled his arm away.

"No, me neither," he said, shaking his head making his blonde curly hair bounce around his face, "I came with a couple of mates but I think they've left me for the pub."

"My mates are still here but I think they'd be happier if I wasn't."

"Well, do you fancy coming on the bumper cars wi' me, it's no fun on your own." I could hardly believe it. He was asking me to go on a ride with him. My breath caught in my throat as I tried to speak so I nodded instead. His big brown eyes twinkled when he laughed and I thought I must be dreaming.

"I'm Darren," he said, holding out his hand as if he was going to shake mine.

"Rosie," I responded, holding out mine. He switched hands quickly and took mine and pulled me gently towards the ride. As I climbed into a car beside him, I caught sight of my friends getting out at the far side, they had definitely clocked me but I just started laughing and pretending I hadn't seen them. As I started to open my bag to get some money out, he said "Let me pay, you're doing me a favour."

As soon as he'd paid, he slipped his arm around me and I thought I would explode with the endorphins shooting through my body. I put my hands together and dug my longest thumb nail into the palm of the other hand to make sure I was actually awake.

The ride was fun; I laughed, I screamed, I felt amazing. Darren talked to me, although I've no idea what he said, everything around me was blurry; the bright lights, the quickly moving cars and other riders' happy calls. At the end, he helped me out of the car and we were just going down the steps when Julie and Karen were suddenly at the side of us, all super friendly. Karen in particular was giving Darren the eye as she pretended they'd been worried they'd lost me.

"Well you've found her now," Darren said with a wink at me, "and as you can see she's safe and sound." He put his arm around me and gave me a little squeeze before dropping his arm and looking directly into my eyes, "I should get off now. Rosie." I felt my shoulders drop and tried to stop my smile from collapsing as he tilted his head and to my delight added, "Well, unless you want to come on the Big Wheel with me?" My eyes lit up and I nodded enthusiastically.

"We were just about to go there an' all," Karen piped up.

Ignoring her completely, he took my hand and we walked like that all the way to the ride. Karen and Julie were in the carriage behind us, their seat swinging around as they tried to see what we were doing.

What we were doing was talking. He put his arm around me as we started to rise and asked me how old I was. I thought he looked about seventeen, eighteen maybe.

"Nearly fifteen."

"Oh", he said with disappointed surprise, "I thought you were older than that." I was suddenly terrified I'd spoiled it and wished my lie had been bigger. "I'm old for my years," I blurted out what Nana was always saying about me.

"Okay," he laughed and cuddled me and with a raised eyebrow asked, "So when will you be fifteen?" and after a pause he added, "Truthfully?" I felt like I had butterflies swarming in my stomach.

"July," I said sheepishly, my eyes lowered to my lap. He burst out laughing. "Okay so you're fifteen in ten months time, oh my Giddy God."

"Yeah, I know but I'm not a kid or anything," I said a little petulantly, oblivious to the irony, "Anyway how old are you?"

"How old do you think I am?" He was still cuddling me.

"Eighteen?" I guessed.

"Near enough," he laughed, gave me a kiss on my forehead and asked me where I lived. He knew The Swan as his Mum lived in Horbury but he had never been in there. He lived at the other side of Wakefield where he worked as a mechanic.

"But I might be moving back soon," he said, "so maybe I'll come and see what the beers like."

"Then you'll have the pleasure of meeting my stepdad, Billy the Bully," I said.

"He doesn't sound very nice." His eyes creased and he reached for my hand.

"He really is not," I said and was annoyed with myself that I had to blink back tears at just mentioning him, "he's actually a right bastard."

"Right, well, I'll look forward to meeting Billy the Bastard Bully," he laughed and we were quiet for a few seconds before he asked if I had a boyfriend and I told him no, not yet, but I'm hoping that's going to change soon, which made him laugh again.

"You are a right tonic, little Rosie," he said, squeezing me again, "you've proper cheered me up today."

"And you've made my day really good," I replied. He shook his head ever so slightly as he seemed to be conversing with his thoughts. We were just starting the rise of our final accent as he put his hand under my chin, leaned in and kissed me, just lightly but enough to set off the butterflies again and making me tingle all over. He stroked my face and kissed me again. As soon as the barrier was released on our carriage, he leapt out and took my hand.

"Come on, let's go and get a toffee apple or summat and you can tell me more about life at The Swan and we can carry on cheering each other up."

We wandered around the fair for a while, deciding on candyfloss instead of toffee apples and sat on a patch of grass on the perimeter chatting as we pulled at the cotton candy and licked the sugar crystals from our mouths. I was so happy.

I told him how my life had changed when Mum married Billy and about Davy and then about Grandad dying and how much I relied on Nana. He asked about my friends and I told him how close Julie and me had been before Karen turned up. As he listened, his expression wavered between concern and sadness and he said the occasional word, which were mostly about Billy and mostly derisive.

It didn't occur to me that I was telling him my full life history while not finding out anything about him. He didn't reveal a single fact about himself other than he had left school at fifteen and worked at a garage. I can maybe excuse my completely naive and self-absorbed chat by reminding myself that I was fourteen and had led a very insular life and, as he asked me so much, there were no gaps for me to ask him anything. In hindsight I should have noticed the red flags that were flapping like the wings of a pterodactyl on speed.

It was all so new and intoxicating, this good looking lad interested in me, listening, smiling and occasionally touching my face or stroking my arm. We stayed there for probably the best part of an hour when he said he needed to get going. We stood up and I felt my euphoria slump as we walked towards the road. As if sensing my disappointment, he caught my hand and said he really liked me.

"Would you like to go out to the pictures or something with me?"

"That would be great, but …" My emotions were going crazy, I would love to go out with him, I wanted to go out with him, but could I get a pass to do this, how many lies would I have to tell?

"Mmm, maybe Billy the Bastard Bully wouldn't be happy for you to go out with me," he said, tilting his head, stopping our walk and leaning in to kiss me again.

"How about we meet up, in a couple of weeks, one Saturday in Wakefield and we can have a coffee or summat, go to the Wimpy maybe?"

"Yeah, I'd like to do that," I said, thinking that really might be possible.

He said he had stuff going on he needed to sort out but he gave my hand a tight squeeze as he added that he really wanted to see me again. He suggested we meet in three weeks' time, on a Saturday, under the clock in Wakefield bus station at half past eleven. I tried to hide my disappointment that it wasn't sooner and he hugged me and said he hoped I'd think he was worth waiting for. I said I hoped so too and we both laughed.

He walked me all the way to the bus stop and waited with me, saying he was off to find his mates in the Duke of York pub. Kissing me again as the bus approached, he gave me another of his twinkly smiles and said, "Thank you, little Rosie, for cheering me up, you really are lovely."

I paid my fare, rushing to sit down and look through the window. He was still standing by the stop, waving, and I could not stop smiling.

Nana was surprised when I got back to her house more than an hour before my curfew and, as I'd walked from the bus stop, I had been practising my not so happy face as I told her how Julie was now best friends with Karen and I had felt like a spare part. She nodded knowingly and said that if Julie was a real friend, she wouldn't leave me out and I wasn't to get upset and did I want a slice of Victoria sponge. Inside, I was tingling with suppressed excitement and a happiness I had never experienced before.

## **Ten**

I remember the next three weeks as torturously wonderful. The calmness of Mum coming home from hospital soon switched back to the charged atmosphere as it became clear that Shirley Blenkinsopp's role was not just as a barmaid. I spent practically all my time laying on the bottom bunk, daydreaming about Darren and formulating a plan of escape. The anticipation of seeing him again, and of course the secret nature of the arrangement (I didn't' tell anyone, not even Julie and especially not Karen) was like a bubble around me, cocooning me from the hard realities.

Julie and Karen remained as thick as thieves and although still superficially friendly, their chatting during playtimes and dinner break was mainly a two-handed affair. They hadn't stayed at the fair until the end but left just as it started to get dark. Their money had run out and, disappointingly, the good looking fairground lads weren't offering free rides and soon transferred their attention to other girls. Julie asked me about Darren a couple of times but gave up after I kept repeating he'd been nice but I wasn't seeing him again and had no idea where he lived.

When I opened my eyes on the morning of Saturday 16th October, the sun was only just rising through the trees and Davy was still sound asleep as I tiptoed into the bathroom. I knew I had to work hard and not let anyone notice how coiled up I was inside; it was only three and a half hours until I would be seeing Darren again. I'd been practicing kissing on my arm and in the bathroom mirror when Mum and Billy were both downstairs. I was certain he would notice the improvement in my ability and smiled at myself before practicing some expressions that I felt made me look more grown up and attractive.

Mum was going to spend an hour down at Nana's with Davy after we'd finished the cleaning. I told her I was going into Wakefield to meet a new school friend and we were going to have our dinner in a Wimpy cafe. Nana was delighted to hear I had a new friend and gave me fifty pence to pay for my dinner.

I arrived at the bus station at twenty past eleven and walked quickly to the clock. Standing under the large semi-circular awning to avoid a fairly heavy shower, I was beyond excited. I remember trying to look nonchalant, not that I actually knew what that meant, but found it hard to keep still. People were dashing around trying to get out of the rain and I walked slowly around, moving between the three large brick pillars that held up the shelter. My face was starting to ache a little from the fixed smile as I peered out, watching for Darren, waiting for our eyes to lock and for us to then wrap our arms around each other.

The longer I waited, the stupider I felt and finally at quarter to one, I admitted to myself he wasn't coming and as the rain had stopped, I decided to make my way over to the Wimpy anyway to spend the fifty pence Nana had given me. I bought a Wimpy Grill and followed that with a Knickerbocker Glory. It meant I had to use another eleven pence but it was worth it. I ate slowly, enjoying every mouthful and not making eye contact with anyone else as I daydreamed a different outcome.

I thought about why he hadn't turned up, I mean why would he, when had anything really gone right for me? This wasn't self-pity, it was pragmatism. I'd always known, deep down, that no one was going to save me from this life, I was going to have to do that for myself. The little scenarios of me and Darren running away; my hidden stash, which was by then quite substantial, would be my dowry and pay for us to rent a flat as we started our lives together or I'd go and live with him at his Mum's house and she would love me, declaring I was the perfect daughter-in-law as she helped me plan our wedding. It was all ridiculous. I needed to stop these flights of fancy and start making plans of how I was going to save myself.

I felt a bit sick on the bus as I travelled home and there was still a little bit of disappointment trying to push its way into my mood but I managed to suppress it by remembering how I'd dealt with The Widow. I needed to remember I was the master of my own destiny and to get on with it. I needed to apply myself and get a plan together.

I had always liked school, it had been a kind of refuge for me, even though I didn't have many friends and was definitely not popular. But I did work hard and enjoyed most subjects. The bigger school had been a double-edged sword for me at first. There was a bigger library and more focused learning but more kids and different social groups weren't so great. Karen arriving and, as I saw it, taking my best friend from me was only the start but in the first two years I'd done well academically, keeping my head down in an effort not to become a target. Happily though, this had the bonus effect of making me fairly popular with some of the teachers, particularly Mrs Thackeray our English teacher. She'd encouraged me to read books from the library and although she said there was nothing wrong with Jackie magazine, I should broaden my world with other forms of literature.

After the Darren incident, I became more focused on improving my chances of a better life. Mum never asked me about what I wanted to do after school, she never actually asked me anything, but one Sunday afternoon at the end of November, Nana asked me. We were in the kitchen; she was making Christmas puddings, one for us and one for her neighbour.

"So what do you want to do when you've finished school?" she asked and even though, up until that moment, I hadn't been fully sure, I said,

"I think I want to be a nurse." I was doing pretty well at school with most subjects but science was my favourite. I had a bit of a girl crush on the teacher and my interest and keenness in her lessons made me one of her favourites. Even though she was quite old, late thirties at least, she wore short skirts and trendy clothes and smiled and laughed a lot, unlike most of the other teachers.

Nana smiled and said she was happy to hear that.

"You'll be stopping on at school and doing your O levels then?"

"Yeah, course," I nodded, "my form teacher says I'll do well in Science and both Englishes. I'll have to work a bit harder in History and Maths but she says I'm more than capable."

"I'm so glad you're enjoying school," she smiled but looked a bit wistful, "Your Mam couldn't wait to leave."

"It's not all great," I said, trying to distract her from her thoughts and wanting to remind her that I was not Mum, "I mean I hate PE and Games and I'm rubbish at Geography but stopping on an getting O levels gives me the best options to make summat of myself."

"That's great luv, I'm so glad you're not wanting to leave next year to work in a shop or a factory." I raised my eyebrows at this and she smiled and shook her head,

"Oh well, there's nothing wrong with that, I mean some folk are happy to just stay put an' some lasses are only looking for summat to do till they get married and start a family," sighing heavily and I saw regret and lost chances cloud her mind again, "but you're a bright lass an' you could go far, college or university even and if you change your mind about nursing, you can do whatever you want with your life." She put down her spoon and turned to the sink and even though her back was to me, I could see her wiping away a few stray tears with her apron.

In 1972 the UK Education Act of 1944 was changed to raise the school leaving age from 15 to 16, meaning that all children in state schools would sit GCE'S or CSE's from that point on. My year was the last year allowing children to leave school with no qualifications and I was really shocked at how many of my peers had the mindset to do that but it was that Julie was one of them which surprised me most.

"Oh my God, why do I want to stop on here a minute longer than I have to?" she exclaimed when I asked her why, "I mean, me Dad says I can easily get a job at Empire Stores, it's a good company to work for." The talk of the village was about the new site for the catalogue company opening up just off the High Street.

Karen had made it known, right from when she first arrived, that she had her future all planned out. She was going to be a hairdresser, working in a shop until she got married and had children after which she could work from home as and when she wanted. At the beginning of the year, she'd got a Saturday job at Sandy's Hair Salon in Kettlethorpe and Sandra, the owner, had offered her an apprenticeship.

"You've been saying for years all you wanted was to get a job and earn some money so you could get away from Billy and The Swan?" Julie said, her arms folded in front of her. I tried to explain about how important qualifications were, telling her I was trying for nursing or maybe something really well paid if I could get into college. When I added that Miss Metcalf had said I was bright enough for university, she shook her head.

"You're mad if you think you'd ever get to university, it's not for the likes of us an' what's the point anyway?" she laughed scornfully.

"You'll probably still end up packing at Empire Stores," Karen added nastily.

Late in the evening on Saturday 1st April 1972, I was watching the TV and attempting to do my maths home work as I heard Mum stumbling upstairs. She was muttering drunkenly about being *sick of all this* and generally crashing around. I put my books aside and went to see what I could do to get her to bed before she woke up my brother. After getting her a cup of water and helping her take her shoes and cardigan off, I turned to leave.

"Rosie," she called after me, "Rosie, I need to tell you something."

"Shh!" I hissed at her, walking back into the room, "What, what do you need to tell me?" I moved to stand in front of her.

"You're a good girl Rosie, I don't know what I'd do without you."

"I know Mum and you're very drunk, lay down now and go to sleep."

She smiled at me, turned and put her legs on the bed and lay on her side facing the wall. She was still fully clothed but that wasn't unusual on these increasingly frequent gin-soaked nights. I left the door ajar and went to the kitchen to get myself a snack and had just taken my first bite out of a chocolate digestive when I heard a crash from her room followed by the door slamming shut. I crossed the hall and looked at my old bedroom door, imagining her on the floor behind it. It took me a while to force open the door, she had become a dead weight, but I managed to push her enough to get into the room.

"What are you doing?" I asked as I tried to move her towards the bed.

"I've left me bag downstairs, I need it, it's got me pills in it."

"You don't need them tonight; you've drunk too much anyway."

"No, I have to have them, I'll just..." lunging herself forward. I pushed her back and sighed.

"I'll get it, you stop here," shaking my head in frustrated despair as my anger rose. This wasn't fair, Mum drinking away her sorrows and leaving me to deal with the reality of this miserable life. I was so engrossed in self-pity, I didn't notice the unnatural silence from what should surely have been a noisy lock-in. The door to the storeroom was slightly open and it was only as I pushed it open and stepped inside that I realised my mistake; there was no lock-in. The door to the bar was open and the only light in the pub was from the three lava lamps, amplified by the mirrored wall behind them. I froze for a second, fearing I was about to catch Billy in the throes of passion with Shirley Blenkinsopp and was about to turn and run back upstairs when my stepfather suddenly appeared in the door way. He looked momentarily surprised and unnervingly strange in the orange glow.

"Mum needs her pills, she left her handbag down here," I said quickly. He looked to the side of him, nodded and took a step back. I swallowed. "Will you bring it up when you come?" I said weakly.

"It's just here," he nodded his head to the left, "you might as well get it." His grin exposing his yellowing teeth. "I'm just finishing me drink. It's been a busy night and your Mam's been a right pain."

"Has Shirley gone home?"

"Aye, she were a bit upset, your Mam had a go at her," shaking his head and frowning as he let out a long breath, "I'm gonna have to get her back to the doctor's, we can't keep on like this." He turned and moved out of sight towards the right. I closed my eyes and took in another breath before opening them and stepping forward and into the bar. I moved as quickly as I could towards Mum's high stool placed in the corner; her brown leather handbag was placed on top. Grabbing it, I was aware of him moving behind me and felt fear rising. Clutching the bag tightly as I turned quickly to face him, my absolute terror must have shown on my face as he burst out laughing.

"Bloody hell Rosie, I'm not some bloody monster; you don't have to be so scared of me." He tilted his head and smiled. He had a large measure of what was probably whisky in his right hand and he took a sip before putting it down on the bar.

I couldn't speak. I just stood rooted to the spot, staring at him. He was blocking the doorway to the storeroom and my escape route. I watched his expression change back to a frown as he leaned on the door frame and then he completely wrong footed me as he started to speak.

"I know your Mam's not well, what wi' losin' babby and her fall an' that but she's gonna have to sort her sen out. She were awful tonight."

"What Happened?"

"She threw a drink in Shirley's face after calling her some right choice names. Oh, and this were after tellin' a couple o' regulars that she were gonna bar 'em cos she knew they were sayin' stuff about her." He gave a small laugh, "and to be fair, they probably were an' they definitely will be now."

"I wish she didn't drink so much," I managed to say quietly.

"Aye, me an all," he shook his head sadly "we've got to do summat to help before she really hurts herself." He picked up his drink and knocked it back without the least sense of irony before turning to push it under the optic for a refill. Turning back, he took a slight step forward and, noticing me cower, he shook his head again and ran his free hand through his thinning hair.

"I'm not gonna hurt you, ya daft lass." He turned to walk towards the end of the bar and leaned into the open hatch, speaking without looking at me, "You best take her bag up to her and get your sen to bed."

I didn't need telling twice and was out of the bar, through the storeroom and back upstairs in a couple of seconds.

The next day Mum was badly hungover and slightly contrite but insisting she only remembered shouting at Shirley and had no recollection of throwing the drink at her. She chain-smoked at the kitchen table, refusing toast as she said she felt sick. Billy told her he was sick as well.

"Sick of the way you drink your sen stupid then start shoutin' at the customers. Summats got to change." He said Shirley was refusing to come back and that was leaving them in a right mess.

I was in the bathroom getting ready to go down to start the cleaning as his shouting got louder, fuelling his temper. He told Mum she had to go round and apologise to the 'bottle blonde busty barmaid' – not his words but that was how I always thought of her. Mum screamed back that he must think she was stupid, she knew exactly what was going on as did half the village and she wasn't going to apologise to that jumped up fat tramp and he would have to do a bit more work himself or get somebody else. This exchange ended with the inevitable slap and Davy starting to cry. I came out of the bathroom as Mum stormed by me, pushing me out of the way and slamming and locking the bathroom door behind her.

I gave my brother a cuddle and asked him if he wanted to come down and help me with the cleaning, promising him a trip to the park later. Billy was leaning on the sink, rubbing his chin and looking deep in thought. He didn't speak so I hurried Davy downstairs with me.

He came down to start stocking up the bar about an hour later as I was just finishing. He seemed a bit distracted but I was just glad his anger seemed to have worn itself out.

"Do me a favour, Rosie," he said as I came through the bar. He reached into his pocket and pulled out his wallet, "take Davy with you an' go round to Shirley's house and ask her if she'll come up." He took out two pound notes and held them out to me, "Here, this is for you, for the cleaning and for helpin' out an' that." I stood looking at the money. "Call it a bonus," he laughed, "tell Shirley ya Mam's not well so she's stopping in bed so there'll be no trouble and I really need her help." I took the money and nodded. "If you want you can go straight round to your Nan's after an' you can stop there for your dinner, I doubt we'll be havin much here today."

"Okay," I answered in a low whisper, "I'll just go and get our coats." I folded the two notes in half, ran upstairs and put the money in my running away jar which I now kept under my bottom bunk, feeling a sense of relief that things seemed to have calmed down.

Much later, I tried to recall what I noticed as I deposited the money and collected our coats. Were the bathroom door or Mum's bedroom door open or shut? Was I aware where Mum was? But the answer was no, I do not remember noticing anything. In my keenness to get away while my stepfather was in this equitable mood, I am almost certain I did not give Mum a second thought.

Shirley Blenkinsopp was a bit sniffy when she opened the door, standing with her hands on her hips. As I relayed the message, she stared at me with a makeup-free face that looked like she had been sucking a lemon.

"I'll be wanting double time," was all she said. I nodded and feeling that my errand was complete, I took my brother's hand and walked down the road to Nana's house.

She was pleased to see us but guessed of course that there was a problem. I told her that Billy had said Mum needed to go back to the doctor's.

"Billy's right," she said nodding, "she can't go on like this, she's drinking herself into an early grave. I'm going to have a good talk to her later." She ushered us both into the kitchen to help peel potatoes and carrots to go with our braising steak.

"Can we have Yorkshire puddings an' all, Nana?" Davy asked.

"Well of course, it's Sunday so it's the law," she laughed as she got out her bowl to mix up some batter. Davy was equally delighted to discover we would be having apple pie and custard for afters and she let him cut up some bananas to put in a jelly that she said we could take home.

While the dinner was cooking, we played a game of Ludo and two games of Snakes and Ladders and that is the image I try to keep in my mind when I think back to that day. The three of us sat around the table laughing, Davy cheating at every opportunity he got, Nana letting him win and winking at me, and the lovely smell of cooking as we sat in the warm and cosy kitchen.

Davy had just asked if he could have third helpings of pudding when there was a loud knock at the door. Nana was shaking her head and telling him not to be greedy as she frowned and stood up. I stood up as well and glanced over at the carriage clock on the mantelpiece. It was quarter past two. It had been a very loud knock and as she walked to the door, she laughed a little nervously,

"Goodness me, that sounds like a policeman's knock." It wasn't; it was one of regulars from The Swan.

I was in the doorway of the kitchen where I had a clear view down the hall. I couldn't catch all that was said but I heard him say '*your Barbara*' and '*ambulance*' but then he glanced over her shoulder and saw me then moved his head nearer to Nana and lowered his voice so I heard nothing else, just Nana starting to shout, "*No, no, please not that.*"

I haven't counted Mum in the tally of people I killed, although I have never lost the feeling of guilt about her death. By not being brave enough to see Billy off, the way I had The Widow, I was ultimately responsible for her death and it was that, the feeling of culpability, of Billy having somehow won, that caused something in me to shift.

## Eleven

According to the death certificate, Barbara Ann Flynn, my mother, died on 2nd April 1972 from a severe blood loss after severing both her ulnar and radial arteries. She was 32 years old.

When I asked Nana why there was an inquest, she explained it was because it was a sudden and unnatural death. I was hoping that it was because the police had realised what seemed as plain as day to me; Billy had murdered her.

There was an autopsy and, remarkably, the bruising and broken bones where attributed to her alcoholism and not her husband's fists so the body was released back to us for her funeral two weeks later. At the funeral, which was arranged by Nana, Billy cried his crocodile tears as he accepted condolences from practically all of the village, most of who could not get enough of the final chapter in *'that Barbara Cooper's scandalous life'*.

Nana retained sorrowful damp-eyed dignity during the proceedings, wiping away my brother's confused and anxious tears, his father barely acknowledging his presence. I remained completely dry-eyed throughout, as I had been since hearing of Mum's demise. I didn't need to mourn for her, I'd been mourning for her since the day she married Billy. Instead, I watched my stepfather in his charade of sadness and saw clearly that he was a murderer and he had got away with it. It takes one to know one.

The statement he gave to the police and then repeated at the inquest three months later was that he had gone back upstairs shortly after Davy and I had left. Mum had been asleep on her bed and so he had left her and gone back to the bar. Shirley arrived at half past eleven in time to help him open up. They'd been busy up to last orders when he told Shirley, and there were several other witnesses to this, that he was going up to ask Mum if she wanted to come and apologise for what had happened the night before. He ran upstairs but after a few minutes, started shouting. He'd found her in a bath full of blood with her wrists cut.

When asked about the evening before, he said she was in a funny mood all night and drinking even more heavily than normal. With this statement, he gave half a laugh and opened his eyes wide in incredulity, seeming completely oblivious to the sombre atmosphere of the room. You can put a villain in a suit and tie but he's still a villain and that's what he looked like to me as he stood up there with his hair all Brillcreamed back and his jaw line showing off small shaving nicks from a semi-blunt razor.

He told the coroner how Mum had suddenly turned 'nasty' shortly before closing time, how she began shouting and swearing at a couple of regulars who were sitting at the bar and, when Mrs Blenkinsopp had tried to calm her down, she had thrown a drink in her face and began to shout and swear at her. Mum had stormed off upstairs to bed at that point but he didn't go after her as,

"There were still a bar full of folk wanting serving and Shirley, Mrs Blenkinsopp, who were right upset, not to mention covered in gin and bitter lemon, had gone to the ladies." He went on to explain how, upon her return, Mrs Blenkinsopp had said she didn't think she could carry on working at The Swan until Barbara sorted herself out. He gave her a double brandy to calm her nerves and she left with the last of the customers. After clearing up the bar he got himself a drink and was standing alone in the bar having a *couple of minutes peace* to think about what he could do to help his wife.

"Rosie, me stepdaughter, came down to get her Mam's bag an' so I thought, she's alright an' I stopped down in the bar for about another half an hour afore I went up to bed meself." He explained that since Mum had miscarried, back in the summer, they had slept in separate rooms because, "to be honest, she's been a bit funny since then, you know just not right, sayin' stuff, imagining things, crying and doing nothing 'cept drinking. Well, I'm not sure she's been sober for the last couple o' years but I think losin' the babby was what tipped her over the edge."

I just stared at him, the lying evil bastard. The words flowing freely, his attempt at playing the devastated grief-stricken husband was surely fooling no one. I turned to look at Nana, her eyes lowered as she focused on her fingers, pulling at the hard skin around her nails.

"Nana," I started to say but she shushed me with a shake of the head, "but Nana, we can't just let him say these things..."

"We have to," she whispered, dipping her head close to my ear, "he's made sure it's what everybody thinks," picking up my hand and squeezing it, "don't make a fuss love or he'll make things bad for you and Davy." Sighing loudly, she added, "You and me know the truth." And I did.

Thinking through what Billy had said, how odd he had been, standing in the closed pub on his own, drinking whiskey, this wasn't the Billy I knew. And his concern for Mum, this wasn't real, I knew that deep down to my core, he had never really loved her; she had just been useful. Painting him in a good light for his *'taking her on'* and her initial gratitude and servitude as she became his workhorse until she had become a liability and, of course, Billy had clearly now found a replacement.

Just for a split second, as I'd stood trying not to shake with the fear he filled me with, I almost fell for his *'we have to do summat to help her'* but then I saw that look as he turned from the optics with his refill, I saw him look slightly to the left of me, just over my shoulder, and I noticed the other short glass with lipstick marks and I knew he had not been on his own in the bar.

After I'd fled back upstairs, Mum was still lying where I'd left her, drooling and snoring gently. I put her handbag on the bedside table and got her a cup of water and, after rolling her onto her side, I went to bed.

I'd heard the back door open and close sometime later and slipped silently out of bed and looked from the edge of the window to see Shirley Blenkinsopp scurrying away like the streetwalking strumpet she was.

When Shirley stood up and walked to the front to give her requested account at the inquest, Nana muttered, *"doesn't she look a sight,"* as she turned to face the coroner with all her goods out on display and plastered in makeup. The whole time she spoke, she held a white lace handkerchief in her left hand and occasionally pretended to dab away non-existent tears as she concurred with everything Billy had said, adding, "Me and Barbara have been mates for years an' we alus got on but this last year, she's not been right and God help me I tried to help her but well," dab, dab, "well there were no helpin' her." She dropped her head before lifting her handkerchief to her cold, dry eyes.

The coroner ruled that Mum had taken her own life while the state of her mind was disturbed and I could tell that was what everyone was expecting but Nana and I squeezed each other's hands and said nothing. We got up and left the court in silence and walked out onto the road where one of Nana's neighbours was waiting in his khaki green Austin 1300 to take us home.

Davy and I stayed with Nana right from the moment Mum had been found. It made it easier for Billy to deal with all the day to day stuff and his *'grief'*, us being out of the way. Nana had been careful around him, placating almost, which at first made me mad until I worked out what was going on.

As he had never officially adopted me, I could choose to stay with her now and not go back, but Davy was a different story.

"Of course he can't look after Davy," she explained, "but that won't stop him using him to get at you or me if we cross him. We have to let him think we believe him and play along." She looked so tired and worn down by it all.

"I'm never going back to live there," I said stubbornly.

"And I don't want you to go back there but let's just not go in with all guns blazing. That'll get us nowhere, well it will get Billy's back up and make him insist that Davy goes back to The Swan."

"But he'll hate that," I declared, looking at my eight year-old brother engrossed in the television as we stood in the doorway, "and it's not like he'd look after him on his own, even if he didn't have the pub to run." Nana jerked her head away from the door as a signal for me to follow her into the kitchen.

"No, he won't, but that's not the point with Billy," letting out a deep sorrowful sigh, "and I'm sure it won't be long before he's not on his own." After the slightest of pauses for us both to take that in, she straightened up and shook away the painful thought.

"So shall we have egg, chips and beans for our tea today?"

"That sounds great, shall I peel some potatoes?" I brought out my practised smile as I went over to the pantry.

The week after the inquest, I celebrated my fifteenth birthday with tea and cake when Davy and I got home from school. It was a Wednesday and the last week before we broke up for the six week holidays and Julie came up for the evening. We were chatting all the way home and Davy was full on laughing as I opened the front door. All three of us were struck dumb as we walked through the hall and saw Billy sitting in Nana's kitchen, a mug of tea in one hand, a cigarette in the other. Davy's face crumbled as he took in the scene and he sat on the floor to take off his shoes but stayed there.

"Here she is, the birthday girl," Billy said jovially, treating me to a massive grin. "Happy birthday Rosie! Fifteen now!"

"Thanks," I said, taking my shoes off. Julie stayed behind me, she was terrified of Billy and even before I told her that I was certain he had murdered Mum, she said she thought he was a really bad man and probably capable of doing terrible things. I was unsure what to do and looked at Nana who gave slight nod and a tight smile.

"Here you are love," holding out a white envelope, "there's a bit of summat inside to get your sen summat nice." All his yellow stained teeth were on show and I could smell the nicotine on his breath as I reached to take it with as big a smile as I could manage and a thank you that I hoped sounded real.

"Go on then open it," he said, nodding his head eagerly. I tore it open to reveal a card with a drawing of a girl in very bright clothes walking a dog. As I opened it, two five pounds notes fell out and I bent to retrieve them quickly before reading the inside. In capital letters and blue biro was written, 'Happy Birthday Rosie, love Billy' with three x's below his name.

"Thank you, Billy!" I said with further enthusiasm, "that's really generous."

"Yeah, I know but, well with all that happened and that, you deserve a bit of a treat." He took a swig of his tea and wiped his mouth on the back of his hand before lifting his cigarette and drawing in a big lung full of smoke.

"Come on in Davy lad, come an' give your Dad a big cuddle," he said, leaning past me to see in the hall.

"Julie just needs to go to the toilet, Nana," I said quickly, seeing my friends eyes shiny with tears and nodding at her saying, "You go on up to the bathroom, Julie." She took the stairs two at a time. Davy got to his feet and came into the kitchen. He walked robotically towards his father and stood in front of him looking very much like the condemned man. Billy didn't press him for a 'cuddle', instead he just ruffled his hair and asked him how he was getting on at school. I could see Davy struggling to answer with more than one word but Billy didn't seem to notice, or if he did, he didn't seem to mind his son's discomfort.

"So me an' your Nana's just been talking about what's best for you two, now well, you know now your Mam's not here to look after you." He cocked his head on one side and assumed a serious expression. "I mean, it'd not be easy you two back at home, I mean, I work long hours an' I don't think it'd be fair on you Rosie luv, having to stop in all the time and look after our Davy." He paused to take a last long drag of his cigarette before stubbing it out in the ashtray.

"So for the time being it'd be better if you stopped here with your Nan," as he said the words, I felt relief soar through my body, he saw it too.

"This is only temporary mind you," he added with his not so friendly grin, "We can't be relying on your poor old Nan forever, so just while I sort out running The Swan an' get back on top of things, we'll leave things as they are." He ruffled Davy's hair again and I could see my brother's effort in trying not to flinch. "I'll see you both Saturday and Sunday mornings when you come up to do the cleaning an' we'll see how we get on. That alright with you, our Davy?" My brother smiled at him and nodded.

"Right then, that's sorted," standing up and giving me one of his looks, "Course, if gets too much for your Nan then we'll have to have a think about a better solution." I nodded, my face was hurting from the forced smile and I could see my brother just wanted get away.

Julie crept back downstairs as the front door slammed and we all sat down at the table, avoiding sitting in the seat Billy had just vacated. Nana picked up the ash tray, emptied and cleaned it before putting in back on the sideboard and cleaned the table before getting out some glasses and bottle of Dandelion and Burdock.

"Right," she said brightly, "How was school today?" Davy told her it was okay and asked if we were having cake straight away. She got out a plate of potted meat sandwiches, cut into triangles, bowls of crisps and finally, to top off the savouries, there was a cheese and pineapple hedgehog made from an orange and cocktail sticks.

"Wow," I said, "This is great."

"Good," Nana said, nodding her head and looking pleased as the atmosphere continued to lighten and we all began chatting.

Julie was full of excitement about starting her new life as a working girl the following week, still telling me that I was wasting my time stopping on and doing exams but, since Mum died and the circus of events that followed, she'd been a lot more like my old friend.

Karen had also been nicer to me although she seemed to have quite a large group of friends now and a lot of them were older. It was her idea that the three of us should go into Wakefield for a night out to celebrate my birthday. Both of them were already fifteen and had been to the Mecca on Monday nights quite a few times but Karen was suggesting we go on a Friday night when *'there won't be so many kids'*.

"I'm not sure me Mam and Dad will let me go," Julie said and I knew for a fact Nana would not be giving me her blessing.

"Well don't tell them," was Karen's solution. "We'll tell them we are going to a party. You can say it's my cousin's and even say me Mam and Dad will be there if you want."

"What if they don't let us in, you know, cos we don't look eighteen?" I asked.

"We just have to make sure we do look eighteen," she beamed at us, "it'll be a right laugh. You should both come round mine and we'll get the bus into Wakey from there." She giggled, "I'll ask our Laney to help tart us up a bit before we go."

Laney was one of Karen's older sisters and very glamorous. She was already a fully qualified hairdresser and worked in one of the big shops in Wakefield.

I did ask Karen to if she wanted to come to Nana's for tea and cake but she'd already started her hairdressing apprenticeship, signing her indentures the Monday before and missing the last week of school, *"Well there's no point going to school for the last week, not like I was gonna learn anything..."*

The prospect of a night out was really quite exciting. I didn't like lying to Nana but knew she'd never let me go if I told her the truth.

When Julie and I got to Karen's house that Friday at half past six, it was her Mum that opened the door, holding her lit cigarette with two fingers close to her face and having just exhaled, we couldn't see her for the cloud of smoke.

"Ready for your big night out then?" she said, stepping aside, "Come on in an' get yourselves tarted up." As we stepped past her, she gave a cackling laugh and, turning to go back into the living room, muttered, "Like bloody lambs to the slaughter."

Karen was sitting at the kitchen table, already heavily made up, as her sister stood behind her backcombing her hair. There was an array of makeup; hair brushes, clips and pins all laid out in front of her as well as a big black box with a red light on.

"They're me Mam's 'lectric rollers, she says we can use 'em, I've already had 'em in." She stopped speaking as her sister gave a very liberal spay of Harmony lacquer around the large mound of hair she had created to start her beehive. Now we had full view of her face, including the very bright blue eye-shadow and false eyelashes.

"Wow, you look so different," I blurted out, "so grown up."

"I am grown up," she retorted sharply, "I've left school and got a job and tonight I'm going to get a boyfriend."

Laney put the electric rollers in Julie's hair next while I put on my makeup. I had brought my newly acquired makeup bag which had been Mum's. I had taken it out of the top drawer in her bedroom when I had been back at The Swan the previous weekend to get the rest of my clothes. I had already taken a bottle of Anne French moisturiser and the tail comb she always used for poking her hair back into shape and they were hidden at the back of my underwear drawer at Nana's, along with my running away money and the wedding picture. There weren't a lot of items in the bag, Mum didn't wear a lot of makeup, but I knew there were some other things on the dressing table in Billy's room. I didn't dare go in there.

Karen was looking suitably impressed as I started to get a few bits out. She particularly like the unused lipstick, the label at the bottom stated it was Mulberry and she declared it be fabulous. I declined the offer of her eye-shadow, preferring my own not quite as bright, and also decided against the false eyelashes but I gratefully accepted some of her Rimmel foundation, powder and rouge and agreed to her request to try my lipstick which looked okay on her but much better on me.

Laney did Julie an up style but with much less backcombing than Karen's, and I said I didn't really want mine up so she took the sides back in what she called a semi-up style with a small bit of backcombing on top.

"Right," she said, as I stood up, "I think you're all good to go, you look eighteen no problem." She turned to her sister who was pouting at herself in the mirror, "Don't you forget what I told you, don't be letting some lad think cos he's bought you a drink he can start mauling you and, for Christ's sake, don't get too drunk an' miss the last bus home."

We got off the bus at the bus station and I gave the clock tower a small glance as we tottered down the road and walked into The Mite pub.

"Everybody goes in here first for a few drinks before the Mecca," she informed us with a big smile, walking confidently to the bar. Keeping her smile fixed in place, she was soon served by a fairly old bloke who grinned a lot; we stood close behind and I was keen not to make eye contact with him or anyone else. We drank our halves of lager and blackcurrant fairly quickly, standing slightly to the left of the bar as we looked around. The pub was getting fuller and I saw a couple of girls I recognised from our school who were actually in the year below us and, to me, looked nowhere near the legal age to drink but saw them served with Martini and lemonade.

"Shall we have another?" I asked as I took the last mouthful of my drink. They both agreed we should and I made my way to the three-deep queues of drinkers and found the hint of a gap to move my way into. My friends followed and I was soon handing them both another drink which we managed to make last a little bit longer.

One of the people I brushed against at the bar was an older bloke who looked almost Billy's age and equally as creepy. As we stood close to one of the side walls, he edged his way over and started trying to chat us up. I was very wary of him so I semi-turned away and fixed what I hoped was an aloof, bored expression. Julie looked like a rabbit in headlights and Karen was just plain rude, telling him to piss off and find some girls who weren't too choosey. He retorted with a forced laugh saying we were frigid lesbians and he had actually been feeling sorry for us as we looked like prozzies who needed some work; I actually though that was funny but Karen was not impressed.

We edged our way through the throng a bit closer to the door where a group of five lads were standing and Karen shamelessly pretended to trip and knock into one of them. She had cleverly picked the one without a drink in his hand, who also happened to be the best looking. She was quick to apologise and bat her very long eyelashes at him so fast I'm surprised the over bright strip lighting didn't make her have some sort of a fit.

We were soon in conversation with the lads, Karen practically glued to the good looking one as they told us they were on a pub crawl. We somehow, courtesy of one or more of this gang, had a third drink in our hands as our shouted chatter managed to keep going amid the rising background noise. Karen was keen to tell them we were going to the Mecca and the conversation moved to us going to another pub with them to see where that would lead. Julie looked like she was about to pass out at such a suggestion but Karen was really up for it. I shook my head and said I was looking forward to having a dance at which one of them put his arms round me in a kind of bear hug and said he could dance with me somewhere a bit more private if I liked. I broke away and put my almost untouched drink down on a table and said, 'Thanks but no thanks," and stepped to the side, linking arms with Julie before looking directly at Karen.

"We're off to the Mecca now, you coming?"

She did come with us, reluctantly, but not before having a bit of a snog with the good looking lad and practically begging him to come with us, saying she'd be waiting for him. I didn't hear his response but did see her pick up the drink I had put down and gulp almost all of it down before following us out.

I really enjoyed the Mecca, it seemed so grown up and I felt a bit like I was on top of the pops as we were dancing. Karen insisted on another drink as soon as we got in and told Julie it was her round. She asked for a Martini and lemonade so Julie decided to have the same. I said I didn't want one which is just as well as the drinks were so expensive, Julie only just had enough left for her bus fare home.

We danced around our handbags for a bit but Karen kept walking off the dance floor just looking round. I'm not sure if she was looking for the lads from the pub or just sizing up all the males of a suitable age to be her boyfriend. After a long spell of dancing to four songs in a row, Julie and I came off the dance floor to where she had left her drink. The glass was empty and Karen was standing at the bar with a couple of lads talking quite animatedly. Julie shrugged and held up her watch to show me it was gone half past ten. We needed to leave in fifteen minutes to get the last bus home. We went over and told Karen we were going to the ladies as it was nearly time to go. Karen shrugged us off, saying there was loads of time. After we came out of the ladies she was still standing at the bar and seemed to be in some sort of an argument with another girl. After a couple of minutes, the girl threw a drink at her and she stepped back in shock, covered in something dark and sticky. We later found out it was cherry brandy and lemonade. The girl was the girlfriend or actually the fiancée of the lad Karen had been trying to chat up and she was not impressed. She had been even less impressed when Karen had told her to piss off and called her a slag when she had demanded to know what she thought she was playing at.

We got to the bus stop with seconds to spare and all the way home we had to listen to Karen complaining that we had ruined her night. Julie and I exchanged looks but said little. We went to the Mecca again quite a few times after that but we never went with Karen.

## Twelve

The seasons changed again and things carried on pretty much the same, although Billy did start to give Nana ten pounds a week towards our keep. When I saw the relief on her face the first time he handed over the two five pound notes, I was worried she might be struggling with money. I'd no idea about her finances, I knew she collected her pension every Monday and was fairly keen for food not to be wasted but this started me worrying.

A week later, I got a Saturday job at the chemist over at Painthorpe. The pharmacist was a really nice lady called Miss Alderson who had only just bought the shop and lived in the flat above. She offered me the shop assistant job straight away when I said I wanted to go into nursing and I thought learning the names of medicines and lotions would be helpful. The other lady who worked there looked down her nose at me, clearly knowing who I was, but luckily my appointment wasn't up to her. The shop's opening hours were 9.00 to 15.30 on Saturdays and my hours were ten until three.

Taking the job meant getting to The Swan a bit earlier to do the cleaning first, so Billy gave me a key to the back door. I told Nana that I wanted to contribute towards my keep so was giving the money I earned at the chemist to her. She hugged me with tears in her eyes at this announcement and I thought it was because she was relieved and I'd been right about her not having enough income to look after us; it was some years later before I discovered this was not the case.

It was around then she told me of Billy's long term plan for Davy's future. When she told him I was staying on at school and she was hoping

I might be the first person in our family to go to university, he was surprisingly impressed. Saying I was a clever lass and, if that was what I wanted, it would be good but it would be expensive. After the pretence of a bit of thought, he said the perfect solution would be for her to sell her house and move into the pub with Davy so she could look after him. Seeing the horror on my face, she laughed and said obviously she could not imagine a worse fate than living at The Swan, cooking and cleaning for Billy and it was never going to happen. However, what she actually said to him was,

"I think, long term that'll probably be the best thing, let's get through the next year and see how she does in her GCE's," and he'd smiled and nodded contentedly. "Hopefully, he'll leave us as we are for now," sighing deeply. "He's been trying to get his hands on my savings and the house since your Grandad died," she said, pouring herself a cup of tea. I nodded before asking her what would happen to The Swan if Billy died. She looked up startled and took a couple of seconds studying my face before saying she wasn't sure but it would probably belong to Davy. I nodded slowly as she narrowed her eyes, still looking for something in my expression. I shrugged and said with a laugh,

"Anyway, he's not going anywhere is he, it's only the good that die young."

This seemed to ease her concern and she smiled and nodded. I picked up my school books and packed them back in my bag, wondering what would happen to The Swan if Billy went to prison but deciding not to ask.

Throughout November, it was hard not to be aware of the gossip around the village about Billy and Shirley Blenkinsopp. He had taken on a second barmaid a month or so before, an attractive young married woman with a baby. She only worked three shifts before her employment came to an abrupt end. According to local gossip, started by a couple of the regulars and passed on via the village shop, Shirley wasn't happy about this appointment and was 'right hard on the lass', making her cry, telling her she was useless and the likes. Her husband had turned up the day after and told Billy she wasn't coming back as his fancy woman was 'a right cow' and he wasn't paying her enough to put up with the way she treated her. Billy wasn't too happy with this turn of events but it was somehow smoothed over and the next new barmaid was a much older and less attractive woman who Shirley got on with much better.

It was about this time when the charade, pretending Shirley had just got there before me when I arrived to do the cleaning, stopped. I shrugged as Billy began to explain they'd had a late lock-in and so she'd stopped over, like it was the first time, sleeping on the sofa; as if I was stupid. Shirley stood in the doorway, a smug expression on her fat, makeup smeared face and wearing a tatty lacy nightdress that might have at one time have been white. She made sure she caught my eye before turning and going back upstairs. I finished my cleaning in record time that day, needing to get to the chemist a bit early. As I was about to leave, he came up from the cellar.

"Still working hard at school your nana tells me?" I nodded and forced a smile. "Well any road, it's been an 'orrible year for us all and I know you do a lot, looking after our Davy," he reached in his back pocket and brought out his wallet, "so here's a bit of extra spending money for ya." He held a five pound and four one pound notes. My payment for the one hour on a Saturday and the two hours on a Sunday morning had recently been raised to £2.50 a week. "Let's call this a bonus cos of how hard you're working," he grinned, clearly delighted in my quiet compliance. I took the money and said thank you and left quickly. I put two pounds in my running away money and gave the five pounds to Nana along with my chemist money, leaving me two pounds to spend. When I told her about Shirley having 'slept on the sofa', Nana laughed.

"So the extra was hush money then?" she said, "Stupid man, Shirley's telling everybody she's moving in after Christmas, it's all over the village."

"He won't try and take Davy back will he?" I asked.

"Not a chance, Shirley won't be wanting to look after him and I think Billy'll get a bit of a shock once she's got her feet under his table. She won't be as obliging as your mother was."

"Well let's hope she doesn't come to any harm then," I said, going into the kitchen to put the kettle on. I didn't look back at her but I felt her eyes on me.

"Is it okay if I go out tonight with Julie?"

"As long as you get the last bus home and don't be drinking too much!" We had stopped pretending I was going to under-18 discos with no alcohol after I confessed the truth following the Karen incident. She had been okay about it, saying as long as I worked hard, she was happy for me to have a night out at the weekend, if I was careful.

A few weeks before, Julie and me had gone into Wakefield with the intention of going to the Mecca but had instead stayed in The Mitre until closing then come home. We'd managed to get seats this time, close to the jukebox and there were a couple of other girls there that she knew from work. It was a really fun evening and a lad called Mike turned up after a bit and asked her for a date the following week.

She'd been out with him twice since and said he was really nice. She was meeting him at The Mitre that night with a friend who she was sure I'd like. I was reluctant at first but she had promised that if I didn't like the look of him, she would go to the Mecca with me. Mike had agreed to this, saying there was no way I wouldn't like his mate.

As soon as we got our drinks, we moved over towards the jukebox. Julie immediately spotted Mike who came over with another lad. He was introducing us, well mainly me to him, but I didn't hear his name, or take in anything about him. My attention was focused totally just behind him, slightly to the left. Standing with a pint in his hand, smiling and nodding at something someone beside him had said, was Darren, my almost first boyfriend.

He looked slightly out of place and very much on the edge of the group and I stepped back and to the side to get a better look at him and his gaze drifted my way. I gave him what I hoped was an encouraging smile and he frowned and tilted his head slightly before making his way over to me. Julie was tugging at my sleeve but I shrugged her off saying I just needed to speak to someone and moved to meet him.

"Hey," I said quickly as he stopped in front of me, still looking puzzled, "don't you remember me?" I gave a little laugh, "Maybe if I go and stand under the clock at the bus station?"

"Bloody hell! Little Josie!" he laughed and held his hand out towards my face.

"Rosie," I corrected, "or am I just one of lots of girls you promised to meet under the clock?" I turned my mouth down in a mock despair, "or maybe I'm the only one you stood up?"

"Rosie, yeah, course, I promise you're the only one and I really have a good excuse for not turning up." He nodded at my almost empty glass, "Let me get you another drink."

"Well I'm here with a friend..." I started to say but then quickly changed my mind, "Yeah okay, I'll have half a lager and blackcurrant."

"Yuk," he pulled a face and shook his head.

"It's great," I replied, "tastes like Spangles."

As he moved towards the bar, I turned and stepped back to speak to Julie. She clearly wasn't too pleased with me. I didn't even look at Mike or his friend. I told her I was just having a drink and a quick chat with an old friend, to which she snapped,

"You don't have any friends 'cept me."

"Julie!" I exclaimed, surprised and annoyed by her sharpness.

"Look, you came out with me to meet Mike's mate so stop messing around."

"I've seen somebody I haven't seen for ages and I'm..." I started to say.

"Right well enjoy your chat, we're off down to Friar Tucks now so you'll have to come and find us if you're stopping here." She finished the last of her drink and the two lads did the same and they walked off. I stood for a second, wondering what I should do before turning back to the bar. Darren was just getting served and I waited until he'd paid and picked up the drinks. As he turned round, his face lit up to see me waiting there. Stepping away from the throng at the bar, I told him my friend had gone on to another pub.

"What? And she's left you on your own, like at the fair?" he shook his head, "You need to get yourself some better mates, little Rosie."

We moved nearer the door where it was quieter and he took a big slurp of his beer and wiped his mouth with the back of his hand before grinning at me.

"I have thought about you loads since that day at the fair."

"Oh aye, you didn't even remember my name," smiling, I took a sip of my drink.

"Course I did, I were just teasing." He stopped smiling and looked down for a second before saying, "I've had some stuff goin' on, the last year's been a bloody nightmare," taking in a deep breath, his smile returned, "but now, as of this minute, I think it's starting to get better."

"Right, well that's nice but you were telling me why you stood me up."

"Yeah, well it's a bit of a long story..." he started to say, his smile fading a little.

"You better start telling it then," I interrupted, wanting him to keep smiling at me. He took in a deep breath and looked down at his beer, his frown back as he seemed to be choosing his words.

"Okay," he began, "well the first thing I better tell you is I wasn't telling the truth when I met you at the dodgems." He took a small sip of his drink and I kept my eyes on his expression. He didn't meet my eyes as he said, "I wasn't there with me mates, I was there with me girlfriend."

It took a good half hour for him to tell me about Tina. Not only had she been his girlfriend then, but he was living in the spare room of her parent's house at that time and they were engaged. She was seventeen and he was twenty-five. They had gone to the fair in her car but had a massive argument on the way, which continued as they got out of the car. They had not even been on a ride together when, according to him, she stormed off and left him.

"You lied about your age!" I said with a sharp intake of breath, "So how old are you now?"

"I didn't lie, I never told you how old I was, you just guessed I was eighteen." He held up both of his hands in surrender, "Yeah, I know, I should have told you but, well the actual truth is you really did cheer me up. It had been a really shit day, I mean really shit and then suddenly there you were, a little ray of sunshine and that couple of hours we spent together was actually the only highlight of that year." He took another drink and I kept quiet as I took in the complement. "So even when I knew you were way too young for me, I sort of thought we could maybe have a laugh or something."

"So you're twenty-five now then?" I asked and he grinned and said, "ish, I was twenty-six last week." I shook my head, he certainly didn't look that old.

"So you ask me on a date, after snogging me, twice, and then you went back to your girlfriend?" I shook my head, "I don't even know why I'm still here." I made to turn away but he grabbed my arm.

"Please don't go, let me finish." I looked from his hand up to his face and he immediately let go of me. "I didn't go back to Tina's, she'd told me she didn't want to see me again, we'd been arguing for weeks and it was actually a relief when she said she was finished with me."

"Right, so where did you go?"

"I went to Mum's," taking another drink and shaking his head, he continued, "it were a tricky situation all round, see, Tina's Dad is my boss, he owns the garage where I worked then, that's how me an' her got together."

"Alright," I said slowly with my eyes narrowed, "and are you and Tina still engaged?"

"No," he said but with extra emphasis on the o. He finished his drink in one mouthful. My glass was still three quarters full. "Do you want another drink?"

"No thanks," I said, "I don't drink a lot and I don't really want to get drunk now it looks like I'm getting the bus home on my own."

"Do you fancy some chips then?" he asked, putting his empty glass on the ledge just behind him, "We can go and get some and I'll get the bus with you and walk you to your door." He gave me that cute smile and I felt the butterflies flapping around my insides again.

"I'll think about it while you tell me why, if you and Tina had finished that day, you stood me up three weeks later."

"Yeah, well it were all a bit tricky," he started to say.

"Yes, you've said that, you lived in their spare room and her Dad was your boss but she'd just finished with you and you were relieved, so...."

"Well, like I said, we hadn't been getting on for ages so I stayed with me Mam for a bit but then on the Friday, the day before I was gonna meet you, she told me she'd missed two periods and was pretty sure she was pregnant."

"This gets better and better, you're going to tell me next that you're married to her," I laughed but stopped sharply, noticing his expression. "Oh my God," shaking my head in disbelief, "you are, you're married!"

"Yeah well, we did, yeah, we got married. Her Mam and Dad and my Mam an' all, they were all keen we should," he shrugged, "but I don't think she really wanted to, well she wanted to get married an' stuff but just not to me."

"What about you, did you want to?"

"I didn't know what I wanted but me Mam said I was to think about the kid, that it were my baby and I should do the right thing."

"So you got married," I said, nodding my head at him and locking eyes. He nodded and moved his hand towards his empty glass then paused for a second before picking it up.

"I'm more than ready for another pint if I'm gonna tell you the rest." He gave me a straight mouthed smile and asked, "Do you want another one? I promise I'll take you home after."

"What about the mates you came with?" I said, suddenly remembering he was with a group when I'd first spotted him.

"They've already moved on," the skin around his big sad brown eyes crinkling as he attempted a smile, "and to be honest, this is the first time I've been out for ages an' I'm not that bothered."

"Okay, go on then I'll have another lager and blackcurrant please," I nodded and took a gulp of my existing drink. He took a step away and then turned back,

"You're not gonna run off while I'm at the bar are you?"

"Course not," I laughed, "I'll wait here and just hope you actually come back." I was trying my best to sound confident and forthright and remind myself how let down I'd felt when he hadn't turned up that day. A lot had happened in those fourteen months, to him as well as me, but no matter how much I liked him and was flattered by his attention, I wasn't the same young girl he'd flirted with then; now I had an agenda.

He came back with our drinks and tried to distract me by asking if things had got better with my 'orrible' stepdad. I told him they had got worse but I still needed to hear his story. So he told me about getting married the week after Christmas at the registry office, about Tina's parents giving them the deposit for a house two streets away from them which they moved into in January. He said it was hard living with her parents and he'd hoped it would be better in their own house.

"If anything, things got worse," he said sadly, "She was really sick a lot with the baby and was unhappy, which of course was all my fault."

Their son, Daniel, was born on the 3rd April and she had a hard time of it. When she brought the baby home, he seemed to cry constantly, day and night, and *he* was, according to Tina, useless. We left the pub and walked to the bus station as he finished the story.

He had come home from work one Friday at the end of June to be met in the kitchen by his in-laws and all his belongings were packed up by the door. His father-in-law, who had barely spoken to him all week, told him he no longer had a job and gave him an envelope of money. This was his wage up to date plus an extra month in lieu of notice. He was told to take his bags and leave. When he asked where Tina and Daniel were, his mother-in-law said they were somewhere safe and his father-in-law added that if he ever tried to bother them again, he would break both his legs and maybe even his neck.

"I asked them what I was supposed to have done but they just said don't try and pull that one, you know right well what you've done." We had just taken our seats on the bus, upstairs at the back. "So that was it. I took me stuff out to the car and they didn't say another word to me."

"Oh my goodness, what was it you'd done."

"I swear there was nothing I could think of, I'd yelled a bit occasionally, you know, short of sleep and that, but not half as much as she yelled at me. It was completely out of the blue, although afterwards, I realised I should have noticed summat weren't right."

"What do you mean?"

"She were a bit funny about Daniel. Sometimes when she couldn't get him to settle, I'd try to help and she didn't like it. She didn't like it at all if I picked him up when he were crying and managed to sooth him," he shrugged, "I did not hurt her or Daniel, ever; even when she lashed out at me." He took in a deep breath, "She hit me with her shoe once on my shoulder, although she were aiming for my head."

"Did your in-laws know about that?" I asked.

"All they knew was what she told 'em, a pack of lies from start to finish. She really went to town about how I hit her, which I never did, not once, she just hated me and wanted me gone."

"Wow, and they just believed her?"

"At first, but they know now she made it up," he said, shaking his head.

"And is it okay now, I mean, do you get to see your son?"

"Yeah, it took a while but I get to see him, once a week." His face lit up, "I go over and collect him and take him back to Mum's," rubbing his temples, "the in-laws are a bit less blinkered now about their lovely daughter."

"That's terrible," I said, feeling embarrassed by my understatement.

"Yeah, it's pretty shite but hey, my little man is incredible and I don't have to put up with Tina's violent temper anymore. She'll always be my son's mother so I can't get her out of my life completely but at least her Mam and Dad know now I wasn't the one throwing the punches."

"So are you divorced now?" I asked.

"No, not yet, we've put in for irretrievable breakdown so we have to wait two years," he shrugged, "crazy eh, we were only married seven months before she chucked me out. Anyway, there you have it, my whole sorry story." He turned towards me, his face really close, "I honestly forgot all about our date on the day I was supposed to meet you but I've thought about you loads since." He held up his hand, "Honest, I swear on my mother's life."

"Well, that's sort of the opposite to me," I replied with half smile, "I thought about you lots in the two hours I hung around the bus station that day waiting for you and quite a bit as I ate my dinner, on my own in the Wimpey, but I haven't thought about you again until tonight." He chuckled and shook his head.

"Oh Rosie, you are really a one off, seeing you tonight must be some sort of payback to me for all the bloody awful times I've had over the last year." He lifted his left arm to check the time on his watch before tentatively putting it along the back of the seat but he did not touch me. "Do you think we'll get to The Swan before closing time so I can meet the infamous Bastard Billy?"

"Ah well," I said leaning slightly into him, enjoying his warmth and the smell of his aftershave, "the last year's been bloody awful for me as well, maybe even worse than yours. Now's not the time for you to meet Billy but if you really mean that you want to see me again, well maybe I'll tell you about it, but I don't want to be messed about again."

"I do want to see you again, I absolutely do, and I want to hear about your bloody awful year, although I honestly don't think it can be worse than mine," he shrugged and then gave me a hug, "but whatever's happened, I want to try and make it better."

"We'll see," I said, smiling at his twinkling eyes, "let's start by seeing if you turn up for a second date."

"But surely this is our second date," he said laughing.

"No!" I replied quickly, "In actual fact this isn't even our first date."

"Okay, I'm working tomorrow but only till half one, and I work in Wakey so do you want to come an' meet me when I finish and we can go and have that a bit of dinner in the Wimpey?"

"I work on a Saturday till three," I said and saw his face drop, "but I could ask if I can finish a bit early and get the half two bus."

"Alright, I can hang around for a bit but how will I know if you'll be on the bus?"

"I guess you'll just have to stand under the clock and wait."

I gave him one of my sweetest smiles.

## Thirteen

The day after I'd met Darren again, I did get the two-thirty bus and we had a wonderful afternoon although there was still a disagreement about whether it was our first, second or even third date. Whatever, it was a great and he drove me home to Nana's although I got out of his car at the bus stop. I was still smiling as I thought about him the next morning when I was cleaning. I was brought out of my daydream by Billy's pretend friendly voice asking me if I'd pack up all Mum's knickknacks and stuff from her bedroom.

"It's daft it all just sat here in your old bedroom an' some of it might be alright for you."

I told him I would come back the next day after school and sort it out, thinking this must mean that Shirley Blenkinsopp was about to move in like she'd been telling everyone that she was. Nana, however, wasn't so sure that Billy was as committed to this arrangement.

"I'd better come with you," she said and I agreed enthusiastically. We set off as soon as I'd got home that Monday evening, leaving Davy watching telly. Billy was stocking up the bar as there was a darts match that evening and he was doing *'a bit of a stock take while he were at it'* so we could just go on up and get on with it and we were immensely relieved. He handed us two empty crisp boxes he'd saved for us as we walked by the storeroom.

"There's not much, I mean, she weren't one for tarting her sen up. I've left her stuff where it was so take what you want." He looked solemn and spoke like he actually had some feelings for her. Nana and I exchanged the briefest of looks; he wasn't fooling us.

We quickly filled the boxes with her things; some makeup, a lot of it unused, three bottles of unopened perfume, four boxes of bath cubes, soap and talc, all Yardley's Wind Song which I knew was her favourite, and some bits of jewellery, necklaces, bracelets and earrings. She had pierced ears but had a small box of clip on ones that I remembered dressing up in when I'd been small, in my life before Billy. There was a framed wedding photo of her and Billy with a beaming Grandad shaking hands with the groom. Nana was smiling sadly as we picked our way through the remnants of her lost child. There were a dozen or so magazines, mostly Woman's Own or Woman's Realm although there was a more recent copy of Cosmopolitan, along with a small pile of birthday cards. In the bottom drawer, I found a boxed dressing table vanity set comprising a hand mirror, hairbrush, clothes brush and comb. Nana said it had been a present for Mum's fifteenth birthday. She picked up the mirror and examined the beautiful needlepoint embroidered flowers on the back.

"I never realised this was such good quality," turning the mirror around, her brow furrowed, "its silver plated." She was voicing her thoughts and her eyes narrowed as she struggled to pin down a memory.

"I'm surprised Billy isn't keeping it then," I said, hoping to bring her out of what looked like a painful recollection. She glanced up at me but her eyes were far away. I picked up the hair brush and felt the weight of it as Nana suddenly tilted her head to look at the box and snapped out of her daze. She put the mirror down on the bed and began pulling up the satin-lined cardboard of the inner box.

"Careful, Nana," I said quickly, "you'll spoil it."

"I just need to look and see," she began as she eased her hand inside the lining and pulled out a piece of folded paper and a metal badge that looked like a French horn with a white Yorkshire rose in the middle of it.

Her face was horror-stricken at the sight of the badge and she dropped it back into the box and carefully opened out the note. It had clearly been folded and refolded many times. I watched as the colour drained completely from her face and her mouth opened as if she were about to scream but instead she let out a small stifled "oh" and closed her eyes briefly, releasing two massive tear drops.

"What is it Nana?" I stood up and leaned towards her.

"Oh my God, why didn't I see it?" I knew she was talking to herself which was alarming me even more that her tears.

"Nana," I tried to make my voice sound harder, "what is it, what's wrong?" I reached for the note. I was half expecting her to pull it a way or at least not let go but she released her hold and I took it as she gave out a shuddering sob. I lifted the flimsy piece of paper and read the words, silently.

*To my beautiful Barbara Ann, you are so special and one day very soon I will show you just how much you mean to me. Love A x*

"Who's A?" I asked as I lowered the note, "One of Mum's early boyfriends?"

"Your Mum didn't have any boyfriends," she said flatly before looking at me and adding, "except the one we never knew about." I held her stare; suddenly realising she was looking for a resemblance in my features. I was about to speak when we heard Billy calling up from the bottom of the stairs to ask if we were nearly done. I got up and called from just outside the door, telling him yes, we were just finishing off and would be done in about five minutes. When I turned back, Nana was putting the note and the badge back where we had found it. She put Mum's good nightdress on top of it and placed it in the crisp box.

"Anything else?" She was back to herself, if a little too brusque, "Will there be anything of hers in the big bedroom?"

"Nana, who's A? I think you need to tell me."

"Yes, I do need to tell you but not now. I need a bit of time to sort my thoughts," looking around and giving an involuntary shudder, "and not here."

"Okay," I nodded, "but today, when we get back." I didn't make it a question.

"Yes, tonight after Davy's gone to bed," giving me one of her gentle smiles, "Do you think there's anything in the other bedroom?"

"Maybe," I said, crossing the landing. I had a quick scan around Billy's room, fully expecting to see evidence of his bottle blonde barmaid and I was not disappointed. On the dressing table, next to a bottle of Old Spice aftershave were Mum's engagement and wedding rings in a clean, chunky, glass ashtray. I stood and looked at them for a second before turning away and catching sight of a pair of pink fluffy mule slippers peeping out from the side of the bed in a much bigger size than Mum wore.

Closing the door, I went to check the bathroom. Opening the cabinet, I could see toothpaste, Steradent, Brillcream and a box of tampons, behind which were three small bottles with Mum's name on them; her antidepressants, her sleeping pills and some I hadn't seen before. I grabbed the antidepressants and the ones I didn't recognise and dropped them both in my pocket, leaving the sleeping tablets, and nudged the other stuff back in place, closing the door.

Nana was at the top of the stairs as I came out. She still looked a bit odd, but neither of us wanted to spend any more time than we needed in Billy's domain so we picked up a box each and went downstairs.

My stepfather had already emptied the wardrobes of Mum's clothes and they were in a suitcase, not a big one, waiting for us in the storeroom. Billy offered Nana a sherry, which she declined, while we waited for her neighbour, Mrs Davis, to arrive on her way home from the chemist. She was helping us carry the boxes and suitcase back to Nana's.

I'd also taken the opportunity to get more of my things. I left enough to maintain the illusion that my brother and I would be moving back at some point although every night we prayed that would never happen. At no point had Billy suggested he might help us, it would never have occurred to him, as we struggled to the door and set off back. He had been in a noticeably good mood which just kept my hatred and malice towards him simmering nicely as I tried to arrange all the thoughts in my head.

I knew once we got in, Mrs Davis would have a cup of tea with Nana while she passed on all the latest gossip so I got on with tea before retrieving the pill bottles from my coat pocket and taking them upstairs. I hid them in a grey sock at the back of my underwear drawer. When I came back downstairs, I glanced at the two boxes and suitcase in the hall but Mrs Davis was still in full flow, clearly not noticing Nana's glazed expression. Standing at the back of the room, willing her to realise she'd outstayed her welcome; it was all I could do not to tell her to bugger off. There was so much I wanted my grandmother to tell me and it occurred to me that something that hadn't mattered before, something that wasn't important, was now the most important thing in my life. I didn't have to be a genius to realise that the note we had found had given her the missing piece of the puzzle. I was on the verge of discovering who my father was.

As soon as she came back from seeing Mrs Davis out, I told her I couldn't wait until Davy went to bed, I needed to talk about it now. She was having none of it and shaking her head and raising her index finger to me.

"No Rosie, it has to be later." Davy looked up on the sharpness of her voice and she smiled quickly and suggested a game of draughts while we waited for our tea.

"I really need to get it straight in my head," she said softly to me as my brother set up the board on the table, "and it's important that I check something first so you two have a game while I just pop upstairs."

"Okay," I responded, sulkily.

The game of draughts turned into three as my board games wizard of a brother beat me ridiculously quickly and then actually suggested we stop as I was too easy. While we ate our tea, he chatted about how he had discovered that there was a boy in his class at school who played chess and how he was going to ask his parents if he could go round there one day and he'd teach him. We both agreed that was a good idea and Nana said we would ask Father Christmas to bring him a chess set of his own. The minute she put her knife and folk down, I was on my feet and clearing the table. She asked me if I had any homework to do and I lied that I'd done it in my dinner break and said I'd wash and dry the pots if she wanted to take a turn at getting beaten at draughts.

At eight, my brother went to bed. He was allowed fifteen minutes, which he timed himself with his bedside clock, to look through the Guinness Book of Records Santa had brought him the previous Christmas. I was sitting in front of the television not watching 'Softly, Softly', my head full of questions and half formed ideas, when Nana came down. I'd heard her moving above me after she had said goodnight to Davy. I got up and turned the sound down before returning to the sofa and watched her place a large photograph album and tatty brown envelope on the table at the side of the armchair. Before sitting down, she put more coal on the fire and used the poker to move it around, focusing on the glowing embers. Finally, she sat down heavily, took in a deep breath and looked at me.

"Right, I think I've got things straight, although I'm still struggling a little bit…" I think she only meant to pause but I cut in quickly, I couldn't wait another second,

"Who's A? Is it my Dad?" I felt my cheeks burn as the words came out far more aggressively than I'd intended. She looked up to the heavens before dipping her head slightly and letting out a loud sigh, giving me a small nod and replying,

"Yes, I think in all likelihood, he is."

## Fourteen

"His name was Alfie, he was a friend of your Grandad's," she said, looking down at her nails, "they met in Burma during the war. Oh Rosie, I promise you, we never dreamed, never once considered that it could have been him."

"What do you mean he was a friend of Grandad's; how old was he?" I snapped.

"Well he was a lot older than her, I think he was about, let me think, eight or was it seven years younger than Grandad, yes eight," she nodded and half smiled, "yes, he was eight years younger."

"So, what, twenty, twenty-five years older than Mum?" My anger was growing,

"Yes, of course. He was a grown man and she was just a girl but we didn't know, we had absolutely no idea, I swear to you." I saw the pain in her face as I took in a breath to calm down. "He were fond of her, we knew that but he was like her uncle, he made a fuss of her." She stood up and said she was going to have a small sherry before she said anymore.

"I want to tell you about Alfie and how we came to know him and then maybe you'll see why we never suspected," she began, sitting back down with what couldn't be described as a small sherry by anyone's reckoning.

Grandad had served in the Light Infantry of the 2nd King's Own Yorkshire Regiment during the war. As an engineer on the railways, he was in a protected occupation and wouldn't have been called up but he'd enlisted in the spring of 1940, even though they had only just found out Nana was pregnant.

"His father had fought in the first world war," she told me, as she'd told me before, and there was always bitterness in her voice when she spoke of her in-laws, my great grandparents. Luckily, they were dead and buried before I made my scandalous appearance in the world.

"His father told him it was his duty to serve his country, that his family bred heroes and not cowards." She took in a breath and added, "I hated that bloody stupid man, cold and hard-hearted and she were not much better."

Grandad was twenty-six when he enlisted and after the shortest of training, he was sent out to Burma where, six months later, he met Albert Lachlan Fairclough, known to everyone as Alfie, an eighteen year-old, wet behind the ears lad, who, according to Grandad, was scared of his own shadow. Alfie was from Leeds and was terrified, not that Grandad wasn't but, as Grandad was a bit older and, according to Nana, a soft-hearted man despite his upbringing, they became great buddies and Grandad swore he'd look after Alfie.

Grandad never really talked much about the war except to say that *'It were bad and the first couple o' years in Burma, they had it rough, but not as bad as some of the poor buggers in Italy and France'.*

In 1942, his battalion retreated to British India where he hardly saw any active service, just spent most of his time marching around getting a suntan.

"But he were desperate to get home, hearing the news about what was going on round Europe, he felt bad. I was just relieved he was safe there and hoped they wouldn't post him somewhere bad. I got a few letters from him, not many really when you think he was away six years."

"So he didn't see Mum till she was six?" I was astounded by this news. "I never knew that."

"No, well, he didn't like to talk too much about it, I think he saw some bad things at the beginning. In fact, it were Alfie told me about seeing bodies floating down a river, women and little kids who'd been hacked to death. Your grandad pulled him up sharp about that, said it were to be left in that place and not brought back here."

Six weeks after VE day, May 8 1945, the government started plans to decommission soldiers and to bring them home but the war in the Far East didn't end until 15th August. Grandad's return was almost held up again by a minor mutiny at RAF stations in the Indian subcontinent but, luckily, he managed to get home just before Christmas. Release and transportation was based on age and length of service with married men given priority. He arrived at the barracks in York at midday and the next morning he, along with ten other lucky lads, were each given £83 and a demob suit along with the promise that they had the right to return to their old jobs.

"It were such a shock when he walked through the door," tears glistening in Nana's eyes as she spoke. She reached out for a large brown envelope beside her and tipped a pile of sepia photographs onto her lap, "and course our Barbara didn't know him, I saw how hurt he were that she was shy of him them first few weeks but we were lucky, your Grandad were lucky, he got back as soon as he did."

The process of demobilisation became laboured and even stalled in some places. The post war government, after six years of bombardment and blockades and the shortages they brought, struggled to fulfil their pledge of the welcome home that had been promised to all who'd fought for their country.

"Alifie, not being married, missed the boat," she gave a slight chuckle, "literally! He didn't get demobbed for another twelve months."

Nana handed me three small square pictures that Grandad had brought back with him. He was smiling at the camera in two of them as he stood in the middle of two other soldiers, all wearing khaki shorts and shirts, knee length socks and rounded wide brimmed hats. The third one, he was on his own in a different, more formal, uniform, standing to attention with a serious face, his gaze slightly off to the left of the camera.

"That one was taken just before they left for Burma," she said, "the other two are in India." I went back to the first two pictures.

"Is Alfie one of these?" I asked.

"Yes, he's the one on the left." She nodded her head. I looked hard at the grainy out of focus picture. I could recognise Grandad as he was looking square on in both pictures but the other two were shaded by their hats and slightly blurred. Then she held out a small metal badge, the same as the one that had been in the vanity box.

"That's your Granddad's cap badge, it's been in my jewellery box since he got back from the war. The one we found in your Mum's stuff must have been Alfie's."

I examined it carefully as she sorted through more photographs. I peered at the picture of Grandad in his regimental clothes and saw the badge. I nodded and went back to the other pictures.

"They're not very clear; I can hardly make out the faces of either of them," I said, screwing up my eyes in an effort to see better. Nana continued looking through the dozen or so others before selecting one, she stared at it for a while before turning it over and, shaking her head a little, handing it across to me.

"This is him, taken the first time he came here," her eyes narrowing as she processed her thoughts. On the back was written *Jack and Alfie July 1951*. Grandad had given him our address and told him to come and look him up as soon as he got home. He hadn't made it back to his family until the spring of 1947.

"His Dad was quite poorly and they'd had a telegram about his brother the week before Alfie got conscripted." She sighed loudly, "they'd kept hoping there'd been a mistake and he was in POW camp, hoping he'd just walk through the door, poor devils," dabbing her eyes on the back of her wrist before searching up her sleeve for a handkerchief. "He told us his Dad died three weeks after he got home and his Mam died the following year, both still hoping…"

"Hang on a minute, so he was in his late twenties when he first came?"

"He'd just turned thirty," she said with a nod.

"And Mum was..."

"Ten, she were ten. Alfie had written a letter to your Grandad telling him how both his parents had died and he'd moved in with an aunty. Things had been hard for him since he got home." She shook her head before swallowing as if suddenly remembering why we were having this chat. I pressed my lips together deciding not to interrupt. She began rubbing her fingers up and down her temples.

"Anyway, he'd wrote to your Grandad, like I say, he'd been struggling to find work afore the war; he'd worked for his Dad on a market stall but his uncle had taken it over and they didn't get on, but he wasn't complaining," she sighed, "It was a nice letter, lovely handwriting," she smiled and nodded, "it cheered your Grandad up and he wrote back straight away."

The best china had come out for Alfie's visit two weeks later and Nana had managed to find enough coupons to bake a Victoria sponge. She seemed determined to reminisce about the details rather than get to the point but I let her carry on. Over the next hour and two refills of her sherry glass, I learned how this man had ingratiated his way into my grandparent's lives. He was charming and kind, apparently, and really good company and over the next five or six years had been a constant visitor, even staying in their box room.

"And what about Mum, how was he with her?" I finally interrupted her recollections of what a great bloke he was and how he made her and Grandad laugh. She looked up suddenly with a confused, narrow-eyed frown.

"Well yes, he made a fuss of her, always bringing her a bit of summat," her eyes still slightly glassy from the thoughts, "he never had much money, he got bits of work here and there and your grandad put a word in for him with a couple of his mates but it didn't work out." She stopped suddenly as another truth dawned on her, shaking her head, "he were like an uncle to her that's all," her voice catching slightly in her throat, "that's all. We never dreamed...."

Mum had always been fairly quiet but generally happy. As a war baby she had learnt not to complain and was never in any trouble. She didn't have many friends or play out with other children, always seeming shy and reluctant to join in.

"But then she started hanging around with Betty Marsden," Nana said with a clear dislike, "She were a proper madam and there was another lass, don't remember her name, Pauline summat, anyway she must have been about fourteen an' suddenly she starts wanting to go out and getting all moody and secretive."

"Was Alfie around then?" I asked, feeling some annoyance at her deflection.

"What, well yes he was but not so much then actually, he'd got a good job around then, working at Tetley's but that weren't anything to do with your Mum going off the rails," waving her hand dismissively and raising her index finger.

"One night she'd told us the three of them were going to the pictures, it was nearly midnight when she'd come home," she said, her face slightly challenging.

"And where had she been?" I asked, taking up the gauntlet.

"She said they'd missed the bus home and had to walk. We wanted to know how they'd missed the bus, the stop was nearly next to the picture house. She said they'd seen some school friends and been talking and forgot the time."

"So was that it? Was that her coming off the rails?"

"No, course not but that were the first time she lied, we knew that cos I saw Betty Marsden's mother the next day in the chemist. Their Betty hadn't been out that night, she'd stopped in babysitting with that Pauline." She gave a nod to emphasis her point so I asked,

"So what did she say when you told her you'd caught her out?"

"She said she'd never told us she was going with them, she'd gone with some other lasses and got all stroppy, saying she was sick of us treating her like a kid. That was the first time your grandad lifted his hand to her." She suddenly looked stricken. The slap Grandad had given her for talking back had hurt all three of them. Mum apparently cried out in pain before stepping back and staring through angry tears at him. Grandad, shocked by his own action, looked down at his hand as if it didn't belong to him before looking up to see the hostility in his daughter's face. Nana had stood motionless, looking from one to the other, wondering how this could have happened. Grandad had managed to pull himself together, ordering his daughter to go to her room before striding off into the garden.

"Did you ever find out who she was with on that night?" I asked.

"No," she shook her head. "Things changed after that, she was sullen and sulky a lot of the time and she didn't ask to go out again for ages and she were different and that's when we realised she were up to no good."

"Did you think she had a boyfriend?"

"There were a couple of lads used to hang around, local boys, but she didn't seem that interested. Course she'd started working at the shirt factory then; me and your Grandad had tried to get her to stop on at school and get some exams but she weren't interested." She paused and took a breath.

"She made some new friends there, not that we ever met any of 'em." She paused and stared across the room towards the old fake Christmas tree. "We alus thought it were somebody from there."

She pulled out a couple of pictures of Mum and gave them to me. They were all dated on the back, *Summer 1954*. The first was a picture of a tall girl looking very self-conscious in shorts and a t-shirt standing next to a trellis of roses in the back garden. The next one was a similar pose but this time she was flanked by her parents, all standing, straight arms by their sides with the half smiles of a formal family portrait. The third showed a man beaming at the camera, his right arm around a slightly flustered looking Nana while Mum stood closely to his left. I scanned the image and could just make out the fingers of his left hand on Mum's shoulders.

"So why don't I know him?" I asked, "Was he still around after I was born?"

"No," shaking her head she suddenly looked distraught, "No, he'd moved away by then." I said nothing as I stared at the photograph. She sighed loudly. "There was never anything to make us wonder," she said and I knew she was convincing herself not me, "He'd got a job down south, Leicester I think, he'd told us he was leaving weeks afore we found out about your Mam." I just nodded, there was no point labouring this now. I asked if there were any other photographs of him. There was another half a dozen, all black and white and not all in focus. I was wondering what she'd say if I asked her if I looked like him when I saw the picture of him and Grandad standing in front of a small car.

"Is this Grandad's first car?"

"No, that's Alfie's, it belonged to a friend of his and he borrowed it now an' again; he took all of us to Doncaster races once." She smiled again at what was to her a good memory.

"Did he have girlfriends?"

"No, he never seemed interested even though here were plenty of women would have liked to go out with him." As soon as she'd finished speaking, her face changed.

"He took me an' your Grandad for fools," she said sharply. I said nothing and waited. "He borrowed twenty pounds off your Grandad the last time we saw him, it were a week or so afore Christmas. He'd told us he were starting this new job but he'd be back to see us over the holiday. He were coming for his dinner." Lifting her hands to her face and rubbing both her eyes, "Your Grandad thought such a lot of him, we were both upset when he didn't turn up, thinking summat must have come up. He'd been stopping with a cousin and things had been a bit rough, that's why he'd gone for this job down south. We were sure he'd get in touch once he'd settled in." She let out a big breath, "But we never heard from him again."

I asked about the dressing table set and she remembered him giving it to Mum and Grandad telling him he shouldn't have spent so much. She also remembered how Mum had been delighted and hugged him, throwing her arms round his neck but he'd backed away and looked embarrassed.

"So I was born in July, nine months after Mum was sixteen." I was counting backwards trying to calculate my conception. Estimating that I must have been conceived around the end of October, I asked when she'd found out Mum was pregnant.

"I walked into her bedroom one morning and she were standing by her bed, just in her brassiere and knickers. She grabbed for her clothes as I walked in but I saw it, I saw it straight away."

An outraged Nana and Grandad demanded answers from their distraught daughter who swore she had not been with any boy.

"She kept saying she'd no idea how it had happened. At one point, a day or so later, I was upstairs getting ready to take her to the doctor's when I heard her screaming at him, insisting she hadn't been messing about with any lad. I heard your Grandad's voice yelling back but couldn't make out what he said but she responded, not screaming this time so I didn't catch what she said. I was on my way downstairs then and heard him call her a bloody liar. He said that twice and as I walked into the room, they were standing, facing each other, his hand raised and I thought he was going to slap her but instead he dropped his hand, turned round and walked through the kitchen and into the garden."

"When was this?" I asked.

"Beginning of February so she were already four month's gone. Course, once I realised, there'd been other signs I'd not picked up on," dabbing away more tears, "I just never dreamed, I never thought he were like that...."

"Do you think she told Grandad then that it were Alfie?" I asked as gently as I could. I didn't think she'd heard me as she fished her hankie out again and wiped her eyes before blowing her nose but she nodded.

"That night, he said we had to just get on with it now, she were never going to tell us so we should just leave it, and so we did."

We spent the rest of the evening looking through the old photographs. Every now and then she'd get teary and, after another glass of sherry, she said she was sorry that this hadn't come out while Mum was alive and I should never have had to grow up not knowing who my dad was, even if it turned out he was a bloody 'wrong un'. I tried to comfort her a little, telling her I'd never worried about who my dad was, it hadn't been important and still wasn't. But now I realised this wasn't true.

## Fifteen

My courtship with Darren up to this point had been very laid back. Apart from the odd kissing and holding hands, it was platonic but I never for a moment doubted his commitment to it.

He'd been in my life almost constantly since the night we'd met up again. Although we had been to the pictures a couple of times and I met him in The Mitre again the Friday after Christmas, our other meetings were mainly him picking me up from school on Wednesdays and Fridays. He'd be at the school gates in his orange Ford Cortina, arm resting on the wound down window despite the weather being cold and wet, waiting for me with a beaming smile.

Since starting back in September, I'd made a couple of other friends who were keen to get good marks in their O levels and go on to college. I'd known them both for years but it was only when we were a smaller class and I didn't have Julie to sit next to anymore that we became friends. Just before the Christmas holidays, I told them about Darren, well not the bit about him being married and having a child, and they were so impressed and I really enjoyed their envy as they eagerly asked to hear more about my older, good looking boyfriend who had a car.

The first time he picked me up was the Wednesday before we broke up for Christmas and just forty-eight hours after the revelations about the probability of my paternity. It was teeming with rain as I dashed to his car and he could tell straight away there was something wrong. I'd almost not gone to school that day or the day before. What I had wanted to do was spend the days going through the rest of Mum's things and understand why the questionable actions of a family friend had not been discovered earlier.

Darren drove us down one of the small roads near the canal at Calder Vale and we sat watching the rain bouncing off the windscreen while I told him. The words poured out of me and I cried but my tears were of anger. He held and squeezed my hand as he listened, not interrupting or asking questions, just listening. Once my words dried up and I'd wiped my eyes, he gave me a cuddle and told me he could not imagine how I was feeling after everything I'd gone through over the past year. He told me that he hated seeing me cry, his own eyes brimming with tears as he said he wanted to look after me, to protect me and help me start a new happier life. It was exactly what I wanted to hear as he held me close and stroked my hair.

Christmas Day had been okay, almost nice, and by nice I mean there were no incidents or arguments, but the shadow of loss still hovered around the day. I'd bought Nana perfume I knew she liked called Pagan. Grandad used to buy it for her every year, and I got a new Guinness Book of Records for Davy. Nana bought him the much wanted chess set and gave me a silver charm bracelet with two charms.

"I thought it would be nice to collect new charms for all your special occasions," she said, looking slightly embarrassed, "The two that are on, well there's a wishing well, that's to bring you luck and the little lamp's got a ruby in it, that's your birth stone."

"Oh Nana, I love it so very much." I gave her a big hug and she helped me fasten it and I shook my arm to make it jingle.

Billy came down to have his dinner with us after a short two hour opening, putting us all on edge the whole time even though he was on his best behaviour.

He gave Davy a board game he'd been wanting for ages called Mouse Trap, a new set of Meccano to add to his growing collection and a Corgi model of a white Volvo car with Roger Moore's Saint symbol on the bonnet. He was delighted and surprised at such perfectly sourced gifts and gave his father a wide, if slightly confused smile. I was not surprised at these gifts, or mine. I knew Nana had chosen them, bought them and wrapped them before secretly handing them to him as he arrived. My gift was slippers, a bottle of perfume and a vanity case. I thanked him in the required way, telling him they were just what I wanted and I saw the look of satisfaction he gave Nana along with a nod, his money well spent. I nudged Davy to put down his new model car and get the gift from behind the Christmas tree we had wrapped for him, a bottle of Brut aftershave. Nana gave him a nicely wrapped jumper from Littlewoods which he held up to himself and smiled his approval before handing the last present to her. She opened it with a smile and feigned surprise, a set of Yardley bath cubes, soap and talc, which she had also bought and wrapped herself. I wasn't sure that the £25 he had given her for 'his shopping' had actually been enough to cover all the gifts but knew better than to ask. To be fair to him, he did bring her a bottle of Harvey's Bristol Cream which made her smile go all the way to her eyes.

I didn't get to see Darren on Christmas day but managed to get out for a couple of hours on Boxing Day evening on the pretext of going to Julie's. Ever since the night we'd split up in The Mitre, she had been frosty with me but had to started come round. Darren was waiting for me in his car, about 200 yards down the road, at half past six as arranged. He drove down to Julie's where I ran to her door to give her the cassette of David Cassidy's latest LP, Rock Me Baby. She had already told me her Mam and Dad were getting her a new hi-fi with cassette player for her bedroom. Darren waited in the car while we swapped our gifts on her doorstep but she walked back to the car with me to say hello; I was forgiven.

He drove us to towards Wakefield and we went into a pub on Barnsley Road where we were hoping we wouldn't see anyone we knew. I'd stressed about getting him a Christmas present, I'd no idea if he would get me one and didn't want to be embarrassed by not having one to give him if he did, then worrying it would be equally embarrassing if I gave him a gift and he didn't have one for me. In the end, I got him a record token from Woolworths which I wrapped in a piece of Christmas paper and fit easily in my handbag; If he didn't give me a present, I'd keep it for later. This was all academic though. As soon as we sat down with our drinks, a pint of bitter and half a lager and blackcurrant, he handed me a small oblong parcel wrapped in very bright red wrapping paper adorned with snowmen, Santa and Rudolph.

I was slightly giddy as I took it and held it for a few seconds before opening it. I pulled the paper off as carefully as I could, trying not to tear it, while he kept nodding encouragingly, his excitement growing. It was a small oblong leather box that had 'Collingwood the County Jeweller' written in gold on top. It looked so expensive. I felt my face flush and opened the lid slowly as a lump formed in the back of my throat.

"I hope you like it," he said shyly as I stared down at the beautiful golden heart necklace, shaking my head in awe. My silence clearly unnerved him and he said my name.

"It's beautiful, really beautiful," I finally managed to say, "I love it, thank you so much." I ran my finger over the smooth surface of the small heart. "I just wasn't expecting anything like this; no one has ever bought me such lovely present."

"Well, that is a shame," he said, leaning forward to cuddle me and kiss my hair, "you deserve it," holding me now at arm's length, "and so much more, you are very special; let me see it on you." I took it out of the box and held it out to him with slightly shaky hands. He stood up to fasten it around my neck and sat back down and took both my hands in his. "Perfect, you now have my heart," he smiled. I let go with one hand, raising it to touch it with my thumb and forefinger.

"Thank you," I managed to whisper, "thank you." He gave me another big hug before sitting back down, looking pleased with himself. He said he was equally delighted at the record token which dissipated my embarrassment a little.

He had been to see Daniel the day before, being allowed into his in-law's house for one hour in the morning but ushered out well before their festive meal. He'd taken his Mum with him but Tina, his *'soon to be ex-wife'* as he kept referring to her, stayed out of the way. They had both been offered a drink; his Mum took a glass of port but he declined.

Daniel, only being eight months old, was far more interested in the wrapping paper than the Fisher Price telephone on wheels he'd received with a romper suit and hand-knitted matinee coat from his mother.

Having been only just on the pleasant side of polite and staying in the room for the visit, as soon as the allotted hour was up, both his in-laws got to their feet, indicating it was time for them to leave. He said he got the impression that they were embarrassed about the way they'd treated him.

"Her Mam told me to look after myself as we got to the door an' her dad just nodded, not really able to look me in the eye." He looked thoughtful as he spoke, "I wished them a Merry Christmas and said I'd see them in a couple of weeks." He shrugged and I wanted to say something comforting but couldn't think of anything to say. I took a big gulp of my drink and, as I put my glass back down, he took my hand.

"Anyway, how was your Christmas day?" his smile back on full beam.

"It was good thanks," I smiled, "even though Billy came round for his dinner." I told him about the presents and that I'd been on my best behaviour, having been warned by Nana not to provoke him or mention the rumours about Shirley having moved in.

"So has she?" he asked.

"Dunno, Nana was surprised when he said yes when she'd asked him if he wanted to come for his dinner. We'd been a bit scared he might bring her with him but he came on his own, arrived at quarter to two and stopped till half past four." I paused and then laughed as I added, "Nana had to pour herself a very big glass of sherry after he'd gone." I laughed again, "Seriously though, it was so stressful, he was being so nice and even played Mouse Trap with me and Davy while Nana washed up."

"That's good though in't it?"

"You have no idea what a bastard he is," I began, "he's never played a board game with us before or managed to be properly civil for that amount of time." I took a breath, "and do you know what, I'm sure he knew his behaving so nice was making us tense."

"It must be hard for you, first Christmas without your Mam," he said softly, "but it'll get easier."

"I don't think it will," I said, suddenly sure I was right, "I know he killed her and he's got away with it." I blinked back fat tears catching the overspill on the back of my hand. "She weren't great as a Mam, she really didn't have a clue half the time, but none of it were her fault."

"Yeah," he nodded his head," she just got in with a wrong un - twice!"

"And I don't like the way he is with Nana, it's like he enjoys seeing her squirm around him, and me for that matter. He knows what we think, it's pretty hard to hide sometimes, but we kowtow to him, pretending we believe the ridiculous story cos if we make a fuss he'll take Davy back."

"But would he really do that?" he asked, tilting his head, "I mean how would he look after him, get him to school an' stuff?"

"He wouldn't look after him, he'd be shut upstairs on his own and left to feed himself and I can't see that mucky old trout treating him very well, she certainly won't want him cramping her style," shaking my head and wincing at the thought of it, "but he'd still do it just to spite us if he thinks we're not playing ball."

"He really is a bastard," he said with a nod before picking up his drink. I took a big breath through my nose and took hold of my emotions, "Anyway there's no point me moaning and crying about it."

"It's alright though, to be sad, you've had a lot of stuff happen and finding out about your dad, it must be bloody awful," he said, nodding his forehead towards me.

"Yeah, but I'm more mad than sad, in fact I'm furious."

He took me back to Nana's shortly after that but not before some passionate kissing in the car park.

I didn't see him again for a couple of days but I found a lot comfort touching the golden heart that hung around my neck and thinking about him. As soon as I got to my room that night, I examined the box and discovered that this wonderful and thoughtful gift was actually real gold, fourteen carat in fact. I couldn't wait to get back to school and show my friends this expensive and romantic gift, the very thought of how jealous they'd be was enough to make me laugh out loud. It was a lovely feeling but only a temporary reprieve from the dark thoughts that were circling my mind, gaining strength and becoming more and more tangible each day.

I told Nana I had a boyfriend the next day. I confessed I'd met him at the start of December had seen him a few times and I thought it might be serious so I wanted to ask him round to meet her. I reassured her again that I was not going to do anything silly with him and he wasn't that sort of boy. She was, of course, suspicious, even more so when I showed her the necklace he'd got me.

When, two weeks after Christmas, I introduced Darren as my boyfriend to my grandmother and brother, we decided not to mention that he was still married. It was a Sunday afternoon and she welcomed him with her best china, a large slice of double layered chocolate cake and three cups of tea. Davy stared at him for a few minutes before agreeing to come and sit at the table with us and managed a smile. Darren turned on his charm; smiling, listening and asking questions and helped by a copy of The Beano he gave him, soon won him over. However, I sensed Nana wasn't quite so sure about him.

During our little tea party, she'd been friendly and warmly hospitable, asking him about where he lived, wondering if she might know his family, which she didn't, and where he worked. He told her he was a mechanic at Charlie Brown's Garage on Northgate and he had his own car which he used mainly to get to work and back and take his Mum out. Davy had left the table at this point and was sitting on the floor, his back up against the sofa, reading his comic. Darren went on to say how hard his Mum had taken the loss of his Dad nearly four years before. Nana commented how much she understood that and she would never get over losing Grandad. There had been a slightly uncomfortable silence at that point and I felt a small surge of panic thinking she was about to cry. Instead, she blinked hard and added,

"And then of course we lost Barbara, last year, I'm sure Rosie's told you about the circumstances of that." He nodded vigorously and opened his mouth to say something but she held up her hand, "so my grandchildren are all I have left in the world and they're very precious to me."

"Yeah," he said nodding, "I told my Mam about it and she said 'no mother should have to bury her child'. I'm right sorry Mrs Cooper, you've all been through a lot." I smiled at him, although I was holding back tears too. He smiled back at me then turned back to look at Nana,

"Rosie's a lovely lass an' she's precious to me an' all." He reached over and picked up my hand and squeezed it briefly before letting go. "You don't have to worry about me, I'll look after her." Nana nodded just once and went to put the kettle on again to freshen up the tea. After that she had been fairly quiet and I thought she was probably thinking about Grandad and Mum. I was thinking how well it had gone and how impressed I was with Darren, hoping she was too.

He left fifteen minutes later and I walked out to the gate with him where he kissed me very tenderly, right there in the street. When I came back in, Davy was clearing the table and Nana was in the kitchen, her hands in a washing up bowl full of Fairy bubbles. I had just picked up the tea towel to start drying the china when she asked,

"How old is he?" without looking at me. I suspected she wouldn't like to hear he was twenty-six so I added yet another lie to the tally I had built up over the past month; I told her he was nineteen.

"He seems older," she said, still not looking at me. I didn't dare speak and continued to dry the pots. As she lifted the last plate from the suds and placed it on the draining board, reaching for the hand towel, she turned to look at me.

"Promise me you'll be careful Rosie, you've got a chance to make something of yourself, don't throw it away on some lad with a cheeky smile who tells you you're lovely...," holding up her hand to stop me interrupting, "I'm sure he's a nice lad, he's got good manners and it sound like he's got a good job an' all, I'm just saying, don't get too serious." She took in a deep breath and as she exhaled, she looked so sad, "He's your first boyfriend and you're only fifteen and, well boys can sometimes want more and well.... it's a dangerous age."

"I know and I know why you're saying this but Darren isn't like that. He knows I'm working hard at school cos I want to go into nursing and he knows I'm not like that either. Honest, Nana, you don't have to worry, I promise."

I almost added that I wasn't my mother but her expression stopped me. I knew she felt she shared the blame for Mum's fall from virtue so my adolescence was a tightrope she was doing her best to tread. I wanted to make it easier for her, that's why I lied to her, well that's what I told myself anyway.

She didn't say anything else and I turned to look at my brother. He was back on the floor with his comic, his cute little boy face smiling at the antics of Billy Whizz. Her voice, behind me, made me jump,

"Do you want to go upstairs and finish going through your Mam's boxes while he's so engrossed in his comic?"

The boxes and suitcase were now on the floor in the corner of Nana's bedroom. Shaking my head as sadness swept over me, I said, "Maybe next weekend."

When I first met Darren's Mum, a week or so later, despite her friendly 'Hello Luv' as she stood up, her smile and body language left me in no doubt about her unease. Mrs Norton patted the bottom of her dark, permed hair and with a nervous smile and instructed me to sit down on the sofa while she went to make us all a cup of tea. Darren nodded at me before following her. I clearly heard her ask how old I was and him replying I was seventeen; he had already said it would be better if she thought I was older and I agreed but I was hoping she wouldn't ask me. I was working out in my head how old she was, she looked quite a lot older than my Mum and probably nearer to Nana's age.

When they both came back, Darren sat beside me on sofa, looking completely at ease. I was perched right at the front of the seat, straight back, cup and saucer held tightly in front. As soon as she sat down, facing me, his mother cleared her throat before saying,

"I'm right sorry to hear about your Mam, Luv. Our Darren said it were sudden?" She raised her eyebrows on her last sentence like it was a question.

"Yes," was all I could manage, I was so taken aback. Darren had told me that she hardly went out and didn't meet up with many people but I was certain she would know about Mum, only living in the next village. I frowned and shook my head, looking quickly at Darren. He nodded and leaned forward,

"It's been a really horrible time for Rosie, she were really close to her Mam." He squeezed my arm and then changed the subject, suggesting she could show me the jumper she was knitting for him.

It was an awkward hour that the three of us chatted through intermittently with Darren talking the most, filling in the empty silences and managing the topics. When she asked me if I had a job, he quickly said I was at college and training to be a nurse, which seemed to both impress and satisfy her.

At quarter past six, exactly an hour after we'd arrived, she glanced over at the mantle clock and exclaimed it was nice to have met me and stood up. I looked at Darren who smiled and got to his feet as well so I did the same.

"Mam's next door neighbour, Betty, comes round every Sunday night," he said, just as someone knocked once on the back door before opening it and coming in. "They're making an eiderdown or something," he added in a slightly lower voice.

"We're making a couple of patchwork bedspreads," his mother corrected, "Betty used to be a needlework teacher so she's helping me with it and I'm helping her do some knitting for her grand kiddies."

The next time I saw him, he told me his Mum liked me, she thought I was pretty and seemed very sensible.

"She never took to Tina," he added, "thought she were a right little madam, which she were to be fair, she is actually."

I wasn't sure I believed him about his Mum liking me, it certainly hadn't felt like that but I was hoping I would grow on her. As for Tina, the mother of his child, I already knew I didn't like her. In fact, hearing about all she had done to Darren made me hate her. Now, as a much older and better-informed human, I understand the phenomenon of anger by proxy. Back then, we had no social media to spread and infuse the rage. Back then, as a fifteen year-old in small disconnected world, fake news was spread by gossip. Back then, I was susceptible to hatred spread through personal vendettas and make no mistake, anger by proxy was then and is still very much today, a dangerous thing.

## Sixteen

The weather in January of 1973 was fairly mild with above average temperatures for the time of year and, for almost everyone around me, the year began well. Then along came February with an anticyclonic calm bringing us frost and fog.

Shirley Blenkinsopp moved into The Swan as Billy's officially acknowledged girlfriend but not as landlady. It had been my stepfather's reluctance to put her name above the door that had stalled her taking residence. He had painted over Mum's name only a week after the funeral and declared his intention that he would remain the sole licensee of pub. In fact, he told Nana that the only other name that would go up there was Davy's.

"Soon as he's old enough, it'll say *William Flynn and Son proprietors. Licensed to sell beer, wine, and spirits to be consumed on or off the premises,*" he had declared with a pride in his voice that astounded me.

In the end, Shirley must have decided she stood a better chance of persuading him to make her the landlady once she was fully moved in. She didn't bring much with her and she didn't put her house up for sale straight away, suggesting she wasn't sure how long the arrangement would last. Two weeks after she had got her feet properly under the table and her clothes hanging in the wardrobe space recently vacated, she came down to see Nana. It was half past four on a school night; the three of us were eating in the kitchen when Nana let her in. The food in my mouth seemed to expand as she came in with her heavy makeup and coiffured yellow hair.

"I've just come to say, well to tell you," she said, pausing, and I could see her doubting her decision to come as her bravado waned, "Look, I know you probably don't like me an' think what happened has summat to do with me," stopping again and I could see the effort she was putting in as her eyes darted around the room, eventually settling on the doors of the kitchen cabinet, "but I am right sorry about what happened to Barbara, she were a nice woman but I'm sure you don't need me to tell you her an' Billy weren't happy."

If she expected some response to that, she was disappointed as the three of us stared at her. I managed a quick glance at Nana as Shirley did something odd with her shoulders, a sort of half shrug, half shimmy as she searched for her words.

"Anyroad, I don't expect you to like me but well, as Billy's David's dad," nodding at my brother then with a sudden jolt, adding, "an' Rosie's stepdad." She held up one of her hands as the flash of colour around her neck subsided, "So The Swan's still your home an' I'd like us to get along."

The stunned silence continued for a few more heart beats before Nana shook her head, belying her words, "Of course we will try and get along. There's been enough unpleasantness."

"Right, yeah, well that's good so I wondered if the three of you want to come up on Sunday afternoon for a bit of tea, after the bar shuts. I'll get some stuff in, and make sandwiches and...." her voice had started to trail off as Nana cut in.

"Do you mean this Sunday?" Shirley could only manage a nod.

"Well we've got plans for this Sunday, but maybe next week?"

"Yeah that's fine, good, yeah, that's good," her relief physical, "Right then, I'll get off an let you get on wi' your tea."

Nana was laughing as she came back from seeing her out. Davy who had been sitting holding his knife and folk and staring at his plate, looked from me to Nana.

"Bloody silly woman," Nana laughed, "as if a potted meat sandwich and piece of shop bought cake'll make us all 'get along'."

"I can hardly believe she had the cheek to come here." I put my knife and folk down, my appetite lost, "What are we doing this Sunday?"

"Nowt as I know but we can't have her thinking we'll just go round when it suits her," she picked up her knife and fork, muttering, "thinking she can start playing happy families? Well she's got another think coming."

I said nothing out loud but a little voice in my head whispered, "Oh yes, she certainly has."

Two days later, Darren came round for a cup of tea and a jam tart, straight from work, before driving all four of us back to school for the parent teacher evening. Mum and Billy had never been to any of these progress meetings throughout the whole of our education. When I told Nana this, she'd said crisply 'well it's about time somebody did' and signed both the forms. Darren came into the school hall with us but stayed at the back with my brother while Nana and I chatted to my form teacher. Nana wanted to know straight away if I was keeping up with the work or if, since Christmas, my attention had been slipping. Mrs Jackson assured her I was fully focused and if anything, I seemed to be working harder. She said I was well on track for some good results and would be surprised if I didn't get at least three A's. Satisfied with this, she went over to talk to Davy's teacher while I took advantage of the public setting and lots of my school friends around and wandered around the hall holding hands with my boyfriend. I was feeling quite smug from all the praise for my schoolwork and being there with Darren.

Davy's teacher told Nana how she'd noticed an improvement in his concentration after a poor year previously which, given all that had happened, perhaps was understandable. Now, though, he was doing better and seemed a bit happier. Nana sniffed, thanked the teacher and gave Davy one of her smiley nods.

When we got back, she told Darren he could come in for half an hour but that was all as I had some homework to do and needed to be in bed at a decent time.

"It's okay Mrs Cooper, I need to get back home as I'm helping me Mam do a clear out of me dad's shed, there's all sorts in there that probably needs chucking out," he said, word perfect on the script I'd given him.

"Oh right, well that's good," said Nana, clearly surprised, but also his words had triggered something and just to be sure, I gave Darren a nudge for the last bit.

"I've been keeping the garden tidy, not much to do over the winter so now's a good time to clear out some of the big shrubs and stuff."

"So do you like gardening?" Nana asked.

"Oh yeah, I love pottering," he lied, "I'm not much of a gardener, that were me dad, he loved his garden but I know enough to keep it tidy."

"Right, well, when you've finished helping your Mam, maybe you could spare a couple of hours to help sort out our garden? Jack was the gardener in our family and I'm finding it a bit much lately," raising her eyebrows.

"Yeah, course, I'll see how I get on this week, I'm sure I can fit it in." He gave a nod, emphasising his broad smile which transferred to Nana as she got out of the car.

When I got home from serving people at the chemist that Saturday, Darren's car was parked outside the house. The temperature had dropped substantially during the day and the clear skies and chilly air had begun to make the pavements sparkle. I felt buoyant opening the door as the warmth of the kitchen hit me along with a lovely smell of cooking. Nana was standing at the worktop, rolling out dumplings and singing along to the radio as a big pan of casserole bubbled on the cooker. As I walked in, she turned, brushing the flour from her hands.

"Hello luv." She looked a little tired but seemed happy. "Darren's here, he's out in the garden with Davy, I'm making us all some stew and dumplings for when they've finished."

"It smells lovely, has he been here long?" walking over to the window.

"He turned up about two and I took him a cuppa out just after that but he's not stopped since. He's cleared down the far side by the shed." She walked over to stand next to me. "I've told him I don't expect him to do it all in one go. It'll be getting dark soon."

"I'll go out and tell them to come in now," I said, moving back toward the door, "It's a bit parky out there."

I told Davy he needed to go in and wash his hands and that I'd help Darren put the gardening tools back in the shed. Once we'd got inside, we had a bit of a smooch behind the old wooden door.

"Thanks for doing this," I said as his hands went inside my coat and his fingers started to trace my spine. I let out a gasp of pleasure, knowing it would make him smile and kiss me again. He pulled back with a half moan and we touched foreheads before he kissed me lightly on the nose.

"I think you must be ready for something hot," I said playfully.

"I'm ready for summat," he laughed, "but I can wait." He gave me a quick squeeze as we turned to leave and, catching sight of two shoe boxes on the shelf above the door, he reached up and took one down. "Oh yeah, I meant to ask if you knew what this was." He removed the lid to reveal a collection of dried dark green and brown leaves and stalks.

"I dunno," I lied with a fake frown, "I remember helping Grandad with some planting the spring before he died and I thought those boxes had bulbs and stuff in."

"Right," he nodded, replaced the lid and put the box back.

I gave him a quick kiss stepping out of the shed and lead him back up the garden path to the house.

A week or so previously, he mentioned an Aunty May who lived in Leeds but who he hadn't seen for years. It was the first time he'd mentioned any other family apart from his parents.

"So, what other family have you got?" I asked.

"I've got two aunties, two uncles and four cousins. They all live in Leeds but we don't see them anymore."

"How come?"

"Dad and his brother, Uncle Duggie, had a big argument and well, Uncle Jimmy sided with Uncle Duggie, mainly cos they live close to one another so it were easier."

"Wow, what was it about?

"I can't remember," he said, looking to the right before rubbing his hand across his forehead and shrugging. I could sense his reluctance but asked about his cousins.

"My Uncle Jimmy and Aunty May live in Armley with my cousins Martin and Margaret. Aunty May is me Mam's sister and she writes to Mam now and again," he paused and dropped his gaze again before adding, "Uncle Duggie and Aunty Dorothy live in Wortley with Cheryl and Tracey."

"So when was the argument?"

"Years ago, ten, eleven maybe, anyway Uncle Jimmy's in hospital and really poorly. Mam's thinking of going over to see Aunty May."

I'd said it would be nice to meet some more of his family but he'd suddenly looked alarmed at the suggestion and said he wouldn't be going. If his Mum went, she would be getting the bus.

Nana put some sheets of newspaper down just inside the door for Darren to put his boots and my shoes on and we both washed our hands at the kitchen sink with the bar of Wrights coal tar soap. We sat round the table and Nana spooned us all a big ladle of stew; Davy, her and me getting two very large dumplings each while Darren was given three which lit up my face with a smile, this act of acceptance.

"Eat your dumplin's first so they don't get sad," she said, as she always did. I loved some of the things she said as she put her meals on the table,

'It's lamb and it sets quick' and 'get that on your chest an' you won't take much harm' were my favourites. Dumpling getting sad was up there too.

"This looks wonderful, Mrs Cooper, thank you," my boyfriend exclaimed, making her cheeks flush with delight. As we ate, he told her he'd finish the main clearing the next day and leave the big pile of dead and overgrown plants and shrubs he'd made by the back fence, behind the Laburnum tree.

"I can come back and make a bonfire of them in a couple of weeks. Just keep forking them down as they mulch up and we can use some for compost," he said between his mouthfuls of food.

"Well I'm not a fan of bonfires in the garden," Nana said, "We had a bit of a fall out with the next-door-but-one neighbours a few years ago when Jack made one. It were a Saturday and the wind took the smoke all through her washing," shaking her head at the thought, "so let's leave it to rot, it's out of the way in that corner."

Darren played draughts with Davy while Nana and I washed up and then Darren went home. I went out to his car with him and asked,

"Did you get it?" He nodded passing me the telephone book that was on his passenger seat.

"I nicked it out of a phone box near Elland Road," he said proudly. I kissed him, turned and ran back inside, taking it straight to my room.

Nana was going to Crigglestone Club with Mrs Davis that night so Darren was coming back round to watch telly and play board games with my brother and me.

As soon as Nana had left, I abandoned the Mouse Trap game and went to the sideboard to look for her old address book. It was exactly where I thought it would be and, taking it and ignoring my brothers' cries to hurry up as it was my turn, I quickly turned to the F pages and was immediately crestfallen to see there was no Fairclough listed. Thinking, of course, that would have been too easy, I was about to put it back when I turned to the beginning and there it was, second entry down under the

A's; Alfie Fairclough.

The ink of Nana's beautiful cursive writing was faded in parts and there was a cross through the entry in a different pen with a firmer hand, making it hard to fully make out. Number, 28 or maybe 38, and the street began with War. The rest was a little hard to see but it was definitely War something Mount. I took the book over to show Darren and asked him,

"What do you think this says?" He squinted at it for a few seconds before declaring it looked like Bramley. I jotted down 28 or 38 War???? Mount, Bramley, Leeds on a clean page in my note book. Then I put the address book back and the paper into my cardigan pocket before going back to finish the game.

Later, while Davy was watching a western film on telly, cowboys being his latest fad, I went into the kitchen to make us all some cocoa. Darren followed me in.

"Why do you want that address? Your Nana told you he moved down south."

"From what else she said about him, I doubt he always told them the truth, if ever," I replied, slightly irritated, "He could be still in Leeds or he might have lied about his family," shrugging, "I don't know, I just feel it's a start to tracking him down."

"And then what?" he asked, putting his hands on my shoulders, "If realising your Mam was pregnant was what made him disappear, well do you think he'd be happy about you turning up now?" he added, reasonably. I shrugged his hands off me and turned back to the pan of milk on the gas ring, not wanting to be reasonable.

"I haven't worked out what I'll do when I find him but I'm not looking to play happy families with him," I said, turning off the flame. I didn't mention it again but Darren's comment had riled me and to hide my annoyance, I suggested we watched the film. As soon as it finished, Davy went up to bed and not long after, as my mood hadn't improved, Darren went home and I went up to bed carrying my notebook and a glass of water. After changing into my nightie and brushing my teeth, I thought about my project to find Alfie. I knew I couldn't do too much on this project for a while, I had other pressing matters to deal with, but I was pleased I had a tenuous lead. Shuffling down under my flannelette sheets until my feet touched the hot water bottle, my smile got bigger and I felt naively confident of being in control of my life as I fell into a dreamless sleep.

## Seventeen

The following week was a busy one, it was coming up to exam time and I was bringing home lots of homework, telling Darren I could only see him at weekends, an arrangement that started on a Friday when he met me outside the school gates at four. Climbing into his car with a big smile, he leaned over to give me a quick kiss before revving up the already running engine and pulling out into the road.

"I was wondering if you fancied coming to meet Billy the Bastard on Sunday afternoon," I said casually. Giving a quick start, he glanced at me before laughing and saying he would absolutely bloody love to.

As he parked by the kerb outside Nana's house, I told him about the invite from Shirley, about how she hoped we could all get along.

"How'd you feel about that?" looking at me as he took the keys from the ignition.

"Oh, I'm sort of looking forward to it," I said, getting out of the passenger seat, "there's more than one way to skin a rabbit." I pulled my school bag out and slammed the door, laughing at his puzzled expression as we walked towards the house.

As usual, we had haddock and chips from the fish shop down the road which Darren drove Nana to collect while I buttered four slices of Mothers Pride and Davy set the table. While we ate our well salted and vinegary tea, we chatted about the impending Sunday afternoon tea and whether or not Billy would actually be in a hospitable mood. Davy, who had made his reluctance to attend clear ever since Shirley's invite, was now on board since realising that Darren was coming too.

"What do you think she'll give us?" he asked, forking up his last chip.

"We'll probably get dripping sandwiches and a stale Swiss Roll from Parkes," I suggested.

"Oh well," Nana shrugged, "we don't have to stop long and I'll bake a Victoria sandwich in the morning for us to have when we get back." She stood up to start clearing the table. "I don't know what he's gonna make of you though," nodding at my boyfriend. It had been her idea to take Darren along, even though we were fairly sure that Shirley had only intended for the three of us go.

"It'll be a nice surprise for them, meeting your young man," she laughed.

I cleared up and Darren helped me wash and dry the pots while Nana went to get ready to go to the club with Mrs Davis for what had become her regular bingo and sherry evening. Darren stayed to play Cluedo with Davy and me until half past nine when he went home and Davy went to bed. I opened my school bag and started some revision.

The next day, I got up really early and was letting myself into The Swan at half past seven. Not making too much effort to be quiet, I hung up my coat and was just heading for the storeroom for the mop bucket when Shirley appeared in the doorway; I took great delight in seeing how haggard she looked. With a weary smile, she told me to *'get your sen' a cup of tea'* before picking up a pack of cigarettes and lighter and going back upstairs. Billy came down as I was finishing, an hour and a half later, his heavily painted floozy close behind him. I smiled and told him how grateful I was that he was letting me keep the cleaning job, even though Shirley was there now, as the money was coming in handy. Clearly pleased at my subservience, he said it wasn't a problem and that I did a good job. I could see Shirley's face behind him, the heavy layer of makeup creasing as she attempted a smile.

Having moved my cleaning forward by half an hour, I was early for the chemist's and Miss Alderson, the pharmacist, was delighted to see me when she discovered me waiting by the door as she arrived to open up.

Since learning of my desire to be a nurse, she'd taken me under her wing. Mrs Baxter, the other shop assistant, was visiting her brother in Scarborough so I was looking forward to chatting with my new mentor.

I made us both a cup of tea and then asked her where she was from; her accent didn't sound like a Yorkshire one.

"Oh, well yes, as people keep mentioning, I'm not from 'round ere'," she said, laughing at her own attempt at the local accent and, as I helped her get the back room ready, she told me an abridged version of her life story.

She was born in North Yorkshire and her father was a colonel in the army as was his father before him. He had been disappointed at having a daughter and not the son he desperately wanted and, for the rest of his life, resented her and his wife, who never managed to conceive a second child.

"The old arrogant fool," she said with shake of the head, "he knew nothing about biology. It was his bloody chromosome that made me female and most probably his low sperm count, not that I know for sure, of course, but it had taken almost ten years to conceive me. By that time, Mum was in her early forties anyway and she never properly recovered from the long and arduous labour; it's a wonder she survived another fifteen years."

Between customers, Miss Alderson was more than happy to chat to me. Even though she wasn't a local, she was well aware of my back story, no doubt fully informed by Mrs Baxter, but unlike the locals, she seemed far less interested in pumping me for gossip or information and, somewhat unexpectedly, was far more keen to tell me her story.

Having only known an ailing mother and a disinterested father, she decided from the age of five, she claimed, that she was going to be a doctor. However, when her mother died, her father 'put her straight'. He would not facilitate or even allow her to train for a career in medicine. It was not a job for a girl, it would take far too long to qualify not to mention the cost and for what? Girls weren't supposed to have careers, they were supposed to get little jobs to tide them over till they got married. She was upset but soon rallied, declaring she would go into nursing instead. Her father's objection to this was he was not having any daughter of his emptying bedpans or hanging around men in their pyjamas. It was her science teacher at school who had suggested she train to be a chemist and so in 1947, at the age of sixteen, she started a two year apprenticeship at the Leeds branch of Timothy Whites on Briggate and loved it. So much so, she became so absorbed in her work she forgot to have another life. As she told me this, the corners of her mouth forgot to smile, but only for a second or two. She shrugged and then gave a hearty laugh.

"While I was training, I lodged with my mother's sister in Headingley. This was my father's idea; Aunt Joan had a room so he wouldn't have to pay for digs. At the time, he was still pretending to be grieving for my mother. It was supposed to be a temporary arrangement but within a couple of weeks of me moving out, my father took up with some woman," she shrugged, "although it turned out he'd taken up with her years before, while my mother was alive." She shook her head, smiling sadly.

"So I stayed with Aunt Joan for the duration and we rubbed along nicely."

Later, when the shop was quiet again, she told me I should call her Judith. I said I was sure Mrs Baxter wouldn't like that and she laughed and gave me a hug.

"You are such a tonic Rosie," she declared and, slightly embarrassed, I asked if she still lived with her aunt.

"Goodness no, she died some years ago. She was a lovely woman, very like my mother," she said sadly, "Of course, my father was both furious and relieved about me not going back."

"Why?" I asked.

"Well, he was relieved as I'm certain neither he or his 'lady' friend wanted me in the house again but furious that I was now so close with Aunt Joan. You see, she was the elder sister and Mum's family was quite well off, probably why my father married her I shouldn't wonder, he certainly never seemed to care for her at all," pausing and taking a deep breath, "Grandad had set up his will mostly in favour of Aunt Joan. Once he'd seen Mum married, he assumed she'd be alright but as Aunt Joan had always been bookish and far too interested in studying to attract herself a husband, she'd need his money more, so he left it all to her."

"Right..." I said, not actually following.

"My father assumed the money would come to him when she died, thinking her foolish enough not to see through his pretence of a grieving widower or his 'help' with her investments, but she didn't, she left everything to me."

"That's brilliant," I said with a laugh, "it's really good that you had her, she sounds a bit like my Nana, only richer." She nodded and laughed but I saw her eyes get a little glassy,

"I missed her terribly when she died but she'd told me in no uncertain terms that I was not to mope. I was to sell up and move somewhere and give myself a chance to start again, so I moved out here, although of course that wasn't easy, being a woman."

"What do you mean?"

"Oh my dear, the law is an ass with regards to women. My father tried his best to contest the will using the 'woman's rights to own property and finance laws' but my Aunt Joan had made sure it was all watertight. Anyway, there is talk of the laws finally changing, which will be good news for you."

Mrs Baxter did not miss another Saturday; I kept wishing her brother would invite her back but understood his possible reluctance. Anyway, the break seemed to have done her good and she seemed a lot friendlier.

Miss Alderson started asking me to help with labelling and was delighted with my interest in the names of solutions, ointments and creams. Prescriptions were in abbreviated Latin and many drugs on the shelves were labelled in Latin and my employer was elated at my 'inquisitive mind', happily explaining what things were and their uses.

"I wanted to ask you something," I said the following week, as soon as Mrs Baxter was out of earshot, "It's about my Mum."

"Oh my goodness, well yes of course dear," she said straight away. I took a piece of paper out of my pocket and gave it to her, watching her read what I'd copied from the small bottles I still kept in a sock in a drawer under my underwear.

"These are the pills she was taking before she died, I just wanted to know what they were and if they could have caused her to...to...do what she did." The catch in my voice and my lowered eyes worked exactly as I hoped. She looked up, her concern magnified, and pulled me into a hug.

"Oh, my dear girl, you poor thing," giving me a squeeze before releasing me but remaining close, "would you be able to stay on for half an hour or so after we close? We can have a chat upstairs in the flat."

"Yes, that will be nice," I said nodding, her warmth and the lemony smell of shampoo in the shop lifting my spirits, making the corners of my eyes leak with a flash flood of emotions.

Darren was taking his Mum to see his little boy that afternoon so I was in no hurry to get home. I told Mrs Baxter I was staying behind so Miss Alderson could help me with my chemistry homework and she was happy to leave half an hour early. When we got upstairs, my host told me to make myself comfortable in her small sitting room and she turned on the gas fire before going to make us both a cup of tea and then coming to sit opposite me.

"First of all, Rosie, I want to tell you how sorry I am about your Mum. It's heartbreaking she died so young," she paused, considering her words, "but I really hope you don't think that you are in any way responsible for what happened."

I lowered my head and let my gaze rest on the brightly-patterned carpet, my hands so tightly clasped on my knees that they were turning white.

"She was very unhappy and her confusion led her to do what she did," she told me in her soft, full-vowelled accent and for a second I thought about telling her what I was sure had really happened, how Billy had got away with murder. She must have taken my silence for upset and came over to sit next to me on the sofa, placing her hands on mine. "I don't want to speak out of turn here," she said after another small considered silence, "but I understand your stepfather isn't a very nice man."

"He was horrible to her," I managed to say, lifting my head and locking eyes with hers, "He's not a nice man, he's evil." As the words came out, I caught my breath and started to sob.

Over the next hour, I told her what life was like living with Billy. I told her about the miscarriage and the physical and mental abuse and how Billy encouraged her to drink so much but I stopped short of telling her I was certain he'd killed her.

She was clearly shocked and, after giving me one of her lovely white lace-edged handkerchiefs, she told me that Billy sounded very much like her father, a nasty bully. She told me I was lucky to have Nana and agreed totally that we should try anything to stop Billy taking Davy back to live with him. She got herself a brandy after that, hesitating as she asked me if I would like one and looking relieved when I refused.

"So, the pills Mum was taking when she died...." I said as she sipped her rather large small brandy.

"Yes," she nodded, "yes, well the Prothiaden is an antidepressant, the doctor most probably prescribed that after her last spell in hospital," pausing and looking thoughtful, "Hopefully, she would have been told that it's not advisable to drink alcohol with them though."

"My mother generally drank herself unconscious every night," I said flatly, "encouraged by him," I sighed, "I even saw him give her a double gin to wash them down with a couple of times."

"Christ!" she muttered before taking a large sip of her drink, her eyes rolling up towards her forehead before placing the glass down and turning to explain.

"Consuming alcohol with this medication would cause excessive drowsiness and almost certainly be damaging her liver." She rubbed her temples slightly as she picked up the slip of paper.

"Tetracycline is an antibiotic." She paused again, looking slightly uncomfortable before asking, "Was she given this when she was discharged from the hospital?"

"I don't think so, I think the doctor prescribed her these the week before she died," I said.

"Right, so do you know if your stepfather got any medication at the same time?"

"I don't know," I shook my head. "What is it for?" She breathed in deeply and reached for her drink, which she knocked back in one.

"It's generally prescribed for UTI's, urinary tract infections," she said, looking pained, "this particular one is quite strong," shaking her head then adding quickly, "most probably it was for an infection linked to her miscarriage."

I left half an hour later, having convinced her that I was okay and in no way worried about what she had told me. I even managed to change the subject to tell her about Darren and how we were going to the pictures that night. She said she hadn't been to the cinema in a long time but remembered it being quite an experience. Walking downstairs to let me out of the back door, she touched my arm and said,

"I'm glad we had this chat and I want you to know if you ever want to talk to anyone or need any help with your school work or anything, just let me know." I thanked her and said I'd liked it too before adding,

"If you mean it about helping with school work, it would be good if you could help me with some revision in science before my exams."

"Of course," she beamed at me, "it will be fun, and I'm free most evenings."

"That's great," I beamed back, "maybe Tuesday?"

"Absolutely, come round after the shop shuts, about half past five."

"Thank you," I repeated. She nodded and smiled and I set off home at a quick pace. I had things to do. I had decided I was finally brave enough to kill Billy.

## Eighteen

I usually got to The Swan for nine thirty on a Sunday morning, by which time the lights were on and Billy was already in the bar, checking the shelves and counting the float. However, on this particular Sunday, I'd given myself an extra ten minutes, going through my plan and making sure the jar of Robertson's strawberry jam was securely wrapped in an old t-shirt in the bottom of my shoulder bag, so I was almost twenty minutes late but the pub was still in darkness. Letting myself in, I called hello up the stairs to the flat. After a second of silence, I walked to the storeroom door which was double-locked and I had no key.

Something felt very wrong. I walked back to the bottom of the stairs and called up again.

"Billy, Shirley, it's nearly ten, are you up yet?" Nothing.

Hesitating, I raised my hand towards the banister and shrugging the shoulder strap of my bag behind me, I leaned forward, lifting my leg to ascend the stairs, calling out again. Before my foot gained purchase on the worn carpeted surface of the third step, I heard a muffled sound followed by a thud of something falling to the floor heavily.

"Billy?" I called again as a surge of adrenaline swept through me. The silence shattered as my stepfather made a half groan, half cough sound before calling out,

"Rosie, yes, we've just slept in, stop where you are I'll be down in a minute."

The hairs on the back of my neck were raised and my mind went into overdrive as I moved away from the stairs to stand near the storeroom door. Billy thundered down the stairs in his old trousers and a string vest a couple of minutes later and unlocked it to let me through.

"Shirley's had a bad night," he said, not looking at me, "I think she might need to stop in bed for a bit." I watched him run his fingers through his greasy thinning hair. I nodded and went to pick up the sweeping brush as he mumbled something about him needing to get dressed and he turned and dashed back upstairs. I took my coat off and put my bag across my body as I processed the emerging situation.

I'd been there almost an hour when he came back fully dressed and as he passed close by me in the storeroom, the smell of stale whiskey and nicotine indicating to me he had not had a wash or brushed his teeth.

"Have you got much else to do, Luv?" he asked. I looked up at him, startled. He hardly ever called me 'Luv'.

"I've just got to mop behind the bar and swap the bar towels but I can stop on a bit an' give the flat a clean if you want, if Shirley's poorly?" I replied in my meekest tone, my eyes downcast. It took him only seconds to respond and I could hear the relief in his voice.

"Yeah, mebe that'd be a help," he nodded, adding sharply, "but don't go in the bedroom, leave her to sleep." I raised my head and gave him a small smile as he nodded and added, "Don't bother wi' the bar, I'll sort that, you go up now, it's a bit of a mess but I'll pay you double for today." As he finished speaking, his tongue quickly flicked round his dry cracked lips and, if I didn't know better, I'd swear he looked scared.

"Okay, I'll be as quiet as I can so I don't disturb her," I replied with a nod as I moved away.

"Good lass, an' I don't think she's gonna be up to this tea an' cake thing this afternoon," he said with a smile, exposing his yellowing teeth as he reached for his cigarettes and lighter, "we'll do it another time."

I nodded and turned to walk quickly upstairs, recalculating my plans, this might be easier than I thought. I hadn't been sure Billy would be keen on me cleaning the flat, assuming this was Shirley's job, so him accepting my offer was a bonus. However, her being up there was a bit risky so I needed to tread carefully.

I went straight into the kitchen which was in a terrible state. All the surfaces had dirty pots and pans on and the sink was full of stagnant, grimy water and more mugs and plates. The table was covered with a layer of sugar and food crumbs with an overflowing ashtray in the middle. On the cooker, a frying pan was half full of congealed lard and bacon fat and the room stank of stale cigarette smoke and refried food.

I opened the cupboard above the bread bin and saw the half full jar of jam that Billy had on his toast every morning and most nights when he'd had a skin full. I took it out and put it on the side before reaching into my bag to make the switch. The jar I was leaving had a bit of something extra special that would certainly end his hangovers for good; ground laburnum seed pods.

I had no idea if Shirley also partook of the strawberry preserve as well but I had shrugged at the thought of her also being poisoned. I mean, her dying also wouldn't even just be collateral damage as I couldn't be certain that she wasn't in on Mum's murder; she was definitely a right cow and had made Mum unhappy so, well, maybe she had it coming. As I closed the cupboard door, I shook away the thought that it might be seen as suspicious if both of them died then I heard a noise from the bedroom. I quickly went to see the door was still closed but turning my ear close, I could hear her groaning then she coughed, cried out a little in pain and went quiet again.

I stepped away towards the bathroom door which was ajar. Lifting my hand, daring myself to push it open and trying to block the imagined images, the ones I had never actually seen, of my mother laying bloodless in a bath of red water. Finally, I got myself together and pushed it open, taking a step inside.

It was empty of course and the dark ring around the inside of the bath made it clear Billy had no qualms about getting in there. I surveyed the rest of the room; wet towels piled up behind the door, half a bar of soap on the wash basin covered in hair and an open bottle of shampoo on its side spilling out on the floor. I bent down to pick it up but shot back upright before my fingers got purchase. There were several small splashes of blood on the floor in front of the washbasin which looked fresh. I backed out of the room and closed the door. It took a few seconds for my heart rate to calm down but as soon as I felt able to move, I went back to the bedroom door. Gently turning the knob, I edged it open.

She was snoring gently, her hair piled up on the pillow above her head exposing fresh bruises on her face. I stepped a little closer and noticed an open bottle of pills on the bedside table; they were Mum's sleeping pills.

I think perhaps that was the final straw for me.

I leaned across the sedated body and picked up the pillow, stained with Brillcream and nicotine, from the other side of the bed. Holding it stain side down over her recently punched face, I leaned forward, smelling her pungent sour breath, and pressed it to her face. It took a second before she reacted and began to struggle but not as much as I expected, rage fuelled adrenaline sustaining my determination to smother her out of existence. I climbed on top of her, kneeling on her chest to stop her lungs inflating. She tried to cry out, clearly in pain, but the noise was muffled by the pillow under my fully extended arms. I watched the second hand on the alarm clock pass the number twelve eight times before I climbed off and moved the pillow, placing it back on Billy's side. Then I rolled her on to her side, facing away from the door and with a feeling of immense satisfaction, I left the room.

With adrenaline still coursing through me, I went back to the kitchen and began cleaning. Moving everything out of the sink before filling it with hot soapy water as I thought about the little surprise I was leaving for Billy. With very steady hands, I washed and dried all the pots and pans and put them away. I cleaned the surfaces and the table and then swept the lino floor before swopping back the unadulterated jam and putting the laburnum-spiked one back in my bag.

This time I walked straight into the bathroom, hung up the towels, picked up the shampoo, wiping up the spillage with blue toilet paper, but I left the blood. The sitting room wasn't too bad, just messy with sofa cushions on the floor and newspapers strewn about. The carpet could have done with a hoover but I decided not to do that, the bag was probably full and I decided I'd done enough.

It was quarter past twelve when I came downstairs and walked through the storeroom. I could see a couple of the regulars in the bar and Billy nodded at me as he finished pulling a pint. After ringing up the fourteen pence, he came over to me.

"I'll be off now," I said, "I cleaned up the kitchen and sitting room but I didn't run the hoover round as I didn't want to wake Shirley, I think she's still asleep."

"That's all reet, she can do it after," he said with a nod as he pulled his wallet out of his back pocket. I watched him pull out two pound notes before murmuring,

"There was some blood on the bathroom floor."

"Oh yeah that, yeah," pausing then glancing up at me quickly before his eyes darted around the room, he then gave a throaty cough and said, "yeah, it's her monthlies, sorry...," stopping as he saw my tears.

"Oh Christ, yeah, your Mam," He froze as his panic returned and his emotional immaturity rendered him helpless. I sniffed and wiped my eyes with the back of my hand.

"It was a bit of a shock, so I didn't finish in there," I said.

His relief was palpable as he quickly pulled out another two notes and handed all four over to me.

"No problem, Shirley'll sort it out after." He cleared his throat and tried for a smile which just looked creepy. I nodded my thanks and went to get my coat. "Tell your Nan we'll do the tea party thing next week when Shirley's bucked her sen up."

I nodded, agreeing and used up the rest of my will power to walk calmly through the pub and out through the front door, walking briskly down the road.

The house smelled of roasting beef and cabbage and as I walked in Davy was in the hall putting his shoes on.

"I was just coming up to look for you, Nana was worried," he said.

"Rosie, where have you been?" Nana asked, walking in to the hall wiping her hands on her pinny, "The dinners nearly ready," not waiting for an answer and turning to go back in the kitchen, "I'll just put the Yorkshire puddings in…"

"Nana," I interrupted her with a choked sob of emotion, making her turn back, "I think Billy's done something to Shirley."

"What on earth do you mean?" she asked sharply.

"He says she's not well, she's in bed and he asked me to tidy up the flat," clearing my throat, I dropped my eyes, "there was blood all over the bathroom floor."

"The bathroom!" she yelled. I didn't look up but nodded. Davy shuffled from foot to foot not knowing what to do and she stepped forward and embraced us both.

"Come on Luv," she said, "don't be letting it all get to you." Giving a tight squeeze of my brother and me, she let go and nodded at us, "Let's go and get our dinner down us and talk about it after."

"Do we still have to go up there this afternoon?" Davy asked fearfully.

"No," I shook my head, "he said they'd rearrange it for another time."

"Is Darren still coming round here though?" he asked, clearly relieved.

"Yeah, he'll be round a bit later. I'm just gonna run upstairs and get out of these mucky clothes. I won't be a minute."

After a lovely dinner which I pretended to be struggling to eat, Davy went to play with his Meccano and I told her about the morning, well, my edited version. How the pub had been in darkness and how I had to shout upstairs, how Billy came down in his vest looking like he'd just got out of bed, how he'd told me Shirley wasn't well and not to wake her up. I told her it was after I'd seen the blood in the bathroom that I opened the bedroom door and saw her lying there.

"She was really still and I think there were blood on her face."

"Oh well," Nana said, nodding her head, "maybe now she'll realise what your Mam had to put up with."

"Yeah, and we don't have to go up there and eat her stale buns and pretend we like her," I nodded in agreement.

Before Darren arrived, I went down to the bottom of the garden and tipped the strawberry jam on to the pile of garden rubbish in the corner behind the shed, putting the empty jar in the dustbin.

"As we're not going out to tea, shall we have a drive out to Newmillerdam and have a walk?" my boyfriend suggested when he arrived, "all of us," he added, smiling at Nana.

"Well that would be nice," she said, displaying a grateful smile that I suddenly realised I hadn't seen for some time, "and when we get back we can polish off that Victoria sandwich."

It was cold but bright and we wrapped up well and enjoyed our stroll around the dam. The sun that had brightened the early afternoon started to fade as we arrived back at the car and the dullness of the greying skies made it seem like the night was drawing in, even though it was only just after four.

As we pulled up outside the gate, Mrs Davis came running out of her house in an excited state and I had to suppress a smile, composing my face to surprised and alarmed, preparing for how this was going to pan out.

On hearing her neighbour utter cries of 'Billy, ambulance and police', Nana quickly suggested that Darren go into the front room with Davy and play draughts with him. Over a cup of sweet tea, which Mrs Davis insisted on giving us, she recounted what we had missed while we had been out.

I actually struggled to hide my frustration when I realised Mrs Davis didn't actually know much but, mistaking my irritation for upset, Nana reached out and held my hand. All she knew was that an ambulance with lights and sirens on had raced up the high street sometime after two and stopped outside The Swan. The pub was still open and the dozen or so regulars that were just finishing off their pints saw Billy in a right state, shouting at one of the paramedics before suddenly throwing out all the rubberneckers. Soon after, two police cars arrived and, *"It dint look much like a lock-in'* according to our narrator. Mrs Davis put on her coat and walked up the high street where two of the regulars were standing outside the Spar shop surrounded by several other concerned villagers, all listening intently to the '*goings on'*.

The ambulance and one of the police cars were still parked outside more than an hour later and they only left about twenty minutes before we got back. Here, Mrs Davis's theatrical leaning came to the fore as she announced dramatically, *'The Swan's locked up and in complete darkness!.'*

"Well it should be locked up, it's Sunday afternoon," Nana said curtly.

"Well yes but...," she tried to respond.

"Did anyone see the ambulance and police car go?" I cut in, "Did Billy go in the ambulance?"

"Well no, neither of them had their sirens on when they went," responded Mrs Davis, "but Don Varley says Shirley weren't there at all. Billy said she'd had a few too many the night afore and was sleeping it off." She took in a big breath, nodded her head and tapped the side of her nose with her index finger, "Ring any bells?"

"Mavis!" Nana stood up, "Thank you for letting us know but I think you need to go now. I've got to get the tea on."

"Oh right, well it were just," crestfallen that her bombshell had not been received in the way she had expected, "I mean, it just proves...," she trailed off as Nana walked past her, opening the door and leaving no doubt that the conversation was over.

## Nineteen

I had been expecting a visit from the boys in blue that evening but it wasn't until Tuesday morning that we had the knock at the door. We were in the kitchen eating breakfast and on hearing the knock, Nana and I exchanged glances and I leaned forward to get up but Nana said firmly she would get it. Mrs Davis had been round Monday afternoon with the latest from the jungle drums. Shirley was dead and Billy had been kept at the police station overnight as it was as plain as the nose on his ugly face that he'd '*dun her in!*'

After allowing in the two officers, one in uniform who looked familiar, and one in a dark suit which looked like it had seen better days. Nana told Davy to go upstairs and brush his teeth. I followed her and our visitors into the front room as they explained they wanted a chat about what I'd seen at The Swan on Sunday morning.

Nodding meekly, I sat on the edge of the armchair while they sat on the sofa and introduced themselves as DS Todd and PC Bailey.

"As I'm sure you know, Shirley Blenkinsopp was found dead on Sunday afternoon and we are treating her death as suspicious," the DS began, "Now your stepdad tells us that you were up there that morning?"

I nodded but said nothing and looked to Nana who smiled.

"Tell them Rosie, tell them what you told me," she said.

I gulped loudly before going through the same narrative that I'd given Nana, my voice quiet and occasionally hesitant as I openly struggled with emotion, although I made sure to keep eye contact as much as possible. I ended with how upset I'd been when I got home. Nana started to explain about how Mum had been found and was saying how seeing the blood on the bathroom floor had upset me.

"You mean because we know it was him that killed her," I said, raising my voice as my eyes glistened.

"Now, luv," Nana said soothingly but the plain clothed policeman held up a hand asking, "What's this?"

"Billy Flynn's wife slashed her wrists in the bath last year, Sergeant, afore your time. She were a bit of an alkie." The uniformed plod sounded pleased to impart these facts. I was livid.

"She did no such thing and you all need to stop saying she was an alkie, like well, that's alright then, he can slap and punch her. Billy drugged her and then put her in the bath and cut her arms, how in God's name did she cut both arms so straight and so deep?" I took in a deep breath and avoided looking at what I knew would be Nana's terrified face. "He wasn't happy just knocking her about, pushing her downstairs; he wanted rid of her so as he could move Shirley in, everybody knew." Rage continued surging through me and I couldn't stop and, pointing at the policeman, I shouted,

"You and your mates knew an' all, just cos Billy was a mate, serving you beer after hours, you let him get away with it." My yelling was punctuated with sobs and I am almost sure I had genuine tears.

"Now then lass, you want to be careful...," warned P.C. Bailey, springing forward and wagging his finger at me.

"That's enough, Constable," the good cop said sternly, then looking at me he tilted his head slightly to one side and, in a gentle but still firm voice, he told me they would be going back to the police station and he would be making more inquires but they would need to talk to me again. They would also want me and Nana to make a statement; we would need to go into the station for that, perhaps later that morning? But I could rest assured he would look into what I had said. I raised my tear-stained face to look at him.

"If you let him out he'll come after me, I know he killed me Mam and I'm sure he'd started hurting Shirley, if you let him out he'll kill me next."

As they left, what little bit of professionalism PC Bailey may have had seemed to have completely deserted him. He glared at me as they got to the door and looked like he was about to say something but the DS indicated to him to leave and turned and said again, he would be taking a look at the investigation into my mother's death.

As soon as she closed the door, Nana turned and looked at me, shaking her head, "Oh Rosie, what did you have to say all that for?" stepping forward and engulfing me in her arms. Over her shoulder I saw my little brother standing at the top of the stairs, his face devastated with sorrow.

It was plain that his young brain was overloading with contradicting emotions as he tried to understand what was going on and what would happen to us. Nana was fully in the camp of her generation; he was a child and should be kept in the dark as much as possible. She seemed to think that unless anyone spoke directly to him, he'd be unaware of what went on. The circumstances of Mum's death had not been divulged to him and she and I had only voiced our concerns when he wasn't around. He did tell me later, much later, that he knew Billy had hurt Mum, lots of times, but had more or less chosen to believe that her dying had been an accident and found that easier to deal with.

However, hearing my very loud and angry accusations, he allowed the truth to sink in and become more terrified that Billy might get away with it again and would come after me.

Once she had released me, Nana went back to the kitchen and I went upstairs to try and comfort my little brother. As I got to the top step, he flung himself at me, clinging fiercely to me as I shunted us both into his bedroom. We lay side by side on his bed, his arms still wrapped round me. I asked him if he wanted to talk about it but he shook his head, his voice still lost behind his emotion, so we laid like that for a good half an hour. I saw Nana peep round the door at one point but then heard her pad back downstairs.

"Well, I guess neither of us are going to school today," I said eventually.

"Will I have to go to an orphanage?" he finally managed to ask.

"No! Absolutely not, you're going nowhere, you're staying here with me and Nana." He managed a weak smile and squeezed me. I squeezed him back.

"Come on let's go down and see if we can get Nana to do a bit of baking as we're staying home today."

"Do you think Dad will stay in jail?" he asked quietly. I took in a deep breath and managed to stop myself from saying, 'I bloody hope so' and instead shook my head.

"I don't know but whatever happens, nothing's gonna change, I promise."

As we walked downstairs, we could already smell the warm aromas of baking sponge cake. What I remember about the rest of that day was wondering if I'd gone too far. I'd not slept well the night before, not through remorse for what I'd done but with the excited satisfaction of perhaps killing two birds with one stone. Smothering the already beaten up Shirley and leaving Billy to try and explain how he wasn't responsible was just too wonderful. But that, was of course, also a problem; Billy had managed to talk his way out of these things in the past, what if he convinced them that she'd just died of natural causes, of a heart attack or something. This was why I needed to make sure that the lazy 'nothing to see here' plods connected the dots and did not believe a word he said.

That afternoon, once the Victoria sponge was out of the oven, the three of us, Davy not wanting to stay on his own, took the bus to the Wood Street Police Station.

Nana went first, giving her statement in a small room to the side of reception while my brother and waited. I stood up when she came out, expecting to go in, but the policeman behind the desk said that DC Todd was coming down to speak to me as he had a few more questions. I saw the colour drain from Nana's face but I gave a shrug and sat back down. Davy grabbed my arm and pulled himself close.

We only had to wait a few more minutes and as soon as the detective arrived, smiling and apologising for keeping us waiting, he took me down a corridor and into another room where a woman police constable was waiting at the door. This was a proper interview room but I was assured that he just wanted to get all the details right and that the WPC would be making notes that would be used for my statement but I would have a chance to read and check it before I signed it. He then mentioned, as if it had just occurred to him that, because of my age, I could have an adult in with me if I wanted one but I said 'no thank you, it's fine' which was the answer he wanted.

"So, let's start with what time you actually got to The Swan shall we and what happened then." He smiled and nodded. I told him again about being a bit later than normal and being surprised to see no lights on.

"So usually, your stepdad is already in the pub when you arrive?"

"Yeah," I nodded emphatically, "he'd be in the bar most times, stocking up the shelves and checking the optics, specially on Sundays as Saturday nights are alus busy with bottles, you know cos there's a lot of couples in."

"Right," he nodded "but last Sunday he wasn't in the bar?"

"No, I don't think he were even awake." I opened my eyes as wide as I could, scratching my head, "It were really strange but I've got a key to the back, you know to the flat. I let myself in and it was really quiet so I called upstairs, saying I was here and it were nearly ten o'clock."

"Did you go upstairs?"

"No, not then," leaning forward a bit, "it was strange, you know, it being so quiet and the storeroom door being locked, I actually felt scared. I was thinking I should go home and tell Nana but then I heard a noise upstairs. I called up again and Billy shouted he were coming and to wait there."

"How long did it take for him to come down?"

I shrugged, "I'm not sure, five minutes, maybe a bit longer."

"And how was he? What sort of a mood would you say he was in?"

"Well he weren't in a bad mood, which is what I was expecting, you know cos I'd shouted upstairs," I said.

"What do you mean, why would that put him in a bad mood?"

"Cos I'd shouted him up and I thought if he's slept in it won't be his fault, nothings ever Billy's fault, so I was half expecting a slap when he came down."

"But he wasn't annoyed?"

"No but he was a bit weird, you know like...I don't know, not really with it and he just had his vest on."

"What! He was just in his vest?" DS Todd's face actually coloured up.

"No," feigning embarrassment, "he had his trousers on, well he was still doing them up as he came downstairs but it's the first time I've ever seen him in just his vest. I mean even in the flat he alus had a shirt on." I stopped for a second, screwing up my face to show my concentration, "In all the years I've known, that's the first time I've seen him without a shirt." I glanced over at the WPC who was scribbling away on her notepad before suddenly saying, "Flustered!"

"What?" DS Todd looked confused.

"He seemed flustered, yeah that's it, maybes cos he'd just woke up or something and he looked like he'd had a skin full the night before." I smiled at him and then as if the memory was just coming back, I said, "So I got the impression they must have slept in, which is really unusual for Billy." I ended with an emphatic nod. Then I explained how Billy had told me Shirley wasn't feeling right and was stopping in bed so we wouldn't be having our tea party that afternoon, "Then he laughed and said it was just as well as the kitchen *'were a bloody tip'*."

"Tea party?" he looked confused.

I told him about how Shirley wanted us to go round and play happy families and how that was the last thing we wanted to do but we had to keep Billy happy so he wouldn't take Davy back to live at the pub just to spite us.

"So what happened then?"

"He went back upstairs and I got on with the sweeping up and emptying the ashtrays. He came back down about half an hour later, dressed in a clean shirt and trousers, but I could still smell last night's beer on him".

The DS nodded at that and looked thoughtful for a second so I added that I'd offered to do a bit of tidyng up when I'd finished in the pub and how he'd thought about it for a minute before saying I could go up and clean the kitchen and bathroom but not to go in the bedroom.

"He said that, he told you not to go in the bedroom?"

"Yeah, he said I weren't to put the hoover on or be banging about and disturb Shirley."

"Did he say what was wrong with her?"

"No, he just said she weren't feeling right but...," letting my voice fade.

"But what?" he asked sharply.

"Well, I thought at first she'd maybe had a skin full, you know at the lock-in, but then I saw the blood."

"What blood?" he asked leaning forward.

"On the bathroom floor and around the wash basin." I felt my eyes start to brim over with tears, "I started to clear it up but I..., I thought about me Mam and I had to come out." I wiped my eyes with the top of my wrists, "So I guessed Billy had given her a good hiding, like he used to give me Mam."

"Right," he nodded, "so when you came out of the bathroom what did you do?"

"I went over to the bedroom door and just stood there for a bit, listening, but I couldn't hear anything."

"So..."

"So I opened the door, quiet as I could, just to have a look and see how bad she was," I said, trying to swallow the rising sob.

"And what did you see?"

"She were laying in bed, her back to the door and the cover right high up, so I said her name, just softly but she didn't move and I knew if Billy came up and caught me he'd give me a right good hiding an' all so I pulled the door shut and went back downstairs." I took in a deep breath and tried to expel the image of her bruised dead face as I'd lifted the pillow.

"Then what?" he asked with a straight mouth smile. I shrugged and made a show of attempting to control my emotions before replying.

"Billy was serving one of the regulars," pausing, I took in a lung full of air, "and when he'd finished, I stepped into the storeroom so he'd follow me. I told him about the blood in the bathroom, he said it was...," I trailed off, slightly embarrassed.

"It was what?"

"He said it was Shirley's monthlies," I said quietly, head bowed over the desk but after a split second I raised my head and added, "but I knew it wasn't."

"Did you tell him you didn't believe him?"

"Course not! I learnt a long time ago not to talk back to him," I exclaimed, "I just nodded and he paid me, paid me extra an' all, told me to get meself summat nice." The WPC looked up for a second and asked, "How much did he give you?"

"Four pounds," I smiled at her and noticed the DS frowning, "he normally gives me a pound for each day, Saturday and Sunday, so he gave me double."

She nodded and wrote it down as DS Todd shook his head before asking, "Did he say anything else about Shirley?"

"He asked me if I'd been in the bedroom and I told him I hadn't." I watched the biro scribble on the pad some sort of shorthand and a small silence rested on the three of us before I asked, suddenly, almost making the policeman jump,

"Was she dead, when I looked in on her, had he already killed her?"

## **Twenty**

Darren came round that evening straight from work and brought Nana a bunch of daffodils wrapped in newspaper. She opened the door to his knock and he started straight away telling her how sorry he was about all this stuff that was happening and if there was anything he could do, she only had to ask. In that moment, I saw her lower her shoulders and she nodded her head slowly. She took the flowers from him and I knew, with that gesture and few words, he had extinguished any of the niggling doubts she'd had and, like my little brother, she was completely taken in by him.

When I first met him, I was infatuated with him and then quickly devastated by what I thought was his rejection of me. Meeting him again and hearing his explanation for standing me up had sparked a spectrum of emotions. On first catching sight of him in The Mitre, excitement coursed through me and as we talked, his good looks and cheeky charm were certainly having an effect on my teenage hormones. When he abandoned his mates to stay with me, my confidence grew as he flirted and teased me and I realised he could be the catalyst I needed to ensure a safer future for me and my brother.

He was relieved at my reaction to his troubled past and my doe-eyed keenness had been too sweet for him to resist but what had made me so perfect for him was my own family issues and what he saw as my vulnerability. He, like everybody else, thought I was completely besotted with him. However, right from the start, I was aware he was not who he seemed. Don't get me wrong, I did like him and I was immensely flattered by his attentions and loved the way my friends were jealous of me, especially Julie, but I was not taken in by him. The things he told me had a ring of truth but I suspected it wasn't the whole story and in the same way he thought I was perfect for him, I saw him as very useful stepping stone.

However, my plan seemed to be in a constant state of flux. First the bombshell of discovering Alfie, the cad who had taken advantage of my mother before disappearing and then Shirley, making herself available for the victim role, hence saving me the trouble of killing Billy. So while Darren was working his charm on Nana and Davy, fully ingratiating himself in what was left of my family, I was frantically rethinking my plans.

Thankfully, all these distractions didn't seem to affect my school work as luckily, I am quite good at compartmentalising; I suppose you've already noticed that. One thing I knew for certain was I needed to do well in my exams although, at that point, I was starting to reconsider nursing as a career following my chat with Miss Alderson; I was wondering if training as a pharmacist might be a better option.

I was processing these thoughts, the saga of Shirley's murder, which is what the police were calling it following the medical report, and Billy's culpability, as I walked to my now only weekend job on Saturday morning. Mrs Baxter's face lit up as I walked in, quickly changing to a frown of concern. Miss Alderson was shocked that I'd turned up and told me that I could go home at any time if I wasn't feeling up to it and she would still pay me.

"I'm alright. I would rather keep busy than sit around at home thinking about it," I told them both, "I'd like to not think about it for a few hours," I concluded with my head lowered and my eye blinking away imaginary tears.

"Of course, you poor thing, you've gone through enough," my employer stated and then with a very pointed look at Mrs Baxter, "We'll just get through the day and all this unpleasantness won't be mentioned."

The little shop saw one of its busiest Saturdays ever with lots of people calling in for over the counter medicines and toiletries. One or two people did ask me how I was or say they were surprised to see me there but I just gave them a small shrug, refusing to be drawn. Mrs Baxter seemed to have changed her mind about me and became quite protective, so much so that when the old harridan Edna Brooks just came out and asked me if I'd seen what Billy had done to Shirley and was it like what he'd done to my Mum, she told her to shut up. Later, just before the shop closed, she put her hand on my arm and her face began to colour up as she spoke,

"I just want you to know that I'm right sorry for all the terrible things that have happened to you." For an awful moment I thought she was going to cry and I had no idea what to do. I stood staring at her hand still on my arm as she went on, "I didn't know your Mam, only what I heard," shaking her head, "but I do know Billy Flynn and I know he was alus a nasty sod, so any road," another emotional pause, "just look after yourself, alright?" I smiled and she withdrew her hand, satisfied.

As I walked home, and Nana's house was now truly my home, there was still light in the sky and, as it was the last few days of February, I felt hopeful of longer warmer days ahead. I went straight up to my bedroom to get washed and changed but as I was about to pull my bedroom curtains closed, I saw something at the bottom of the garden. I crept downstairs as quietly as I could, Davy and Nana were playing chess in the sitting room and the door was half closed. I stealthily made my way through the kitchen and out of the back door, walking purposefully toward the bottom of the garden. Just a couple of feet from the pile of garden rubbish lay Tabatha, Mrs Davis's fat, ginger cat, sprawled with her legs stiff and straight and a pool of bloody vomit around her open mouth. Looking a little closer, I could see traces of jam on her whiskers and nose. I poked the rotting vegetation with the garden fork to cover up the remaining sweet poison before going back into the house to tell Nana the sad news.

## Everything in the Garden

Knowing how devoted her neighbour was to her cat, Nana made the decision not to tell her of Tabatha's demise. Instead, the three of us went back to the garden, now quite dark, and dug a shallow grave close to the laburnum tree, which I thought was quite fitting, and made a vow not to mention it again. Davy said he'd never liked Tabatha and had seen her trying to kill birds and that she hissed a lot, then wondered if our neighbour might now get a dog.

Over the next couple of weeks, Mrs Davis could be found sitting at our kitchen table dabbing her eyes at the absence of her Tabby. Nana consoled her with the fickle nature of felines, suggesting she had temporarily taken up residence somewhere else and would more than likely come back. I was impressed at her duplicity and the sincerity with which she lied.

The Swan was closed and locked up and, although back then, the West Yorkshire Police force was not as careful with or vigilant of crime scenes, for almost a week I fought my urge to let myself in for a look around. Instead, I phoned Wood Street station to ask if it was okay for me to go and collect some more of mine and Davy's things and was given the affirmative from the duty desk sergeant. Nana said she wanted to come too and, surprisingly, Davy said the same. Darren drove us up as I'd insisted we should take everything so we never had to go back there again.

There actually wasn't much of my stuff left, mainly clothes that I'd grown out of and some books and games. There was a lot more of Davy's stuff which we packed up quickly. In the kitchen there were two half full mugs of cold tea on the draining board and a chunky whisky glass smeared with finger marks and honey-coloured dregs next to a large piece of the shop bought cake, and a full ashtray. I opened the fridge and Nana muttered something about having to clear it out and get rid of all the other perishables, "I mean well, if he's not going to be back for a while." I said nothing and walked into the hall.

The bathroom was exactly as I'd left it although the seat was up. Nana came up quickly behind me and pulled me back.

"Don't go in there, Luv," she said softly.

I turned back to the passage and made my way to the big bedroom. The door was closed and, as I put my hand on the handle, Nana shook her head and started to object but I told her I wanted to be absolutely sure there was nothing of Mum's left there and opened the door and walked in.

"Do you think you should be in there?" Darren asked from the kitchen doorway.

"The police said it was alright," I answered without turning round.

Nana was leaning on the door frame and although, initially, she questioned the correctness of my search, she seemed to make her mind up, telling me to get Mum's engagement and wedding rings this time.

"Me and your Grandad paid for them anyway." The rings were still where they had been before. I lifted them out of the ashtray and turned and dropped them into Nana's open hand. Darren shrugged and went back to Davy's room to help him get the last of his things.

I checked the wardrobe but all it contained was Billy's shirts and trousers and his two jackets along with three frocks that were far too large a size to have been Mum's. However, on the shelf at the top, pushed right to the back, I could feel a screwed up bundle of clothes. I moved the dressing table stool over to stand on and reached inside. It was her wedding dress and I felt a lump in my throat as the tips of my fingers took purchase, my eyes filling with tears. I half turned to hold it out so Nana could see but as the dress unfurled in my hands, I caught sight of something else that had been behind it. Nana stepped forward and took the dress from me. It was dirty and creased and some of the lace was torn but all both of us could see was the vision of a delighted Mum standing outside St James Church beaming at us.

"Oh my," Nana said shaking her head, "I never knew she kept this."

"Hang on," I turned back, "there's something else up here; I think it's her hat and veil." I had to lean forward on my tiptoes and only just managed to feel the netted fabric to slide it forward. As it got to the front, I grasped it properly and, turning, I registered that it was surprisingly heavy. As I stepped down, I saw a small oblong tin inside. Expecting it to be keepsakes from the wedding day, I walked across to Nana and, passing her the hat, I opened the tin. Inside there was a wad of assorted bank notes. Nana stifled a gasp and I touched my lips with my finger and tilted my head towards Davy's open bedroom door before closing the tin, placing it back in the headdress and taking it out to pack in one of the boxes we'd brought.

I checked all the drawers and cupboards but there wasn't anything else that had belonged to Mum except the chrome plated cigarette lighter Billy bought her when she was trying to give up smoking. He'd claimed not smoking was making her a 'miserable cow' and gave it to her with two packets of Benson and Hedges. The lighter was in Billy's bedside drawer along his own bits and bobs; cufflinks, coins and a large box of condoms. I had a sudden urge to flick the lighter and set fire to the bed and see the whole pub go up in flames. Davy's voice asking if we could go home now please brought me out of it. I dropped the lighter back in drawer and slammed it shut.

"What'll happen to the pub now?" Darren asked as we carried the boxes and bags out to his car, "I mean, if Billy goes to prison, for like a long time."

*"If he doesn't go to prison for a long time I will go up there and burn the bloody pub down with him in it,"* is what I wanted to say but, instead, I shrugged and said I had no idea, I supposed it would belong to Davy and me.

I missed quite a lot of school over those few weeks but the teachers were amazing and, along with Miss Alderson, I had plenty of offers of help with revision for the coming exams. I'd been predicted mostly B's but an A in science, as long as I could keep my focus while all the drama unfolded around me.

I still have a copy of the Yorkshire Post dated Tuesday 6th March 1973 in a box in my loft. Oh, don't get me wrong, I haven't kept it as some sort of a trophy of my handy work, no, far from it, it is just a symbol of how it was over and finally, we could move on. But anyway, I've kept the newspaper bearing the headline 'Man Charged with Murder' and, although it wasn't my mother's murder he was charged with, it felt good to see it. Billy murdering Shirley, suffocating her after a sustained and brutal attack, apparently wasn't a big enough story to make the nationals but six months later, after a very short trial and a unanimous guilty verdict, the story finally got countrywide coverage.

I had a lovely few minutes in the paper shop next to the bus station in Wakefield, just standing in front of the paper rack, seeing his face and the word GUILTY in block capitals on the tabloids; it gave me a tingle of satisfaction.

Throughout the trial, Billy maintained his innocence – admitting to giving her a slap or two but insisted she were fine when he left her in bed. He said they had been 'making up' when I had arrived which is why he was flustered. He'd given her the sleeping pills he'd found in the bathroom cabinet and told her to 'stop in bed' until she felt a bit better. She'd been 'pissed up' the night before so she had a massive hangover, that's what they'd been fighting about and that was when he'd given her a couple of slaps but she had been 'well out of order' and 'needed putting in her place'.

The coroner's report had a different story. Shirley Blenkinsopp had substantial bruising to her face and body that was consistent to her having been punched, not slapped, and she had been asphyxiated. She also had a high content of the sedative Flurazepam in her blood along with an excessive amount of alcohol which would most likely have rendered her unconscious. When he had been arrested, he'd had scratches on his neck and arms that he couldn't explain and allowed his temper to get the better of him as he attempted to defend himself against the charges.

I, on the other hand, was a star witness and, even if I say so myself, I put on a brilliant performance. DS Todd and one of the barristers had been concerned about how I would hold up during cross-examination or how I would feel with Billy sitting staring at me while I gave my evidence, but they need not have worried. I responded to the sharp and condescending questioning from Billy's defence team with almost, but not quite, teary bemusement. Since I was six years old, I had been a witness to him beating my mother and to his lack of self-control. But for me my best moment was when I managed to say I was sure he'd murdered Mum as well. The whole court erupted at that and even though DS Todd had warned me not to say this in the witness box, I saw him smile as the judge shouted for order.

The headline on the Yorkshire Post dated Thursday 27th September was 'Man Given Life Sentence for Brutal Murder'. The picture of Billy underneath looked like a typical police criminal mug-shot; hard faced, unshaven and looking every bit a murderer. There was a smaller picture of Shirley, smiling with her hand on a beer pump behind the bar of a pub but, on closer inspection, I could see it wasn't at The Swan, clearly her flirtation with Billy wasn't her first rodeo. I didn't bother keeping that one.

Even though we knew that a life sentence would not necessarily mean life, *'he could be out in fifteen years if he keeps his nose clean'* DS Todd told us, The Swan and what to do about it became our problem in the first week of 1974 and it was then that I saw, very clearly, what the effect of the last few years had had on Nana. She had only just turned sixty-two, her birthday not long after Billy was charged, but she looked ten years older than that. I knew she had been worried about money; she had wanted to put the money we had found in Mum's tin, £120, in my newly opened Post Office savings account. But I had insisted it be spent on getting a telephone installed to make our lives a lot easier and the rest on bills. However, money worries aside, I could see she wasn't well.

It took a lot of encouragement to get her to go to the doctor's, *'they never really give you good news'* she had insisted and, as always, she was right. She refused to go to the hospital for more tests until we'd been to see a solicitor. Making sure all her affairs were in order, most importantly, making sure her house and the few saving she had would be left to me.

All in all, 1974 wasn't a great year for most people living in the United Kingdom, not just me. I mean, it started with the three day week, and the blackouts and the TV going off really early and the news seemed to be forever bad. The IRA bombings continued, 180 Briton's were killed on a Turkish Airlines flight in Paris and the Flixborough chemical plant exploded. Although now I think about it, that was the year we first saw Abba at the Eurovision song contest and of course Leeds United won their second Football League First Division title. Manchester United were relegated three days later. Not that I was remotely interested in football at that time although I did become an armchair supporter some years later.

But there was not much romance in the candlelit evenings at our house. Now Billy was out of the way, I no longer needed Darren and so was planning on dumping him.

Just before the trial, I'd been elated with my O level results, all grade A except for geography and needlework where I had only managed to scrape a C and a D. I was still a little unsure about whether or not to pursue a nursing career but had started on a two year course as a nursing cadet at The Wakefield School of Nursing based at Pinderfields Hospital. Three days on the wards doing practical training and two days in the classrooms. My original plan was to try and get into St James's Hospital in Leeds once I was eighteen but with Nana being ill, I was keeping my options open as she was about to start some initial treatment at Pinderfields.

Three weeks after Billy had been sentenced, he told his lawyer that he did not want the pub to be sold. There was no mortgage on it and he was hoping to appeal against his sentence, still insisting he was innocent of Shirley's murder. He had this hair-brained idea that we; Nana, me and Davy, could all move in. I was surprised at this given the visual daggers he'd given me throughout his trial. He wanted us to hire staff to run it and Nana to be his proxy landlady; it was, after all, Davy's legacy.

When Darren heard this, he had the ridiculous idea that we could run it, him and me, and I was shocked at how excited he was at this prospect, especially when he saw no problem with the fact that I was only sixteen and not old enough to be a licensee. Nana refused and I once more stated I never wanted to step foot in the place again while Davy went white at the prospect of ever moving back there.

When Billy was told of her refusal to comply with his wishes, apparently, he was furious. Even when he was told that Nana had been diagnosed with debilitating emphysema, he accused her of being an evil witch. He raged for days, getting himself into a proper tizzy which must have spilled out into his general behaviour, causing him to get on the wrong side of a couple of the 'harder' inmates. Although the injuries from the beating he took were not life threatening, two weeks in the prison hospital did give him time to reconsider.

We got the news via a phone call from his lawyer explaining he had informed 'Mr Flynn' that there were no grounds for an appeal and had therefore advised him to sell the pub; he had outstanding legal fees that needed settling. Billy finally agreed but wanted Nana to handle it all and put the money in trust for Davy so that he would be able to access it when he was released. This set Nana off wringing her hands in panic and shaking her head.

After a cup of tea and a lot of worried sighing, I told her she should call her solicitor to ask about the legality of this arrangement and what it would involve but the receptionist claimed her boss wasn't available and this would need to be a face to face appointment, the first available one being in a week's time. She had an appointment with the consultant at the hospital the following day to discuss her prognosis and treatment plan and had already told me she wasn't letting me go with her but she agreed to Darren driving her there and back.

The day before this appointment, at seven thirty in the morning, there was a very distinct knock on the door. Nana put her hand to her chest and I jumped to my feet, touching her on the shoulder and telling her I would go.

DS Todd and a different WPC stood on the step and, for one horrible second, I thought I'd been found out.

"Sorry to come round so early Rosie, can we come in? We've got some bad news." I stepped aside to let them in, gestured for them to go through and followed them into the kitchen. I offered them tea, which the DS refused. He cleared his throat and repeated that he had some bad news for us but it wasn't bad news at all. It was good news, really good news. Billy was dead and a thought flashed into my head, he was dead and I was ultimately responsible. That cheered me up no end.

## Twenty One

Because The Swan had been empty for almost a year, it wasn't in great shape. There had been a couple of attempted burglaries but the alarm and the surprisingly quick response of the police had thwarted them. Nana and Mrs Davis had gone up again shortly after Billy had been charged and cleared out the flat upstairs, taking all the bedding and soft furnishing and giving them to the Salvation Army. The contents of the fridge, freezer and cupboards were all thrown out and they had given it all a good clean, *'even the bathroom'*.

As Billy was dead, from undiagnosed complications following his previous beating, by the time Nana had her appointment with the solicitor, the process had become easier in some respects but harder in others.

"As he is intestate, the next of kin should inherit the estate," explained the law man. He paused here and looked at me, "However, as I believe you were not formally adopted that would mean young David would be his sole heir?" I nodded and he looked pleased. "Right, well that will mean we shall need to set up a trust fund as he cannot inherit until he is eighteen."

"I'd like Rosie to be in charge of that," Nana said quickly.

"I'm afraid under eighteens are not allowed to be trustees," he said, frowning, and Nana slumped in her chair.

"However," he held up his hand and gave us a broad smile before suggesting a solution. After exactly fifty-five minutes, the meeting was brought to a fairly satisfactory close. The solicitor, although a little bit pompous, was actually quite helpful. He was drawing up the trust fund documents which would make Nana sole trustee but would make me an officer of the fund until I turned eighteen. As trustee, she could legally sell The Swan and, once all debts had been settled, the money would be placed in an account for Davy.

Just before we left, he gave us another bit of 'free' advice. He suggested that we contact the brewery who had supplied beer to The Swan as they might well be interested in purchasing it, saving a lot of hassle with lots of nosey public wanting to view the place for their own ghoulish curiosity, but we should get a couple of valuations first. It was good advice and would see a quick end to the sack of worry Nana had on her shoulders. Although her health continued to deteriorate, she seemed a little more at ease for a few weeks before she finally got round to addressing the other issue.

It was a warm May evening and I had just got in from the hospital after a particularly taxing day of washing bed pans and making beds. An hour before my shift ended, one of the patients had thrown up all down my purple uniform dress while I had been, under supervision, feeling her pulse. I'd changed into my spare dress and put the soiled one in a carrier bag, needing to get it washed, dried and ironed for the next day. Davy was out at his friends, playing chess no doubt, and I had no plans to see Darren that night. It was only the worry of Nana's health that had stopped me dumping him.

I knew as soon as I stepped over the threshold that something was wrong. There was no delicious smell of a warming meal for me and the sitting room door was closed. Dropping my bags, I opened the door to see her asleep on the sofa. In full repose I could see just how much she'd aged, her face lined and grey, wrinkled far beyond her years and I felt a devastating sadness. I sat down in the chair opposite her, unable to take my eyes off her face. She opened her eyes as if sensing my scrutiny. Her facial muscles rearranged into a smile and she started to push herself up.

"Hello Luv. Goodness, what time is it?"

"It's half past six, but don't worry, stop there and I'll make us both a cup of tea." I returned her smile and went to the kitchen. While I waited for the kettle to boil, I rinsed my uniform in the sink ready to wash later. After we'd had a cup of tea along with a slice of not quite stale Victoria sponge, I told her how worried I was about her.

"Well I don't need you to worry about me, Rosie, that's really not going to help. I'm not going to get better but," pausing, she placed a hand on her chest, "I'm just hoping I'll hang on long enough to see you through the next couple of years." She gave a deep cough, causing her to wince slightly with pain. "Course you're gonna be here, we just need to take care of you," I said.

"Anyway," she said, getting up and picking up our plates, "while Davy's out I want to talk to you about your Mam." I followed her into the kitchen with our mugs. "When we found those things, stuff she'd kept," she went on, turning to me while leaning on the kitchen sink, "it was a shock to me and I don't think I'm ever going to be able to forgive myself for not realising what had happened." She sniffed back a wave of emotion.

"I think it sounds like this Alfie was a bit of a conman who took advantage of you and Grandad," I said with a shrug.

"That's as maybe but we should have protected your Mam better." She swallowed, "Anyway, nothing I can do about that now but what I can do is tell you to be careful." She narrowed her eyes as, "I know you were trying to find him, before all this awful business started." I tried to interrupt but she shook her head, "Oh don't deny it Rosie, I'm not quite as daft as you think I am but all I ask is that you wait until I'm gone, please."

Unable to find my voice, I nodded and wiped away the few stray tears.

"Promise me?"

"I promise," I said, stepping forward to hug her.

"One more thing though. If by some miracle you do find him, don't be taken in."

I nodded, still in her embrace, and said again 'I promise.'

"Right then," she said, letting go of me, "let me get you something to eat, you must be starving."

"I really fancy beans on toast but I can sort it," I said.

"I'm fine now I've had a bit of a rest," waving her hand as the front door opened, "Sounds like your brother's home," she said with a smile.

Later, as we watched TV together, I glanced over at her laughing at Dad's Army and realised my grandmother really didn't know me at all if she thought for one moment I would be taken in by Alfie Fairclough, or anyone else for that matter.

When I turned sixteen in the previous summer, there had not been much in the way of celebrations; we were at that time gearing ourselves up for Billy's trial. However, Nana made me a cake and Miss Alderson called in after she closed the shop to bring me a lovely set of Blue Jasmine soap, talc and bath cubes, which she said was from both her and Mrs Baxter.

Nana persuaded her to stay for tea and cake and she was still there when Darren arrived to take me into Wakefield for a meal. He was wearing a brown suit, a light blue shirt with a big pointed collar and wide mustard-coloured tie.

"My goodness, don't you scrub up well?" Miss Alderson said as he came into the room, making him blush slightly as he muttered 'thank you'. When she was leaving shortly after, I saw her to the door but when I opened it she suddenly looked uneasy as she thrust an envelope into my hand.

"This is just something to help you over the next few years. I know you'll be successful with whatever you decide to do but I'd hope you'll be happy as well." She gave me a very self-conscious hug, taking me by surprise, before muttering *'don't be a stranger'* and walking briskly down the path.

Opening the envelope, I found a lovely card with a garden full of forget-me-not's on the front and inside she had written, 'Walk confidently into your future and let the past go, make your life count. Best wishes Judith Alderson xx'. Folded inside were five ten pound notes. I ran upstairs and put the money on my dressing table ready to put in the Post Office and, after quickly getting changed, I went back down to show Nana and Darren the lovely card and stand it up next to the others on the mantelpiece.

I had full intercourse for the first time that night. After a lovely pub meal of steak, chips and peas followed by sherry trifle and slightly more than half a bottle of Blue Nun wine, Darren took me to the darkest spot of the car park at Newmillerdam where he deflowered me on the back seat of his car.

It was nothing like I had expected, not even close. Over the nearly two years we had been going out, our kissing and cuddling had progressed fairly quickly to some very heavy petting and, on occasion, even some touching of each other's private parts. However, every time we were in the deep throws of passion he had pulled away, insisting that it wasn't right. He had stated almost at the beginning he did not want to *'go all the way'* with me until I was sixteen and, at first, I thought this was lovely and because he cared for me. As the months had gone by, I had become bolder, reading a couple of articles in Cosmopolitan about 'How to excite your man' and I'd found myself experiencing the not unpleasant tingle of arousal on these encounters, only to become frustrated by his quick withdrawal from our embraces and insistence that it wasn't right and rushing this with Tina was what had spoilt it.

All the way through my meal my anticipation of what was to come was building. As we clinked our glasses, his foot touched mine under the table and his eyes shone giving me a delightful expectancy of what was to come.

The moon was two days full, only three weeks after the summer solstice and the air was still warm. Apart from being on the back seat of a five year-old Ford Cortina, it was quite romantic as he started to kiss me and my eagerness for it to happen made me almost squeal. He ran his fingertips gently on the outside of my thighs and I felt his nervousness as he traced them around my leg to the front. But that was when it all went wrong, for me anyway.

The actual act of penetration was unbelievably painful and I don't want to go into too much detail but, well, let me just give this bit of advice to any men reading this; a bit of spit on your fingers before poking them into a virgin vaginal opening will not add to any arousal, nor will it prepare for a forceful insertion of a condom covered erect penis on the verge of eruption.

So, in summary, it was not a good experience but it was memorable, for two reasons. The first, how quickly Darren became excited and then unexcited, if you know what I mean, and the second was how he cried afterwards before asking me to marry him.

I was more than a little confused at this turn of events. I had hardly begun to process how disappointed I felt, not to mention sore, and suddenly he was sobbing on my chest and telling me he loved me, begging me to say it back. I did of course, I felt I had to really, but I knew I didn't; my feelings for him were purely mercenary. The fact that he was good looking and my friends fancied him was a bonus but I'd worked out pretty sharpish that he was a pathological liar. But I agreed to marry him, once his divorce was through and he could show me the decree absolute.

He thought I believed everything he told me. I let him think that and, at first, I thought his mother was going to be a problem. I thought she didn't like me although Darren had insisted she did but I realised that she probably understood more about her son than she let on and her attitude towards me was more of concern than dislike.

In recent years, since we all became 'woke', I believe there would be other names for what Darren was but I want to stress, as firmly as I can, that I did not enter that relationship not knowing who and what he was.

My invite to a Sunday afternoon cup of tea and a bit of cake with his Mum was, according to Darren, an indication that she liked me. I thought it was more so that she could see how serious he was about me and was rightfully checking me out. It was the Sunday that Darren was allowed access to his son. Daniel was delivered to the house by Tina and her father at ten o'clock with strict instructions that he needed to be ready for collection at four thirty. My invite was for sometime after two. My knowledge of Daniel was only what his father had told me. I'd seen a couple of pictures of a small infant with standard issue baby features and fine blond hair but I got the feeling that Darren wasn't that paternal towards his son so I was keen to see how these visitations played out.

I arrived at the house at quarter past two, insisting on making my own way there. Darren opened the door with a welcoming smile and led me into the small cluttered sitting room where a small child sat on the floor surrounded by building blocks. His mother was in an armchair by the fire and looked up as I walked in, the curl of her smile straightening slightly. I only stayed for an hour, although it seemed so much longer.

After saying hello, she said would I please call her Gloria. This was unexpected but I smiled, nodded and blushed a little. Darren went to make the tea and her next words wrong-footed me again. She claimed to have known Shirley, '*I knew her afore she were Shirley Blenkinsopp, Shirley Gaunt she were and a right stuck up madam, it's not surprising she came to a sticky end...*"

I was saved from responding to this nugget of gossip as my boyfriend came back into the room with a tray. I refused the shop bought Battenburgh cake and after a tiny sip of the scalding tea, I told her how much the whole thing had upset me and how I wanted to just leave it all in the past now. I managed a few tears, real ones, and she nodded and said that was the best thing to do. When I stood up to leave, her smile looked genuine and she said it had been nice to see me.

I found the visit extremely enlightening. Darren's interaction with his son was practically none existent. He barely acknowledged his presence, instead sitting next to me on the sofa, smiling at me and touching my arm or my hair throughout. When I said I needed to go, he wanted to drive me home, much to his mother's annoyance, but I had to insist he stay and play with Daniel. I saw a flash of confusion cross his face at this suggestion, quickly covered by a grin, and then a glance down at the child before he nodded.

Much later on, I discovered these access visits with his son had been insisted on by Gloria and not by him. She had begged Tina and her parents to allow them to see Daniel. Tina's parents had not been keen, stating that their daughter was getting no maintenance payments from him and he seemed to take little interest in the child so what they wanted was a clean break, but Tina had been swayed to allow the visiting agreement to stay in place, at least until the divorce was finalised.

As I walked back home, I decided it was time for me to tell Nana the truth about Darren, his marital status and his age. I prepared myself for her displeasure and disappointment, rehearsing my regret at not being honest while declaring my love for him. It wasn't required; she was amazing. She really liked him and could see he really cared about me and Davy and it was a weight off her mind to know that there was someone who would look after us both should the worst happen.

Things pretty much rolled along a fairly smooth path for the next year. I was enjoying the training at the hospital, even though it was hard and not all the senior nursing staff were friendly. Davy was growing in confidence and doing well at school and although Nana was becoming frailer, she was still cheerful and had something of a calm halo surrounding her now that money had stopped being a worry for her.

All the bills were paid, including Billy's cremation, which she and I arranged, without a service. There was a lovely big pot of money held in trust for my brother but there was a generous allowance, arranged by the solicitor, which was paid to Nana monthly to provide for his upkeep and general expenses.

I didn't see Mrs Norton, Gloria, again until almost the end of the year when she unexpectedly invited all three of us for a Boxing Day tea. The invite came the week before and Darren was particularly coy about asking us. I was instantly suspicious but Nana said it would be lovely and to ask his mother if we needed to bring anything. I discovered the reason for this jolly little gathering on Christmas Day morning when Darren arrived with my present. He had bought me a four diamond, boat-shaped engagement ring which he presented to me in a navy blue jeweller's box, along with his official proposal, in front of Nana and Davy. He didn't get down on one knee or anything but he did tell me he had already asked Nana for her permission in the week before and she had been happy to give it.

## Twenty Two

The two year separation, allowing the divorce to be finalised, was due to end on the 30th of June, 1974, and Darren wanted to plan our wedding for the day before my seventeenth birthday on the 20th of July. I said I would prefer to wait until August or even September. I was due to finish my first year as a cadet at the end of July and start my second year training in the third week of August.

Also, at my insistence, Darren had promised to give me driving lessons as soon as I turned seventeen. He took some persuading, insisting that he could drive me anywhere I wanted to go, but agreed in the end. As soon as I'd had three lessons, I put in for my test and got a date booked for the middle of September which I didn't tell him about.

Darren was immediately thrown into panic at my reluctance to book a wedding date, pleading for reassurance that I really did want to marry him, so I agreed to early afternoon on Saturday 31st August at Wakefield registry office on Northgate. It turned out this was just as well as, although his decree nisi was issued mid-June, due to administrative errors, he did not receive his absolute until 29th July.

The registry office was actually situated in the old coroners building, the same place the inquest into Shirley's death had taken place, where I had heard the coroner declare Shirley's death as an unlawful killing. It was also opposite Charlie Brown's garage, Darren's place of work, so there was a lot of cheering as we arrived and again when we left.

Getting married so quickly after the dissolution of his first marriage set tongues wagging, wondering if I was pregnant. I was not but I did choose to not to wear white and went for a pink sundress which Nana made for me. She also re-modelled Mum's little pill box hat and veil, dying it to match the dress and the pink rose button-hole on Darren's suit jacket. I invited Miss Alderson and Mrs Baxter and was thrilled that they closed the shop so they could both attend. Miss Alderson and Darren's boss Clive were our witnesses and, after the short ceremony was over, our party of twelve went to The Roundabout pub for a small and very boozy reception.

Darren did not request that his son, who was by then three and a half years old, be allowed to come to the wedding, much to Gloria's angry disappointment. He would have pretty much ended any pretence of wanting a relationship with little Daniel at that point too if I had not insisted that he continue to see him regularly. My new husband's definition of regularly was different from mine and his visits became monthly rather than weekly.

Before the wedding, I had not met any other members of Darren's family other than his mother and his son. Having told me they were not a close family, I was surprised when he said two of his cousins were coming. His mother had insisted on inviting them, he told me, even though they hadn't seen or spoken to each other in years. In the days leading up to the big day, I began looking forward to meeting Martin and Margaret, brother and sister in their late twenties, and finding out why they didn't see much of each other as Leeds wasn't that far away and they, like Darren, had cars.

I had recently discovered a taste for vodka and lime and although I was always cautious about drinking too much, never wanting to lose control of my mouth or my senses, on my wedding day I did partake in a little more than normal.

"I don't drink much," I told Martin as he handed me my second glass.

"Are you legally old enough?" Margaret asked with a smile.

"Near enough," I laughed, "but I grew up in a pub, saw a lot of drunk men and women and realised it's not a good look."

"Wow, very sensible," she looked impressed, "but you are allowed to let your hair down on your wedding day." She clinked her glass to mine, "Cheers."

"So how long have you and our Darren been going out?" she asked, after downing her own vodka and lime in one. I only sipped mine.

"Just over two years." I mirrored her knowing smile and added, "I met him in one of the pubs up the road, just before Christmas, about six months after him and Tina separated."

She nodded and asked if I knew Tina. I said I'd never met her but I'd heard lots about her. "Me too," she giggled, "None of it good though. We didn't get an invite to that wedding and actually, if we had, I'd be wanting my present back."

We moved on to jobs then; Margaret worked as a clerical officer for Leeds City Council and enjoyed it. There were lots of perks apparently and her office was in the city centre so she went shopping most dinner times. Martin worked in the civil service but was hoping to get into the fire service before the end of the year. He was engaged but his fiancée couldn't make the wedding as she was a hairdresser and couldn't get the day off at such short notice. I was just about to ask what he meant about short notice as we'd booked the date back in May but Darren appeared at my side and gave me a hug.

"Int she great?" he said loudly in my ear. He wasn't slurring just then but he'd had certainly had a few, "In fact she's bloody wonderful, she makes me happy." He gave me a big wet smacker of a kiss on my lips, "Right, who wants a drink? I'm getting one for me Mam."

He ordered and paid for another round of drinks, buying me one even though I'd declined, before going back to his boss and workmates who were standing by the juke box. I handed Gloria her gin and tonic and she put it on the table behind us saying she was off to the ladies.

"So what's your job, nursing is it?" Margaret asked vaguely.

After telling them about cadet training at Pinderfields, I confided in my new cousin-in-laws that I wanted to do my SRN training at St James's Hospital in Leeds as I'd heard it was the best in Yorkshire although it's a bit far and I wouldn't want to be too far away from my Nana while she's poorly.

"And your new husband!" Margaret said with a chuckle.

"Oh yeah, course, I meant that as well," I said quickly, realising the alcohol was affecting my normally cautious persona, "although Darren told me he can get a job at any garage and, if I really want to go to St James's, he'd be happy to move." This actually was true, he had said that. I wasn't a hundred percent sure he meant it. I had soft drinks after that and went over to speak to Miss Alderson and Mrs Baxter as they looked like they were getting ready to leave.

"My Stan's coming to pick us up in ten minutes," Mrs Baxter said as I sat down beside them, "We've had a lovely time though and I know I've said already but you look lovely."

"Thank you and thank you for coming and," I looked at Miss Alderson, "thank you for closing the shop."

"No problem at all Luv," she smiled, "It's been a smashing day and your brother is such a lovely young man. I wish you'd told me before that he played chess; I haven't had a decent opponent in years. He's invited me to come round for a game or two while you're off on your honeymoon, with your grandmother's permission of course."

"That's great and really kind of you, he's a bit obsessed with it and we've never quite got the knack." I felt a great surge of affection towards this lovely lady and was pretty sure this was her way of telling me she would be visiting my increasingly frail Nana while I was away. Nana looked shattered; it had been a long day, so I asked if Mr Baxter would mind giving her, Davy and me a lift home.

"Well yes of course," she glanced over at Darren who was leaning on the bar talking to his boss and cousins, "but wouldn't you like to stay with your husband?" We can take Mrs Cooper and young Davy home, they both look like they're ready."

"No, I'm pretty tired myself and by the look of Darren he's in for a long session. I want to get my things ready for tomorrow. I'll just go and tell him I'm off."

The following day we were going to Whitby for six nights in a B&B for our honeymoon. I'd never been to the seaside before and Whitby had always seemed like a magical place so when he had asked me where I wanted to go, I knew straight away.

Darren looked shocked when I told him I was going home. His face morphed into a naughty school boy who'd been caught out. I assured him I was happy for him to stay as long as he wanted and although the plan had been for us both to stay in my room on the first night of our marriage, I said he should stay at his mother's and then come and pick me up in the morning. His boss slapped him on the back and congratulated him on having married a good 'un, *'one what understands a man needs his nights out'* and then ordered them both another pint and whisky chaser.

Mrs Baxter's husband was waiting outside for us and, just as I was about to climb into the back to squash myself in between Davy and Nana, Margaret came running out. She gave me a folded piece of paper, said it was her work phone number and I should keep in touch and if I ever needed to know anything, I only needed to ask. I stuffed it in my little pearl-crusted handbag and got into the car. Mrs Baxter, who was sitting in the middle of the front bench seat with her husband and Miss Alderson remarked, *'that was an odd thing to say,'* to which I agreed and said I thought the whole family was odd, including Darren, which made everyone laugh.

We had talked about looking to rent a place of our own but only briefly; Darren had raised it soon after we got engaged. I pointed out that we would be much better off saving for a deposit to buy a house and should stay living with Nana. I could tell he wasn't too keen on that, I assumed he was still bruised after his previous experience of living with in-laws but, after a bit more encouragement and me telling him firmly that I would not live at his mother's house, he agreed.

He arrived the next morning to pick me up just before eleven and he looked dreadful. His eyes were bloodshot and he had an unpleasant aroma of stale alcohol and cigarettes. His cousins, he told me, were chain smokers and Martin had given him a cigar, which he claimed to have enjoyed, just before they left the pub. I said I should probably drive as it would be good practice but he looked stunned by this suggestion, saying he just needed another cup of tea and he'd be fine. Nana insisted on giving him a cup of Camp coffee and a bacon sandwich before we set off.

As he drove us towards the east coast, still very much over the limit I was sure, he told me what a great night he'd had and how brilliant it had been to see his cousins again. They'd stayed at The Roundabout until closing time and then he, his equally drunk mother and cousins all got a taxi back to her house where they had carried on drinking until the early hours.

"It was such a laugh, Rosie, you would have loved it," he chuckled, looking straight ahead. I would have hated it, I thought, but said nothing.

It was warm and sunny when we arrived and continued that way for the whole of our stay. Having not had sex on my wedding night, I had assumed our first night in the Riviera Guest House would be one of some passion and I would finally experience some sexual fulfilment. Since that first time, which I had told myself was just to get the whole cherry popping experience out of the way, there had been lots more occasions of steamy, sensual kissing and touching but not much in the way of penetrative sex. Despite trying all the 'little tricks and flicks' I learnt from magazines like Cosmopolitan and Viva, which incidentally had been quite an eye opener, Darren seemed to shy away from actual intercourse. If anything, my arousal and eagerness only dampened his desire and although he almost always climaxed, it was on me rather than in me.

Once, after a very amorous session on Nana's sofa, we were alone and it was the end of a particularly stressful week at work, I had felt his desire very quickly as he pressed himself against me, kissing my neck. Both of us fully clothed, laying side by side on the maroon draylon cushions, his fingers started to trace the contours of my chest before moving down my body. I almost yelped with pleasure and he covered my mouth with his other hand as he continued, firmer this time, exploring my inner thighs, still fully encased in my fifteen denier tights, moving his mouth back to my neck and breathing heavily in my ear.

This kissing, touching and panting went on for quite some time. I tried to move my hand down to touch him but he kept pulling it back before holding both my wrists above my head with one hand while the fingers of his other hand undid the studs on his 501's. I gasped at the sight of his phallus and he smiled and groaned slightly before leaning in to kiss me again, his fingers rubbing the crotch of my very wet pants and tights. As a tingle of a spasm began to travel up my body, he groaned again and I felt him shudder as he ejaculated onto my red velvet dress, leaving a stain resembling the shape of West Yorkshire which I could never get out.

After Darren signed the Riviera's guest book as Mr and Mrs Norton, we unpacked and I saw him put a condom under his pillow. We went for a walk up to the ruined abbey where, as we climbed the 199 steps, we talked inevitably about Bram Stoker and his literary creation. Darren had an old camera that had belonged to his Dad and he took a few snaps along the way of me posing in the graveyard of the old Norman church and he even asked someone to take one of us both with the sea view behind us. When we came back down into the town, we went in a cafe and had tea and cake before spending half an hour in an amusement arcade. He had been in a really good mood up to that point. I could see he was tired and suffering from the previous night's excesses but he was jolly and laughing, swinging our arms as we walked hand in hand. Even in the tearoom, he'd held my hand across the small, lace covered table. It was his suggestion to go into the amusement arcade, he was a 'Pinball Wizard' he told me, making a b-line for the three flashing machines on the back wall.

He said I should watch him first and I laughed at how animated he became, his fingers and wrists moving quickly as he operated the paddles to keep the ball ricocheting around the bumpers, making the lights flash and the score pinging its way up the leaderboard. A small crowd of teenagers hovered just behind us, watching in quiet admiration as my husband played on, seemingly oblivious to anything but the game. As the last ball was lost, he let out a loud sigh, depleting his concentration, and he dropped his hands and stepped back, suddenly becoming aware of where he was. The little group were all talking at once, asking me if he was some sort of professional and if I played too. He looked startled and embarrassed as they continued to praise him but managed a smile and a nod as he put his arm around me and started to walk away. One of the lads called him back saying he'd won a free game but he just shrugged, calling over his shoulder they could have it as he firmly pulled me outside.

"What's wrong?" I asked but he shrugged again and said there was nothing wrong but his mood was clearly darkened as he dropped his arm from my shoulder. He took my hand again after a few minutes as we walked back to the guest house and, once inside, he said he wanted to close his eyes for half an hour, the drive had taken it out of him, so suggested that I go and sit in the lounge until it was time for our high tea. The mood he was in, I was more than happy to do that.

The landlady banged a gong in the hallway at half past four and a few seconds later, Darren appeared with his smile fully restored. He kissed me lightly before walking me into the dining room where we were allocated a small square table, covered with a crisp white cloth, in the bay window. The table was set with beautiful bone china crockery which would have made Nana envious and I said as much, loudly enough to make the landlady smile and flush with pleasure.

We ate our way through salmon and cucumber sandwiches, fairy cakes and biscuits, talking about how lovely our wedding had been.

"Your cousins seemed nice, has all that family stuff been sorted now?"

"Yeah, well a bit but Uncle Duggie's never gonna come round," he shrugged, "Him and Aunty Dorothy didn't even come to Dad's funeral. Aunty May and Uncle Jimmy came but they didn't stop for long."

"Wow, so your Dad's brother," I said with a frown, "your Uncle Duggie didn't come to his funeral?" He shook his head. "Well that's awful, and you've no idea what they fell out over?"

"No," he said irritably, "it was a long time ago. Anyway, Mam decided we should invite Aunty May and Uncle Jim. I wasn't sure but she was really keen."

"But they didn't come," I stated unnecessarily.

"No. She phoned them last week, they said they couldn't make it."

"Last week!"

"Yeah, she'd sent them an invite as soon as we booked the date but they never responded so she had to phone them up."

"Well, they sound charming," I said with indignation. Darren's Mum didn't have a phone so she would have had to go to the phone box outside the Post Office.

"Yeah, well, me Mam says it's Uncle Jimmy cos him and Uncle Duggie are mates so he'd not wanted to come and fall out with him." I was dumbfounded by this and just shook my head. Darren shrugged and said two days later his Aunty May had sent a letter saying she couldn't come because of the trouble it would cause but was it alright if Martin and Margaret came as they really wanted to.

"And they came back to your house after the wedding?"

"Yeah, they stopped over. I slept on the sofa so Margaret could have my bedroom and Martin slept on the old mattress in the box room. They were still there when I left to come and get you," he smiled "me Mam was cooking them breakfast."

After walking along North Parade as far as The Royal Hotel and posing under the Whalebone Arch, we walked back into the town and went for a drink in The Black Horse. This drink turned out to be three before we left, shortly before last orders, walking hand in hand back to The Riviera Guest house where our landlady sat in the guest lounge in her dressing gown and curlers. She asked in a tone indicating she could not care less, if we'd had a nice evening and then, talking over Darren's reply, said that in future, if we intended to be out later than ten, could we have the courtesy of letting her know as that was her bed time. Darren apologised and assured her we would not be staying out this late again as I tried really hard to hide my vodka induced giggles.

Once in our room, I fell onto the bed contorting with laugher as my husband sat on the bed with his back to me, taking off his shoes and laughing along. As the hilarity subsided, I told him I was going to get ready for bed, picked up my towel, wash bag and, what I had thought, a very sexy see-through lacy nightie along with the old candlewick dressing gown I'd had for years and left the room to use the small bathroom along the corridor.

After getting ready I gave myself a quick spray of perfume before padding barefoot back to our room. Opening the door, I was instantly aware of the faint, evenly spaced, snoring of my husband as he lay at the far side of the bed. Laying my clothes and things on the chair behind the door and pulling off the scratchy night dress, I pulled back the covers and climbed into bed.

## Twenty Three

Of the six nights we slept together under the flowery eiderdown on the lumpy double bed, we were intimate just the once. On the second night, all dressed up, we walked to The Duke of York but after two drinks, making sure we didn't break the curfew again, we left to get back shortly after nine. Not bothering with the sexy nightie this time and half expecting it to be a re-run of the previous night, I climbed in between the cool flannelette sheets and waited for Darren to come back from the bathroom. He returned with a smile, took off all his clothes and climbed in next to me and I felt a tingle of desire as he pulled me towards him and began kissing me. However, the kissing, cuddling and almost tentative brushes against my nether regions stopped abruptly when he let out a small moan. He then quickly moved on top of me and very roughly inserted his erect penis inside me, ejaculating instantly.

I was young and inexperienced but I knew there should be more to intercourse and a healthy sexual relationship than this. Even though I had only married him to give myself and Davy security and because it stopped Nana worrying about what would happen if she died, I had hoped for better than this. I was just about to say something to him when I realised he was crying. I was at loss as I tried to comfort him, asking what was wrong. In between saying sorry and begging me to say I loved him, I said what he wanted me to say and he promised it would get better. Finally calming down, he fell asleep, leaving me wide awake and deep in thought. My husband had more faults and flaws than I'd realised but marrying him had been a means to an end and so I didn't mention it again and the remaining nights of our honeymoon were almost platonic.

On our last day we went to a small jewellers on Church Street where

## Everything in the Garden

he bought me a small carved heart in Victorian Whitby jet edged in silver for my charm bracelet. Funny really, that even though I never loved him, I still have fond memories of his smiling face and how pleased he was to buy that small black heart for me.

Darren drove us home after a bacon and egg breakfast on Saturday morning. I called Nana from the phone box near where Darren's car was parked to tell her we were setting off and that we'd had a wonderful time. Just before the pips went off, she asked if I was alright. I said yes, I was fine but she asked again, rephrasing it to say 'was everything okay, are you, I mean, do you feel okay?' I laughed and told her I felt fine and would see her soon.

As I walked up the path of the familiar semi-detached house in Crigglestone, carrying my small vanity case and a carrier bag with gifts for Darren's Mum, Davy and Nana, I felt massively relieved that I was home. At the threshold, I turned to see Darren following behind with the big suitcase also looking pleased to be back.

Nana, of course, had made a cake and had asked Gloria if she wanted to come up to welcome us home but she had declined, saying she'd be happy to have a bit of cake later if there was any left.

We had ham and tomato sauce sandwiches and large slices of cake, during which we gave Nana the round silver brooch with chips of jet and crystals that I'd chosen for her and Davy a copy of the Chess Players Handbook that Darren found in a little book shop near the jewellers. After taking our things up to what was now 'our' room, I suggested we went down to see my new mother-in-law. It was such a sunny afternoon, we walked, holding hands most of the way.

Darren knocked before opening the back door and walking in, calling out to her. She was in the sitting room and called for us to put the kettle on as we came through. I was still unsure if Gloria liked me or not but the welcome we got as we walked in left me in no doubt. She jumped to her feet and embraced me – something Darren told me later he had never seen her do to anyone before. Telling us both how we looked well and was so happy to see us and tell her all about Whitby. We passed an unexpectedly pleasant couple of hours, discovering another reason for her buoyant, bordering on manic, good mood. On the mantelpiece was a white and gold card, given pride of place in front of the clock. She was invited to the marriage of Martin and Donna Louise on Saturday 25th January 1975.

"I expect your invite will go to your Nana's house," she said and then suddenly frowned "although I didn't think they had your address."

Darren insisted I gave her our small gift adding to her happiness. It was a small wooden box decorated with shells which Darren had picked, saying his Mum would love it; personally I thought it looked cheap and tacky but as she began to unwrap the tissue paper, her face lit up.

"I picked it out specially for you Mam," he said with a grin and her eyes went a bit glassy as she nodded her approval at both of us.

"It's lovely but you shouldn't go spending your money on me," she responded with a forced firmness which in no way hid her delight. "You need to be saving up for your future."

It was a massive relief to me that Gloria seemed completely genuine in her friendliness, her hospitality and warmth making me think things might work out okay after all. The only little cloud that caused a low moment was when she realised that Darren and I were not invited to Martin's wedding. I was a little disappointed myself but Darren said he wasn't bothered and didn't really want to ask for a Saturday off work. Gloria phoned her sister who told her it was just about the numbers and they were keeping the cost down. A day or so later, she said she thought maybe she wouldn't go as she didn't want to be on her own. I talked her round in the end but only after I had phoned Margaret and discovered the real reason.

"Duggie and Dorothy are going to be there with Tracey and Cheryl," she said after a pause, "and I'm fairly sure that Duggie would still like to punch Darren's lights out over the 'unpleasantness." After a longer pause she asked, "You do know about what happened, or what Cheryl claimed happened?"

I didn't tell Darren or his Mum about the phone call or that I now knew the reason for the family feud, I just filed it away for future reference.

We soon fell into a routine which encompassed all of our different lives. I passed my driving test first time which Darren pretended to be pleased about but clearly was not. Davy worked hard at school and the majority of his spare time was spent playing chess, mainly with himself as the frustration of games with us lesser mortals was leading him to despair. One of his teachers noticed this dissatisfaction at the lunch time chess club and offered to take him to a tournament in Leeds which was literally a game changer. This was a gateway to other clubs, both regional and national and the change in him was both incredible and comforting as his previously small group of friends now grew. His weekends were full of meetings and games and strategy talks, most of which took place in or near Leeds. I saw the pleasure and relief in Nana most Saturday mornings as he dashed around the house packing his duffle bag for another day out. He had found his tribe.

Nana's health continued to deteriorate as the chronic obstructive pulmonary disease continued to reduce her oxygen intake. At the end of November, a nasty cold she had been fighting off for over a fortnight, developed into pneumonia and she spent some time in hospital. I went to see her before and after my shifts and after a couple of days, she did begin to rally although she had lost even more weight. They were trialling some new drugs on her and giving her twenty minute sessions with an oxygen mask so she improved enough to be discharged after eight days. She was sent home with a bronchodilator; her condition now diagnosed as chronic bronchitis, and told not to catch any more colds.

Tina also remarried shortly after her divorce from Darren, he told me.

What he didn't tell me was that her new husband wanted to officially adopt Daniel and he'd agreed. This bit of information came from Gloria who also visited Nana in hospital and made stews and pies to feed us during her incapacitation.

She told me how upset she was that she'd lost her first grandchild. Her emphasis on first wasn't lost on me but I chose to ignore it and sympathised with her loss. This was shortly after our first Christmas as a blended family and, to be honest, I was almost certain Darren and I would never conceive a child.

Our sex life had settled into a regular pattern; once a week and mainly on a Saturday. Intercourse was exactly the same as on our honeymoon, lots of foreplay, followed by a rushed conclusion which mostly resulted in his bodily fluid on the bed clothes or on various parts of my lower anatomy.

I tried to remonstrate with Darren on Gloria's behalf but he was having none of it, at first insisting that Daniel would be better off with the Mummy and Daddy he lived with and it would only make him confused having him in his life. When I didn't let it drop, he became annoyed and in a very rare show of anger said he wasn't even sure that Daniel was even his son and it was his business not mine. I was astounded by this news but given our physical relationship I began to wonder if he might actually have a point.

On the stroke of midnight on New Year's Eve, I hugged Nana, then Davy, then Darren and finally his Mum. We were all in the concert room of the working men's club and, although I had not had a drop of alcohol, I felt drunk on the possibilities ahead. This was the year I was turning eighteen and finally all my ducks would be in a row.

As the months passed and the fairly dry spring turned into a warm and dry summer, we talked about having another week away at the seaside. I was keen to take Davy, who had never seen the sea and at eleven he was now shooting up, taller than me and thin as a bean pole, despite having an appetite like a horse. Miss Alderson gave me the phone number of a guest house in Scarborough called The Sandcastle where she had stayed a few times over the years, telling us,

"It's handy for South Bay and the landlady is very friendly."

I wanted Nana to come and the doctor agreed the sea air might do her good. She wasn't up to it but keen for the three of us to go. Mrs Davis and Gloria both said they would keep an eye on her for the week we were away and Miss Alderson said she would pop by a couple of times, everyone telling us that we should have a holiday and Nana seemed to have rallied the week before we went. So on Saturday 9th August, I got into the back of Darren's car, leaving the passenger seat for Davy, while Nana stood at her garden gate with Mrs Davis waving us off.

The guest house was clean and comfortable and Davy's single room was next to ours. It was on a long street of guest houses, a short walk from the beach and our landlady was very friendly but it was far from a jolly holiday.

Darren was moody and kept going out for walks on his own, sometimes being gone for hours. The initial reason for his bad mood began the first night when, in the evening, I wasn't happy to leave my brother on his own at the guest house while we went to the pub. Davy had said he didn't mind but I insisted we all went out together; there were lots of amusements and music and shows at the Spa.

Darren became ridiculously annoyed at this suggestion but said we could go to the Spa and he'd go to the pub and meet us later. On the first night, Darren did come and find us after about an hour and a half and walked back with us. As soon as we got into bed, he cuddled up behind me but I was still cross with him so I kept still and slightly rigid until he fell asleep.

He was perfectly normal the next morning as the three of us ate our cooked breakfast and was happy with my idea of going to Peasholme Park for the day. It was hot and sunny and I suggested we walk, it was about two miles and the landlady told us there was a bus we could take to come back. I saw Darren's mood changing as we left the guest house and started to walk down the Esplanade. I think Davy did too as he suggested getting the bus both ways but I foolishly said a walk would do us good, that it would make us ready for some ice creams, maybe even 99s, when we got there. My husband said nothing but the pace of his walk slowed as he started to lag behind; there had been no question of him holding my hand. Davy and I were walking side by side and I became more irritable myself as I sensed my brother's anxiety so, as we got to the Spa, I turned around and, with my hands on my hips, asked him if he was going to sulk all morning. He said he wasn't sulking but was just tired after a busy week at work and was frankly getting fed up with my bossiness.

The Peasholme Park plan was abandoned as we sat on deckchairs in the open air theatre eating ice creams and listening a brass band. Later, we watched a Punch and Judy show on the beach and Darren tried to get Davy to have a donkey ride but he wasn't having any of it. At mid-day we ate fish and chips sitting on a bench looking out at the sea and Davy asked if we could go in the amusements. Darren didn't object but his sullenness returned as we crossed the road and walked towards the bright flashing lights. I was opening my bag to get out my purse when Darren handed me two pound notes and said he was going for a walk and he'd see us back at the guest house for our tea at half past five. I was happy to see him go, to be honest.

Davy and I had a lovely afternoon. After losing the two pounds of change on the slots, we walked down to the harbour where we had another ice cream and sat in the shade, as the sun was baking hot, until it was time to go back.

After devouring a substantial amount from the selection of assorted sandwiches, two fruit scones and a massive piece of cream cake, Davy asked the landlady if she had a chess board.

She said she had lots of board games but didn't think chess was amongst them but invited him to have a look. Darren went upstairs for a lay down and I went with Davy to look. There was a boxed compendium of board games which included Snakes and Ladders, Ludo, Tiddlywinks, Draughts and Chess although some of the pieces were missing. There were also some playing cards and dominos and I said I'd go and get Darren to come down and play with us.

No one else came into the lounge and the three of us played cards until around eight and then switched on the television at which point Darren stood up and said he was off for a walk and a pint before bed.

When he came in, well past eleven, he made a big deal of trying to be quiet, drunkenly stumbling around the small room. I was furious. Even more so when he climbed into bed, stinking of beer, and immediately started mauling me from behind. I tried to shrug him off, hissing that he was drunk and I just wanted to sleep but was caught completely off guard when he roughly pulled me over onto my back. I was shocked, confused and actually a little frightened as he pulled at my nightie and despite, or maybe because, of my struggles and attempting to fight him off, he became more and more aroused. I won't go into any more detail, I'm confident you've got the picture.

When he'd finished, he kissed me lightly on the forehead and told me he loved me as he pulled me towards him. I said nothing as I lay silent and still encased in his tight embrace. He stroked my hair, my face pressed into his chest as he sobbed quietly, his tears running into my hair until he fell asleep.

As soon as it was light the next morning, I got out of bed and went to the bathroom where I took a shallow bath, noticing bruising and dried blood, before getting fully dressed and going to sit downstairs in the visitor's lounge. Darren came down at just before eight and cautiously asked if I was alright.

I told him, no, I was not alright and that he needed to explain to me why he had been so violent with me the night before and if he couldn't promise me he wouldn't do anything like that again, I was going home straight away. He sat down next to me and pulled me to him telling me he was sorry. He'd had too much to drink and it would never happen again. We sat like that for a few moments more before I pulled away and asked him to get Davy up ready for his breakfast.

Sitting at the table, I watched my husband and my brother eat their full English with gusto. I didn't have much of an appetite and slid most of mine on to Davy's plate. As soon as we'd finished, I announced I wanted to check how Nana was and was going to phone her.

We found a phone box and called home to discover Nana was fine and keen for us not to worry about her before insisting we didn't phone again and got on with enjoying ourselves. As we walked from the phone box, Darren took my hand, saying we were going to have really fun day.

We finally made it to Peasholme Park. As soon as he suggested going, I said we should get the bus there and back which was a good shout as the day was even hotter than the previous one. I managed to keep my concerns about what had happened in the bedroom buried under a forced cheeriness that made my jaw ache. My husband was on good form, joking around with Davy and being very attentive and nice to me. That evening was much like the previous one, the only difference being Darren didn't stay in the pub quite so long and when he came to bed he kissed me lightly on the cheek turned over and went straight to sleep. The rest of the week went by in much the same way.

The weather broke on the Friday evening and so we drove home through some heavy showers and Darren was in one of his surly moods. I remember him snapping at me when I said I wanted to call Nana and tell her we were setting off. I saw how Davy looked upset so I just got in the car. This of course meant there was an uncomfortable silence for the first five minutes or so until I turned the radio on. Darren seemed to come round after a bit but, as I sat there, I decided that was the last time I was going on holiday with him but said nothing.

Once back home we settled back into our routine of working, going for a drink in the club most Saturday nights, occasionally Nana coming too but she mostly seemed happier to stay in and watch TV. Davy was working hard at school and out most Saturdays from early doors, meeting up with his friends from the chess club, but we always had Sunday dinner together with alternate weeks at Nana's and Gloria's. The only thing that changed was that there was no more fumbling under the covers, my husband always came to bed after me and I was generally so tired I hardly knew he'd got in beside me. The weeks trundled on like this and although, as I think of it now things clearly weren't right, I was fairly content. But then the wind veered in a different direction and along with the colder weather came change.

I was now in my first year of training as a State Registered Nurse, on the male orthopaedic ward, It was the 8th of October and I was halfway through my shift, making up the bed of a patient who had just gone to theatre, when the staff nurse, the one that seemed to criticise everything I did, came over. It was a Wednesday and I clearly remember glancing up at the big wall clock at the other end of the ward. It was five past one.

"Leave that Norton," she never gave me the courtesy of calling me nurse and was always brusque but this time there was something slightly softer in her tone, "I'll finish it, Sister wants to see you."

I nodded and straightened up, smoothing down my dress and apron with the palms of my hands before walking towards the office but came to a quick stop as I saw Darren standing in the corridor. I felt the blood drain from my face as I ran the last few steps toward him. He went to put his arms around me but I shrugged him off demanding to know what was wrong and I could clearly see it was something bad and knew before he said the words.

We had left the house together that morning at quarter past six, as we did every day when I was on the early shift. He dropped me off at the hospital and then went on to work himself. We were both really quiet getting up and out so as not to disturb Nana and Davy, although my brother could generally sleep through anything. That morning he had slept through our leaving and his own seven thirty alarm. The postman dropping two bills onto the parquet floor in the hall, shortly after eight, also failed to disturb his slumber. It was Mrs Davis knocking loudly on the door at a quarter to nine that finally roused him. With his head still full of sleep, he leapt out of bed and ran downstairs to open the door wearing only his underpants and the top of his green paisley pyjamas. After the initial confusion and embarrassment from both of them, the fact that Nana was not in the kitchen, or in fact anywhere in the downstairs of the house, finally dawned on them.

Mrs Davis was ahead of him heading up the stairs and after opening the bedroom door, she told Davy to go downstairs and call for an ambulance straight away. She later told me that she had actually thought it was too late for an ambulance but wanted Davy out of the room. The ambulance took twenty minutes to arrive and after a few moments looking her over, surprised our concerned neighbour by putting an oxygen mask on Nana's face, carrying her by stretcher into the ambulance and blue lighting her all the way to Pinderfields. As soon as they had gone, she phoned Darren at work and he had come back straight away to collect Davy and bring him to the hospital. They'd been to check on her and leaving Davy at her bedside he'd come to get me.

The normally strict sister looked a lot more like the caring professional she was, telling me I was excused for the rest of the day and telling Darren to telephone her first thing in the morning to let her know the situation. She actually touched my arm slightly, giving me a straight smiled nod, before turning to walk into the ward.

Nana lasted just one more day, twenty one hours to be exact. She never regained consciousness as her organs failed one by one and she drifted off into oblivion.

## Twenty Four

I was devastated, we all were, but it really blindsided me even though I'd known it was coming. I tried to be strong, mainly for Davy's sake, but inside I was awash with grief. The funeral took its toll on all of us but Gloria and Miss Alderson were real towers of strength. Darren tried to be comforting but I would not allow him and there were times over the next few weeks that just being in the same room as him filled me with a burning rage in me.

It was the day after the funeral I realised that not only did I not love him but I actually didn't like him very much. As I washed up Nana's best china after everyone had left, I decided I didn't even need him and it was time to for him to go.

I was now nineteen and the law had changed allowing me to have my own bank account and financial freedom. There was no issue with me being my brother's legal guardian, I could drive and afford a car of my own so I didn't need Darren at all.

My plan was to spend a few weeks freezing him out before orchestrating a row and telling him he had to leave. I had no doubt, when faced with a few home truths, he would go, especially when he learned I knew all about what had really happened with Tina and coupled with what his cousin had told me, I had plenty of ammunition if he decided not to comply.

However, two days after the funeral, a shocking realisation put a massive hurdle in the way of my plan as I brushed my teeth that morning. Putting the toothpaste back into the bathroom cabinet and catching sight of the box of tampons at the back, it occurred to me that I had missed a period and a shockwave jolted me partially out of my grief. As I sat at the kitchen table with the calendar in front of me, a further swell of panic caused a nauseous feeling to rise up from my empty stomach. I remembered the last start of my menstrual cycle had been the week before our trip to Scarborough.

"Noo!" I cried silently in my head, trying to swallow down the bile. This cannot happen now and I remembered the nice staff nurse at work who was surprised when I told her I wasn't on the pill. "You don't want to get pregnant before you've finished your training," she'd said, shaking her head. But I had smiled and told her we were careful, actually thinking it would be a miracle if I did conceive. She had shrugged and shook her head. *Well, miracles do happen,*' she'd laughed. And it seemed they did.

I think both of my children would agree, I am not the maternal type, in fact I don't really like children, well other people's at least. I did always want to have one, or two, who I knew I would love and protect but I didn't want one yet and I certainly didn't want one with Darren. But it was even worse than that, this child had been conceived through force and not love, not even affection.

After another fifteen minutes on a rollercoaster of emotions, most probably the hormones kicking in already, I managed to stop berating myself for my arrogant stupidity and get a handle on the simmering rage I felt towards my inadequate husband who had already proved to be an inadequate father. I decided I needed to get control back of the situation.

I was due back at work the next day after taking three days holiday on top of compassionate leave and, as Davy had gone back to school and Darren was at work, I pulled myself together, got dressed and went down to the doctor's surgery.

I had to wait for three days before I could go back and get the result, although I was pretty certain it would be positive. I was tearful and emotional but I had just lost the only permanent individual that had known me all my life, which is actually what helped me keep my condition under wraps.

Dr Walton, a fifty something, overweight Scotsman whose breath suggested he had a dram or two of whisky with his mug of tea, congratulated me on my pregnancy before saying it was a shame Nana hadn't lived to see it, *"but there you are, the circle of life."* He went on to tell me, according to the date I'd given him of my last period, I was about ten weeks gone but the hospital would confirm that and I'd get an appointment through the post. I think he put down my lack of excitement or, indeed, my inability to look anything but miserable with this news, down to my recent loss, telling me I should accept that life goes on and I was now living proof of that, along with the child growing inside me.

I decided not to tell anyone, especially Darren, until I worked out a plan. I mainly wanted to talk to the Sister at work about what would happen with regards to my training. I knew the answer really but had hoped for a different one. I was not entitled to maternity pay and it would be unlikely that I could resume my training once I had a baby.

She expressed her disappointment that I had not been more careful, telling me I had the makings of a good nurse and if I decided to 'go ahead with this pregnancy' it would be a terrible waste. There had been some restructuring throughout the whole of the NHS and nurses were about to receive much better pay and recognition but the work would be hard and we were expected to do forty-two hour shifts and I would struggle as my pregnancy progressed. She said she would speak to the training office but even if I did have full time care for the baby and could return quickly, I would be so far behind, I would need to start again.

I got the bus home that evening. Darren had said he had things to do and wouldn't be back until after seven. It was good to have the commuting time to think through my options. Surprisingly, I never considered the option of not having the baby; my choices were about the best way to bring it up. Mainly, it was staying married to Darren or ending it now. I knew his mother would be a big help, having lost contact with her first grandchild. I imagined her face at hearing of another grandchild and then seeing it crumble when I threw Darren out.

I was still undecided as I walked towards the house and was a little surprised to see Darren's car parked by the gate. My face morphed into an involuntary smile on seeing him at the kitchen table playing chess with Davy. One of his mother's casseroles bubbled on the cooker, filling the kitchen with a wonderful aroma, and I thought perhaps we could do it, maybe we could play happy families. I decided I'd wait until after we had eaten and tell them both my news.

As he plated up our stew, there was a loud knock on the door followed by a series of thumps. I stood up and Darren took the pan back to the stove. Davy was in the hall putting his chess set away and went to open the door. In my peripheral vision, I saw my husband move to the back door as I stepped into the hall.

"Where is he?" Demanded an angry voice as the door opened and a man I'd never seen before pushed past my brother and walked towards me. "Where is the fuckin' bastard?" he yelled into my face. I raised my hands in an effort to keep him back from me,

"Who?" I shouted back, "Who are you looking for and why are you in my house?"

He seemed suddenly confused as he narrowed his eyes and looked at me, still in my nurse's uniform, before looking back at Davy. He remained standing inside the open front door, in front of a young girl looking just as terrified as my brother. I turned slightly to see the kitchen was now empty and the back door slightly ajar as the man took another step forward.

"Darren Norton," he said with barely controlled rage, "He lives here right?"

"Yes, he does," I replied, fearfully, "Why do you want him?"

"Cos he's been messing with my little lass and when I get my hands on the pervy bastard I'm gonna kill him."

And just like that there was no further need for my deliberation on what I needed to do.

After convincing the burly Painthorpe man that Darren was not in the house, I walked him to the door, telling him he should go to the police. I told him that I would call the police myself if Darren came back to the house. I leaned on the closed door for a moment after he'd gone before realising Davy had stayed stock still at the bottom of the stairs looking terrified, his eyes full of tears. I pulled him in for a hug and told him I was going to sort this out and he was not to worry. I ran upstairs to see if Darren's car was still parked on the road but it had gone. Then I went back into the kitchen and locked the back door, leaving the key turned, and slipped the bolt across the double locked front door before picking up the telephone to call Gloria.

She was of course, beside herself, saying it wasn't true, this man was lying and she would come up but I told her to stay where she was. I said Darren had run off through the back garden and so would probably turn up at her house so she would need to be there for him. She kept saying that it wasn't true, that this girl was lying and so I yelled at her to stop.

"I know about what happened when he was seventeen; what he did to his nine year-old cousin and why you moved from Leeds." Although I wasn't shouting, my voice was loud and her sharp intake of breath perfectly relayed her pain. I took a breath myself and told her, firmly and unambiguously, her son was not welcome in my house and if he tried to come back, I would call the police and I hung up.

Davy was sitting at the kitchen table and I asked him how long Darren had been in before I got home. He said *he'd* got in just before five after calling at a mate's on the way home. He was surprised to find Darren in the kitchen when he got in and even more surprised when he asked him if he wanted a game of chess.

"He didn't really want to play," he said quietly, "he was even more rubbish than normal, sort of just moving pieces without thinking, well he was pretending to think but he wasn't, you know."

"Yeah, I know," I said, nodding encouragingly, "Did he say anything about why he was home?"

"No, he was just, you know, a bit wound up." He shrugged and then took a deep breath, "That girl..."

"What about her?"

"She goes to our school."

"Jesus Christ!" I exclaimed, "Please tell me she's not in your year."

"No, I think she's two years above me," lowering his head with his eyes closed. He took in a breath to help him with his next words, opening his eyes, he slowly raised his head, "I think it's true what that man said."

And of course it was. I won't go into the sordid details, which I discovered at length from the girl's Dad and also from PC Bailey who came round to talk to me two days later.

"Bad luck seems to follow you lass," was his opening statement to me before he asked me if I had any idea my husband had been hanging around the playground at Painthorpe, giving cider to young lasses. I denied knowing anything about his predilection for young teenage girls, not in any way to save him but to save us.

There was an investigation, of sorts, but the way it was back then, the girl's character and appearance were brought into the mix. Some of her friends were all too keen to come forward with tales of her easy virtue and how she'd bragged about having an older boyfriend. She became less of a victim and more a cock teaser, bringing it on herself. The fact that she was fourteen and Darren was thirty-one, even if he did look younger, didn't seem to be important. Of course, I knew the picture being painted of her could not be accurate. I knew his tastes, if she had been forward and tarty, as how PC Bailey suggested, Darren wouldn't have been interested, but that's all by the by.

After he left, I called Gloria, telling her that I was putting all of her son's belongings outside our gate so she'd better arrange to get them collected before somebody set fire to them. She said I was being silly and I should remember that he was my husband and I should be standing by him, insisting that me throwing him out was making it worse. I laughed and put the phone down.

After three weeks, the charges were dropped; Darren was living at Gloria's but keeping a low profile and coming nowhere near me. His boss accepted his word that it had all been lies so he managed to keep his job. However, the majority of the local folk were not so sure and Mrs Baxter told me she had heard there'd been other rumours about him, even before we were married. I had no direct communication with him, only speaking to Gloria on the phone. I told her that I wasn't planning on divorcing him - yet, leading her and him to think that there was a chance of reconciliation at some point. There clearly was not.

Davy was finding it hard at school and so, after a long chat with Miss Alderson, the only person apart from Davy that I had told about the pregnancy, I put the house up for sale, bought a small car, an Austin 1100, and started house hunting in Leeds. When the local jungle drums conveyed this news, I got another call from my mother-in-law, pleading with me to take Darren back. She told me he was in a bad way, that he wasn't eating and he just wanted a chance to talk to me, to explain what really happened. I said I did not want to hear anything he had to say, I just wanted to do what was best for my brother and the consequences of what Darren had done had made it impossible for him to stay at that school so we were moving.

The hospital told me I could work up until four weeks before my due date and they would allow me back into training if I wanted to return to work but I would have to start the three year SRN course again.

Miss Alderson said she would help me make a fresh start in Leeds. As a single woman, she knew about all the problems and pitfalls in buying a house on your own but the recent introduction of the sex discrimination act should, in theory, make it easier but she warned it might still be difficult.

I was selling a three bedroomed semi-detached house with a garden and I wanted something similar and with as small a mortgage as possible, as I soon wouldn't have a job. The reason I wasn't going to divorce Darren was mainly about the money. Still being only nineteen and a soon to be single parent with a young brother to provide for, my status as a married woman was much more preferable to the building society. No one needed to know we were separated.

The week before I married Darren, I got Nana to change her will; leaving her house to both Davy and me. This had been my idea as 'a safeguard', just in case. She had given me a funny look when I suggested it but, after a few seconds, had agreed it might be for the best. I never told Darren about this and, to his and his mother's credit, there was never any talk of him being entitled to half.

In the end, we did it without a mortgage. As Davy's guardian and trustee of his estate, I sold the house for £12,800 and we bought a newer, slightly smaller three bedroomed semi with garage and small garden on the Spring Valley Estate in Bramley for £11,500, which was absolutely perfect. It was at the end of a cul-de-sac and there was a footpath to the bridge over the railway line, just at the side, giving easy access to the bus routes. It was perfect.

The timing of our move could not have been better for three reasons, even though it was more luck than management. The first one was getting Davy into a school as quickly as possible. As soon as my offer on the house was accepted, I contacted schools in the area for him to start at straight after the Easter holidays. The first school I called that had space was Hough Side, a twenty minute walk away and knew it was meant to be when we discovered that there was a chess club twice a week.

The second reason was, as I approached the eighth month of my pregnancy, the effect of a child growing inside me began to take its toll. Although I never had morning sickness, I did have regular heartburn and felt almost permanently exhausted. The training sister at work had been sympathetic to my circumstances but the work was becoming harder and, as the staff nurse told me very pointedly, I was becoming a hindrance rather than a help. Having not had much of a bump for the first five and a half months, the sudden growth spurt from the end of February took me by surprise and at the antenatal clinic in mid-March, I was told I needed to rest more and given a sick note for a week. This prompted the training sister, who took me into her office on the day of my return, to bring my leaving date forward by two weeks and, to be honest, this was a relief.

The third reason was my estranged husband. Amazingly, I had managed to keep the news of my pregnancy quiet for some time. My fabulous surrogate family were wonderful at keeping the secret and I didn't start to show until well after Christmas when it was so cold I was multilayered when I was out and about in the village. I'm not sure how Gloria and Darren found out but it was a very cold evening in early February when, as I arrived home from a classroom day at work, I discovered my mother-in-law standing at the side of our gate.

She was almost blue with cold and had clearly been waiting for some time. After a deep intake of breath and a roll of my eyes, I told her she had better come in for a minute. She gave me a heartbreakingly thankful smile and followed me into the house. I put the kettle on before taking off my coat and she sat at the kitchen table, keeping hers on. I made two mugs of tea in silence, fully aware she was staring at my baby bump.

"It's true then?" she said finally as I placed the mugs on the table and sat down. I managed a smile and nodded, seeing her eyes soften and sparkle with building tears, "When are you due?"

"Middle of May." I broke eye contact, picking up the scalding tea, holding it close to my mouth and blowing gently. She didn't respond and I guessed she was calculating dates.

"Look Gloria, I'm sorry, really sorry for you but I'm not letting Darren have anything to do with this baby." I was expecting her to protest, for her to get angry and shout but she just sat there, tears silently falling down her cheeks as she stared down at her mug. I was completely wrong-footed, feeling like crying myself and not knowing what to do or say. We sat like that across the table, me hugging my tea in both hands and her with her head slightly bowed, both hands on the table, quietly weeping.

## Twenty Five

Gloria's reaction had unnerved me to begin with but after a few minutes of a shared quiet sadness, she took a deep breath and rummaged in her coat pocket for a handkerchief. I started to drink my tea as she blew her nose and took control of herself, managing to tell me what she had come to say.

Darren had gone; he'd stormed out of the house after a row the week before. He hadn't taken anything with him so she assumed he would come back the next day but he had not. After four days, she came back from shopping with her neighbour to find a note from him. He had gone to see a mate in Newcastle and see if he could get some work there and would be in touch when he was settled.

He had lost his job after his boss finally lost patience with him, just before Christmas, and had been out of work since, just sitting around, not getting dressed most days except to go up to the off-licence to buy beer. He had been wallowing in self-pity and declaring his love for me and still insisting he was innocent. She had been worried about him but was also worried about herself. The drink made him argumentative, bordering on violent, and it was her money he was buying it with.

Things got much worse when she told him she'd heard I was pregnant. It was this that had started the argument between them. He had raged and insisted I could not be pregnant, certainly not by him, he had made sure not to spoil it this time. When she'd asked him what he meant, he screamed that a baby would spoil everything, it would spoil me and I wouldn't be any good. She knew then that she had to stop lying to everyone and to herself. She discovered that morning that not only had he emptied the old tea pot she kept her bills money in but he had actually cleared out her Post Office savings and taken some of her jewellery.

"I've been at me wits end," her hand shaking as she lifted her mug, "but I just wanted to let you know, I'm sorry, for not saying anything, you know," pausing to sniff and dab her nose, "I mean, that time when you first came round, I should have said summat then but he seemed to be alright, you know, he stuck with you and well." She paused again to swallow down the emotion catching in her throat, "Well, turns out he never really stopped."

Looking at her anguished face, I decided she didn't need to know the full story so I told her I must have conceived while we were in Scarborough.

Davy came in while we were drinking our second cup of tea and she got up to leave straight away. At the door, she told me she was moving in with her neighbour. Everything that had happened had shaken her and she was going to be struggling to pay her rent so Betty from next door had suggested she move into her back bedroom.

"It makes sense," she managed a smile, "it'll be company for us both."

"I suppose so," I agreed as I walked her to the door.

"I don't blame you for moving away, it's the right thing, but will you keep in touch?" she asked weakly.

"I will," I agreed and smiled.

"I'll be moving next door in a fortnight and we're getting a telephone installed so maybe you will let me know how you get on?"

I went to see her the week before we moved. I didn't give her my address, only telling her it was in Leeds, but promised to call her with my phone number as soon as we had moved in and got connected. She mentioned she was now back in touch with her sister in Armley and wondered if perhaps she might visit sometime after the baby had arrived. I said 'we'll see' and she accepted that.

Davy and I moved in on Friday 9th April 1976, the day after I left my position at Pinderfields School of Nursing. We had a lot of help. Mr and Mrs Baxter organised the furniture removals for us then turned up that evening, along with Mrs Davis and Miss Alderson, to help us settle in and start the unpacking. They brought tea bags, coffee, milk, sugar and a large Quiche Lorraine along with lots of other groceries to help us over the weekend.

The following week was the first week of the Easter holidays so Davy and I had plenty of time to settle in and he was an absolute star. We chatted and actually laughed quite a lot during that first week and one night, the night before Good Friday, we finally talked about Mum and he managed to tell me how scared he had been living at the pub.

Even before the lead up to her death, he had never felt safe living with Billy. Having witnessed so much of his father's cruel and selfish behaviour, he had been terrified of the prospect of him ever getting out of prison. I understood fully his concerns; I still woke up sometime in the middle of night, my subconscious accessing my memories and playing scenarios that left me in a state of terror.

I told him that this was a fresh start for both of us and we were leaving the past – all of it - behind us. He went quiet for a few minutes before he nodded and said, as this was a fresh start, he wanted to change his name and wondered if I was going to change mine back now too. I explained that it would be better, in the short term, for me to be Mrs Norton but agreed if that was what he wanted, he could change his surname and so he started his new school as Davy Cooper.

It was no coincidence that we moved to Bramley, the village where my father had come from. Of course, I had no idea if there would be any trace of him or how I would go about finding him and I had no idea what I was going to do if I did, but I just knew that I had to.

I decided to use the time I had before the baby arrived to scope out the area. I still had Nana's old address book and the Leeds area telephone directory to start my research. There were seven Faircloughs listed and none of them were in Bramley, which was disappointing, but I jotted the details into my old exercise book before closing my eyes for a few seconds to consider what would be the best thing to do next. Maybe I could just phone each of them and ask for Alfie, see where that got me, and decided I would do that when Davy was at his friend's house the following evening.

I had registered myself and my brother at the doctor's surgery on Town Street and had an appointment for an antenatal check-up that week on the Tuesday morning. Davy had insisted on walking to school that day so once he'd gone, I washed up our breakfast things before putting on my coat and comfortable shoes.

Wanting to familiarise myself with the area, I had spoken to my new neighbour about the best way to get to the surgery on foot. She had offered to drive me but I said I really wanted to walk so she said she would walk with me as far as the shops. Our route took us along the footpath over the railway bridge, coming out on Elder Road, then up Avondale Street and crossing Stanningley Road where we parted ways as she pointed me towards Bath Lane and telling me to turn right onto Hough Lane at the junction. My progress was slower than I had hoped and I was starting to regret not bringing the car or even accepting a lift.

Quickening my step to make sure that I wasn't late for my appointment, I hurried along the road and, just as I got to the library, across the road I saw a street sign that that gave me a little surge of excitement; Warrels Road – could it be the street beginning with 'War' in Nana's address book?

Following my appointment with a lovely lady who, after checking my blood pressure and having a brief feel of my bump, assured me that everything seemed fine but said I should make sure I had my hospital bag packed as the baby was very low. I left with a spring in my step as I set off back, retracing my journey home. Being eight months pregnant, the foresaid spring in my step did not last long and so I went straight home, slowly.

After managing only a couple of bites of my corned beef and brown sauce sandwich - my appetite had been poor for the last few days - I washed down my Preg-a-Day iron tablet with a glass of orange juice and got into my car. Working out my route from the estate back to the library didn't take too long and my frown turned to a smile as I turned down Warrels Road. After ten or so slightly stressful minutes of driving around the rows of houses, I finally turned into Warrels Mount and a small twinge of excitement began in my stomach as I parked the car and got out to try and see the numbers.

I stayed on the side of the odd numbered old stone houses, whose front doors opened right onto the street, until I got to the end, number 33, and I stood thinking for a few moments. Dare I just go and knock on the door of 27 and see if anyone answered but what then? I needed a plan. I decided I would go back home and think about it just as I noticed the corner shop over the road.

The shopkeeper, a very smiley man, and a customer he was serving both turned to look at me as the bell above the door announced my arrival, their conversation stopping mid-sentence. I took only a few steps before stopping to look around the packed shelves when the customer, an elderly lady with a blue rinse perm, asked,

"Are you lost, Luv?"

"No, well yes, a bit," my voice a bit squeaky and my mouth suddenly dry, "I was wondering if the Fairclough still lived over the road, on Warrels Mount?"

"You mean Norma at 27?" she smiled and I nodded but then grimaced a little as I felt another flurry of excitement, stronger this time and oddly uncomfortable.

"Yeah, well maybe," I said as my right hand moved to support my baby bump, "My Mum and Dad used to have a friend. Dad was in the army with him and he's gone now but Mum asked me if I'd see if his friend was still around." I grimaced as the feeling in my stomach changed to a tightening ache and I put my hand on the counter to steady myself.

"Well you're about ten years too late for Alfie," the old lady said, "died back in 67 weren't it Len?"

"Aye about then, just after his youngest were born, a sad affair it were." the shopkeeper confirmed.

"Well not entirely," the old woman said acidly, "I know you're not supposed to speak ill of the dead but he weren't a nice man. Poor old Norma's better off wi'out him."

"Well aye, he were a bit of a bad lad," the shopkeeper replied, shaking his head.

"A bad lad!" the old lady exclaimed, narrowing her eyes, "He were a cheating, lyin' chancer. Gambled away every penny he had and some he didn't." There was no hiding her dislike, "Took me for a fool borrowing money he'd no intention of paying back, an I weren't the only one."

"How did he die?" I asked quickly, managing to stand up straight and take a deep breath.

"They said it were his appendix." Clearly Alfie Fairclough was the woman's specialist subject, "but he'd been in a fight a couple of days afore, tried to argue with Billy Brayson, local bookie, about the odds on some bet an' it got nasty. Course, Billy's two lads didn't take kindly to him giving their old Dad a hard time so they gave him a right pasting."

"Right, well he doesn't sound very nice, not the bloke my Dad described," I said moulding the truth to fit my narrative.

"He were a scumbag and you'll not get many to disagree with that."

"Maybe you won't want to tell your Mam all the details," the shopkeeper cut in with a friendly smile for me and a small scowl at his customer. I smiled but could feel another wave of pain building and let out an involuntary groan.

"Are you alright Luv?" he asked, quickly lifting the flap from the counter and coming over to me, just in time to stop me crumpling to the floor as my knees gave way. They wanted to call an ambulance but I insisted I was okay after I'd sat down for a few minutes on the hard wooden chair brought from behind the counter and taken a few sips from a glass of water.

"We've not long moved to Bramley and I think I've been doing too much, I had a check up this morning and everything's fine, I think I just need to get home an' have a lay down," I explained.

"Do you want to come next door with me for half an hour?" The old lady's voice now soft and concerned, "You can put your feet up and I'll make you a cuppa."

"No, no, I'm okay, I just need to get home thank you though." I turned to go as the pain receded. It had not been as bad as the previous wave so I managed to get gingerly to my feet.

I hare-tailed it out of the shop as quickly as I could manage after that, realising the folly of my spontaneous investigating. Uttering my thanks, I walked a little stiffly back down the road to my car. Once inside, I realised I was shaking and took a few deep breaths to calm myself.

At least I knew now; my father was dead and he had been a nasty piece of work. Trying to be as pragmatic as I could be, I managed a smile as I said to myself, 'clearly my mother liked a bad boy.'

Putting the key in the ignition, I felt the pain building again and realised that the twinges and butterflies I'd been experiencing might actually be contractions. Rather than sending me into a panic, this actually cleared my head and gave me a calm sense of purpose; there was stuff I needed to do and checking my watch, I started the engine. Driving away, I saw the worried faces of the old lady and the shopkeeper who were standing on the pavement outside the shop.

As I drove home, I made a plan. I may not have gone to any antenatal classes but I had read, very thoroughly, the two books I'd been given. Although I hadn't covered the subject of childbirth during classroom sessions, I had worked on the maternity ward for a couple of weeks and heard stories of Braxton Hicks contractions and how the first stages of labour could take hours before anything happened *and* that first babies were mostly late and not early. However, I decided to err on the side of caution and start timing the waves of pain that were really getting stronger. I was going to have a little lay down before sorting out Davy's tea and then phoning the hospital. I just needed to prepare myself.

It makes me laugh now I think about it, how I thought I could control everything. Well, it was almost a rude wakeup call. Luckily, my lovely neighbour Gill saw me attempting to get out of the car and came to me. It was shortly before four as she helped me into the house and tried to persuade me to phone the hospital straight away. I tried to argue that the contractions were still about ten minutes apart and I needed to make Davy's tea and I hadn't actually got my hospital bag ready yet. I just needed a minute then I'd get it sorted. I sat down heavily on the sofa, leaning back, lifting my legs. Shaking her head, she said she'd make me a cup of tea but only got two steps towards the kitchen when I let out a gasp as the next contraction hit me, not so much a wave of pain this time, more like a tsunami. That's actually not a bad metaphor as my waters broke.

It was Gill who called the hospital, the contractions now around three minutes apart, and told them they needed to send an ambulance. She put together a bag for me and tried her best to hide her surprise when I told her I had no idea where my husband was so she could not phone him *and* that I didn't actually have anything for the baby. I asked her to call Miss Alderson, telling her she was my aunt but as the contractions increased in strength I could barely speak.

I was sitting at our small kitchen table with my coat on and overnight bag at the side of me when Davy got home from school ten minutes later. Gill was washing up mugs and generally fussing about on the draining board. My brother's pallor changed as he took in the scene and we all heard the sound of the ambulance driving up to the house.

"It's okay," I began with a smile although I could feel a contraction building, "the baby's decided not to wait till next month so I'm off to the hospital, Gill's gonna make you your tea an' stop... with.. you...tonight..." my words spaced as I tried to breathe through the pain. The ambulance drivers did not hang about, one of them practically carried me out and we sped off with blue lights and sirens towards Leeds General Infirmary.

My daughter was born in the ambulance before we had even got off the estate. The paramedic, they weren't called that then but he was clearly much more than an ambulance driver, pulled into Spring Valley Walk and parked up quickly before rushing through to help deliver my daughter, there and then.

I had to battle with the ward sister to allow me to go home – word had got out that my husband had abandoned me and so my perceived strange behaviour during the first couple of days was put down to that. I will admit, I was a bit of a mess and struggling to understand my feelings. Once I had given birth and the excruciating pain had stopped, I thought I should be back in control but instead I was flooded with hormones and my emotions were all over the place. I struggled with breast feeding and was terrified of holding my little girl. The sister thought I was indifferent and not wanting to bond with her, my not having a name for her after the third day only added to this. She could not have been more wrong.

Having spent the whole time since learning of the conception thinking only of the baby growing inside me as an inconvenience, I had been sure from the onset that I could not abort it; it was a hurdle to be overcome but something I would take in my stride. However, from the moment I laid eyes on that beautiful screwed up and tiny face, I knew I loved her. I believe my initial reluctance to hold her was caused by her being whisked away from me the moment we arrived at the hospital and my losing consciousness because of the massive blood loss and not seeing her again for almost twenty-four hours.

Gill came into see me the next day with Davy; she had made the executive decision to phone the school and tell them he wasn't well and, to be fair, he did look pale. She pushed my wheelchair to the premature baby ward where we all looked at her through the see through walls of the incubator. She weighed 5lbs 6oz which they thought was a good weight for three weeks early and she was breathing fine but just a little jaundiced. The nurse offered to take her out and let me hold her but I shook my head, terrified at the prospect. She was too small, too precious and I burst into tears.

They insisted I would benefit from the full eight days in hospital, to which I finally agreed, before I was allowed to go home with my baby girl. On the advice of Miss Alderson, who brightened up one evening visiting hour, I had phoned Gloria to tell her of the arrival of her granddaughter and to ask her if she would like to come and stay with me for a week when I first got home. She was delighted to accept, even with the proviso that if she heard from her errant son, she would not tell him where we were.

While I was in hospital, Gill had sourced a cot from a friend who didn't want anything for it and her husband, Roy, had put it up next to my bed, fully made up with new mattress and sheets. Mrs Baxter and her husband brought Gloria over on the afternoon when I got home. Davy had reluctantly gone to school; he had been staying next door with Gill and Roy, who claimed it was lovely to have a young man in the house again and had thoroughly spoilt him. He had loved it too, especially as they were both keen to learn how to play chess.

The Wakefield posse arrived just after midday while I was adjusting to the strangeness of being home with my tiny girl and knowing that my life was now completely different. Miss Alderson was working so couldn't come with them but she sent a gift, a navy blue Silver Cross pram, which had made it a tight squeeze in the Baxter's car. I don't think I will ever feel so much pride again in my life as I did as I pushed my baby in it for the first time.

Gloria ended up staying for nearly three weeks and was mostly helpful and didn't try to interfere with how I bonded with my child. Instead, she arrived with a bundle of lovely baby clothes and a beautiful handmade cot blanket, made lovely meals, hung out our washing every day and also joined Gill and Roy in Davy's local chess tuition group.

She also provided a non-judgemental sounding board as I tried to pick a name for my child. Although, to be honest, she wasn't that good at hiding her disapproval of certain names. She came with me to register Angela Amy Norton, our little Angel, and the delight on her face as we left the council offices created a warm glow which surrounded her for the rest of the stay.

Mr and Mrs Baxter came to collect her on the Sunday of the last weekend in May. They brought Miss Alderson with them and we all had a lovely tea of quiche, sausage rolls and other party-like food, mostly made by Gloria but aided and abetted by Gill. Roy came round with a five pint can of beer for him and Mr Baxter to share and a bottle of sherry for the ladies. When I refused a glass from Gloria, even though she suggested it would help Angela to sleep through the night, Gill suggested I try Guinness as "It's full of iron and did me the world of good when our Stephen were little." I shook my head and said I'd stick to orange juice, quickly blinking back a terrifying memory.

Davy set up a chess tournament while the four women played pass the baby until it was time for them all to go. Gloria had filled my fridge with mostly ready to heat meals although there was enough left over party food to last the week. We had a nice hug before she got into the car and I promised to go over to see them all, along with Mrs Davis and Gloria's friend Betty, in a few weeks. It was a lovely day with lots of smiles and even a few happy tears. Darren was not mentioned by anyone and I truly believed that life was going to be good from then on.

## Twenty Six

Life was good for us for the next few years and that isn't me looking back through rose tinted lenses; it really was. That first year, the famously long hot summer of 1976, was glorious.

When Angela was six weeks old, I took her out for a walk up to the park and called in at the little shop on the Warrels. The shopkeeper was delighted to see us, telling me he'd been worried about me since the second I left. He got his wooden chair out again and asked me to sit down a moment while he went next door to get Mrs Backhouse who would definitely want to see the lovely little miracle.

The old lady seemed as delighted to see us as the shopkeeper, declaring my daughter a very bonny and healthy looking baby. They enjoyed my story of her sudden arrival in the ambulance and agreed we had picked the perfect name for her.

"What a shock your husband must have got that day," the old lady said as she sat down on the chair I'd just vacated.

"Yes," I said, peeling back the white woollen blanket to lift Angela from the pram, "Yes it was quite a shock for all of us. Would you like a cuddle?"

I stayed for half an hour, getting a few groceries, while Angela slept through her cuddle and Mrs Backhouse told me,

"I mentioned to Norma, Alfie's widow, about you coming in asking after him. Told her you'd said your Dad knew him from his army days."

I nodded but didn't say anything.

"Well, course, that were afore her time and he were quite a bit older than her but she said, from what she knew of him, he'd probably 'borrowed' money off your Dad," she said, raising her eyebrows.

"Oh, I don't know about that," I said vaguely, "I mean, I suppose he might have, Mum's not mentioned it."

"Well, anyroad, she said as how it were the biggest mistake of her life marrying him and him dying saved her from more years of misery." She nodded her head, emphasising that what she had already told me about Alfie was indeed the truth.

Angela began to wake up as I put her back in the pram and Mr Webster, the shopkeeper, handed me a bottle of Lucozade and a bag of Maltesers to keep my strength up. Mrs Backhouse took a fifty pence piece out of her purse and put it momentarily inside Angela's hand before handing it to me.

"There you go my love, crossed her palm with silver to bring her good luck and good health." Her smile was warm and, just for a second, I thought I saw the suggestion of a tear before her no-nonsense expression returned and she told me not to be a stranger and pop in any time I was passing.

I made a few friends via the health visitor and baby clinic and discovered that, comparatively, my gorgeous girl was a very easy baby as well as being the most beautiful, in my opinion anyway.

We celebrated each of her early milestones with pride and she was adored by Davy who had immense patience with her for a teenage boy. He talked about her to our adopted extended family in tedious detail in our weekly phone calls and the adoration was very much reciprocated. Her little face always lit up at the sight of her uncle and I am pretty sure her first word was Davy.

We went over to Crigglestone a few times, once visiting Julie who was expecting her second baby by then. Her life was chaotic and she seemed far from happy although she was keen to tell me she was. She also told me how well Karen had done for herself, marrying somebody that worked for a bank. They were planning on coming over to see me and would call the following week to arrange it. I pretended I believed her but knew that she wouldn't ring and they would never visit.

As my angelic baby girl grew, she began to look more and more like her father, although of course no one mentioned this, especially not Gloria who we saw almost every other week. She started coming over on the bus and just spending a night or two with us before going back to her shared house, claiming she thought the two bus journey was quite an adventure. She was a big help to me and of course idolised her granddaughter. She even helped me tidy my small back garden the following spring so Angela would be able to play safely outside once she found her feet and bought a blue shell sand pit and paddling pool that we fixed at the edge of the patio. Once that was finished, she turned up the following week with packets of seeds and a tray of pansies and started working on the front garden, creating a flower border around the small patch of lawn.

"Everything in the garden is just rosy," she laughed as she stood back to admire her hard work and I agreed. She laughed when she said it and give me a hug before going in to wash her hands and start her batch cooking. I smiled warmly at her, grateful for her help and what I thought to be her immense restraint in not mentioning her son.

However, our Gloria would never have made a poker player, bless her; she had so many tells in her it was like she had speech bubbles above her head.

I might need a minute here; I really want to get this all off my chest, but this next bit is actually going to be hard and I'll need chemical cotton wool to soften my addled brain so I think I'll come back to this in a bit. You see, I did see my feckless husband just one more time and it didn't end well; not for him anyway.

## Twenty Seven

I think they might have increased my medication this morning as it seems to be taking longer for my head to clear, probably because of last night. Almost as soon as I closed my eyes, in that pleasantly decorated room, the demons crawled out of the corners, taunting me with images and thoughts that I'd allowed to resurface after so long.

There is someone coming to see me this afternoon, I've already forgotten who, I only remember that it's some official but, apparently, it's nothing to worry about, it's just to clear up a couple of things. So I want to use this time to continue the story while it's fresh in my mind and not do what the nice young nurse suggested which was to and try and get some more sleep. Instead, I'll grasp the nettle, I'll tell you about Darren; I am, after all, the only person who really knows what happened to him.

He made contact with me just after ten o'clock, one Tuesday morning in March 1977. Angela was teething and I had just got back home from walking her to sleep in her pram. Leaving her outside in the enclosed back garden, I was in the kitchen, the washing machine had just finished and I was about to start hanging out the nappies when the telephone rang.

It's strange but I remember not being surprised when I heard his voice at the other end of the line. There had been a couple of silent calls during the previous week and I half guessed it might be him plucking up courage to speak to me. I suppose I knew he would turn up again at some point and I think a little bit of me was relieved that the day had come. Now I could finally close the chapter properly and not have the worry of him being in the background waiting to come and spoil things.

"Hello Rosie, it's me."

"What do you want Darren?" I asked coldly. His pause telling me he wasn't expecting that but he soon regained his demeanour, still believing he was able to manage me.

"I want to come and see you," a pause, "and my daughter."

"Well you can't," I said simply.

"Rosie, we're still married and I'm Angela's Dad," he said with what sounded like gritted teeth patience, "Look, I know it looks like I ran away but all that stuff with the police and that lass making up stuff really got to me."

I remained silent, slightly curious to hear how he was going to explain his lack of communication for nearly eighteen months.

"Look, I just want to talk to you, to explain what happened. It was a mess, I was a mess, I had to get away." I still said nothing. "But I'm back now and I'm alright and I'm gonna get a job and be there to help you." He paused to see if I would react; I didn't. "You can go back to your nursing; we can be a proper family..."

"How did you know her name?" I interrupted him.

"What?"

"Who told you she's called Angela?" I rephrased my question. I could just about hear the shrug in his voice as he told me Gloria had told him.

"When?"

"What?"

"When did she tell you?" I demanded.

"Last week when I phoned her, I didn't know she'd moved next door to live with Betty."

I took in a breath and let it out slowly waiting to see what else he had to say, my mind quickly working through all scenarios I had imagined for my husband's homecoming, none of them ending well for him. I realised he was still talking.

"I've been living on the Isle of Man but I'm coming back tomorrow. I can't go to Betty's, she won't have me there."

"So you thought you'd come here," I said quietly.

"Yeah, look, I've told you it's gonna be different, I'm different. We can be a family. I can't wait to meet my little girl." The bubble of laughter in his voice made my blood run cold but I swallowed and managed to keep calm.

I pretended to be reluctant for a few more minutes, letting him persuade me, telling me how much he'd missed me and how things were going to be so much better. Finally, I managed what I feel sure was an Oscar winning performance, allowing him to believe that he had won me round and admitted, my voice catching slightly, that I'd missed him too. I agreed to let him come to the house but only after making him promise he wouldn't tell his mother that he'd called me. I said we could phone her and talk to her together when he was back, saying how thrilled she would be by this. He made the promise which I'm fairly certain he kept.

After telling me his flight got in at quarter past seven the next day, I said I would pick him up from Yeadon Airport. He seemed to be getting a bit emotional as he told me he had never stopped loving me and hung up quickly.

Putting down the receiver, I sighed heavily, shaking my head. Gloria had been over at the weekend and I had detected something slightly off about her. When I'd asked, she said everything was fine, she was just happy to see us. Now I knew she had spoken to Darren and chosen not to tell me. I was disappointed in her but that was for another day. I shook myself before glancing at the clock and went to hang out the washing while making mental notes of what I needed to do for the next day.

Gill was happy to babysit Angela for me, I told her I was going to see an old friend from Wakefield and wouldn't be back too late. Davy was at a friend's house and was being dropped off home at eight. She said she would have a game of chess with him when he got in.

I remember a feeling of calm washing over me as I got into my car shortly after six; it was like I was playing a part in a film. I knew the plot and I knew my lines, all I needed to do was stick to the script and make the ending convincing. I know now of course, that I really had not thought it through but nevertheless, I set off down the road, feeling a sudden frisson of excitement as I exited the estate and set off towards the airport.

The clocks hadn't yet sprung forward and so it was dusk as I set off and, turning into the airport shortly after seven, it was getting quite dark. His plane was on time so I didn't have to wait long for him and his shabby looking suitcase to pass through the nothing to declare channel. His face lit up when he saw me and I was instantly relieved that his boyish looks were no longer even slightly appealing to me. His skin had a yellowish pallor but he clearly thought his smile would melt me as he stepped forward to hug me. I let him, barely responding, which I sensed threw him as he turned up the charm and I pretended to be taken in.

After putting his luggage in the boot, he asked me if I'd like him to drive, as I had known he would. He hadn't had a car all the time he'd been away, *'not really had the cash'* and I said okay, he could drive, even though he wasn't on my insurance. As he got into the driver's seat, I suggested that we drive up the track off Bayton Lane to the viewpoint. It was only just after eight so there hopefully wouldn't be too many courting couples there already. He was clearly excited by the prospect and took my suggestion as a willingness to take him back. He actually beamed at me as we set off, saying it was just like when we first started going out.

I was relieved to see there were no other cars as he switched off the engine and applied the handbrake. I had no idea what I would have done if there had been anyone else there. Like I said, I hadn't thought it through but luck seemed to be on my side.

He was very talkative and sat sideways in the seat to look at me and, as we sat in the darkness, I listened as he tried to impress upon me how he was a victim in everything that had happened. How girls had always thrown themselves at him but I had been the only one that had ever mattered.

I didn't say much, letting him talk, nodding my head occasionally and uttering a word here and there to let him think I was listening. When finally, he stopped, he looked me full in the face and I think he might have had tears in his eyes. He reached across and touched me on the arm and asked if he could cuddle me. I nodded and smiled as I shuffled sideways in my seat and he lifted both his hands to hold my face, brought his lips to mine and kissed me gently. I think I may have waivered slightly at that point, I'm not sure, I mean, I sort of want to think I did, you know, consider giving him a chance but then he spoiled it all. Just as he pulled his hand away he groaned his arousal and I knew he was never going to change.

In one swift movement, I moved my left arm slightly behind me to the door pocket and folded my fingers around a syringe, quickly swinging it round and injecting the contents into his neck.

During the last week of work, I'd been on the women's surgical ward and was helping with the medication being given out. Half way round, the sister and the staff nurse were distracted by a suddenly hysterical patient who had managed to pull out her cannula then became more frenzied at the sight of the blood dripping from her arm. The Sister instructed me to stay with the trolley and not allow anyone to touch or remove anything while she dealt with the patient. In the five or so minutes this took, I managed to help myself to two syringes and two vials of fentanyl which fit securely in my deep pocket.

It had been a spur of the moment compulsion, purely opportunist with no forethought whatsoever although I was fairly sure they would come in handy sooner or later and I just hoped the fentanyl wouldn't degrade too much in the meantime.

Even though I was aware the drugs were catalogued and audited regularly, nothing was ever said and I took that to be a sign that it had been a good decision and that evening when I collected the purloined items from the little tin box that I kept in a secret drawer of my dressing table, I congratulated myself on my forethought.

I can still see the shock on his face as the needle pieced his skin and the liquid opioid entered his bloodstream. He opened his mouth to shout or cry out but as the narcotic surged through his system, his brain receptors reacted to the increased dopamine and he raised and then dropped his arms, the hint of a smile on his confused face.

"What, wha,, Ros...." he tried to form the odd couple of words as his eyes struggled to focus and as I removed the syringe and pierced the second vial with the needle, in case the drug had lost its potency in the 18 months I'd had it, I told him softly not to worry, this was for the best and in a few minutes he wouldn't feel anything. I've always considered that I have a good bedside manner and, like I've said, I am not a monster.

I was home shortly after ten and, after thanking my neighbour for her kindness and having a brief chat with Davy before he went to bed, I went up for a peek at Angela, sleeping soundly in her cot. I got a bath, washing my hair and leaving it to dry on its own, and went back to my bedroom where I lay on my side, watching my baby girl in her slumber until I fell into a dreamless sleep.

The next day after giving Davy a lift to school, I drove with Angela in her new car seat to Newmillerdam. It was a reasonably warm day but there weren't too many people around as I took her for a walk in her pushchair around the large expanse of water. Things were quite different back then and people weren't so conscious of fly tipping or dumping of their unwanted stuff. It didn't take too long before I discovered all sorts of detritus in the trees close to the path. Taking my time and being as careful as I could not to be seen, it took me just over an hour to get round to the other side, discarding my husband's few belongings as I went. I felt this was very poignant, shedding his material remains in an area where we had done our courting. Of course, by then, I knew that I had not been the only underage girl he had parked up there with but, as I say, it was quite cathartic for me. I'd left his battered suitcase in the boot, deciding that, as it had no identifying marks, I didn't need to be too thorough in its disposal.

In the end, I took it to a second hand furniture shop on Armley Town Street and while I was there bought myself a new, well new to me, wooden ironing board. I've still got it actually, been through countless new covers but the old wooden structure's survived really well. I was using it right up until the week everything......oh dear, here I am, off again. I might need a minute to get my mind straight; I'm going to ask the nurse if I can have a cup of tea.

Right, so where was I? Oh yes, back to that spring, and what I saw as my final act towards my goal of taking full control of my life, a last step toward the better future I had promised my brother and my child.

I've told you what I did with his stuff, a sort of ritual disbursal, although I did keep the money I found in his wallet before dropping that in the dam. He was actually carrying very little that would identify him apart from his passport, driving licence and the letter from Gloria, all of which I burned in my kitchen. I put the remnants; bits of pungent, charred plastic, amongst the ashes in the dustbin along with the teabags and vegetable peelings which gave me a lovely sense of calm.

I'm sure you're wondering what I did with Darren, well here's the thing; this was yet another case of things just falling into place, I honestly had no plan of what to do with his body. My only purpose had been to put him out his misery and prevent mine, but I hadn't worked out what I was going to do with him after that. I'd been so fixated on the fentanyl doing its magic, the getting rid of him was, well, I guess I sort of thought as things had worked out so easily before, I'd figure something out. So I had no preparation for his disposal but had not allowed myself to be concerned by this fact.

I sat in the car with him for a good half an hour, once I knew he was dead, enjoying the stillness and even smiling at him when the lights from a Britannia Airways plane lit up the interior as it took off on its way to Alicante. Glancing at my watch, I realised I probably should be getting a move on and I roused myself to search his pockets.

It was the letter from Gloria I found in the inside breast pocket of his jacket that made me really sad. She had sent him the money for his plane ticket plus '*a bit extra*' so he could buy me and Angela something and not to forget to get something for Davy *'as he's a nice lad and he's had put up with a lot cos of what you did'*. She warned him he would need to mend his ways, telling him he had not married a fool but a lovely lass who was a good mother. She went on to tell him how stupid he was to spoil everything but that she loved him despite his faults and wanted desperately to see him again and for us to all live as a family, if I'd have him back.

I folded the letter back into the envelope and slipped it into my handbag along with his passport and driving licence. The last thing I found was a small pink box containing a silver locket. I smiled at the thought he had actually spent some of Gloria's money on a gift for his daughter. Closing the box, I dropped that into my bag as well, knowing that I would never give it to her.

Getting his coat and his jacket off was easier than I had anticipated but the buttons on his shirt, which I noticed was quite new, were a bit problematic and I ended up ripping it before throwing the pile of clothes on the back seat along with his shoes and socks. I unfastened his trousers but left them on him as I pushed him across to the passenger seat and fastened him upright with the seat belt. Then I got into the driver's seat and checked my mirrors before starting the engine.

As I turned back onto Bayton Lane, I considered going right towards

Yeadon Tarn but didn't think I would be able to get the car close enough to the water and wasn't sure how far I could drag him or if I could do it quickly enough not to be seen. So instead, I turned left, thinking through all the possible places I could dump him as I made my way back to Bramley.

Just as in every sticky situation I've found myself in throughout my life, the solution just presented itself. I remembered a walk I'd had with Angela the previous week when I chatted to an elderly man who was walking a small brown dog. He was keen to tell me how much the area had changed, and not for the better. I told him my anecdote about having given birth in the ambulance, parked almost where we stood, but he was not to be distracted as he told me of what it was like before all this *'modernisation'*.

The redesigning of the ring-road to incorporate the Stanningley Bypass at the bottom of Spring Valley estate was an ongoing project. The bypass itself was not without controversy and had already seen several fatal accidents in the short time I'd lived there.

The place of birth, now written in neat fountain pen handwriting on Angela's birth certificate, was actually a cul-de-sac but there was a footpath that led to another road where four blocks of maisonettes were still under construction. Opposite them was what the old man described as a 'bloody eyesore and dangerous an' all'.

"There were an old tannery just down there, been there more than a hundred years, properly built it were though, but it were derelict an' needed knocking down, but they've not done it properly, left lots of bits of walls an' God knows what else, it's a proper death trap," he said and paused for breath, "I can't let my little lassie off to run around down there." He looked down at the dog who wagged her tail hopefully but the old man wasn't finished with his critique of the local council and department for roads.

"It's like a bloody bombsite. They've started building, digging holes and the like afore they've properly cleared it and they're having to shore up the railway bridge with ugly looking concrete pillars. You mark my words, it's not gonna end well," shaking his head and waving his finger at me as if I was in some way responsible, "an' there's nobody to keep the kids out, bloody little vandals making it worse."

Perhaps that was when he realised I had said nothing for some time and he started to move away. He seemed to shake himself back to the fact that we were just passing strangers and he cleared his throat and set off up the hill.

On the evening of Thursday 10th March 1977, on my return from Yeadon Airport, I drove down to the bottom of Hough End Lane where I did not encounter a single soul. I backed my car as close as I could to the end of the building site and then, albeit with difficulty, pulled my semi-naked husband out, leaving his underpants on, from the passenger seat onto the muddy ground. It was at that moment I felt a slight stab of panic. Although Darren was only of slight build, he was now, of course, a dead weight and although there was no one around, I was conscious that it was going to take some time and effort to get him to the disused footpath and launch him over the edge. I stood up straight, stretching out my back and looked around. It was a fairly overcast night but the moon was still half full and, as it found a small gap in the clouds, it highlighted the half-erected building to the side of me and, specifically, the collection of tools and materials. I smiled as I walked across towards a large pile of sand covered by damp plastic sheeting that glistened in the moonlight; this was yet another sign that I was doing the right thing and fate was on my side.

Although it was still tricky, once I'd rolled him onto the plastic, my adrenaline levels soared, giving me the strength to drag him along the uneven terrain. As soon as I got to thinnest part of the path, which traversed the steep drop, I yanked the sheeting up, tipping him over the edge and almost losing my footing in my exhilaration, but managing to right myself just in time to see him ricochet down over stones and bushes to the other building site below. I couldn't see where he landed but I thought there might have been a yellow JCB not too far away and I could just about make out bits of scaffolding and old brickwork. I stood still and waited but the silence was broken only by traffic travelling on the new concrete road surface below. I took a deep breath and quickly went back towards my car, returning the plastic to where I had found it, carefully covering the sand. Then I used Darren's clothes to wipe my hands before throwing them in the boot, climbed back into the driving seat and changed my shoes before returning to my new life.

I was, I remember, apprehensive over the next few days, watching the news, waiting for one of my neighbours or even Davy to ask me if I'd heard about the naked dead bloke being found down by the bypass, but there was nothing. As the days passed, I started to wonder if I had dreamt the whole thing. Occasionally, I would rummage in my underwear drawer to find the small box containing the silver locket, snapping it shut quickly once I had assured myself it was true. As the weeks passed and I took almost daily walks around Hough End Lane, occasionally walking down to the footbridge over the bypass, there was still no sign of any police activity and I decided that yet again, luck had been on my side.

To this day, I have no idea how the body of my feckless husband did not come to light. I did wonder if, perhaps, it had fallen into a hole filled the next day with concrete, or maybe it was just covered in mounds of earth and flattened before rotting away. I would chuckle to myself sometimes, thinking that perhaps it had been beamed up by aliens but it didn't matter. All that mattered was that he was gone and we were now free of him completely.

## **Twenty Eight**

So there I was, a twenty year old widow, although of course to the world I was still the abandoned wife, struggling to make ends meet but actually coping well. Gill from next door told me on several occasions how brave and strong she thought I was, coping on my own after my husband had run off and me being so young. I never told anyone about Darren's skirmish with the police and the real reason he had taken off, I may have hinted at there being another woman, although that was preposterous; Darren was never interested in women. I did tell her how foolish I felt as I'd learned he had already abandoned one wife and child before he met me.

Gloria remained tight lipped about him but I realised that she had fostered some hope that her prodigal son would one day return and things would be fine.

The weeks after I had made him disappear, I noticed she was unusually distracted and her mood was low. On a couple of occasions, I was sure she was on the verge of telling me she had spoken to him weeks ago but her courage failed her. I watched her come to terms with what she believed was yet another total betrayal from him. Darren had taken more of her money and not come back as promised.

I did feel quite bad about that, I knew she had been desperate for her boy not to be the person people had said he was and she was struggling to finally accept that he was beyond redemption. I mean, God knows what he'd been up to on the Isle of Man but I doubted that it was wholesome and I was never going to risk Angela's future with a man like that.

It has occurred to me that you may now be thinking that my killing spree, not that you can actually really call it that, might be escalating, I have to admit, my despatching of Darren was a tad gruesome but he had given me little choice. I could hardly bring him back to the house and cook him special soup or smother him in our bedroom; both those scenarios would be hard to explain. You probably think I should have just divorced him and refused to allow him access to Angela but I'm sure you all know of cases where that situation has not ended well, so he had to go. You also must remember how young I was and all the responsibilities I had, and there was my own rationale; it had worked out okay for me the two other times. And in fact, I was as kind as I could have been in the method I used to kill him.

As the months turned in to a year and there was still nothing, I decided I could well and truly draw the line on any concern and, as no one had ever reported him missing, no one was looking for him, and so our happy life continued. Even the sadness in Gloria's eyes faded a little as she took constant delight in her granddaughter and we got on with our lives, her son never mentioned again. Although actually, now I think about it, there was just one time when someone did mention him and it sent a flurry of emotions through me; a little sadness but mostly relief.

I had organised a small tea party for Angela's third birthday and invited all the Crigglestone gang as well as Gill and Roy and some other neighbours who had young children.

It was a warm Sunday afternoon and I was just standing outside the back door watching Miss Alderson and Davy blowing bubbles for Angela and two other toddlers from down the road. Gill and Roy were in the sitting room chatting to Mrs Davis and our other neighbours. Gloria had just gone into the kitchen to make a pot of tea and Mrs Baxter stood up quickly, saying she would give her a hand. Even though there was a lot of laughter and excited shouting, I clearly heard Mrs Baxter ask my mother-in-law if she'd really never heard from her son. They both had their backs to the door but I actually think Gloria knew I could hear her response, which was that she had neither seen nor heard from him since the day he left. I'd tried to smile but felt the sadness rising, knowing she was lying but that she would never admit it. She would never actually want to address what she thought was his final betrayal.

So the years rolled by and things were good. We were comfortable money wise but I was keen not to run my savings down too quickly so I scoured the local newspaper for any jobs I could do with a baby in tow. I delivered telephone directories, ran a Kay's Catalogue and became an Avon Lady. None of this made me much more than an extra five or six pounds a week but this was enough, along with the child benefit, to keep us. Once Billy had gone to prison, Nana had started giving Davy the child benefit she claimed so he would always have some money of his own. I had kept up this arrangement and he became very good with money and opened a Post Office saving account on his fourteenth birthday with the twenty five pounds of loose change he had saved in a jam jar.

He continued to do well at school and passed all nine of the O levels he sat and, with only a little bit of encouragement from me, decided to stay on at school and do his A levels with talk of university.

In the autumn of 1979, I discovered the world of Tupperware after popping round to Gill's one evening, leaving my capable little brother to babysit and it was a revelation to me. I was impressed with the products and how useful they could be but what I found most impressive was the business model and immediately signed up as a party planner. According to Dawn, the regional manager, I was a natural and would do well. She was a very nice lady who helped me with my first couple of parties and recommended me for her job within twelve months as she was moving onto a new type of party plan – aimed at a different type of young wives.

As a thank you, I had one of her first parties at my house, inviting all the stay at home Mums I knew from around the area. As the gismos, gadgets and underwear were displayed on my sideboard, I was fascinated by the reaction of most of my guests. It was a very interesting evening with lots of hilarity and sexual innuendos but as I helped Dawn carry her stock back to her car at the end of the evening, I declined an offer to join her Ann Summers party plan team.

I was making quite a good income from the airtight and odourless plastic containers through my own parties as well as a percentage from the team I had working for me but after another year, in early 1981, I started to think about what I was going to do when Angela started school. Davy, who had continued his academic success, was all set to start university that year.

I had long conversations with Miss Alderson as well as Gill about what I should do. It took me quite some time to finally admit to everyone, including myself that I did not want to go back to nursing as I had always said I would. Once I had spoken the words, it set me on a path of more indecision.

"I think you are very much a businesswoman," Miss Alderson said, "You are making a good wage from your Tupperware but they are also making a lot of money out of you. Maybe you should start your own business and work for yourself."

"You mean buy a shop?" I asked, startled at the prospect.

"Goodness no, well not yet, but maybe you would benefit from getting an office job if you are sure you don't want to go back to nursing?"

"I'm sure," I said.

"Well in that case why don't you do a course at the local college, in something clerical, you can reinvent yourself and if nothing else you might make some friends of your own age?"

As I got ready for bed that night, I sat in front of my dressing table mirror thinking about what she had said and decided she was right; it was time to move forward and I slipped off my wedding ring and dropped it into the little crystal pot that had come from Nana's dressing table.

September was a busy month. The first week, I went to Park Lane

College in Leeds to check out what was on offer and would also fit in with my other commitments and Davy was packing for university. He'd got a place at Liverpool studying Maths and Physics and, although he promised to come back lots, I knew I was going to miss him.

When he first told me he was keen to go to a different city and not to Leeds, which is where I had presumed he'd go, I'd been thrown into a blind panic, explaining, almost hysterically how, if he didn't want to stay at home, he could live in halls and that Leeds was great university but he stood his ground, making me both horrified and proud. As always, Miss Alderson was the voice of reason, insisting I allow him the choice and persuading me that it would be good for him to have the whole university experience and would give him independence.

Having conceded that it was ultimately his decision, my panic returned when he started to talk about going to Kent because the British Chess Federation headquarters was in Hastings which he said was just down the road. When I pointed out that it was more than fifty miles from the campus he shrugged and said that it was closer than nearly three hundred miles away which is how far away from Leeds it was. In the end he decided on Liverpool as his first choice when he discovered they had an excellent Chess Society and the BBC filmed The Master Game there sometimes, his favourite television program. I would still have been happier if he'd gone to Leeds but consoled myself with the fact that it was only 80 miles away and two of his friends from The Silver Knight Chess Club were also going there.

I really didn't have a clue what course I wanted to sign up for at college and after reading through all the flyers and leaflets I'd brought home, I plumped for a bookkeeping and accountancy course, mainly because it was on Wednesday evening and Gill had said that would be the best evening for her to babysit Angela; not really the best reason to choose a course, I know. It ran from 6pm to 9pm with a half hour break in the middle which meant I would be home by 9.45 at the latest, which worked for her. The lessons were held in a block of wooden classrooms which had been installed as a temporary measure many years before but had now become a cold and damp permanent extension.

I met Rob on my second week; the first week had already left me thinking I'd made a mistake. I was passing the pay phone which hung on a wall in the small corridor outside the break hut. He was standing with the receiver in one hand while the other hand was in his jacket pocket searching for coins.

"Excuse me, have you got any change for the phone?" he asked, stepping back slightly to stop my passing. I shrugged and replied that I didn't think so but started to pull my bag round in front of me so I could check my purse. It turned out I had two five pence pieces which I offered out to him. He took one and apologised that he had no change at all and asked if he could pay me back next week. I nodded and left him to his call.

The following week when I arrived, he was standing just inside the entrance, clearly waiting for me. Holding out his hand to me with a ten pence in the middle of his palm, he said with a smile,

"Here's the five pence I borrowed, plus interest, to repay my debt."

"Wow! Hundred percent interest," I said, the bookkeeping lessons clearly paying off. I took the coin and smiled, "That was a good deal for me."

"And for me too," his eyes twinkling as they locked onto mine and I felt the strangest feeling of anticipation, "I mean it was a very important call I needed to make which might have caused me no end of trouble if I hadn't made it so...." He tilted his head and raised his eyebrows, still smiling, "thank you."

"You're welcome," I was smiling so much I was on the verge of giggling and I tried to reign myself in. Luckily someone knocked into me slightly as they passed and I pulled myself together. "Right, well, I've come with plenty of change this week if you need another loan." I managed to pull my gaze away from him and made to walk past.

"Good to know," as he began walking beside me, "I'm Robert by the way, Rob."

"Right," I said, taking in a deep breath to give me a second to decide, "Rose," I said and in that instant I decided that was who I was going to be; yet another part of my moving on. He was waiting for me at break time, offering to share his Cadbury's Fruit and Nut bar with me and buying me hot chocolate from the vending machine.

One of my granddaughter's favourite words is organic, it's a word I like and it's probably the best word to describe how my relationship with Robert Nicholas Morgan developed.

At first, we talked about our courses; he was doing computing, which he said was a bit intense and he wasn't sure the guy taking the class actually understood what he was teaching but said '*I think computers are really the future*'.

I said I thought my teacher was over-qualified and seemed irritable and bored. I felt out of my depth but hopefully I'd soon start to get the hang of it.

Rob was, or had been, a Leeds United fan and tried to go to every home game. He'd stopped going to away games as the crowd he used to go with had drifted apart. I told him I didn't really understand football and he said that was because I'd never experienced a live game.

The next week, he asked me out. We chatted over hot chocolate at break but this time I'd brought two Jacobs Fruit Club biscuits which he said were his second favourite, "You really can't better the Mint Club but this is very nice."

"My favourite is actually the Orange," I said as I took a bite of the chunky chocolate and raisins, feeling completely at ease with him. He asked if I was getting into my course. I wasn't. I told him I didn't think it was for me and probably wouldn't finish the course.

"Oh really," he said with puzzled surprise, "will your employers be okay with that, I mean isn't it for your job?"

"No, I don't really have a job, well not a proper one, I just picked bookkeeping cos I thought it might be helpful but it's so boring."

"So wait," he held up his hand and looked me in the eye, "you enrolled on a bookkeeping course and didn't expect it to be boring?"

"I know," I giggled, "but I quite like maths and numbers so I thought it might be okay. Maybe I should have chosen a computer course."

"Yeah, well, that's not in the least bit boring," he said sarcastically before adding quickly, "You will still come next week though?"

"I will come next week," giving him my brightest smile; "the break time makes it worth effort."

"Well in that case I wonder if you fancy going out with me, at the weekend maybe?" He leaned forward eagerly and my smile faded slightly.

"Okay, well, before I answer that, I need to tell you something and then you can decide if you're still interested." He listened attentively as I told him the bullet points of my circumstances.

I was still technically married although I had not seen my husband since he ran out of our back door to avoid some trouble almost six years before.

I had been pregnant at the time and I had a daughter.

I also had a younger brother and they were my absolute priority.

I didn't go into any more details and he didn't ask anything else but, as we stood up to go back to our classes, he caught my hand with his and asked if I fancied going to the pictures or would I prefer a meal and what day would be best for me.

After the classes finished, he walked me to my car and I gave him my phone number, asking him to call me the next evening when we could make arrangements.

The following evening, I had just come down from reading Angela a bedtime story, she was tired after a trip to the park after school and had settled down to sleep as soon as Goldilocks had jumped out of the window to run home. I switched the kettle on to make a cup of tea as the phone rang; it was just gone half past seven.

We talked for over an hour and I told him it was a long time since I'd been out with anyone and thought the cinema was a good choice for a first date. I said I had secured a babysitter for Saturday night but couldn't stay out too late so he suggested we went to see Airplane, a comedy and a fairly short film, at Hyde Park Cinema in Headingley. He offered to pick me up but I said I would prefer to meet him there. My babysitter was actually Gloria, who was coming for the weekend, and I was not ready to test out how she would feel about me having a boyfriend.

I met him outside the front door of the beautiful grade ll listed building. He was already there, leaning against one of the greying white stone pillars of the small canopy. He said he'd been at Elland Road watching Leeds lose to Ipswich Town that afternoon and was in desperate need of cheering up.

It was a lovely evening; the film was very funny, we had a choc-ice each and he walked me to my car afterwards. There was a slightly awkward moment when, as we stopped by my driver's door, I guessed he was trying to decide if he should lean in for a kiss and I quickly turned to unlock it. As I turned back he had taken a step back and dipped his head slightly.

"Can I see you again?" he asked quickly.

"That would be lovely," I smiled at him, "I've really enjoyed tonight, it's been lovely but I'm a bit new to this and…"

"It's okay," he interrupted me, "I've enjoyed it too and I'd like to go out with you again, maybe for a meal next time but shall we talk about it on Wednesday?"

Driving home, I thought about my very good fortune in meeting him. He was good looking, funny, clever and kind and for some reason seemed to like me, even though I had no idea why. I knew that I would have to try really hard to take it slowly, and I hoped that he had the patience to stay the course.

On our second date, a meal at Bistro 5 the following Saturday, he told me all about himself and his family. He was six months older than me and lived in Pudsey. His parents lived in Armley and his mother was Dutch but had lived in Yorkshire since marrying his Dad in the early fifties. She had been a model in her younger years but now worked in a clothes shop in Leeds. His father was an engineer, working for the council, and he had a sister, Julia, who was seventeen and worked in the offices at Tapp and Toothill in Bramley. She could, apparently, be a right pain but was basically alright as long as she was the centre of attention.

He was a junior manager at Leeds Permanent Building Society. He'd planned to stay on at school to do A levels and go to university but his childhood sweetheart, who he'd first kissed when they were both fourteen, had been desperate to leave school and get a job after O levels and talked him into doing the same.

They were engaged at eighteen and had a big party to celebrate, gleaning them lots of gifts to make a substantial bottom drawer. As they both worked for LPBS in the offices on The Headrow, they were guaranteed a lower rate mortgage and began saving for their deposit. It was all textbook small town happy ending but then came the plot twist. A month before their wedding, two years later, he was told by a mate that his fiancée and his best friend, who he'd asked to be his best man, were having a bit of a fling.

It transpired to be substantially more than a fling and had been going on for over a year. His fiancée didn't protest her innocence, claiming she had realised ages before that she didn't love him but she really wanted to wear the big dress and have her big day. The wedding was cancelled and he took his half of the savings and bought a terraced house in Pudsey. His fiancée handed in her notice but was told she did not have to work it, so he didn't see her again until he spotted her wedding picture in the Yorkshire Evening Post. She was wearing a big dress and standing beside the ex-best friend who she clearly thought was the best man.

"Was he the one you used to go to away matches with?" I guessed.

"Yeah, there were a couple of others that sometimes came but it was mostly him and me," shrugging with a tight lipped smile, "They still go and she goes sometimes an' all but I'm okay just going to home games and," suddenly smiling widely, "I'm especially glad I didn't go this week as not only would I have had to watch Leeds get thumped by Liverpool three nil, I wouldn't have been back in time to come out with you."

He'd been pragmatic as he told me the story but it was plain he'd been scarred by the double betrayal. I asked if they gave the engagement presents back which made him laugh.

"Now that is a massive issue with my Mum," he told me, "she bought us a set of steak knives, really good ones and I had to stop her from going round and demanding them back."

"Did she get them back?"

"No, I told her to let it go, I wanted nothing from her and just wanted to forget about it and move on." He sounded like he meant that and I liked him even more.

"And anyway," he chuckled, "I did get the ring back and gave that to Mum and she wears it on her right hand." I must have looked slightly surprised at this as he laughed and went on, "She loves to tell anyone who admires it or even just anyone, how her wonderful son bought it for his girlfriend but he found out she was a cheating." He paused to try and stop the corners of his mouth from twitching up, "Ugly tart she calls her or, when she's had a couple of gins, a kutwijf."

"A what?"

"A kutwijf, it's a Dutch swear word, it means a bitch, although this is pretty mellow now. I learned lots more very rich Dutch insults from her after I told her what had happened."

"I've always fancied learning another language," I mused, taking a sip of my water. He had wanted to buy us a bottle of wine but when I said I didn't like wine and that water was fine, he asked for two glasses of water; although we both drank our complementary lemony flavoured liqueur after the meal. It was a lovely evening and I felt incredibly relaxed in his company. As we left the restaurant, our hands naturally found each other as we walked back to his car. Gill was babysitting for me as Gloria wasn't visiting so I'd let him pick me up.

On the drive home, he spoke my thoughts out loud saying he hoped I'd go out with him again and I smiled and said I hoped so too.

## Twenty Nine

Gloria's visits started to be more infrequent when, encouraged by both Betty and me, she realised she had a life of her own. Soon after I'd moved to Bramley, she established contact with most of her family in Armley and I visited them with her occasionally. Darren was never mentioned in my presence except for just once.

Angela would have been about two and Martin was helping me carry my things back to the car after a visit. It was only the second time I'd seen him since my wedding. I'd noticed him looking at me and felt he wanted to say something and he wasn't exactly subtle when he shot to his feet to help me pack up. I opened the boot and he leaned forward to drop in the stuff, took a deep breath and asked quickly,

"Do you worry that he might come back?"

"Sometimes," I said with a shrug, "but as time goes on I'm starting to think he won't, I mean he's clearly happy wherever he is."

"Yeah, maybe," he said with a frown, "but I can't imagine not wanting to see your own kid."

"Well he made it clear he didn't want children, I mean, I wasn't the only pregnant wife he abandoned," I laughed, attempting to combat his frowning concern.

"Do you think Gloria's still in touch with him?" he asked.

"No!" I said, sharply shaking my head, "She's been a great support to me and I'm certain she understands I won't tolerate him our life; she's picked her side."

"Right," he nodded, unable to hide his surprise at my response, "Well that's good, he's a scumbag and you don't want him in your life or anywhere near that little lass," he took in a deep breath, "and I want you to know if he does come back and you need any help to make him understand he's not welcome, just let me know."

"Thanks, Martin."

"I just wish I'd punched his lights out years ago when we were teenagers," he said with passion, "he were always a sly little bastard, looked like butter wouldn't melt but Duggie were right about him, he's a pervert, sorry," suddenly stopping and shaking his head, "sorry, I don't..."

"It's okay," I said, slamming the boot shut.

"Well anyway, I would love to get the chance to..."

"You'll be the first person I call if he dares to show his face again." I cut him off again and gave his arm a squeeze.

"I mean it, Rosie," he insisted.

"Good to know." I gave him what I hoped was a reassuring smile and as I drove home fifteen minutes later, I glanced at Angela in my mirror as the tiredness of her busy morning washed over her little face. Gloria was staying at her sister's for a few days so we were alone in the car as I said out loud,

"It's comforting to know I wasn't the only one that wanted your Daddy gone."

I told Gloria I had met someone that I liked after Rob and I had been going out for four months. It was the end of January 1982 and she and I were watching TV on a Thursday evening. I tried to only see Rob once a week, making it clear to him that I needed to go slowly although our long phone conversations most nights, which I looked forward to so much, made me realise how much I cared for him.

I saw the shadow of sadness in Gloria's eyes at this news but she forced a smile. After a moment's pause, she said she thought something like this was coming.

She had been the first person to notice that I'd stopped wearing my wedding ring but had managed not to mention it for almost an hour before she commented. I told her I could not spend the rest of my life waiting for him to come back and I wasn't sure I actually wanted him back anymore.

I told her I'd been going out with someone occasionally for a little while, I'd met him at college and I wanted her to meet him and tell me what she thought. I told her what I'd told him - Darren had left me and I hadn't seen him since before Angela was born. I said I wasn't going to let him meet Angela yet as it was still early days. She said she understood that I probably should move on and with Davy being away at university, she had been worried about me being lonely.

The fact that I asked her to meet Rob and check his intentions definitely helped her mood and I'm certain she was genuine in her understanding but I'm in no doubt about how much it cost her.

I arranged for him to come to the house for a cup of tea and one of Gloria's wonderful cheese scones the following Saturday. Davy came home especially to meet him and I was anxiously hoping it would go well while trying to give off a confident and fully composed air.

My wonderful neighbour was taking Angela into Leeds to see the new Disney film, The Fox and The Hound, and my daughter was almost bouncing off the ceiling as I got her ready to go. Gloria was nervously fussing in the kitchen after I stopped her plumping up the sofa cushions for a third time. Davy seemed his normal thoughtful self but I noticed he'd put on clean clothes which was unusual for him on a Saturday morning; I didn't comment though. What I did say was it was lucky there were no big chess games on that weekend and he raised his eyebrows and said there was always a big game on every weekend but this week he had something more important to do. I would have hugged him right then and there if I hadn't seen him flush with embarrassment as I'd made the slightest move towards him.

I saw Rob's Ford Escort pull up outside the house from the bedroom window at two minutes before two, just as I'd given myself a quick spray of perfume, and I shot downstairs to the front door as Davy called out,

"He's here Gloria," sitting forward on his seat but not getting up.

Rob handed me a box of chocolates in the instantly recognisable purple box as he stepped into the sitting room.

I pointed to my brother and introduced them.

"Aren't you supposed to deliver them in the middle of the night when we're all asleep?" Davy asked, eyeing the box. Rob's expression of confession made me laugh as I realised he was a nervous as me.

"It's the telly advert, The Milk Tray Man," I said. He laughed and nodded and was quick to add,

"Well I hope the lady does love them."

"She actually prefers Black Magic," Davy replied with a pretend serious expression, "but I'm sure I can help her out with these."

"Right," Rob nodded and his smile broadened, "You're as sharp as your sister then, I'd better buckle myself in for a bumpy ride."

"Oh, just wait till you meet Gloria," Davy chuckled. I shot him a look as I invited Rob to sit in the armchair opposite him before going to see what my mother-in-law was doing in the kitchen. She was standing in front of the sink, starring out of the window, the teapot and cups on a tray on the draining board. I went over and gave her quick hug but didn't say anything. She took in a deep breath and fixed a smile before picking up the tray and following me back in.

"And this is my mother-in-law and very good friend, Gloria," I announced as she put the tray on the coffee table. "Gloria, this is Rob."

The conversation was amicable and light as we drank the mugs of tea and polished off six of the dozen scones Gloria had made. She asked him about his family and was very interested to hear about his mother being both foreign and glamorous. Davy mainly listened during talk of his family but when Gloria asked Rob about his job, he was keen to know more about computers. Of course, I knew exactly where his train of thought was, as always it was on chess.

Rob told him he thought 'computers were the future' and it would not be long before everyone was using them for all sorts although he struggled to come up with an example when Gloria asked, 'Like what?' This didn't matter though as my brother had his own agenda and went on to tell us with great enthusiasm. The chess community in the UK were watching with interest the development in America of computers that were able to play the great game.

Chess engines had, Davy informed us, been around since the 1950's but recently, in the late seventies, they had become more sophisticated and, with advancements in what was termed the technological revolution, a machine named Belle had won the 1978 North American Computer Chess Championship. The engine's special hardware allowed it to analyse over thirty million positions in three minutes.

"Every day's a school day," I said getting up to make another cup of tea. I noticed Rob was not only listening to Davy sharing information and facts, he also seemed to know the right questions to ask. Gloria followed me and, with a shrug, said she had no idea what the two of them were talking about but clearly they were getting on. We heard Rob say he had played chess a bit at school but hadn't had a game in years. I quickly walked back into the room.

"I'm sure my brother would love to give you a game, some other time."

Much to Davy's obvious disappointment, I turned the conversation to how we'd first met. He had finally confided in me, only the week before, the truth of it.

"I'd seen Rose at break time on the first week of the course and noticed her sitting on her own reading through her notes and I quite, well, I quite fancied her." He blushed and took a big gulp of his tea, "I managed to cross the room and was about to speak to her when this old bloke wearing a suit suddenly appeared and sat down next to her."

"That was Alan, he's on my course and although he's probably a lovely man, he has really bad breath and thinks that spreadsheets are the most interesting thing in the world," I said with a laugh.

"The second week, I saw her arrive and spent the whole of the first half of the class trying to think up a way to talk to her without seeming like a weirdo."

"Too late!" I muttered and he coloured up again.

"My plan was to get out of my class first for the break, which I did, and stand in front of the pay phone, right by the door, and wait for her." He looked a bit like a school boy with his slightly embarrassed smile. "When she came out, I asked her if she had some change for the phone." He paused, looking like he was waiting for us all to exclaim 'genius' or something I chipped in,

"He told me he had a really important call to make but didn't have any change, so I gave him a five pence." The listeners nodded.

"That gave me a reason to go and thank her after the call and to tell her I'd pay her back the next week." He looked delighted with himself.

"So who was the call to?" Gloria asked with a frown of suspicion.

"Well I didn't really have a call to make at all but obviously she could see me through the door so I had to make one." He took another mouthful of tea before admitting, "So I called Dial-a-Disc and just listened to the song, while pretending to have a conversation."

"What song was it?" Davy asked with a chuckle.

"Do you know, I've no idea," he laughed and shaking his head, "I was busy pretending I was having a conversation while trying to keep an eye on Rose. I really couldn't tell you what it was."

When he left, I walked out to the car with him, aware that the other two were watching. A brief hug and a small brush of my lips and he looked over and waved at the window before getting in and driving away.

"He seems nice," Gloria said as I came back in, "Rose?"

"I think so too," I laughed, "and I told him my name is Rose, I like that too, I think it suits me."

"Okay, shall I call you that then?" she asked, carrying the tray of plates and cups into the kitchen.

"You can call me whatever you want, although I'd rather you didn't call me Rosemary, you choose, Rose or Rosie," I said, following her. As she started to wash up, I took the tea towel from the hook before walking back into the sitting room and raising my eyebrows at Davy.

"I liked him," he said simply, "What time are we having our tea cos I'm starving an' if it's gonna be ages, I'll have another scone."

Angela burst in just after four o'clock, full of chatter and obviously on a sugar high. Half an hour later, Gloria left to get the bus down to Armley; she was spending the night with her sister. Gill stayed for a cup of tea as my daughter overexcitedly told me about the milkshake and Milky Way she'd enjoyed before the film, the choc-ice during the film and the bag of Quavers on the way home.

Gill looked sheepish as she made a half-hearted apology for spoiling her using an excuse of how good and polite she was and suggesting that she would probably sleep really well that evening.

After eating four minced beef and onion Crispy Pancakes and a massive plate of chips, Davy played draughts for half an hour with his niece before I ran her a bath. As I carried her to her bedroom afterwards, he announced he was going out and asked if I'd washed his Ben Sherman shirt, which I had. As I read Angela a story, I could hear him banging about in his room and when I came out thirty minutes later, the bathroom and landing reeked of Hai Karate aftershave.

He was going round to the Elder Road Working Men's Club with two of his friends to watch the snooker, he said, but I was sure it was that he had recently decided he quite liked a beer or two. He had never seemed interested in alcohol throughout his early teens, even though a lot of his friends had found pubs and clubs where they could get served from as young as fourteen. We never discussed it but I assumed his abstinence was because of what we'd witnessed with Mum and Billy but whatever the reason, he'd avoided it. On his eighteenth birthday, he had gone to

The Daisy pub where he enjoyed two pints of Tetley's bitter with a couple of his mates. He told me he had refused a third as he started to feel a bit odd, not that it wasn't a pleasant feeling he assured me, but decided he wasn't happy about feeling so light headed.

His decision to go out that evening had taken me by surprise and the house felt suddenly strange when I came downstairs. I still hadn't got used to him being away most of the time and, after a busy day, I thought about how lovely it would be to sit on the sofa and chat with someone. Of course, I was thinking about Rob but only for a few minutes before reminding myself it was early days so I phoned him instead.

We chatted for well over an hour, discussing how he thought meeting my family had gone and me reassuring him. I told him he was a hit with my brother and although Gloria would always struggle with me being with anyone else, she was as okay with the situation as she was ever likely to be.

We had no plans to see each other again until Wednesday at college, which was actually my last lesson. I told him I wasn't going to sign up for the next block as I'd got a job working in the offices of the showroom of the Yorkshire Electricity Board in the Merrion Centre. He was trying to persuade me to have a go at something else but I was reluctant and told him the only thing that had kept me going was knowing I would see him at break time, but now the novelty of that had worn off, I'd rather spend my Wednesday evenings at home.

I rang off saying I would see which night I could get a babysitter for the following weekend and switched on the TV, not that I wanted to watch it as my eyes were tired and I was struggling to stay awake.

Davy had a key but I was concerned about him being out so late which was unlike him and was relieved when shortly after eleven, he finally stumbled over the threshold and I knew he had not refused a third pint this time. He grinned at me before hiccupping loudly and I shook my head in mock despair. He was as excited as Angela had been, telling me about the turn they'd watched, a comedian that told the bluest of jokes but was really funny. He tried unsuccessfully to tell me one of them but kept forgetting bits and was laughing so much I had no idea what he was saying.

"I guess I had to be there," I said sardonically which made him laugh more. I told him I was off to bed and he suddenly asked,

"Does it make you feel more grown up, being called Rose?"

"Maybe a bit," I smiled, "but it was meeting Rob and thinking that it was time to be a grown up," I shrugged, "it's hard to explain but it just felt right."

"Do you think I should start being David then?"

"I don't know, would you like to be David?"

"I'm not sure."

"You can be whoever you want to be, I mean you can still call me Rosie if you want, it won't change things between us. I'll always be your big sister."

"Maybe I'll be Dave," he said wistfully before giggling and repeating, 'Dave' a couple of times. I shook my head and as I wandered round the house checking all the doors were locked, I muttered to myself, *'You'll always be Davy to me.'*

## **Thirty**

In the late summer of 1982, I received an invitation to Margaret's wedding. Apart from exchanging Christmas cards and the occasional phone call from her and May, I didn't see too much of them so it was a happy surprise. Angela and I were invited to the wedding of Margaret and Glen in February of the following year.

Gloria was very excited about going but also still concerned about seeing Duggie and his wife Dorothy who would also be there. Wringing her hands, she said she was sure he would bring up '*all that nasty business*' again. I told her I doubted he would want to spoil Margaret's wedding and that she and I would stay close.

Privately, I was also a little concerned about meeting this man who believed his daughter had been assaulted by Darren. As a parent now, I knew how I would feel if anyone harmed my child. I would never forgive or forgot and I would most likely inflict my own retribution. I felt sure though that Duggie and Dorothy would be aware of my perceived situation as the abandoned wife, struggling to bring up a child on my own and thought, in all probability, he would sympathise with me as one of Darren's victims and want to tell me I'd had a lucky escape.

Gloria had hoped that Angela would have been asked to be a bridesmaid or at least a flower girl and had said as much to her sister. The bride had apparently asked four of her friends to be her attendants and originally wanted the wedding to be child free but had been talked out of such a ban by her future mother-in-law.

However, Gloria was not to be out done. She had managed to discover the bridesmaids would be wearing pale blue dresses with flowery skull caps and then taken Angela shopping in Leeds to buy her a new outfit. This consisted of a lovely pale blue calf-length dress with puff sleeves and a full skirt, layered with lots of lacy underskirts. This was topped off with a flower garland for her hair which made her look like the cutest six year old bridesmaid and Gloria was delighted.

"You don't think Margaret might be put out by this?" I asked her as Angela twirled around in front of us in delight.

"What?" She pretended to look puzzled, "I mean we're just following the colour theme, I'm wearing a blue frock as well." Her pretence at innocence was worthy of a round of applause.

The ceremony was at St Bartholomew's church in Armley and, as we arrived, the photographer quickly ushered Angela to stand with the four official bridesmaids where she happily posed, much to the confusion of the other attendants. As soon as he'd finished, I ushered her and a very smug looking Gloria inside before the bride arrived.

Her brother, Martin, gave her away and the ceremony was quite lovely. I had to blink away a tear or two as they said their vows and when we stood up to sing the first hymn, I had to quash a fit of giggles as Angela sang 'All things bright and beautiful' at the top of her voice. It was only as we'd our way out of the church that Margaret and her mother clocked our little scene stealer, when we passed the bride and groom posing for their formal photographs. Gloria shamelessly dashed over to them, holding Angela's hand to scatter confetti over the newlyweds as she gushed out her congratulations. I caught Margaret's eye and she shook her head in good natured disbelief before bending down to say hello to Angela. She told her she thought she looked like a magic flower fairy, which provoked an infectious chuckle from her, giving the photographer some excellent spontaneous shots and Gloria a surge of satisfied pride.

I was quite nervous as we walked into the reception at Armley Liberal Club. Up until that point we'd managed to avoid Duggie and Dorothy but as soon as we walked into the concert room, there they were sitting at the table right by the door. Two young women who looked like they wanted to be elsewhere were sitting gloomily beside them. Even though I'd never seen either of them before, the way the colour drained out of Gloria's face told me exactly who they were and alerted me to this unavoidable encounter. Fortunately, at that moment, May appeared at her side,

"Gloria, why don't you and Rosie come and sit over here with me and Martin," she said loudly, guiding us past them and towards a long table at the front. Martin went to the bar to buy a round of drinks and I saw Gloria knock back her double gin, 'just to calm her nerves', so I made sure to stay vigilant for the rest of the afternoon. It was all fine and, although on occasion I was aware of some looks and glances, they kept to themselves.

At Margaret's request, there were no speeches and the afternoon melted into early evening and other guests began to arrive, along with a DJ who began setting up for the disco. Much to Angela's disappointment, we left at shortly before eight, her excitement was bordering on hysteria as she charged around. Before we left, I managed to catch Margaret to thank her for inviting us and to wish her well. She thanked me for bringing the flower girl she had not realised she needed but laughed at my blushes saying she knew exactly who was behind that.

"I don't begrudge her though," suddenly serious, "Gloria's had a pretty shit life all in all and you and the angelic one are the only bit of happiness she's had for decades." I asked her if they were going on honeymoon and she laughed, acknowledging my change of subject, before telling me about their planned trip to Crete. As I turned to leave, she touched my arm and said she was glad things had worked out for me and that Darren taking off was the best thing that could have happened. We had a quick hug and I said I looked forward to seeing the wedding photos when she got home.

It was tricky to get Angela to wear anything else for the next week. The minute she got home from school, she ran to her room to transform into the magic flower fairy and was looking forward to her Uncle Davy seeing it when he was home for the weekend.

On the Friday after school, I let Angela help me make a lasagne, Davy's favourite meal, and we had just placed it in the oven when the phone rang. I was immediately worried that it would be my brother saying he'd missed the coach or that there had been some other glitch that would stop him from coming so when I heard Gloria's voice, I was so relieved I laughed out loud.

She was phoning to tell me she and Betty were going on holiday, abroad no less, and for ten days. They weren't going until the following June but she was so excited and pleased with herself at making this arrangement although I guessed that Betty had done all the organising. Gloria had never been out of Yorkshire before so this was going to be a huge adventure which had actually started already as she'd been to the Post Office to get the form she needed for a passport.

It was lovely to hear her so happy. She had gone a bit quiet on me after her initial meeting with Rob but, as the weeks passed and nothing had changed, she seemed to have come to terms with my having a boyfriend. I still hadn't introduced him to Angela and was only seeing him once or occasionally twice a week, despite being tempted to see more of him since Davy had left.

Gloria's friendship with Betty had become closer since she finally accepted her son wasn't coming back and that was a great comfort to me. It meant that her visits became fewer and she generally only stayed for one or two night but always offered to babysit when she came. I tried not to take advantage of her though and made sure we had some nice evenings watching telly together.

I met Rob's parents and sister two weeks after he'd met Gloria and Davy. They were so very polite with a clearly forced jovial friendliness masking their concern. I could tell Rob had told them not to ask me any questions about my family. The only thing they knew about me was that I was six months younger than their son and I was a single mother, which was also off the table for discussion, the single mother thing not my age.

After this visit, I decided I needed to get it all out there and told him to tell them the potted version of my family history and to say it was alright if they wanted to ask me anything about it. What I told him was -;

*My mother had been really young when she'd had me and my father had died soon after. My mother had remarried when I was six and my stepfather was a horrible man who beat my mother so badly, she died when I was fifteen. The evil stepfather was later sent to prison when he murdered his next partner and I went to live with my grandmother until I met and married a man eleven years older than me who left me for someone else when I was pregnant. I had no idea where he was and he had never seen his daughter. When my grandmother died, she left me her house and so I was able to move away and start a new life with my daughter.*

I basically rewrote the story of my life in much the same way as Walt Disney did with fairy tales.

The next time I met them, a month later, it was much less strained and his sister, Julia, immediately broke the ice by asking,

"When your stepdad murdered his partner, was it in the papers?"

I told her it was. She wanted to know then if I always knew he was a 'wrong un'. Her mother told her that was enough but I smiled and said, yes, I had always known he was a very bad man from the way he treated me and my Mum. There was a short silence broken by Rob who announced that I had just started working in the Merrion Centre for the Yorkshire Electricity Board. His Dad followed his lead in the change of conversation and said he went to The Highlander Pub in the centre with friends from work sometimes.

"Robert tells me you live in Bramley," his mother said, "Walt and me go to the Bramley Band Club sometimes on a Saturday. Have you been in there?"

"Not yet, I don't go out much, well not before I met Rob," I gave a little laugh.

"We've been in the Elder Road Club a couple of times; it's only round the corner from Rose's house." He beamed at me with a nod.

"Do you take your kid with you?" Julia asked abruptly. I took a deep breath and, seeing her antagonistic smile, turned my own smile up to gas mark 8.

"No, I know they allow children in the concert room on a Saturday night but I think Angela is too young just yet."

"Angela, what a pretty name, how old is she?" Mrs Morgan asked warmly.

"She's six," I replied.

"And where's her Dad?" Julia asked.

"Julia!" Rob and his mother both snapped at the same time.

"I have no idea," I said, raising both my hands and keeping my smile firmly in place, "He left me when I was pregnant and I haven't seen or heard from him since."

"Oh my goodness, that is so terrible, you poor thing." Mrs Morgan tilted her head towards me, "Anyway, that's enough interrogation," glaring at her daughter, "so who would like some more tea?"

As Rob and I were leaving, Julia followed us to the door and asked if I thought the trial and stuff would be available on microfiche in the library. I said it probably would and she said she'd go and see at the weekend. Then she gave me a narrow-eyed smile and said, "You're not much like his last girlfriend." Which I took as a compliment and said so, although I was fairly sure she had not meant it as one.

I think the best way for me to describe my relationship with Rob was as a whirlwind romance that, because of my circumstances, became a long courtship. As my feelings for him got stronger and became more apparent, I took the next step and introduced him to Angela.

We met him in the cafe in Woolworths in Leeds and were already seated when he arrived. I could tell immediately from his expression and forced smile that he was nervous. When I mentioned this to him some months later, he laughed.

"Course I was nervous, this was a potential deal breaker if she decided she didn't like me."

Angela was uncharacteristically shy for the first ten minutes but cheered up when her banana milkshake and a heavily buttered toasted teacake arrived. Rob sat down next to me and opposite her, putting a small plate with a big slice of Victoria sponge and a mug down before smiling at her as he said hello. She murmured a very quiet hello in response, her eyes only briefly flicking towards him before resting on the cake. I gave him a smile and he nodded and picked up his coffee, purposely tipping it too high while leaning into the wide mug to coat the tip of his nose in the chocolate-sprinkled froth from his cappuccino. Putting it back on the table he asked Angela what her favourite fruit was. Lifting her gaze, she noticed the froth and pressed her lips together unsure if she should laugh.

"What?" he declared, innocently looking from her to me and back again, "I haven't got something on my face have I?"

"Yes you have!" she declared with a giggle.

"Goodness me!" He pulled a clean white handkerchief from his pocket and deliberately wiped everywhere except his nose, causing much hilarity. Finally, he rubbed the chocolate off and said, "That teacake looks good," pointing at her plate, "I think I might have one of those."

"You can have some of mine if you want," she said, still laughing.

"Well, that would be lovely, if you're sure, but then I think I'll have to offer to share my cake with you." As she nodded enthusiastically, I knew it was going to be alright.

## Thirty One

On a warm summer evening in 1983, when Gloria was staying with me for a few days, I sat her down with a glass of Blue Nun and told her I had been to see a solicitor about divorcing Darren. It was almost eight years, I explained, since he had walked out and, although I had no plans to remarry, her eyebrows raised slightly as I said this, I'd decided being a divorced woman would be more preferable to being an abandoned one.

She surprised me by agreeing, saying, "Aye lass, you're right, if he's not come back by now, he's never coming back." She touched the corner of her eye with her cardigan sleeve before lifting her glass and taking a sip, allowing the wine to help her swallow her sadness.

I explained the process, I had to prove I had done everything I could to try and find him and asked her if she had any idea, any at all, where he might have gone. I watched her closely as she took another sip of her drink, avoiding my gaze, but I could see her thoughts playing out on her face. Then, making her decision, she lied to me again. I accepted the lie and asked her to provide me with a letter stating she had no idea where he was and had also had no contact with him. After the briefest pause, she agreed.

Before going up to bed, she told me she was sorry for what her son had done and hoped that she'd made up for the pain and upset he had caused me. She said she thought of me as a daughter and Davy as a son, a good son, and always would. I told her I found it hard to believe that someone as kind as her could have had a son like Darren.

"You shouldn't ever think you have to make up for what he did and how he behaved. You have been brilliant to me and Davy and Angela. I honestly don't know how I would have coped without you."

"Do you think you'll marry Robert?" she asked, after giving me a hug, "I mean he's a nice lad, a hard worker and he's good with Angela," giving a false chuckle to hide how awkward she felt, "and of course Davy would love to have him as a brother-in-law. You know he's worried about how you're coping since he went off to Liverpool."

"Well, apart from not being eaten out of house and home or having to keep putting the seat down on the loo, I think I'm doing okay," I laughed, "but please don't think I want this divorce because I want to marry Rob, or anybody else for that matter. I just want to be able to finally end the uncertainty. And maybe it will help you as well." I moved my head to get her to look at me, "Cos he's not coming back, you know that don't you?"

She nodded and blinked quickly.

"It's been eight years," I said quietly, "I don't want to be the abandoned wife anymore."

She nodded again and hugged me before pulling away with a sniff and asking me if I'd like some hot chocolate before bed. I declined but offered to make some which she also declined and, touching my shoulder, she said she was going up. I watched her turn towards the stairs with not quite a smile but a look of poignant acceptance.

I had Gloria's letter and had completed all the forms given to me by the solicitor Miss Alderson had recommended; *"He's an old friend who helped me when my father got a bit uppity, he'll sort it out for you"*. He told me that, as I didn't have any address for Darren to send the divorce petition or the dissolution request to and there was no evidence of him contacting anyone else, it would actually be quicker to petition for a presumption of death.

This meant I would have the documentation that would allow me to remarry but would not provide me with a death certificate so I wouldn't be able to apply for probate of Darren's estate or finances. He quickly added that from what he understood of my errant husband, this would not be an issue for me. He told me I could have a day or so to think about it but I said I didn't need to as I did, indeed, presume he was dead.

I had the paperwork six weeks later. I never told Gloria and she never mentioned it again. It was as though Darren had never existed and all I felt was relief. I didn't tell anyone at all that I was now legally separated from him and I didn't change my name.

As the months went by, it became clear that Rob thought our relationship was long term and I felt the same although I still tried outwardly to remain slightly detached. I remember thinking about Mum a lot during that time, about how different things could have been for her and me if only she had chanced on the right man. That's what I think life is actually, pure chance. Right time, right place, turning the right corner, catching the right train....

Our relationship blossomed and continued to bloom and I finally admitted to myself I was in love with him and that thought terrified me. I began to worry that for the first time in my life I might not be in control of my feelings and because of this, when he asked me to marry him the weekend before our second Christmas, I turned him down.

I knew by then he was the love of my life and Angela adored him, but it was a fear of getting it wrong that was blurring my inner vision, a fear I was reliving the past in a different role.

Even though his proposal was not really unexpected, we'd been out for a walk during an afternoon at Bramley Fall woods, it did bring me up short. It was a crisp and bright December day and Davy was due home that evening. We had brought one of Angela's friends with us, a girl that lived down the street, and they were running around ahead of us as we walked hand in hand. He was talking about how much he loved Christmas and how, when he was younger, his family celebrated two Christmas days. This was a tradition adapted by his mother from her own childhood in Holland. On December 5th, there would be a parade through the town when Sinterklass would ride through the streets giving out sweets and presents to the children. He was aided by an odd looking character named Black Pete who resembled a sinister chimney sweep.

"In the one year we actually went to Amsterdam," said Rob, "I was ten and Julia was four. Mum had built it up to be this fabulous event and of course, at the mention of sweets and presents, we were both up for it." He gave an uncomfortable chuckle, "But there were hundreds, thousands of people lining the streets and the kids were running and jumping about trying to catch the sweets being thrown into the crowds and we were being jostled and pushed, it was quite terrifying. Julia was crying and I wasn't feeling that brave myself." He took in a deep breath, "Then we saw Zwarte Piet - Black Pete - looming over us. There were actually loads of them, men with blackened clown faces carrying big sticks to whack the naughty children with and a bag of sweets for the good ones. Mum, totally oblivious to our petrified state, casually told us that in her day, he carried off the really naughty children in his sack."

"Bloody hell!" I exclaimed, making Angela stop and turn round. I gave her a smile and she went back to skipping after her friend, "That sounds like a horror film."

"Yeah, I don't think Mum ever really knew how scared we were, it's a Dutch thing," he shrugged, "Anyway, she now has her own Sinterklass celebration on Boxing Day."

"Please tell me Black Pete or Zwarty whatever is not part of it!" I said quickly and in a higher voice than I intended. Angela and I had been invited to Rob's parents' house for her traditional Dutch celebration. I had been expecting waffles, pickled herrings and Advocaat.

"Definitely no Black Pete," he laughed, "but poor old Dad does still have to don the wig, beard and robes to bring in the presents before we eat."

"Okay," I said, my pulse returning to normal, "that sounds okay."

"Yeah, it will be good, Mum's keen to impress you," taking my hand, "just like I am."

"You do, all the time," I smiled.

"Will you marry me then?" He said looking into my eyes.

"Oh Rob," I said, in a tone that foreshadowed my answer, "It's not that I don't love you, it's just still early days..." I trailed off, expecting him to tell me we had been going out for over two years but he didn't. He hugged me and told me he understood and was delighted to hear that I loved him and he would wait for as long as it took for me to be sure.

"Maybe next year we could spend the whole of Christmas together," he said, releasing me and continuing to walk then catching my hand in his again.

"Next year?" I laughed, "Let's get this one over with first." This was going to be the first Christmas Day I was doing the cooking. As well as Davy, I had invited Gill and Roy as well as Gloria and Miss Alderson. Rob was coming late morning but leaving mid afternoon to eat a second dinner with his parents and sister in the evening. "I'm going to be the size of the Honey Monster by New Year," he laughed.

One of the many things I loved about him was that he never once said he was going to look after me. Instead, he said we were a great team and joked about my brains and his beauty making us perfect for each other.

The following summer, Davy announced that once he'd finished his final exams, he was going island hoping in Greece with three of his friends. They would be away for six weeks before he started a job he'd secured for himself in the computing department at Royal Insurance in Liverpool. Apart from telling me this much, he was a little scarce on the details, which obviously stressed me out. Rob said he would take him out for a few beers when he came home at Easter and see what he could find out, which he did.

When they came back from the pub, Rob excused himself saying he had to get back for something but would be back in the morning. As I saw him to the door, he quietly told me to listen to what my very sensible and clever brother had to say.

Over cheese and crackers, he told me he was sorry he'd upset me but he was desperate to show me he was a grown up now. He knew he had lots to thank me for but he really needed to fly the nest.

"I promise, even if I don't live here, I'll visit loads," he said, trying to keep his voice light, "You have been more than a sister to me and God knows what my life would have been like if you weren't there, you always made everything alright." He wiped something from the corner of one of his eyes, "You've done so much for me but it's time now for you to get on with your life."

He had met a girl, Sandy from Newcastle, and she was one of the four, the other two being another couple, who were going on this adventure. He told me if it all went well he'd bring her to meet me but it was early days yet. He had no doubt he would get a first in his degree and had a few ideas about what he wanted to do next but wanted to stay in Liverpool for the time being. I managed really well to keep myself calm and convince myself that he was indeed clever and sensible and it was time for us both to move on.

Five weeks later, he phoned me from Speke Airport to say he was on his way to Mykonos. I phoned Rob and asked him if he fancied going to the Greek restaurant in Leeds the next night.

It was early in June of 1984, Scorpio's Taverna in the Merion Centre. After two glasses of Retsina, I spontaneously said that if the offer was still on the table, I would love to marry him. We were pulled to our feet by the waiters to join in doing the Hasapiko to Zorba The Greek after which we were given extra shots of ouzo and congratulated by everyone in the restaurant.

He stayed over at my house that night. This was something that rarely happened, as he was as keen as I was not give Angela the wrong or actually, as it turns out, the right impression. Before we fell asleep, he asked me if I would consider allowing him to officially adopt Angela once we were married. I said I needed to think about that one and talk to her about it and also, of course, talk to Gloria.

At eight years old, my daughter was remarkably sensible when I broached the subject with her. She asked what it would mean and what would change. I explained it meant Rob wanted her to be his daughter and I didn't think much would change except our second names. At the time, I was not as succinct as that, I was quite emotional and struggling not to sob, I was so happy he wanted us to be a proper family. The only questions she asked were; could she still have the same second name as me even if she didn't want to be adopted, which I agreed she could, and would she have to call him Dad or could she carry on calling him Rob. I said she could call him whatever she wanted as long as she didn't swear and was always polite. Finally, she asked if it would make me happy, this is the point at which I almost lost it. I said it would make me happy but l would still be happy if she did not want it. Smiling and nodding her head, she said in a very serious tone, that she wanted to think about it for a bit and would let me know. I hugged her, which she allowed for a second, before pulling herself away and going back to her Sindy dolls.

Even though I was dreading the conversation with Gloria, it went much better than I thought. She actually said it made sense for Angela to change her name and was happy for me that I had found such a good man that clearly thought the world of us and took his responsibilities seriously. When I told Rob, he was delighted, even though Angela was still thinking about it.

My daughter helped me to pick my ivory silk dress and a small flower garland for my hair. Miss Alderson had come with us and insisted on paying for it along with the pale pink satin bridesmaid dress that Angela had struggled to take her eyes off. When she tried it on, I felt a well of tears threaten to spoil my makeup as a memory of that old wedding picture forced itself into my mind.

"She looks so pretty in pink," the shop assistant said, sensing an additional sale, "It looks like it was made for her."

"I agree," Miss Alderson said firmly, "and you obviously need a bridesmaid."

Gloria had declined the invite to come shopping but she assured me it was because of a prearranged seaside trip with Betty.

Once the decision to get married was made, there didn't seem to be any point in waiting and we were to be married at the end of August, 1984, in Leeds Registry Office. There would be more than double the guests at this celebration than at my first wedding and Rob's Mum had arranged and paid for a reception in the upstairs room of Bramley Home Bakeries on Stanningley Road.

Although the wedding was far from formal, I had a bridesmaid and Davy - he'd decided against Dave - was Rob's best man. Towards the end of the meal Rob stood up and tapped his teacup with a spoon. Once he had everyone's attention, he explained that he wasn't going to make a speech but he did want to say a few words.

"I would like to thank you all for coming today to join us in our celebrations and I would especially like thank my lovely Rose for finally agreeing to take me on." This was met with laugher and cheers and my new husband beamed.

"But I would also like to thank two other people. Firstly, my new brother-in-law Davy for his friendship and his immense patience in teaching me how to play chess." My brother's embarrassed delight was obvious by the redness of his face as he smiled broadly before quickly looking down at his plate again. He had recently broken up with Sandy who he claimed had become too bossy.

"And also, of course, I'd like to thank our beautiful bridesmaid Angela Amy, not only for looking almost as lovely as her Mum but for giving us both the best wedding present ever by saying she is happy to be my daughter as well." Lots more cheering and even a bit of whooping and a very smug looking bridesmaid stood up and took a little bow, her cheeks as pink as her dress.

I watched his parents' reaction and was relieved to see they looked as pleased as everyone else. However, Julia, sitting between her father and my brother was looking far from happy. Her eyes first widened in shock but then narrowed as she looked over at Angela. She did have the good grace to try and disguise her feelings with a smile and raise her glass at the toast but, like Gloria, she would never have made a poker player.

The majority of the wedding party went on to the Elder Road Club where there was a group playing. Angela stayed to see the first set but Gloria took her home when the bingo started, even though Angela claimed she wasn't a bit tired. Rob insisted on walking back with them telling me to stay and enjoy myself. When he returned, most of us had moved into the juke box room; we were too loud and boisterous for the regulars in the concert room. Even though there was nowhere near the amount of alcohol consumed as at my first wedding, everyone was in the best of spirits and love was definitely all around.

The only slightly off moment came when I met Julia in the ladies towards the end of the evening. I had just come out of the cubicle and she was standing in front of the mirror. She was clearly drunk and was holding on to the wash basin.

"Well that's it then, you've got him now, my big brother," she slurred angrily.

"Yes, we are man and wife and very happy," I smiled broadly at her.

She tried to study my expression but her inebriated state meant she was unable to process anything other than what was going on in her own head. After a second, she shook her head, narrowed her eyes and almost spat out the words,

"If you ever hurt him, I promise you, I'll make you pay."

"Noted," I said with a laugh before leaning forward, inches from her face and in a calm but equally threatening voice, I replied,

"But just so you know, I have been threatened by some very nasty people in my life and none of them are still alive to tell the tale."

I turned and left her there, her confused expression confirming she really had no idea who she was dealing with.

I went directly to find Rob and told him what she had said, not what I'd replied of course, and how I couldn't understand why she wanted to be so antagonistic. He said she was terrible when she'd been drinking and generally ended up crying so I shouldn't take it to heart. Then he told me that his Mum had just told him that she had been sulky about not being asked to be a bridesmaid.

"Oh no..!" I shook my head, "I wish she'd have said, I mean, I hadn't planned on having any bridesmaids so didn't really think…"

"It's okay, Julia is just being Julia and not happy that she wasn't the centre of attention," he said, pulling me in for a cuddle.

"She is very drunk," I smiled and snuggled into his embrace, "She probably won't remember it in the morning so I'm not going to let it spoil our day."

He gave me a quick squeeze before releasing me and saying she was well out of order and he would have a word with her. I'm not sure if he did as it was never mentioned again but my relationship with Julia moved from cordial to barely civil after that and remained that way for the duration.

We talked at length about where we were going to live. Rob felt uncomfortable moving into my house and wanted us both to sell up so we could buy something together. I was reluctant to move out of my lovely Spring Valley home and tried to explain that it was the first place I had lived that had no bad or sad memories and it was still Davy's home too even though he was living in Liverpool.

In the end he sold his house, put the money in our joint saving account and moved in with me but would not let me put him on the deeds of my house, repeating what I had said, that it was Davy's home too and he did not want to seem like he was taking over.

As soon as the adoption was complete, Rob arranged a party, after asking me if it was okay but insisting that becoming a father for the first time was something he was desperate to celebrate. It was mostly family and close friends apart from Julia who declined the invite, saying she had something else on.

Luckily, the weather was dry and not too cold for our guests to spill out into the back garden. My new mother-in-law made a cake with about a dozen candles on, insisting Angela and Rob needed to blow them out together. It was a wonderful afternoon.

## Thirty Two

Nicholas was born the day before Christmas Eve the following year and, as I watched Angela holding him, I saw the echoes of my past and hoped that my children would have as strong a bond as Davy and I had.

My brother kept his word and visited us regularly, occasionally bringing a girlfriend but always claiming it wasn't serious. All of them bright and lovely young women but none of them lasting long.

Towards the end of 1988, he was head hunted by a big Canadian IT firm in Ottawa. He was always vague about the name of the company but I was fairly sure it was something to do with defence. Rob joked about him now being part of the brain drain but agreed it was an amazing opportunity, adding he could only dream of anyone thinking *he* was smart enough to be headhunted.

Obviously, I was delighted for him, I had always believed him to be a genius but also sad that he would be a minimum of twelve hours and two connecting flights away. When he told me about it, he had already accepted the job but hastened to say that his plan was to go for two years. I made a conscious effort to only show my pride and delight and to help Angela come to terms with him going. She very dramatically announced that her heart was broken and she would never get over her 'favourite person in the whole world' going to live so far away and who she probably would never see again. I told her he would be back in two years and tried to make the prospect of writing letters to him sound exciting which she didn't buy for one minute. Rob managed to cheer her up explaining that instead of letters we could message him with emails on our Commodore 64 computer.

Davy's move half way round the world was followed three days later by Gloria passing away which made a difficult time almost unbearable. It was very sudden; she had not been ill and had seemed absolutely fine when we had spoken on the phone two days earlier.

Betty called me just after nine in the morning, struggling to get her words out through her upset. I could hear voices in the background and she managed to tell me she had called an ambulance and two paramedics were with her; they had to stay until the police arrived.

As soon as I hung up, I called Miss Alderson who said she would go straight round and see what she could do. She told me to call Rob and to stay where I was,

"I'll call as soon as I know anything. You go and give that little boy of yours a cuddle and wait for Robert to come home. There will be things for you to do once you've got over the shock."

Betty had found her when she'd taken her a cup of tea up. They had been out the evening before, playing bingo, and she had refused her cocoa when they got in and mentioned a headache but nothing more.

I crumbled at the thought of telling Davy and so Rob called him, even though it cost a fortune to make the transatlantic call. To allow for the time difference, he phoned before he went to work the next morning. Gloria had been good to all of us and had done her best to fill the gap left by Nana and definitely had a soft spot for my little brother. Rob explained that she had died peacefully and suddenly in her sleep and had not suffered and, no, there was no need for him to come back for her funeral.

In yet another visit to Crigglestone Crematorium, I managed to hold it together and, against my better judgment, Angela came and sat between Rob and me and wept silently, holding both our hands as Doris Day sang Que Sera Sera.

After only one of his two year 'trial period' in Canada, Davy told us he absolutely loved his new life and had decided to stay indefinitely. It was just after Christmas, 1989, and he sugar-coated this decision by promising to come back for a few weeks in the spring. He also admitted he was currently sharing his wonderful new life with a young lady called Celeste. She was French Canadian and they had been friends for a little while but had started being serious six months before and he would be bringing her to meet us.

As soon as I got off the phone, I told Rob that he needed to go into Thomas Cook's with me that weekend so we could book our flights to go and see him straight away and not wait the three months for him to come to us. Rob suggested we wait a while, maybe look at something during the summer holidays so Angela didn't miss any school, or – at this point he raised a finger,

"If we wait till after they have been to see us, we'll get an idea of just how serious he is about her, maybe we could be going over for a wedding before the end of the year."

It turned out that's more or less what happened. Davy brought Celeste over to meet us at the end of March and stayed for three weeks. Two days before they flew back, he asked her to marry him. She was lovely and I could see immediately they were both completely besotted with each other and Angela was captivated by her exotic French accent which she tried to copy, much to everyone's amusement. Celeste was also a champion chess player and extremely bright. I liked her instantly.

Davy had bought the diamond solitaire engagement ring in Canada, which was just as well as it was a little large for her finger and would need altering when they got home. He told us that he had asked her father's permission and he had laughed and said, '*Just as long as you know what you're letting yourself in for, you have my blessing,*' before slapping him on the back and shaking his hand.

They planned their wedding for the end of the following summer and Celeste asked Angela to be a bridesmaid when they phoned to give us the date a month later. However, we had quite a lot going on ourselves at the time.

Although he wasn't headhunted, Rob was offered a job with IBM which he was both delighted and concerned about. It was a great job, a promotion, very good pay and prospects, but it was in Portsmouth.

I could see the anxiety in his face as he told me about it, assuming I would be horrified at the thought of moving away and would refuse. I surprised him and myself by agreeing it was great opportunity for him and also for our family and so in the summer of 1990 we moved to the south coast and, even though secretly I did have my doubts, it turned out to be one of the best decisions we made.

We were both worried about how the move would affect Angela though. She had just turned fourteen and was struggling with teenage hormones, spots and the fact that she couldn't decide who she loved more, Matt or Luke Goss, aka the pop band Bros. Rob and I found this to be hilarious as these boys were twins and almost identical. We were driven crazy listening to 'When Will I Be Famous?' and 'I Owe You Nothing' played over and over again as she lay on her bed, pretending to be doing homework while staring at the posters of on her wall.

I knew telling her about the decision to move away from all her friends and the only home she had known, to start again over two hundred miles away, would be tricky so I called Miss Alderson. She came over on a 'spontaneous' visit, bringing with her photographs from her previous year's holiday in Bournemouth. It had been a coach trip with lots of sightseeing including a day in Portsmouth to see the Mary Rose, a 16th century warship which had been salvaged and was being preserved, along with lots of artefacts and information about its history. Angela was not massively academic but she liked school and her favourite subject was history, particularly the Tudors and Stuarts.

"Apparently, Henry VIII named the Mary Rose after his favourite sister," Miss Alderson told her "and he was standing just here." She showed her a picture of a lighthouse in front of a fortress where she stood smiling into the camera. "It's Southsea Castle, one of the coastal fortresses Henry built to guard us from a French invasion."

"One of how many?" quizzed Angela.

"Well, I'm not altogether sure but I think our guide told us there are a chain of them all along the south coast. I expect your teacher could give you more information." She continued showing us the rest of her snaps, all of which involved some lovely coastline or interesting landmarks. I left the two of them chatting as I went to make us some tea and see how Rob was getting on helping Nicky build his Brio train track along the hall, his favourite place to play.

After lunch, before Rob drove our guest back home, we told Angela we were going to move to this history rich coast. Looking from me to Rob and then to Miss Alderson, she lowered her gaze to her knees. I quickly said we would hopefully move during the summer holidays so that she started her new school at the start of the academic year. Rob shuffled uncomfortably in his seat but didn't speak.

"Is it definitely happening?" she finally asked.

"Well I've accepted the job," Rob said quickly, "I start in two weeks time. I'll stay in digs somewhere down there and find out about the area and the schools."

"Yes," I cut in, "Nicky will be starting school in September as well."

"So we're selling the house?" she asked me.

"Yes, there's an estate agent coming round on Monday."

"Right," she sighed and looked at Miss Alderson, "What do you think?"

"I think it sounds like quite an adventure," she replied, nodding her head, "and I shall enjoy coming to see you and exploring the area with you and hearing about all your discoveries."

I can't say that Angela was excited by the move, she very obviously was not, but she accepted her fate in a slightly martyred manner. On her last day at Hough Side, she was asked to stand up in assembly while the deputy head, who was also her history teacher, said he spoke for the whole school in wishing her well at her new school. He was sure she would be just as happy and popular as she had been there. Her face was tear-stained and blotchy when she came home and she went straight to her room. I went up after a few minutes expecting her to tell me go away and leave her alone but she surprised me by folding into me when I sat on her bed beside her and letting me cuddle and rock her gently.

Our house sold quickly and Rob found us a lovely new home in Locks Heath, Hampshire. He wanted me to go down with him one week to see the house for myself but I had not wanted to leave the children and so, instead, agreed I would leave it to him, my only stipulation was it had to have three bedrooms. The difference in house prices in the north south divide had really shocked me and I was worried about what we could afford but I need not have been. The sale of the Spring Valley House and Rob's considerable savings gave us a substantial deposit and IBM not only covered most of our moving expenses, they also offered a preferential interest rate mortgage. When he told me that, I asked if he was sure he hadn't been headhunted.

He brought photographs of the new house when he came home the following weekend and we were astounded at how wonderful it looked. Our *four* bedroom house was in a leafy suburb, set back from the tree lined avenue by a circular drive. It was a white, twin gabled detached house with leaden bay windows and a good sized enclosed back garden that looked overgrown but had two lovely trees at the bottom and backed on to fields behind a thick laurel hedge.

"It looks great!" Angela couldn't help but comment.

"The nearest secondary school's about twenty minutes' walk away," Rob told her, "and the infant school is even closer and in the same direction."

Our leaving day was extremely emotional, almost everyone cried, even me. Gill and Roy promised they'd come and visit once we'd had a chance to get settled and Miss Alderson hugged me so tight just before I got into the car, whispering in my ear that life was again giving me another chance to reinvent myself.

"You can be whoever you want to be. Just be happy."

I could see her smiling face as I turned to wave. Angela was still trying to stifle her sobs, Rob unable to speak for the lump in his throat and Nicky not quite sure what was happening but feeling awash with everyone else's emotions. I was sitting in the back with him, allowing Angela to sit in the front, riding shotgun as she called it, the large road atlas on her lap to trace our predicted six hour journey.

## Thirty Three

We spent the first night in a hotel in Southampton as the removal lorry with all our belongings wasn't meeting us at the house until the next morning. Nicholas had slept for a lot of the journey down but woke up when we stopped about halfway at a Happy Eater restaurant. Always a good eater, he ate his body weight in fish and chips, but Angela only picked at her chicken burger sulkily. The reality of leaving her friends had become heavier with every passing mile.

Her sulk lasted right up until we pulled up in the drive outside our new home the next day. As she got out of the car, just ahead of me, her curiosity and excitement took over. The furniture hadn't arrived and so we wandered through the large empty rooms, each one making me gasp at the tasteful decor and space. When we got upstairs, there was a bigger surprise; not all the rooms were empty. Angela's room had been decorated and furnished in a style that any teenage girl would be delighted with; pastel shades and white furniture, a bed with a pale pink canopy and bedding to match the curtains. There was even a kidney shaped dressing table with three oval mirrors with ornate gold edging that was practically a copy of the one she had for her Sindy dolls.

"Wow, is this really all mine?" she asked with delight.

"Yes, it is, I hope it'll go some way to making it up to you for the move..." Rob started to say but she interrupted him with a massive hug.

"It's perfect, thank you so much." She glanced at me and I told her it was as much a surprise to me, Rob had done this on his own.

We settled in quickly. Rob had a week off to help us explore the area and show us where all the local amenities and shops were and our new neighbours called round to welcome us.

## Everything in the Garden

In the last week of the summer holidays, Miss Alderson came down for a few days and we had a day out visiting the Mary Rose, Southsea and Calshot Castles, where Angela inquired about getting a Saturday job with National Heritage. She had not made any friends of her own age yet and I was sure she was starting to feel uneasy about the new school year.

On her first day, which luckily was the day before Nicholas started school for the first time, we all three walked with her. Rob stayed outside the gates with Nicky while I went in with her, as instructed, to the admin office. We were both welcomed warmly and two very smiley girls who were to be her class mates were brought in to help her acclimatise and navigate her way around.

I left her looking slightly anxious but with almost a smile on her face. Rob went off to work and I took Nicky home and spent most of the next six and a half hours glancing at the telephone and hoping the school didn't ring which, of course, they did not.

Nicky and I were waiting at the gates for her at three thirty and she came out with a small group of girls, smiling and chatting, and I finally allowed my own nerves to settle. The next day she walked with me as far as the infant school where she met one of her class mates who she walked the rest of her way with. I got to stay for the first half hour with my son as part of his settling in period but he wasn't remotely interested in me being there, so keen was he to explore his surroundings and play in the sand tray, that he hardly gave me a backward glance when I left.

I spent the rest of that day cleaning the house to within an inch of its life, not that it really needed it and I ate nearly a whole packet of digestive biscuits while drinking copious amounts of tea. The following day after the school run, I went to the library and did a little bit of shopping, picking up a copy of the local newspaper; it was time for me to find something to do in this new life.

I applied for three jobs that evening and posted the applications off the next day. I only heard back from two but both invited me for an interview. One was at a firm of accountants as a receptionist and the other was in the promotional department of the local newspaper. While I was waiting for the interview date, we had a visit from Rob's parents and Julia. They stayed for two nights and were very complimentary about the house. Julia barely spoke to me or Angela, except when absolutely necessary, but made a big fuss of Nicholas and was all smiles for her brother. Angela, I noticed, just ignored her in return and was extra warm towards her adopted grandparents, clearly annoying Julia and making me so proud of her.

Just before they left, they asked if we might go up to them for Christmas. This had not occurred to me so I said nothing. Rob said that he'd like to have our first Christmas in our new home but we might go up at Easter. I felt a flood of relief but that was short lived as he said they would be very welcome to come to us if they wanted. Thankfully they declined.

I decided during the interview at the accountants that I did not want that job, which was just as well as I wasn't offered it, but I was offered the position of admin assistant in the newspaper sales and promotions department of the Portsmouth News. I was to join a team of five in their newly refurbished offices at Hilsea and my name changed back to Rosie again when my new boss, Simon, who had interviewed me, introduced me to everyone and gave me a pile of business cards with Rosie Morgan printed on them.

Our first southern Christmas was magical and the first of many. The following summer we flew from Heathrow to Canada for Davy and Celeste's wedding. We were there for the week before the celebrations and then went on a mini tour for two weeks afterwards while the newlyweds went on honeymoon.

My little brother, now a very fine young man, and his very lovely wife, went on to have two boys in the next three years, although we didn't actually meet them until the eldest was almost school age but we kept in regular contact, our family bond so strong, it easily survived the distance.

Julia came to visit a year or so later with her fiancé, a lovely guy named Alan who she had known for only eight weeks but she was telling everyone he was the one. The first time I met him with his beaming smile, I did a double take; he bore more than just a passing resemblance to my husband. They could have been related. I managed not to say anything but I could see Rob noticed too.

They were married six months later in a lavish ceremony in Leeds Minster followed by a reception at the very posh Parkway Hotel in Adel. She had six bridesmaids; two of Alan's sisters, two friends and two ten year old girls who were distant cousins. She asked Nicholas to be a page boy but when Rob explained what this entailed, he flatly refused, saying there was no way he was dressing up in a sailor suit or a tartan skirt.

Years later he admitted that by that time he had started to 'detest' his aunty, seeing how mean she always was to Angela, and although his sister had told him she didn't mind, he said he minded very much.

Our visits up north became scarcer as the years went on and when Rob's parents died within three months of each other in 2010 we only went back once more, for yet another funeral. In 2012, Miss Alderson died quietly at her home after watching nineteen year old Jonnie Peacock win a gold medal in the London Paralympics. I know this because she had tried to call me afterwards, leaving us a message on our answer phone, she knew we were there, all four of us in the stadium, and was calling to let us know she'd been watching. She ended the call with "Right, I'm off up to bed now, I'll catch up with you at the weekend."

Sitting in that Yorkshire crematorium for the last time with all the ghosts of my past, I thought about how lucky I was that this wonderful woman had come into my life. She had made her own provision and arrangements for her funeral. She wanted no mention of God, always a woman of science, and the celebrant opened her eulogy by telling us that Judith Pamela Alderson had left strict instructions for there to be no sadness at her passing, only love and gratitude for a life well lived. After highlighting her many achievements, she finished with her own version of an old poem,

"I'd like you all to remember me with warmth, for your memories of me to be happy and for the smiles to leave an afterglow of love now my life is done. I'd like to leave an echo, whispering softly down the ways, of happy times and laughing times and bright and sunny days."

She also chose three almost jolly songs, all of which I cried through, but as we came back out into the sunshine after passing her coffin, I felt a rush of warmth surround my heart.

She had left her house and considerable savings to Angela and Nicholas, something I had expected her do. However, the actual value of her estate did take me by surprise. I knew in her later years she had enjoyed good holidays and had certainly not lived a frugal life but apparently she had invested well. Her solicitors were instructed to sell the house and contents after we had taken anything we wanted and then for the money to be held in trust, still earning interest for when they each turned twenty one.

Our lives continued happily back on the south coast as the children grew bigger and we all got older. We had plenty of family holidays, visiting Davy a couple of times, annual two week trips abroad and odd weeks in Cornwall, Pembrokeshire and the Isle of Wight, our three favourite places.

We both enjoyed doing a bit in the garden and Rob decided he wanted to create a small rose garden, for me, with an arch and trellis along the back fence and maybe a patio with benches and chairs. However, we never seemed to get round to starting it and the roses he planted kept dying or getting black spot when he put them in the ground. We did have a very thriving wisteria that I said we could train to go over an arch but he said he wasn't giving up on the rose garden idea and maybe, when we both retired, we could get a proper landscaper in.

Angela went to University in Kent, the one Davy had been interested in all those years ago, before going travelling for a year with two of her university friends. She came home for a few months before starting a job in London working for the BBC, where she met Steve who she married two years later. They moved to Southampton after Olivia was born and another granddaughter, Amalee came along within a year. Rob and I couldn't wait to retire so we could help with the childcare and start making more happy memories for the next generation.

Nicholas went to Saint Martin's College of Art and Design where he met Angus who became his partner both in business and life. He had come out to us when he was sixteen. It was no great surprise but it was a massive relief that he had finally felt he could tell us. Angela said she'd always known, probably even before he knew himself. She and Steve were massive fans of Angus, who apart from co-running their design business, sang and played the guitar in pubs and clubs around London.

And that is where I would really have liked my story to end; my husband and I fading gently together as we watched our family grow. However, real life is not a fairy tale. In real life, there are just more stories.

## Thirty Four

Our happy ever after lasted more than thirty five years in all with lots more joyful stories before fate took a turn and my luck ran out.

It was less than six months ago that our world changed, on a cold and grey Wednesday afternoon in April. I had just got home from the shops and was in a slightly irritable mood, tutting as I shook the fine drizzle from my hair. The rain had started before breakfast, it was far from an April shower and more like February mizzle. Walking into the kitchen, I saw Rob sitting in the conservatory as I continued chuntering round, taking off my damp outer clothes and finding my slippers.

"Would you like a cuppa?" I asked, finally brightening up as I picked up the kettle. I heard him say something but the fast flow of water from the tap drowned out his words so, after putting the kettle back on its stand and switching it on, I walked through to the conservatory. He was sitting back with his eyes tightly closed and his face creased with pain.

"Oh my goodness what's wrong?" I flew across to the chair opposite and reached out to take his hands.

"I'm not sure," he began, opening his eyes and trying for a smile, "I just feel not right and I have this terrible pain in my stomach." He rubbed his hands over his face before taking a deep breath, "I think perhaps I should ring the doctor." This suggestion threw me into immediate panic.

My husband was rarely ill, in fact in all the time we had lived in Locks Heath he had called upon our local GP services just twice and both times mainly on my insistence. The first time was for a cough that turned into a chest infection and was clearly not going without antibiotics and the second for an angry and painful rash around his upper torso which turned out to be shingles.

He believed quite strongly that being active and eating a good diet kept us both well and he would also have told you, whether or not you'd asked, that the love of a good woman was also a key factor in his robust health. My cheeks would burn when I heard him say this and I would hide my embarrassment by saying if I ever found out who this good woman was, I'd be giving her a piece of my mind.

So his wanting to call the doctor came as a terrifying jolt. I later discovered that there had been other symptoms he had chosen to ignore and not mention. He'd admitted to being tired recently but always had an excuse, he'd done too much hedge trimming, spent too long on the golf course or it was just a sign he might be knocking on a bit. His appetite had been poor as well but nothing too drastic, just feeling full quickly or not that hungry. I sat for a second, staring at his pale face and watery bloodshot eyes, noticing how gaunt he looked and I was filled with dread.

I picked up my phone and called the surgery. After twenty minutes, I finally got to speak to someone and my patience was rewarded with an appointment for the nurse practitioner to see him an hour later. He put up no objections and meekly got into the passenger seat of the car for me to drive him down. He did say he was feeling a little better since having the cup of tea but I didn't believe him.

He'd asked me to go in with him and in fact I could see by the way he held himself that he was still in some pain but I became numb with shock hearing him answer the nurse's questions and telling her his symptoms.

"So how long have you had the pain?"

"On and off for a few weeks but the last couple of days it's got worse and then today it's really bad."

"Is it just in your stomach?"

"No, it seems to be radiating round to my back as well."

"Any sickness or diarrhoea?"

"Not really but I have been off my food and having quite a lot of heartburn."

After a asking him to lay on the couch and undo the top of his trousers, she excused herself for a few moments before coming back with one of the duty doctors who introduced himself but that was one bit of information I didn't hold on to.

After examining his tummy which Rob found painful, he told him he could sit up and refasten his clothes and explained that he wanted to do some tests, blood and urine and then probably a CT scan.

"Do you think it might be gall stones?" my husband asked, revealing to us all he'd been Googling his symptoms.

"Maybe," the doctor said vaguely, "but the tests should give us a better idea of what's going on. Have you lost any weight recently?"

"A bit," he answered with a shrug, "but like I say, I've not had much of an appetite."

"Okay, can you step on the scales for me please?"

As he stood up, I could see how loose his trousers were and I shook my head slowly. He was a stone lighter than he thought and I began silently berating myself for not noticing. He saw me looking and tried to make a joke, saying maybe he should get some braces to hold his trousers up now his beer belly had shrunk a bit but that was greeted with only a tight smile from the physician and nothing from me.

He asked us to come back the next day with a urine sample and for the bloods to be taken before washing his hands and leaving us with the nurse practitioner. She wrote a prescription for a magnesium supplement and some strong painkillers which she said would help with the pain and emailed it straight over to our local chemist.

When we got home, I warmed up some soup I'd made earlier and set the table in the dining room while Rob lit the wood burner in the lounge. We hadn't spoken much since leaving the surgery; he insisted on collecting the prescription himself while I waited in the car, telling me that he was already feeling better but his face told a different story. He opened the box of Co-codamol as soon as we got in and took two with a large glass of water. I pointedly closed his laptop, which was still open on the table in the conservatory, and put it at the side of his chair, telling him he was not to look up his symptoms again. He smiled and said from what he had already read, it was most probably gall stones which could be zapped by a laser if they didn't pass normally.

After we finished our meal, as per our usual routine, I sent him into the sitting room to switch on the TV and see what was on while I cleared the table. He had eaten most of the soup but not touched the crusty roll and refused anything else, saying he'd have yoghurt or something later.

Neither of us slept well that night, mostly because the three glasses of water Rob had drunk and the diuretic magnesium supplement which had increased his normal one or two trips to the loo to four or five and he never was able to get in and out of bed quietly. The next morning, he insisted that all the fluid had helped, *'probably starting to flush the little buggers out already'* and the pain was much easier, as he filled another large glass with water.

The sun wasn't shining but it was dry as I drove him to the surgery for his blood test. While he went in, I walked across to the small supermarket to buy bananas and wholegrain bread; I had been on Google myself while he was in the shower.

Once he was done, we took a detour on the way home and went for a short stroll round Holly Hill Park. This was something we did regularly and always gave us a much needed bit of calm as the trees performed their magic, decreasing our blood pressure and lowering our stress levels. He was still in some pain but said it wasn't constant and he did seem to be getting a bit of colour back.

That afternoon, I did a bit of tidying up in the garden and the sight of new shoots already on the potted roses and clematis made me smile. By the time we got ready for bed that night, we were almost back to our normal chatty selves, making plans to host a family roast dinner at the weekend.

It was the day after the very nice roast lamb with all the trimmings when Rob got the call from the GP. We had been out shopping and, having left his phone at home, it was only while I was making a pot of tea that I registered he was speaking to someone in the conservatory. I waited until I heard him say, thank you and goodbye before walking to the door to look at him with raised eyebrows.

"I've got an appointment at the hospital tomorrow morning at eight for a CT scan," he said in an even; almost matter of fact voice that I knew was forced.

"Eight o'clock, goodness that's early," was all I dared say.

"Yes," he agreed, "no messing about drinking tea in bed and scrolling on our phones." We stood looking at each other for a minute before he shook himself slightly and said he might go and have a lay down upstairs. I told him I'd bring his tea up and went to start putting the shopping away.

The day after the scan, the surgery called again asking us to go down that afternoon and we knew it was bad. We sat together, holding hands, as we listened to our own GP explaining the results of the blood tests and the scan. The incontrovertible diagnosis was that Rob had pancreatic cancer. She looked as sorry as she claimed to be on giving us this news and I wondered how she coped, having to give people such heart breaking information. I took one of the tissues from the box on her desk; I'd noticed them as soon as we walked in. Wiping my eyes and ignoring the mascara, I looked at Rob, who was sitting very still.

"So what happens now? he asked in a voice that was barely a whisper.

"I've referred you to a consultant oncologist in Southampton and you should have an appointment within a couple of days."

After that, everything became torturously surreal as we attempted to negotiate our way around each other, wanting to say so much and managing to say so little. I was trying so hard to be strong for him and agreed not to tell the children until after the appointment with the oncologist but the truth is, I was not strong.

Looking back, I am mortified that I did not do more for him over the week we waited to see the consultant, Mr Wadley. Instead of holding him and talking to him, I busied myself making meals he could barely eat, doing lots of unnecessary washing and ironing and generally trying to pretend that everything would be alright. I talked confidently about stories I'd heard on the radio of people beating cancer and how - *treatment has come such a long way in our life time, it wasn't going to be easy but it would be effective, we just needed to stay positive.* I felt if I kept saying this and thinking it, it would be true and Rob humoured me, nodding and saying, *"Yes you're right, now we know what we're dealing with I'm sure we can get it sorted"* and *"Southampton specialises in cancer treatment so I'm in the best hands."* Both of us clinging to the vain hope that this was true.

The meeting with Mr Wadley took away any hope completely and left us both devastated. Hats off to the man though; he did not fob us off with one of his registrars or hide behind long words or platitudes. Looking Rob fully in the eye and with immense compassion, he gave him a diagnosis as bad as we'd feared and a prognosis which was worse.

He had advanced pancreatic cancer, stage four in fact, sometimes referred to as metastatic pancreatic cancer. This means it had already spread to other parts of the body. In Rob's case it had extended throughout the peritoneal cavity, which is basically most of the organs in the abdomen.

There was some treatment that might slow down any further spread to his bones or lungs, but there was absolutely nothing that could be done to reverse the damage. At this point he leaned forward and took Rob's hand and asked him if he understood. He just nodded and my heart shattered as I saw a tear roll down his cheek. After a few long seconds he managed to ask,

"How long do I have?"

I didn't hear the answer as a sudden scream followed by someone shouting *'no, no, no!'* filled the room and a nurse, who had been sitting just behind me, dashed forward and put her arms around me and, as Rob stood up, his pale face struggling, I realised it was me. He nodded at the nurse and took me in his arms, taking in a massive breath. He released me for a second and said, "Come on now love, let's let this man do his job."

## Thirty Five

The day after the diagnosis, we sat together on the sofa, cosy after a very brief morning walk and he finally spoke about how he felt. We were looking straight ahead, watching the flames in the unnecessarily lit log burner, morphing shapes, colours and dancing images holding our gaze. Neither of us could turn our heads. I knew he didn't want to look at me as I tried to slow my breathing and stay calm.

"I don't have long left and we have to accept that. I don't want to, I don't want to leave you or our wonderful family and the life we've made together but I know it's going to happen, I can't change that," sighing, "but what I can't accept is this erosion of who I am as I die, the indignity of not being able to do anything, of being a burden. I can't accept that and I won't."

I told him he would never be a burden to me and that helping him through this was a privilege and an honour and that I just wanted to be with him, to do whatever he wanted or needed me to. He smiled and nodded.

"We'll see," he said as I snuggled closer to him.

Telling the children was the hardest thing. We'd been given leaflets and advice on how best to impart the news and, helpful as they might have been, it was something neither of us wanted to do and certainly not to see their pain as they heard the news. Rob phoned Angela first and then Nicholas with the same speech.

"This is going to be very hard but I need to tell you something. Please let me finish what I have to say and then take some time to think about it before we talk some more." Angela had merely asked, "Are you okay?"

Nicholas tried to stop the narrative saying, "I knew something wasn't right when we were round for the roast dinner, all that talk about gall stones, it's not that is it?"

"I told you the other week I'd been feeling unwell for a bit, well I've had some tests done and it's actually quite serious." He did not stray from his script; they both got exactly the same words.

"I have stage four pancreatic cancer. It's already spread to some of my other organs and so there is very little to be done. I have been offered palliative care, which I will take, but I will be staying at home with your Mum. I'm going to put her on now so you can hear she is just about coping but I will want you both to be there for her over the next few weeks." He handed me the phone and I took it with a shaking hand.

Although I don't remember much of what I said, I do know I didn't cry and managed to keep it together, telling both of them to come round whenever they wanted, but perhaps not that night. They both arrived the next morning, Nicholas alone as Angus was away and Angela with her husband and both the girls. Everybody hugged everybody and I tried to make tea while we all fought our way through the emotionally charged atmosphere. Rob seemed to be the only one able to speak. He looked grey and seemed to have aged at least a decade overnight but incredibly still managed to smile. None of them asked what the prognosis was, it was the elephant in the room, and after I had sat down opposite him flanked by Olivia and Amalee, he told them.

"As I said there is nothing anyone can do, the cancer is too advanced and I have four, possibly five months left." Gasps and a strangled sobs filled the pause before he went on, "And I, we," nodding and smiling at me, "have decided that I'm not spending any of that time in a hospital, I'm spending it at home with my family."

He phoned his sister the next morning who declared she was coming down to see him straight away. The intolerance between her and me was still very much alive and so she booked herself and Alan into the local pub. This had been the arrangement throughout the years. Although their visits had been rare, them not staying with us allowed our relationship to remain relatively cordial. They did not come down straight away, in fact it was a week later and they arrived the day after Rob had told the consultant he wanted only the palliative care, at home, and to be made as comfortable as possible.

They had planned to stay only one night but extended it to two after Julia had been shocked at the appearance of her brother, demanding to know why we had not got a second opinion or why we had relied on the NHS in the first place.

"There are so many things they can do these days, how can they be so sure there's no hope – there's always hope!"

Rob had been annoyed, telling her to stop being so dramatic, this wasn't one of her silly soap operas and didn't she think we would have explored every possibility. She was distraught and completely unable to take in his words, insisting she wasn't convinced that there was nothing to be done. Her emotions turned to anger which obviously was aimed at me, saying I should have realised he was ill, I should have got him help sooner and, getting out her phone, saying she would make some calls.

"Julia!" Rob's shouted at her with a force and fury he could barely afford.

"It's alright," I held up my hand and shook my head, "don't be upset, it's fine." I got up to leave the room and Alan followed me, leaving them alone. I went straight through the kitchen and out into the garden, trailed by my brother-in-law, keen to apologise for and explain his wife's outburst. I told him there was no need, I knew how much she loved Rob and how she felt I'd taken him away from her. He didn't dispute my assertion but added,

"She's always idolised him and since their parents died, she says he's all she has left." He gave a sad little chuckle, "I have to keep reminding her I'm still here." He sighed and said wistfully, "Things might have been different if we'd managed to have children…"

Alan and I left them alone for almost an hour and, thankfully, they seemed to have made up when we went back in with tea and cake. As I offered Julia a slice of Lemon sponge, she paused, looking unsure, until I told her it was shop bought, after which she accepted. Rob said he'd love some but it remained untouched at the side of him, managing only to drink his tea. They left shortly after that, Julia turning to wave on the doorstep, not realising that was the last time she would see him.

As the days went on, his deterioration continued quicker than predicted and, although he tried to pretend otherwise, I could see he was in a great deal of pain day and night and I was wracked with guilt that I wasn't helping him properly and tried to get him to reconsider the hospice.

"They have little camp beds I can sleep on," I assured him, "I will still be with you but there will be someone there all the time to help you with the pain and anything else you need."

"I don't need anything else, I just want to be here with you."

I was furiously sad and felt my heart breaking, did you know it is a real thing, heartbreak, I could physically feel the pain as my heart fractured.

The MacMillan nurse, who had been coming twice a day, asked if we would like her to come four times and I said yes quickly before Rob could refuse. She was wonderful and her kindness was a great comfort as was her honesty. She explained that the cancer was in his liver and it was liver failure that would probably take him in the end. As it progressed, I could see that the morphine she was giving him hardly did anything for the excruciating pain although he insisted it did.

When she arrived one morning, shortly after seven, Rob was still asleep, this was only five weeks after the diagnosis. She never asked me how I was, her experience telling her this was not a question that needed asking. Instead she asked instead if I wanted to ask her anything.

"The consultant said he had four or five months, why is he so ill now?

It's only been a few weeks..."

"Unfortunately, people with pancreatic cancer can become poorly very quickly and there's not always much warning when the end is near." Seeing my alarm, she said she would arrange for the doctor to come out and see him that afternoon but I should try and prepare myself.

I called Davy that evening; he had already booked his flight and was due over the following week. He was staying with Angela and told me he would stay as long as I needed him.

The doctor gave Rob something which he said should make him more comfortable and prescribed additional medication for the MacMillan nurse to administer. This definitely helped and his smile managed to reach his eyes that day.

He was really pleased to see Davy although both he and I insisted he went home after almost two weeks. Rob told him how much he had loved seeing him but he should get back to his family. He actually rallied a little during that time and they even started a game of chess but it never got finished. The day after he had gone back, Rob was looking out at the back garden and shaking his head.

"I'm sorry I never got to make you that rose garden," he said sadly.

"Oh but you have given me so much more than that," I told him.

"We have had a good life," he murmured and smiled.

"The best," I agreed, putting my arms around his failing body, hugging him gently and kissing his neck.

He spoke to Julia almost daily and I am confident that he lied to her about how quickly he was fading. I know I should have called her myself and told her but I didn't want her to turn up again with all her anger and resentment. I know how selfish that sounds, but there it is.

The week after Davy had gone back, Rob started to gradually withdraw. At first I thought it was the increased morphine as he was suffering agonising backache. The drugs were helping him sleep better but even when he was awake he was quiet and slightly distant, as though he was drifting away. I sat with him, holding his hand and talking constantly about our happy life, little anecdotes and stories, desperately trying to keep him with me. Watching him dying in pain was the hardest thing I have ever endured in my whole life and I am no stranger to seeing people die.

My charmed life had well and truly come to an end. I had no fight left in me and no desire to go on without him. I've been through tough times before and always thought I could make things better, but this time I knew I could not. I was so very tired and did not want to go on without him. I knew I could not keep my promise to be strong, because I wasn't.

It was two thirty in the morning. I had been lying next to him drifting in and out of sleep when I woke with a start. Gently sliding my hand up to his neck to feel for a pulse, already knowing there would be none.

I didn't phone the ambulance or the MacMillan nurse, I just stayed where I was, at the side of him, clinging to his arm and his shoulder, telling him how much I loved him, crying quietly. I'm not sure how long I stayed like that but it must have been a while as, when I finally managed to lift myself up, I realised there was a crack of light in the sky and the dawn wasn't too far away. I kissed him gently on the forehead and went back to the spare room to get the amitriptyline tablets from the bedside drawer.

## Thirty Six

I'm honestly not sure if my intention had always been to overdose. The doctor had prescribed the antidepressants for me three years earlier when I'd had a very uncharacteristic bout of anxiety. This had started with a bad dream about Billy not actually being dead and, even though the details faded as soon as I woke up, it had unsettled me for some weeks and Rob insisted I go to the doctor's. I had three month's supply of the drug but took only two tablets, deciding I didn't like the way they made me feel. My GP never mentioned them again and I just shoved them in the back of a drawer, but I knew where they were.

Still moving about the house in semi-darkness, I took the box of tablets and a litre bottle of vodka, along with one of our best crystal glasses, back into our bedroom and poured myself a drink.

"To you my love," I said, raising the glass to him before taking the first big gulp, "I'm coming with you."

I had only taken three of the dozen or more tablets I'd pressed out of their foil strips but had drunk a three fingers measure down the bottle when I heard the front door open and Angela's worried voice calling me. After that, everything became confused as I started to drift in and out of reality, a wave of sleep pulling me towards unconsciousness. I was slightly aware of blue flashing lights and Angela crying and possibly touching my face but everything started to spin as faces I didn't know came in and out of focus. Someone was trying to get me to open my eyes but I was so tired and desperate for the blackness of oblivion. My disorientation increased as I felt myself being elevated and briefly managed to open my eyes but all I saw were bright lights so I closed them again and the darkness took me. Surfacing again, my body jolted in a stark and painful awakening as a tube was inserted down my throat, causing me to gag and choke as the medical staff attempted to pump my stomach.

After retching and choking, I was allowed to sleep and it was almost thirty six hours before I opened my eyes properly, even though I had begun to come round hours before. As my head started to clear and I remembered what I had done, how I had been so wretched in my grief and thought of no one but myself, I was suddenly mortified. So I fought the wakefulness, desperately trying to keep my eyes closed and my mind oblivious. I was too much of a coward to face anyone.

But then I heard someone, I think it was Angela, mention the police. I didn't catch all of what she said but her tone was angry and I clearly heard her ask, "Just what is she being accused of?" I didn't catch the response but I did hear her say, very loudly, "That is absolutely ridiculous, my mother wouldn't hurt a fly let alone kill someone, this is total rubbish!"

Panic began to mix with my shame as my addled brain began to remind me, via flash backs, of the things I've done and I desperately began to think how I would explain and defend myself so I kept my eyes closed.

I was wondering if Darren's body had finally turned up, if somehow it had resurfaced. After all these years there would be little left, just bones I guess, if that, and I know they can do some marvellous stuff these days with DNA and carbon dating and the likes but I'm struggling to work out who was left to connect him, there would only be Angela....and my panic intensified.

Olivia and Amalee were here again this morning. Livy is so like her mother, sensible and practical and full of empathy and Amie, normally, is a giggling whirlwind of chaotic fun. They stayed longer this time, telling me all about their day and what they'd watched on TV before telling me that they loved me. Then Livy said she knew I was sad about losing Grandad, they were too, but they wanted me to get better, they needed me to get better as they couldn't handle losing me as well. I can't help but wonder what they'll think of me when the truth comes out though.

When, finally, I stopped hiding and allowed my eyes to open, I was totally confused at the scene I found myself in. As I started to focus on the concerned faces of my son and daughter, I was shaking my head in bewilderment. Angela let out a small cry as she leaned forward to touch my arm.

"Mum, oh Mum, it's okay, everything's okay," she declared with a stifled sob as Nicky leaned in at the side of her, his face lined with worry as he forced a smile.

"Mum," was all he managed to say.

My head hurt and my eyes were struggling with the brightness of the lights and sheets as I took in the hospital room. My eyes lingered on the machine reading my heart rate and oxygen levels before following the line of the drip attached to the cannular in the back of my hand. I tried to speak but my throat was so sore and my mouth dry. Angela reached for a small sponge on a stick and carefully dabbed on my lips with water.

"Don't try and speak yet, let me just do this to try and make you feel better." She dabbed my chin delicately with a tissue to catch the stray drops and I could feel her unconditional love for me as I lay looking into her lovely face. She turned her head slightly to face her brother and told him,

"Go and phone Steve, tell him he can bring Livy and Amie in to see her now and get him to phone Uncle Davy and let him know she's awake." I heard my boy swallow loudly as he looked down at me for a second to reassure himself before leaving the room.

Turning back to me, Angela asked if I wanted to try a few sips of water and when I nodded, she helped me raise my head slightly, keeping one arm around me while she held the small glass to my lips. As she put the glass back down and touched my cheek, she asked if I was in pain and I shook my head, not taking my eyes off her, seeing clearly the devastation of what I had done to her and her brother.

The last few days, since they pulled me back from the brink, things seem very different. As I've purged my soul of the secrets of my past, I've come to realise how lucky and how loved I have been; the telling of this story has been very cathartic. I heard two of the nurses talking last night when they thought I was asleep. Apparently the police want to talk to me, I didn't catch all of what was said but I did hear the word murder.

I know I will have to face up to what I've done, I will accept whatever punishment the authorities decide I am due, but I only hope my family will, if not forgive me, at least understand why I did what I did.

Things started to get clearer today. The intravenous drip has gone but they've left the cannular in to see how I am over the next twenty four hours. They still won't let me get out of bed and I am unbelievably tired in between the fear and adrenaline rushes I get every time someone comes into the room.

A pretty nurse with piercing blue eyes came in to tell me I had visitors. She made me jump actually as I was so deep in thought and I gave a huge gasp which she mistook for pain. She checked my blood pressure and temperature and said all was fine and went off to get me some fresh water as Angela and Nicholas came in. I could see they were stressed, Nicky more so but then he has always been one to fly into a panic when things become a bit tricky.

"Uncle Davy has landed at Heathrow," he declared as he rushed over to my bedside, "He says you're not to worry, he's going to sort everything out, but you mustn't talk to anybody till he gets here."

"Not even you?" I asked with a smile to try and pretend I was not worrying.

"Hello, Mum," Angela said, bending to give me a quick kiss before sitting in the chair at the other side of the bed, "how are you feeling today?"

"I'm fine according to the nurse that just checked me over and my head's not quite so full of cotton wool." I took in a breath and managed a smile, "Do you know what time Davy will be here?"

"He's hired a car and he's driving straight here but don't worry, we're not letting the police talk to you till he arrives…"

"I've spoken to the doctor," Nicky cut in, "he's told them that you aren't in any fit state to be interrogated so they'll have to wait."

"Interrogated," I pushed myself up a little. "Well that sounds dramatic," trying get my expression right while my brain formulates a credible response before I ask what I'm supposed to have done.

"I don't think it's an interrogation," Angela said, rolling her eyes at her brother, "they just want to ask you a few questions…"

"It's bloody Julia causing trouble. I swear if she comes anywhere near me, I'll punch her lights out," Nicky snapped.

"Julia?" I was genuinely puzzled, "What's Julia got to do with anything?"

Angela opened her mouth to reply but my son's agitation could not be contained as he almost spat the words out, "She's told the police you killed Dad."

## Thirty Seven

Being accused of murdering Rob was the last thing I'd expected to hear and, as my head went back into a spin, I flopped back onto my pillows.

"Nick!" Angela exclaimed, holding her hand up to stop him.

"No," I managed to say, "tell me, I need to know." Angela relaxed and looking at me, nodded, and Nicholas started to tell me what had happened.

My lovely sister-in-law had made a formal report to the police within hours of hearing, from Angela, of her brother's death and my hospitalisation. She drove the five hour journey to the offices of the Hampshire Constabulary in Portsmouth to tell them I had murdered her brother. In her statement she claimed she had spoken to him on a very long phone call the day before he died and he was most definitely not at death's door; in fact, he was sounding much better than he had done for a while. She claimed he told her he was worried about me, that I was tired and irritable and he thought I was doubling up his medication to speed him on his way. She told them our marriage was not a happy one and I had made his life a misery and had forced him to move away from his family and friends.

Her final claim, that I had faked a suicide attempt in an effort to deflect what I had done, left me incredulous. Even though I knew she disliked me, I could not believe she could be so malicious.

Neither of my children considered for one second that there was any truth in her allegations, they assured me, but apparently the police were taking it seriously and had begun an investigation.

"Well then," I said as I tried to get my thoughts straight, "they'll soon see what a liar she is." Angela took my hand and squeezed it.

"It's unforgivable. I know she loved Dad in her twisted way and so she's sad, we all are but this is, well, it's just…"

"It's spiteful, that's what it is, what she is, the nasty old witch," Nicholas snapped, shaking his head. I took in a deep breath.

"She did talk to your Dad the day before he died," I said softly, "It was in the morning but it lasted no more than a couple of minutes as the nurse arrived almost at the same time."

"Honestly, Mum, it's okay, really," Angela squeezed my hand.

"Anyway, Uncle Davy will be here soon," Nicholas said with a deep sigh.

"Yes and he's staying for a month. Celeste is coming over in a couple of weeks too," Angela beamed at me.

"So you just need to get well," my son said with a beaming smile.

When my brother arrived a couple of hours later, he asked his niece and nephew to go and get some tea and leave us alone. He told me that he loved me but he was furious with me for trying to kill myself. I told him I was so very sorry, that my grief had made me crazy and I truly regretted my actions.

Once that was out of the way, he said he would deal with 'all this Julia nonsense' and hoped he would get the chance to give her a good slap before he went back. I had been expecting him to ask me if any of her claims could be true but he didn't, instead he gave me a hug and whispered in my ear,

"You're my big sister and you've got through some proper shitty stuff in your life but this time I'm here to help you. You have two of the most incredible children who adore you so stop thinking you have to be strong or that you are on your own."

He explained he'd spoken to the police and they were happy to wait until I was home before they spoke to me which, according to the doctor, would most probably be in the next day or so.

"Obviously, we want it clearing up as soon as possible; we can't make any arrangements for the funeral till they're satisfied," he said grimly, adding, "Rob would be bloody furious with her over this, I hope she realises that."

I was discharged the next day, after speaking to a psychiatric nurse practitioner who made an appointment for me with a grief councillor at our local health centre. Davy took me home and I could tell straight away that someone, most probably Angela, had cleaned the house and removed any traces of the night the only father she had ever known had died. She had been careful though, his clothes and books and other things remained where he had left them along with his presence. For a little while longer, I would be able to pretend he had just popped out for a bit and would be home soon.

The police came the following day; two WPC's who were kind and respectful. I told them that I totally disputed Julia's claims and explained, as best I could, my fractured relationship with her. I told them she had telephoned on the morning before my husband died and that he was a little brighter but... "Rob would never have told her I was irritable, even if I was. He knew my relationship with Julia had always been strained and had always tried to smooth things over." They both listened as one of them made notes.

"His medication was almost always administered by the MacMillan nurse. She did give us a box of 'just in case' morphine and syringes but he never asked for it, it's still upstairs."

I was asked to go and get it and one of them came up with me. It was on top of the bathroom cabinet, the box still sealed. She took a couple of photographs with her phone before opening the box and taking more pictures of the contents. "I'll need to take these away with me," she said and I nodded.

After they had gone, I sat in the conservatory for a while with Davy who asked me how I was feeling and I said I was actually a little bit angry and a little bit sad.

"The thing that's really hurting is the way the police are treating Julia's claims," I held my hand up to stop him interrupting, "It's fine, I did nothing wrong and their investigation will prove that but they are actually looking into her claims, not like how the police dealt with Mum's death, letting Billy get away with it."

"He didn't though, did he?" Davy's eyes locked on mine, his eyebrows raised, "We got our justice in the end." I held his stare and just for a second I wondered if he had some suspicions about that time, if perhaps he had suspected my part in his father's downfall. And I remembered there had been one other time when I'd wondered if my little brother had known more than I thought he had.

It had been back in 1988, just before he left for Canada. It was late in the evening and we'd shared a bottle of wine as I'd helped him pack up his things. He told me he was so happy that I had Rob in my life and how I deserved a good man after all I'd been through. Since the day Darren walked out on us, he had never mentioned him and so I was a little taken a back when he said,

"You were only fourteen when you met him and he was in his late twenties." The deep frown showed me this was something he had thought and worried about. "He groomed you, and fooled us all into thinking he was a good bloke, but he wasn't, he was a..."

"I know what he was," cutting him off and noticing he used the past tense, "We were lucky that he took off when he did. Water under the bridge now though eh?" I smiled and nodded, desperately wanting him to still believe I had been the victim and he looked at me for a few seconds longer, before changing the subject.

It was a further ten days before I was told that the investigation into Rob's death had concluded and there was no evidence to support the allegations made against me. The MacMillan nurse and our GP, who had seen him two days before his death, both concurred with the pathologist. My husband, as predicted, died of liver failure. The WPC who brought me the news told me that it was recorded that Julia's claims had been deemed malicious but as her accusations had not led to me being arrested, she had not actually committed an offence. However, they would be sending an officer to visits her to talk about the wasting of police time.

I won't dwell on the funeral, there have been so many but, thanks to my wonderful brother and children, this one was not as hard as I had anticipated. It was comforting to all of us to celebrate Rob's life with so many of his friends and colleagues.

Julia came for the service, a vision of tragedy in a chic designer black dress and jacket. All that was missing was a large black hat and a veil and she could have been the mistaken for the widow of a mafia don. That's bitchy of me I know but shockingly accurate. She followed the casket into the crematorium, just behind Davy and Celeste and, once inside, took her seat on the opposite aisle to us, Alan at her side. I'm told she wept throughout the service. I did not give her a so much as a glance and once it was over, she strode out with her head high, ignoring everyone, and walked straight to their car, creating her final bit of drama. Alan, who followed in her wake, tried to be his diplomatic self with waves, nods and straight mouth smiles. I felt sorry for him as I returned a similar smile before he got into their car. I had no idea how he was going to cope with her in the years that followed but I was sure she would never stop grieving for the brother she insisted I stole.

I don't expect I'll ever see or hear from her again.

Last Sunday, just before Davy and Celeste went back home, we had a family day. Steve, who is and excellent cook, made an amazing lunch for us all while I project managed the redevelopment of my garden. I had told Nicky and Angus what Rob and I had planned and they'd arranged a delivery of plants, two trellis arches, wood for a pergola and a bench. Angela and the girls, along with my brother and his wife, all donned gloves and we made a start on creating Rob's garden where we will scatter his ashes. This time, I know for sure, the roses will bloom.

## Epilogue

I've lived in the south for a long time, longer than I lived in my beloved Yorkshire but occasionally I get a little home sick for what I left behind. It's a sad fact of getting older how we yearn for a place and time that we can no longer visit. I think as we age, we all start to yearn for our past but perhaps what we are really craving is our youth.

I'm not the person I was back then, I haven't been for a long time, but I'm curious about those other versions of me and from time to time I wonder about different paths I might have trod.

Don't get me wrong, I'm not saying I regret anything I did. In the case of The Widow, I was making everyone's life better and she was so miserable, it could be considered a mercy killing, which I know is still not acceptable but I was very young and had so many other people to consider.

Shirley, well she was collateral damage and, if anything, I think of it as saving her the pain and grief that would inevitably have followed as there is little doubt Billy would have continued to knock her about, like he did Mum. I have never believed that the abuse Mum and Shirley suffered were anything to do with the amount of alcohol he drank; it was just his sadistic and rotten nature. Finding Shirley that Sunday morning, looking like his latest punch bag, then seeing Mum's slippers and bottle of pills – well I took it as a sign.

I actually want to take credit for Billy's death, even if it was by proxy. I mean, by helping Shirley avoid any further abuse, I did start the chain of events that led to it. I'm not haunted by his death, it's what he did to Mum that's haunted me all my life; I know he killed her. But at fourteen and female, the West Yorkshire constabulary were never going to believe me over him, so I found my own, wild justice.

With Darren, well there is some sadness. I did like him at the beginning even though I never actually loved him. My attraction to him was real, mainly teenage hormones I suspect, and I have occasionally wondered, if perhaps he'd been a little stronger, a little more stable, well maybe both our lives could have taken a different path. But it was not to be.

Memories are tricky things, most people think that memory is truth, believing it's what really happened but it's actually just your own truth, that's the way memories work.

Memories are the stories that we tell ourselves, our own narrative, and so I'll leave it to you to decide how much of my story is true.

## **Acknowledgments**

There are plenty of people who helped bring this book to fruition, including the people who just asked me casually how the book was going, providing me with the encouragement to keep going. But I have to give very special thanks to my wonderful husband Paul – my biggest cheerleader who tirelessly helped me with my terrible grammar and spellings, not to mention my occasional tendency to make up words. Also for his wonderful photography skills in creating the cover, I will never tire of being his muse.

As always Andrew, Emma and Sarah have provided me with the happiness and distraction I have needed in times of frustration and despair. I am so very proud of the people they have become and they will always be an inspiration to me.

I want to give a very big thank you also to Bernadette Morrison and John Shires, my very diligent proof readers, for their kindness and attention to detail. The notes and comments they fed back to me along with the corrections, gave me a much needed boost as I prepared myself for this show and tell.

Last but definitely not least thank you to all my friends, old and new. You have not only encouraged and supported my writing but also provided lots of material for future characters and stories.

Printed in Dunstable, United Kingdom

70605439R00190